NIGHTLUST . . .

'I feel a bitch,' Susan

'Hm?'

'Brandon's lying aslee ... d. I've made love with Alicia – and now, here ... with you. I'm like some over-sexed bitch, not caring where I take my pleasure, as long as someone makes me come.'

The pale-skinned, dark-haired man stroked her face. 'Actually, you do care. Too much.' He sighed. 'Stop fighting yourself, Susanna. You're not committing a crime.'

'It feels like it.'

He bit her earlobe. 'Then how about I kiss you until you feel better? And I promise you, you will feel better.' He let the palm of one hand rest against her breast, her erect nipple pushing against him. 'All the places where you ache to be touched, to be licked and stroked and sucked – I'll do it, And you'll feel so much better, afterwards. So very much better.' His voice was slightly hoarse, and very, very seductive . . .

Also available in New English Library paperback

Arousal
House of Lust
The Uninhibited
Submission!
Haunting Lust
Depravicus
The Splits
In the Pink 1: Stripped for Action
In the Pink 2: Sin City
In the Pink 3: Getting It
Lustathon
Vampire Desire
Rock Hard

Midnight Blue

Evelyn D'Arcy

NEW ENGLISH LIBRARY
Hodder and Stoughton

First published in 1996
by Hodder and Stoughton
A division of Hodder Headline PLC

A New English Library paperback

10 9 8 7 6 5 4 3 2 1

British Library Cataloguing in Publication Data

D'Arcy, Evelyn
Midnight blue
1. English fiction - 20th century
I. Title
823.9'14

ISBN 0 340 66644 7

Typeset by Avon Dataset Ltd, Bidford-on-Avon, Warks.
Printed and bound in Great Britain by
Mackays of Chatham PLC, Kent

Hodder and Stoughton
A division of Hodder Headline PLC
338 Euston Road
London NW1 3BH

For Gerard,
with all my love

One

'You look like hell,' Yvonne said, putting a mug of black coffee on Susanna's desk.

'Thanks, I needed this.' Susanna sipped the strong dark liquid gratefully. 'And I'm OK, Yvonne, so stop nagging.'

'Come off it.' Yvonne tossed her dark hair out of her eyes. 'Just look in the mirror. Your hair's dull, there are shadows under your eyes, your face is as white as though you're hung over – and you've written half a dozen words, if that, in the past two hours. Considering that your usual speed's a thousand words an hour, when you're writing something up . . . There's something wrong. Definitely.'

Susanna shrugged. 'Maybe I'm just thinking about my article.'

'And maybe you're lying.' Yvonne's hazel eyes were sympathetic. 'Oh, come on, Susanna. I've worked with you for nearly two years. Don't you think I can tell when something's not right?'

Susanna wrinkled her nose. 'Oh, all right, you might as well know. It's Brandon.'

'Missing him?' Yvonne's voice was all sympathy. It was hard to be parted from your man for weeks on end. Susanna and Brandon had grown used to conducting their relationship long-distance, when his work took him out of London for a few days, but it was always obvious when Brandon was at home.

Susanna literally shone with pleasure then, her blonde hair gleaming, her skin glowing and her green eyes full of laughter which came from a good sex life. Yvonne envied her: not many men were skilled enough to make you come so hard and so many times in one evening that your stomach muscles ached, as Susanna had once admitted to her in the local wine-bar.

'Yes, of course I miss him – he's hundreds of miles away, in bloody Cornwall, at Castle Pentremain – but it isn't that.' Susanna frowned, her pretty face growing hard. 'All I've had from him, in the past week, are these really short postcards. Curt, even.'

'And?'

'Usually, he rings me every night.' Calls which started as a simple 'Hi, how are you?' call, and ended up with them fantasizing to each other down the phone, devising more and more erotic way-out scenarios – not that Susanna was going to start telling Yvonne about *that* at half-past eleven on a Wednesday morning, in the middle of the office. It wasn't the time or the place.

'Maybe he's busy. I mean, we all used to think that interior design was a Mickey Mouse job, but since you've been with Brandon and you've told me how hard he works . . . That castle's huge, from what you told me, and in a real state. It probably needs a lot of effort. Maybe he's just too knackered to talk to you.'

Susanna shrugged. Brandon was one of those people who were never ill, never tired. 'Even so, it's not like him.'

Yvonne paused for a moment, and then decided to risk it. 'You don't think he's fallen under the spell of that woman, do you?'

'Alicia Descourt?' Susanna gave a short laugh. 'You must be joking. She's not his type. He doesn't go for the dark and gothic sort – I mean, don't you think that dyeing your hair black and wearing black nail-varnish and deep burgundy lipstick is just a teensy bit affected, if you're not a teenager?'

'I suppose she earns enough to look like whatever she wants,' Yvonne mused.

Susanna wrinkled her nose dismissively. 'Anyway, Brandon's worked with far more glamourous clients than a middle-aged gothic horror writer.'

'Middle-aged? Susanna, she's only thirty-eight.'

'Which is a lot nearer forty than I am. Eight years nearer, in fact,' Susanna's lips twitched. 'OK, so I'm being bitchy, now. But Brandon's worked with some really stunning models, and he didn't lay a finger on them. He saw them as just another client, and he doesn't mix business with pleasure, ever.' She paused. 'So if he can resist some of the most stunning women in the business, why should he change his mind now, for someone like Alicia Descourt?'

'If you're that worried about it, take a few days off and go down to Cornwall. Surprise him.'

Susanna made a face. 'Who says I'm worried?'

'For a start, you don't usually bitch about other women.'

Susanna smiled wryly. 'I suppose not.'

'Just take a few days off, Susanna. Before you start protesting, I can cope with this place on my own until Madam gets back, and you're owed enough holiday.' Yvonne grinned at her. 'If you get a fit of the guilts at being away from your desk for two milliseconds, you could always do a *Homefile* feature on her castle. I bet it'd go down a bomb with our readers.'

'Some of them, maybe.' Susanna wasn't convinced. *Homefile* readers were more Joanna Trollope and Jane Austen devotees than Alicia Descourt fans. They preferred Agas to vampires, and the only bats they were interested in were those in the attics of tiny cottages being renovated by middle-aged artists, or pretty country church belfries.

'Think about it, hm?' Yvonne gave her a smile, and went back to her own desk, catching up on a pile of correspondence.

Susanna sipped thoughtfully at her coffee, and tried to concentrate on her article. Yet she couldn't. All she could think about were those curt little messages on Brandon's postcards – and the fact that his writing was neat, instead of his usual hasty scrawl. It looked like he'd taken care over them, and thought about the wording for ages . . . No, something was definitely wrong. The question was, what?

She was still thinking about it when she walked in through the front door of their flat. And about what Yvonne had said: that she looked like hell. *Oh, really?* she thought, annoyed; she slung her bag into a corner and kicked off her shoes.

A glance in the hallway mirror told her that Yvonne might just be right. Her fair hair was dull, looking well out of condition; the usual glossy and bouncy curls were limp. Her eyes, too, were a dull grey-green, not their usual vibrant jade. And there were indeed deep shadows under them.

Her figure hadn't altered – she still had the long-legged and curvy look which Brandon liked so much, her buttocks neat and tight from her twice-weekly step aerobics class and her breasts firm and generous. Automatically, she smoothed the short black skirt of her business suit over her thighs. How many times Brandon had met her at work with some flimsy excuse or other, and they'd slipped into a quiet corridor somewhere in the building, unable to keep their hands off each other. They'd even made love in the ladies' loo, once.

Brandon had pushed her skirt up, bunching the material over her hips, and inserted one hand between her thighs. It had been autumn, so she'd been wearing stockings: the lace-topped hold-up type, and he'd smiled with pleasure as his fingers encountered bare flesh. Then he'd pushed the gusset of her knickers to one side, drawing his long sensitive fingers down the length of her quim.

Susanna had shuddered, tipping her head back; Brandon had unbuttoned her shirt, tugging it out of the waistband of her skirt, then pulled down the cups of her bra, baring her breasts. He'd taken one rosy nipple in his mouth, running the tip of his tongue over the areola, then sucking hard on the bud of flesh, while the finger and thumb of one hand manipulated the other nipple, rolling it and pulling it gently until she groaned.

His other hand had returned between her thighs, stroking, one long finger slipping inside her knickers and then easing into her. He'd lifted his head then, smiling. 'Mm. Warm and wet. Do I get the feeling, Ms James, that you're up for a good shafting?' he'd whispered in her ear, knowing that the combination of formality and slightly coarse language would turn her on even more.

She'd pushed against him, feeling the heat and hardness of his cock through the material of his chinos. 'About as much as you are, Mr Rodgers,' she'd replied, her voice husky with wanting him.

'Then maybe we ought to do something about it.' His grey eyes had sparkled wickedly.

'Got any ideas?'

'Just the one.' He'd run his tongue along his lower lip, and Susanna had smiled, knowing exactly what he meant. She'd unbuttoned his chinos, pushing them down so she could free his cock from his underpants. It was hot and hard, the tip dry; she'd run her fingers along its length, squeezing gently, until he'd made a muffled sound of impatience, hoisted her up against the wall, and pushed the gusset of her knickers aside so that he could slide his cock into her.

'Oh God, that's good,' she'd breathed, wrapping her legs round him.

'Mm.' He'd licked her earlobe as he started to thrust; Susanna had buried her head in his shoulder, filling her nostrils with the scent of his skin and flexing her internal muscles around his cock as he continued to thrust into her.

Luckily no one had come in: but if they'd been interrupted, neither of them could have stopped what they were doing. The only thing that mattered was the hot rush of pleasure, the feeling of their bodies joining, and the overwhelming sensations of a mutual orgasm as they came, Brandon's cock throbbing in her and her quim contracting hard round him . . .

She closed her eyes. Remembering that wasn't going to help

anything: all it did was remind her how good it was between them, and how frustrated she felt without him. Her mood darkened when she turned back to check the wire basket on the back of the door for that day's post, and discovered yet another of the curt postcards from Brandon. *You bastard*, she thought angrily. *If you want to finish with me and run off with Alicia Descourt, just do it – don't keep me hanging on like this*. And yet she couldn't see why Brandon would want to finish with her. They shared the same sense of humour, liked the same sort of films and books and music, and the sex had always been good between them.

They looked good together, too. They were both tall and fair; Brandon had grey eyes, an aristocratic face which was emphasized even more by the way his hair flopped over his forehead, and a sensual mouth that made most women shiver and wonder what it would feel like to have that mouth working its way down their body. His shoulders were broad and his chest and thighs well-developed, thanks to his workouts three time a week in the gym: his body promised the toe-curling combination of sensuality and staying power.

Susanna was curvy, with generous breasts and long, long legs; she thought of herself as averagely pretty, not stunningly beautiful, but she and Brandon always drew glances when they walked down the street. Lust, admiration, sometimes a little envy. Really, she thought, it had been a sickeningly perfect relationship, right from the word go. They were compatible in looks, in taste, and in temperament – though Brandon was perhaps a little more laid-back than she was.

She sighed. So what the hell was going wrong with it, now? Maybe Yvonne was right. She ought to go to Cornwall, and find out the truth for herself. Not for the first time, Susanna wished that she'd bothered to learn to drive. In London, you didn't need to – there was almost always a train or a bus. Or you could call a taxi, if it was that late or that urgent. Cars weren't really necessary. But when it came to reaching some stupid castle in the middle of nowhere, in Cornwall . . . She grimaced. Castle Pentremain. Why couldn't Alicia Descourt have found herself somewhere a bit less out of the way?

She forced the thoughts of Brandon and Alicia from her mind, and went into the kitchen. Brandon, who adored messing about in the kitchen, did most of the cooking; when he wasn't around, Susanna tended to live on TV dinners, or yoghurt and fruit and cheese and biscuits. She'd forgotten to go shopping, and the fridge contained a yoghurt just past its sell-by date, about half a pint of milk, and a squashy tomato.

'Oh, bloody hell,' she said. She didn't really want to go out, in case Brandon rang; on the other hand, she *was* hungry. She hadn't bothered with breakfast, and had just grabbed a sandwich at her desk at work; her stomach rumbled, and she scowled. 'Bloody hell,' she said again, and headed for the phone.

She dialled a familiar number, and held her breath as the line buzzed once, twice, three time. Once more, and the answerphone would kick in . . .

'Hallo?'

She closed her eyes in relief as she heard her friend's voice. 'Kate? It's Susanna.'

'Hi, how are you?'

'Average. And you?'

'Fine, fine.'

'Kate, are you busy tonight?'

There was a chuckle from the other end of the line. 'It depends on what you mean by busy. I'm supposed to be drafting an advertorial, this evening.'

'But you're not in the mood?' Susanna asked hopefully.

'Got it in one, Miss Marple.'

'How do you fancy pizza at my place, then?'

Kate chuckled. 'I take it that the gorgeous Brandon is away?'

'Yup – and for another couple of weeks, otherwise I'd offer you something better than pizza.'

'True. Only you could find a man who's as good in the kitchen as he is in the bedroom.'

Susanna laughed. 'Well, he's not here, so it's a choice of takeaway or takeaway. All I've got in the fridge is a yoghurt and a tomato, and I think they're both well on the way out.'

'Open a bottle of something nice, then. I'll be round in half an hour, and I'll pick up a pizza on the way round.'

'OK. See you, then.'

'*Ciao*, baby.' Kate hung up.

Susanna put a bottle of white wine in the fridge, had a quick shower, then tidied up the flat. She'd just opened the wine when the doorbell rang.

She pressed the intercom. 'Hallo.'

'Pizza for you, ma'am,' a female voice drawled in a parody of an American delivery boy. 'I believe you ordered blue cheese and mushrooms, with a little avocado?'

Susanna grinned. Even without the unusual combination of toppings, it could only have been Kate. 'Come up.'

Kate bounced into the flat a few moments later, carrying two large boxes; she looked round, and gave a low whistle. 'Wow. Something's definitely up.'

'What do you mean?'

'*Numero uno*, the flat's tidy – and you're always messy when Brandon's not here, except the day before he comes back. You said on the phone that he's away for a couple more weeks.'

'True.'

'*Numero due*,' Kate tipped her head to one side, her blue eyes assessing her friend shrewdly, 'you look like hell.'

Susanna rolled her eyes. Kate was the second person to say that to her today, and it annoyed her intensely. 'I do not.'

Kate, recognizing the set of her friend's jaw, didn't bother arguing. '*Numero tre*, you didn't suggest going out to see a film, then having munchies and a girly chat in some nice little bistro. Which means that you want to stay at home, in case Brandon rings; which means in turn that you're panicking, in case he doesn't.' Kate spread her hands. 'So. Do we eat first, sink a couple of bottles, and then talk, or what?'

Susanna couldn't help smiling at her old flatmate. Kate had always been quick – both mentally, and in the way she did things. She managed to fit an improbable amount of things into her life; though whenever anyone accused Kate of being on speed or something, to do that much and do it so well, she simply grinned and told people to get themselves a Psion organizer and sort their lives out. Kate, needless to say, always had the very latest model – and a backup of all her data, at home. 'We'll do it your way. Eat, drink, then talk.' Susanna's nose twitched. 'What's with the Italian, then?'

'Just posing. What else do you expect from an advertising bod?'

Susanna grinned. 'Knowing you, I'd say that you've got an Italian client, and you're bedding him.'

'Now, now. I agree with Brandon in that you don't mix business with pleasure. Anyway, you know the cardinal rule: never sleep with your clients or your colleagues.'

'Rules are made to be broken,' Susanna teased, sliding the pizzas onto two large white plates and handing one to Kate. 'My God, you really meant it. Blue cheese, mushrooms and avocado?'

Kate breathed on her nails, polishing them on her sweater. 'My latest find.'

Susanna eyed the avocado doubtfully. '*Hot* avocado?'

'It's gorgeous. Trust me.' Kate grinned. 'And before you ask, no, I'm not pregnant. I'm footloose and fancy-free at the moment, remember?'

'That's what you tell me. Now, the truth about this Italian?'

They walked over to the kitchen table, and sat down.

'I do have an Italian client, yes, but I'm not bedding him.' Kate grinned. 'Though the campaign breaks on Monday night, so he's officially not my client any more, then.'

'What if he loves the ads so much that he wants you to do more?'

'That'll be a separate contract.' Kate winked at her friend. 'He's taking me out to dinner on Monday night.'

'So you're hitting the shops on Saturday,' Susanna guessed.

'With a vengeance. I need some nice sexy underwear, a new little black dress, and new shoes. And shopping for that sort of stuff just *has* to be followed by a facial, and maybe a session in a jacuzzi or a massage.' She paused. 'Want to come with me?'

'Maybe.'

'Ill, depressed, or ragingly angry – which is it?'

Susanna frowned, not following her friend. 'What are you on about, Kate?'

'You've got to be one of them to refuse to go shopping. You're usually worse than me when it comes to spending lots of dosh. And you love going for a girly pamper even more than I do.'

Susanna rolled her eyes. 'I'm not ill, and I'm not depressed, all right?'

'Which makes you angry.' Kate thought for a moment. 'The Bitch Queen is on holiday, so it can't be work. Which makes it Brandon. Who, at the moment, is doing up some mouldering pile in Cornwall for Alicia Descourt.' Her eyes narrowed. 'You don't think he's got the hots for her, do you?'

Susanna sighed. 'I don't know, Kate. It's just – well, he hasn't phoned me for ages.'

'Maybe there isn't a phone, in deepest darkest Cornwall.'

'Even if there isn't one at her castle, he has a mobile.'

'Maybe it's just out of range.'

Susanna shook her head. 'It's a digital phone, Kate. They work virtually anywhere – including the Continent. Even Castle bloody Pentremain's not out of range.'

'Right.'

'All he's done is send me these stupid postcards.' Susanna left the table to find the postcards, then brought them back and gave them to Kate.

Kate read them swiftly, and frowned. 'Hm. This doesn't sound like the Brandon Rodgers I know.'

'Exactly.' Susanna sighed. 'Yvonne reckons I ought to go

down to Cornwall, and see what's going on.'

'Good idea.' Kate topped up their glasses. 'It's meant to be gorgeous in that part of the world – all crags and cliffs. Pixieland. I'd go for it. I mean, it's not every day that you get the chance to spend a weekend in a Gothic castle.'

'I haven't actually been invited.'

'So what? Gatecrash the place! She can't refuse to let you in, can she?'

Susanna swallowed. 'What if she and Brandon are . . .'

'Screwing each other?' Kate waved an expressive hand. 'Maybe he just needs a little reminder of what he's missing in London.'

'Mm.'

Kate squeezed her hand. 'Susanna, don't just sit there and brood about it. It won't achieve a thing. All you'll do is upset yourself even more. Whereas if you go down to Cornwall, you'll either put your mind at rest – or your suspicions will be confirmed. Either way, you'll know where you stand, and you'll know what to do next.'

'Meaning?'

'If he isn't bedding her, you can have a nice sexy weekend with him, in the lap of luxury, and it'll teach him to keep in contact with you properly, in future. If he *is* bedding her – well, then you can join in, and remind him that you're better at it than she is.'

'That's assuming I am.'

'Just assume it, and you'll prove it.'

Susanna was forced to smile. 'God, Kate. If I was half as dynamic and positive as you . . .'

'The Bitch Queen would curl up and die in some dingy little corner, and you'd get her job,' Kate finished, laughing.

'Yeah.' Susanna ate some more pizza. 'Maybe you're right. I might go to Cornwall, after all.'

'You might even enjoy it. I mean, considering what a bookaholic you are – meeting a real live author should be quite a buzz.'

Susanna wrinkled her nose. 'I haven't actually read any of her books.'

'I have,' Kate said. 'I know, I know, it's all Gothic stuff, and vampire novels are ten a penny at the moment. Junk fiction, really. But she's quite good.' A smile curved her lips. 'Quite erotic, in places. Very sensual. She writes as if she really knows what its like to be a vampire. I can lend you one of the books, if you like.'

'Thanks, but no, thanks. And I don't really want to talk about her, if you don't mind.'

Kate winced. Susanna really was worried. 'Sorry. We'll change the subject, hm?'

Susanna was relieved. 'Why don't you tell me about your Italian?'

'Gio.' Kate gave a feline smile. 'He's rather nice, actually. Tall, dark and handsome – the usual cliché, but he really is something, Susanna. He has this terrifically sexy voice, and a mouth that was just made to give a woman pleasure. Definitely the office type, but not a deskbound wimp. He plays a lot of squash, apparently. Oh, and he wears glasses. Those beautiful little round Armani ones which somehow make men look super-intelligent. Though Gio's very sharp. It's not just a pose.' She gave Susanna a sidelong look. 'Actually, you'd like him.'

'I always go for blonds.'

'Yeah, yeah, the aristo type. I know. Julian Sands and Anthony Andrews, eat your heart out. But Gio – let's just say that I'd challenge any woman with blood in her veins to resist him. He's sex on legs,' Kate announced.

'In that case, how come you've resisted him so far?'

Kate grinned. 'It's called masturbating like mad under your desk.'

'In the office?' Susanna's eyes widened. Even Kate wasn't that daring, surely?

'Only when no one else is around. Though I guess the security guy might have had a camera trained on me, once – he's been giving me very funny looks, for the past couple of weeks.'

Susanna couldn't help laughing. Kate was so good for her: always cheerful, always positive, and always with a boxful of outrageous stories. 'You know, you really ought to write one of those erotic novels for women.'

'I might do, one day. You know how we copywriters always have a novel hidden in the bottom drawer.'

'So the rumour goes.' Susanna's lips twitched. 'Though I thought it was supposed to be the all-time literary genius novel?'

'Well.' Kate finished her pizza, and topped up their glasses. 'One day, maybe.' She smiled at her friend, and launched into another outrageous anecdote, about a bet she and her colleagues had been having in the office. The basic idea was that you changed as many words as you dared, in a presentation, and you scored points depending on how much you got away with. 'Simon beat us all hands down, though,' she said. 'He was talking about confectionery.' She grinned. 'He actually exchanged "liquorice" for "clitoris".'

'Never!'

'Yup. The best thing was, he got away with it, because the client didn't dare ask whether he'd really heard what Simon had said!'

By the time Kate left, Susanna was in a much better frame of mind: her sides almost hurt from laughing, and she'd virtually forgotten about Brandon and Alicia Descourt.

Her smile faded when she showered and got into bed. A line from a Joni Mitchell song flashed through her mind, about the bed being too big and the frying pan being too wide when her lover was away; she scowled and turned over, burying her face in the pillow.

The problem was, she was so used to Brandon being in bed with her that she found it hard to sleep alone. The only comfort she had was a vibrator Brandon had once bought her, for a joke, and although it was enough to relieve the deep ache of desire for a while, it wasn't good enough when you compared it with the real thing.

Maybe, she thought, *I should just go out on the town, pick someone up, and have a good all-night fucking session with them. And then again, maybe I can't be bothered.*

'Brandon, you bastard,' she muttered into the pillow. 'You bastard.'

She turned over again, picking up the book which lay on top of the bedside cabinet. It was a medieval murder-mystery, with a complex plot: and although she would normally have found it absorbing, she just couldn't concentrate on it. It was the last book Brandon had read, a couple of nights before he left for Cornwall.

It had been one of the best nights ever, she thought. He needed less sleep than she did, so he always read for a while before he turned the light out. He'd been lying on his side, concentrating on the book and trying to turn the pages quietly so he wouldn't wake her; though she'd actually been awake, and had had this overwhelming urge to feel him inside her.

Susanna put her book down, closing her eyes as she remembered what had happened . . .

She lay against Brandon, cuddling into him. His skin was so soft, so smooth, she just liked touching him, running the pads of her fingertips across his belly and delighting in the contrast of his skin and his silky hair. His thighs, too: Brandon was muscular and long-limbed, and it was a pleasure just to feel the interplay of his muscles beneath her hand.

She couldn't resist curling her fingers round his penis; it lengthened and thickened in her hands, springing to full erection within moments. She made a small sound of satisfaction in her throat: Brandon was so responsive to her. She wasn't sure whether it was the way she touched him, or whether he was anticipating her next move, but the end result was the same. One gloriously long and thick cock, and she could do whatever she wanted with it.

Gently, she began rubbing his foreskin back and forth, letting her fingers play over his cock; eventually, Brandon turned on his back and smiled at her. His smile was full of promise, and it sent a jolt through her.

'Do I get the impression that you want some attention, Susanna?' he asked, grinning.

She grinned back. 'Just a tad.'

'I see. Anywhere in particular?'

In answer, she rolled onto her back, kicked off the duvet, and stretched like a cat, shamelessly offering herself to him.

'I see,' he said again, his voice deep and sensual. 'In that case . . .' He knelt beside her, just running the pads of his fingertips over her body. He had artistic hands, long-fingered and tapering; Susanna shivered, and closed her eyes.

He smiled, stroking her ribcage, and letting his hands drift up to caress the soft undersides of her breasts. 'Mm. Beautiful,' he said huskily, brushing her breasts with the flat of his palms; then he cupped her breasts, bringing them up and together to deepen the vee of her cleavage. He rubbed the pad of his thumb over her areolae, smiling as the rosy tissue became erect.

She pushed against him, wanting more, and he chuckled. 'Greedy girl.' All the same, he bent his head, licking each nipple in turn, and sucking hard on one while he rubbed the other.

Susanna willed him to go down on her. She wanted to feel him kiss his way down her body, rubbing the tip of his nose against her belly and breathing in the musky scent of her arousal as he finally buried his face between her thighs. *Now, now, please now*, she thought desperately; and at last, he seemed to guess what she wanted, dropping a trail of kisses down over her abdomen. She pushed her thighs wider apart, wanting him to lick her until she was at screaming point; knowing exactly what she wanted, he laughed against her skin, and teased her, licking his way down one leg, pausing to kiss the soft skin at the back of her knees and in the hollows of her ankles, then nibbling his way back up the other leg.

At long, long last, she felt the stroke of his tongue on her quim; he drew it the full length of her sex, parting her labia and exploring the soft folds and hollows under his mouth. Susanna was moaning softly, pushing herself up to meet his mouth, when he finally made his tongue into a point, sliding it deep inside her. She gave a small murmur of satisfaction, letting her head rest back against the pillows, and slid her hands into his hair, urging him on.

Brandon smiled, and began to lap in earnest, catching her clitoris between his lips and sucking hard on the erect nub of flesh until she whimpered, her fingers digging into his scalp. He continued to lick and suck until he felt the familiar fluttering of her flesh under his mouth; then, when the tremors of her orgasm subsided, he reached up to kiss her, so that she could taste her juices on his mouth.

'I haven't finished yet,' he promised huskily.

Susanna looked up at him, drowsy-eyed, her pupils a brilliant jade green. 'What did you have in mind?'

'This.' He knelt between her thighs, positioning his cock at her entrance; then he slid slowly inside her, up to the hilt. Just when Susanna had expected him to start thrusting, he leaned back on his haunches, lifting her up so that her buttocks were raised clear of the bed, with her thighs draped over his and her feet flat against the mattress.

When he reached between their bodies and started rubbing her clitoris with the pad of his thumb, she reached behind her to grip the rails of the bed's pine headboard, her knuckles whitening. She pushed against him, but he refused flatly to start thrusting; he merely lay there, inside her, while he rubbed her clitoris.

Susanna reached another sobbing orgasm, her internal muscles spasming wildly round his cock; he smiled then, rolling over onto his back without withdrawing from her. 'My turn to lie back and enjoy it, methinks,' he said softly.

'You bet.' Somehow, he'd moved them both so that she was already kneeling comfortably astride him. She smiled, and leaned back slightly, changing the angle of his penetration to give them both the most pleasure. Then she began to move, lifting herself up until his cock was almost out of her, then slamming back down again onto him, so that the root of his cock rubbed hard against her clitoris.

'Oh,' she said, closing her eyes and swallowing hard.

'Touch yourself,' Brandon urged softly, taking her hands and placing them on her breasts.

She began to massage her breasts, rubbing them gently, and then harder as her movements over Brandon grew more and more wild. She rubbed her nipples between thumb and forefinger, tipping her head back; and suddenly the familiar rush of pleasure was there as she came, rippling through her quim and seeming to explode in her solar plexus.

Her internal muscles quivered along Brandon's cock; it was enough to tip him over the edge into his own orgasm, and he pushed upwards as he came, his cock throbbing and filling her with the warm salty spurts of his semen.

Susanna collapsed onto him, not caring that they were both sweaty, and buried her face in his neck.

'Better?' he asked, stroking her hair.

'Better,' she confirmed.

They fell asleep in a tangled sweaty mass of limbs; the next morning, though she'd had nowhere near as much sleep as she needed, she felt bright-eyed and bushy-tailed, and spent the whole day smiling. Even her boss, who was in a particularly demanding mood, couldn't dampen her spirits; Susanna simply smiled, said yes, and delivered whatever Isobel asked for. It just felt good to be alive, and to have a man like Brandon who could fulfil her every need. Everything from food to fucking . . .

Two

Susanna woke the next morning in a foul temper, with a headache to boot and a mouth that felt sticky and sour. *That's what you get for drinking with Kate*, she told herself crossly. *You know you can't drink anywhere near as much as she can – whatever everyone believes about journalists being old soaks. Just stick to your limits, in future.*

She went to the bathroom, splashing her face with cold water and cleaning her teeth: it made her feel slightly better. Then she glanced at the clock. It was half-past six. *Well, Brandon Rodgers*, she thought, *time for your wake-up call. And this time, you'd better bloody well answer – or else*. She sat on the bed, reached over to the phone on the bedside table, and dialled the number of Brandon's mobile phone.

'The cell phone you are calling is switched off. Please try later,' the smug well-spoken female voice informed her.

'That's it,' Susanna said furiously, slamming the phone down. 'That's absolutely bloody it. I'm going to Cornwall, on the first train I can get. And you'd better have some answers for me, Brandon Rodgers. Good ones.'

She packed swiftly – years of being a student had taught her to travel light – and had a shower and washed her hair, drying it with lots of mousse to make her curls even more pronounced. Then she dressed – *to kill*, she thought nastily – choosing a pair of navy-and-white striped palazzo pants, a navy georgette shirt, and topping the lot with a straw boater.

'Not bad, Susanna,' she said softly as she looked into the mirror. She looked professional, sexy, and dangerous – exactly right for challenging Brandon and That Woman.

She quickly did her make-up, choosing neutral colours for a subtle and professional effect, added a pair of dark glasses, then picked up her bag and went to the office. If she was going to have a five-hour train journey, or whatever it took from Waterloo to the tiny village where Alicia Descourt lived, she might as well do something useful with her time. Like catching up with a few articles she'd been putting off for ages.

It was too early for anyone else to be in, so she carefully downloaded some files from her desktop computer onto her small laptop, then scribbled a quick fax to Kate, explaining that she couldn't go shopping with her on Saturday because she was going to Cornwall, and would ring her later. She left a similar note for Yvonne, and then headed for Waterloo.

The clerk at the ticket office was very helpful, mapping out her route for her and telling her exactly where to change trains, and how long she'd have to wait for her connection. She had twenty minutes to kill until the next train to the south west came in, so she headed for the bookstall.

The one thing she'd forgotten to pack was a book, and although she intended to work on some of the journey, she wanted to relax as well. Besides, the battery of her laptop would only last for about three hours, and the journey would take a lot longer than that. Nearer six or seven, with all the changes she'd have to make. She needed something to keep her going, on the journey.

Sod's law, she thought wryly, as she saw a huge display of Alicia Descourt's latest book in the window of the shop. Though maybe it would help give her some idea of the woman, if she read one of her books. Eventually, she picked up Alicia's first novel, *The Vampire Queen* – it had had rave reviews, although Susanna had never bothered reading it when it came out – and a cheap version of a Dickens paperback she'd been meaning to read for years, paid for them, and went into the snack bar to buy a couple of bottles of water and some fruit.

Thus armed for her journey, Susanna caught her train – which, to her relief, was less than half full, giving her plenty of space. At least she wouldn't have to share a table with anyone, huddling up in a corner to work. She could spread out, to her heart's content.

She settled in at a corner seat with a table, putting her bag on the seat next to her and kicking off her shoes. She spent the first part of the journey working on a couple of articles; then, flexing her tired fingers, switched over to the games file for a couple of games of patience.

Some three-quarters of an hour later, she looked up, to notice the man sitting three seats down from her staring at her. As soon as he realized that he'd caught her eye, he smiled. She frowned, hoping that he'd pick up her 'keep off' signals and not annoy her on the journey. The last thing she wanted was for someone to try picking her up, when all she could think about was Brandon and That Woman.

She packed away her computer and picked up Alicia's novel. She brought out the grapes she'd bought at the station and began munching them absent-mindedly as she read. She was surprised to find that the book measured up to all the hype: Alicia could write really well, spinning a tale about the queen of the vampires which was believable, scary – and erotic, all at the same time.

The description of a scene where the vampire queen first made love to another vampire would have had her sitting with her hand between her legs, had she been at home; as it was, sitting in such a public place, she merely shuffled a little in her seat and pressed her thighs together, hard, to ease the ache.

'Very good, isn't it?' a voice said next to her.

She looked up, startled. It was the man from three seats away; he was standing in the aisle between the seats, leaning against the headrest of her seat.

Part of her wanted just to snarl at him, tell him to fuck off and leave her alone; the other part of her, the part that had been aroused by the book and was still mad at Brandon, thought 'What the hell?' The stranger was attractive, it was a long journey – and what was the harm in it?

She removed her dark glasses, and smiled at him. 'It's better than I expected, I have to admit.'

'After all the hype, eh? I thought the same. Half the time, you buy one of these bestsellers, expecting it to be brilliant – and when you've read it, you think it was good, but not *that* good. Whereas if you'd come across it by chance, without seeing all the rave reviews and publicity notices, you'd probably have thought it brilliant.' He looked pointedly at the seat opposite her. 'Do you mind if I sit down and talk to you, for a bit? I don't know about you, but I get a bit tired of my own company, on journeys this long.'

'Mm, I suppose so.'

He slid easily into the seat opposite her; a shiver of hunger flared up Susanna's spine. He moved well and, although he wasn't quite as tall as Brandon, he had a good body. Muscular thighs, beneath the soft faded denims; nice forearms, sprinkled with a light covering of dark hair, visible below his rolled-up shirt sleeves; and a well-developed chest which suggested that he either worked out or played a lot of sport. *Rugby*, she thought, *and squash. Something masculine and competitive.* He looked the type.

'I'm Paul Beetley, by the way,' he said, holding out his hand.

'Susanna James,' she said, taking it. He had nice hands, too, she noticed. Sensitive, with long fingers. It reminded her of Brandon, for a moment, and her stomach clenched at the thought of Brandon's hands running over her body – or running over That Woman's body.

'So what are you doing, heading towards Cornwall?' he asked.

'Going to see—' *My lover, with the bitch whose book you've just raved over. I think she's screwing him, and I'm not sure if I want to kill her, him or both of them . . .* 'A friend,' she finished lamely. 'How about you?'

'Having a long weekend at my parents' place, just outside Bodmin. I suppose I really could have driven down, but the thought of five hours solid in the car, after a heavy week, was just too much.' He looked rueful. 'Only I'd forgotten how bored I get on trains.'

'Me, too,' she said, smiling. 'Still, at least we're not cooped up on a rush-hour train, standing in a corridor for hours and wishing that the idiot next to us would move his briefcase out of the way, and that the parents of the brat running up and down the aisle, annoying everyone, would just make him sit down and behave himself.'

He groaned. 'Don't even think it!' He smiled at her. 'What do you do? I noticed that you were working on a laptop, earlier. Were you writing reports for the Board?' he guessed.

She shook her head. 'Draft articles, actually. I'm a journalist.'

His blue eyes appraised her warmly. 'Let me guess. You're the editor of the City pages for one of the broadsheets?'

She chuckled. 'I don't think you could have been much further out! No, I'm the assistant editor on one of the women's monthly magazines. You know, one of the lifestyle ones. Cookery, crafts, and the odd interview with someone like Mary Wesley or Felicity Kendal. That sort of thing.'

'Right.' He smiled ruefully. 'I probably haven't read any of your work, then.'

'Probably not,' she agreed. 'Unless you happen to read *Homefile*.'

He shook his head. 'I think my sister buys it, but I've never actually read a copy, myself.'

'No, I can't quite see you being into Agas, appliqué, or couverture chocolate,' she said, smiling. 'So what about you?'

'I'm a dealer, in the City. It's a bit of a rat race, and it's not so much fun now that the markets have gone quiet – you don't get the buzz of suddenly making millions, and waiting until the last possible moment to sell.' He shrugged. 'Maybe one day I'll make my pile, and then I'll retire to a little cottage in Cornwall, spending my days fishing and painting badly, with a couple of red setters bounding round me to remind me when it's time to eat.'

'Nice dream,' she said. Very similar to one of Brandon's – he was always saying that he wanted to move to the Cotswolds, and she could work from home with a computer and a modem and a telephone. An old stone cottage, with bressumer beams and the original bread-oven in the kitchen, apple trees at the bottom of the garden, and the front garden full of delphiniums and daffodils. A couple of cats, a mad springer spaniel, to keep the company and hog the place by the wood-burner in the winter. And the best thing about working from home, according to Brandon, was that they could make love whenever and wherever they wanted . . .

Was it her imagination, she thought suddenly, or was there something touching her ankles? She moved her foot experimentally, and discovered another bare foot close to hers.

'So you don't like wearing shoes, either?' she asked, amusement quirking her lips. It was a long time since someone had played footsie with her. Brandon was far more wicked, managing to sit next to her at dinner parties and sliding his hand between her thighs, the table-cloth covering what he was up to. It had become a kind of game, a challenge between them, for him to try to make her come and her to pretend that absolutely nothing was happening, and the coffee was delicious . . .

Paul smiled back. 'When I'm not at work, I always wear deck shoes. I like walking barefoot across lawns and beaches.'

'Not too many of those in London.'

'That's another good reason for going home to my parents' place, every once in a while. They have an incredible lawn. Dad's a bit of a gardening fiend. It's like walking on – oh, I don't know, a thick velvet-pile carpet.'

He smiled at her again, and she noticed just how beautiful his eyes were: a deep cornflower-blue, fringed by unfairly long and thick lashes. His dark hair was short, slightly curly, and there was a scattering of freckles across his face. His mouth was generous, and Susanna had a sudden shocking vision of herself lying naked on a four-poster bed, with Paul crouched between her thighs, his face barely visible as he licked her quim . . .

She swallowed hard, and hoped that her face wasn't as red as it felt. Even if it was, he didn't make any comment: simply smiled again, that slow sensuous smile which made her skin ripple with desire. She could feel her nipples hardening, and knew that the thin lace of her bra and the even thinner material of her shirt did nothing to hide the fact that she was aroused.

His foot slid very slowly under the wide leg of her trousers, and his toes massaged her calves; Susanna wasn't quite sure what he was intending, but if it was what she thought it was . . . She gave a small shiver as she felt her quim moisten, and moved her thighs further apart.

Still, Paul held her gaze, as though he were mesmerizing her: those blue, blue eyes seemed to know everything. Like the fact that her nipples were so hard they almost hurt, and she wanted him to carry on stroking her, letting his foot drift higher and higher until he was rubbing her quim, giving her the relief she'd dreamed about in the night.

She swallowed hard as his toes massaged the back of her knee, then drifted higher, over her thighs. *He must be able to smell my arousal*, she thought suddenly. *And if his foot goes much higher, he'll find out that the crotch of my knickers is soaking wet.* The thought sent another tremor through her – a mixture of excitement, embarrassment and sheer longing.

Paul smiled at her, and at last his toes made contact with her crotch. *Thank God I'm wearing these and not some tailored affair*, Susanna thought, and gave a small sigh as he wriggled his toes, brushing against her quim. She widened the gap between her thighs still further, and he began rubbing her crotch, stimulating her clitoris.

She swallowed hard, trying not to moan and draw the other passengers' attention to what they were doing. She thought about returning the compliment, bringing her foot up to stroke his cock through his faded denims, but she was enjoying herself too much to concentrate on someone else's pleasure. Besides, she thought, the denim was too thick, in any case.

As a sudden sharp wave of pleasure swept through her, she bit her lip, hard, to stop herself crying out. Another wave followed, and another, and finally she came, her quim flexing madly against his foot. Even the way Brandon teased her at dinner-parties had nothing on this. It must be the added spice, Susanna thought, of true danger. Letting a stranger make her come, in a very public place.

Paul said nothing to her until her breathing had calmed; then he took her hand. 'Susanna.'

'Mm.' Her eyes were sensual and dreamy.

'It's a long way to the next station. We're not in the path of the buffet car, and the conductor came through ages ago.'

A smile curved her lips. She knew what he was going to suggest, but she wanted to hear him say it. 'And?'

'Let's take a little walk, hm?'

She thought about it. While they were gone, anyone could walk into their compartment, take her handbag and her computer, and she'd be completely stuck. On the other hand, the same thing could happen if she fell asleep. It wasn't that much of a risk. After all, a lot of people had left the train at the last station, and the carriages were virtually deserted. A few minutes away from her luggage wasn't going to hurt . . .

She smiled. 'Where are we heading?'

He grinned. 'I would suggest the toilet, but it's a bit sordid – besides, there isn't enough room there to do what I want to do with you.'

She couldn't resist asking. 'And you'd know, would you?'

He ran his tongue along his lower lip. 'Yes. And from experience, before you ask.'

She grinned. 'I see.' She could imagine what had happened. Another woman, maybe one like herself whom he'd just met, and recognized as a kindred spirit, someone who adored good sex . . . 'So where and when do we meet?'

'By the doors.'

'Right.'

'Two minutes,' he said softly, kissing the back of her hand, then standing up and heading for the corridor between the carriages.

Susanna waited for a moment, then followed him. As she went into the corridor, she smiled. He was leaning against the wall, looking for all the world as though he were merely gazing out of the open window, not waiting for someone. What gave him away was the large bulge at his crotch, which wasn't even vaguely hidden by the soft denim of his jeans.

As she walked towards him, he tipped his head on one side. 'Susanna.'

'Paul.' She stood beside him. 'I wish I was wearing a skirt, now.'

'No problem.' He put his hands on her waist, pulling her towards him; then, before Susanna realized what he was doing, he slipped his hands under her loose shirt, and pulled her trousers down.

'Paul! What if someone comes?' she hissed frantically.

He shook his head. 'They won't. And even if they do, let's face it – that couple who were caught making love on the train and hit the headlines were only reported when they lit up a cigarette. Nobody said a thing about the fact that they were fucking.' He paused. 'I don't smoke.'

'Neither do I.'

'Well, then. We've got nothing to worry about.' Gently, he helped her out of the palazzo pants, and stroked her thighs. 'God, you've got beautiful legs,' he said huskily.

'Thank you.'

Some kind of electric spark seemed to run through them, and suddenly she was in his arms, and he was kissing her. His lips were gentle, at first; Susanna, who was still aroused from the way he'd pleasured her under the table, couldn't help opening her mouth under his, nibbling at his lower lip until he opened his mouth, too, letting her explore him. He tasted sweet, and she slid her hands into his hair, holding his mouth to hers. She wanted the kiss to go on forever, just this first moment of anticipation, with all the pleasures to come after . . .

Eventually, he lifted his head. His eyes were a very intense blue, and his pupils had expanded. 'Oh, Susanna. I think we're both going to enjoy this,' he said softly, sliding his hands under her shirt. He eased his hand under the cups of her bra, and smiled in pleasure and triumph as he felt the hardness of her nipples. 'You're so responsive,' he said. 'I want to be inside you. I want to feel your cunt sucking me deep inside, like wet silk wrapped around my cock.' His fingers worked on her breast, making her gasp and push against him.

'That's where I want you, too,' she said, her hands going down to the waistband of his jeans. This was crazy, she knew – making love with a complete stranger, in the middle of a train. If they were caught, the consequences didn't bear thinking about. The publicity would be enough to lose her her job. But the needs of her body were stronger than her attempts to listen to common sense. She was going to do it.

Gently, she unbuttoned his jeans and drew down the fly. His cock was already fully erect; she smiled, easing his jeans over his hips and pushing his underpants down. He looked as good as she'd expected: for a moment, she was tempted to drop to her knees and slide her mouth over his glans, licking and sucking until his body jerked.

Then Paul lifted her slightly, balancing her weight against the wall. It reminded her of the time when Brandon had done that, in her office, and sent a shiver of longing through her.

'Whoever he is,' Paul said softly, 'just forget him, for now. This is for you and me.'

Her eyes widened. She hadn't thought that her face was such a mirror for her emotions. She swallowed hard. 'OK. Just you and me,' she said, kissing him lightly.

He still had one hand under her shirt; deftly, he undid the clasp of her bra, giving him easier access to her breasts. And then, at last, she felt the tip of his cock pressing against her sex; she flexed her internal muscles, and he slid deep inside her. He stayed there for a moment, just letting her body relax and grow used to the feel of him; and then he began to thrust, long slow and deep movements which had her shuddering and tipping her head back against the wall.

Her throat was white and smooth; Paul couldn't resist kissing it, drawing his teeth over her fair skin and licking the hollows of her collarbones. She gave a small stifled moan of pleasure, and he began to thrust harder, faster, pushing into her as if he wanted his whole body to be swallowed up inside her sex.

Susanna felt as though she were spinning, her body completely out of her control; and all the while, cool air blew over them from the open window. *This*, she thought, *is what paradise is like* . . . And then she was coming, her quim convulsing sharply round his cock. It was enough to push Paul into orgasm, too; he buried his head in her shoulder to muffle his cry as he came.

They remained locked together for a while; then Paul tenderly restored order to her clothing, doing up her bra and helping her on with her trousers. Her hair was slightly rumpled, her lips were swollen and reddened, and her eyes were filled with the sparkle which only comes from orgasm, but neither of them cared. If anyone had passed through the corridor and noticed what they were doing, neither of them had been in a state to notice.

'We'd better go back,' Susanna said.

'See you in two minutes.' He couldn't resist dipping his head to kiss her again.

'Two minutes.' She rubbed the tip of her nose against his, then went back to her seat. Everything was as she'd left it; she smiled as she settled back into the seat. Part of her still couldn't quite believe what had just happened. A man had come across to her, introduced himself, and made her come; then they'd gone into the connecting corridor and made love, regardless of who was watching.

Either I'm some kind of sex-craved pervert, she thought, *or it was a temporary blip* – one to rival even Kate's wilder tales. She smiled again as she thought of Kate's face when she told her.

'You look like the cat who's got the cream,' Paul said, sitting beside her.

She grinned. 'I could made a very, very coarse remark, and remind you what sort of cream.'

He laughed back. 'Indeed.'

They chatted for a while longer; then Susanna felt her eyelids growing heavy. She'd slept badly, recently, and the one sure-fire way to a good sleep was good sex . . . Eventually, she gave in, and slept, her head resting on Paul's shoulder.

Some time later, she became aware of someone gently brushing her cheek, saying her name.

She was about to smile, and say 'Brandon' – then she remembered that it wasn't. She gave a small murmur, hoping that the brief flash of disappointment hadn't shown on her face.

'Susanna, I'm sorry to wake you, but this is my stop.' Paul took her hand, kissing her fingertips, and pulled a business card out of his wallet. He scribbled two numbers on the back of it. 'The top one's my parents' number – in case you find yourself at a loose end while you're down here. The other's my home number in London. When you're back, if you feel like looking me up, I'd like to hear from you. Or ring me at work – maybe we could do lunch.' A flicker in his eyes added for him: and repeat what we did earlier, but this time under a table with a cloth covering it.

Susanna smiled at him. 'Thank you. I might just take you up on that.'

'I hope you do. Take care – and enjoy Cornwall.' He kissed her cheek.

She raised her hand in a shy wave as the train pulled out, then glanced at his card. Paul Beetley, Investment Analyst. It was a well-known City firm: she was impressed. He didn't have the brash demeanour of some of the City yuppies she'd met, and the way he'd made love to her had been thoughtful, concerned as much for her pleasure as for his own. Well, if Brandon really was playing around with Alicia Descourt, maybe she'd ring Paul when she got back to London. And if Brandon wasn't with Alicia – well, she could ring Paul anyway. She could introduce him to Kate, if her Italian didn't work out.

The sleep had done her good – not to mention the orgasms – and she felt much better for it. Smiling, she returned to her book, which kept her absorbed through another two changes of trains. She finished it just as the light started to fade; and then, at last, she found herself in Pentremain.

She got up, feeling stiff, and picked up her bag. She was the only person getting off at the station, and the platform was deserted, with the exception of two tubs of scarlet geraniums. There wasn't even a guard in sight.

Well, here goes, she said to herself, stepping onto the platform. There was bound to be a taxi nearby – there were *always* taxis, near train stations – or at least a telephone. And, in a few minutes' time, she'd be back with Brandon . . .

The first thing she noticed was the castle. Perched on a steep hill, it overlooked the village: it looked like something out of a movie-set, she thought wryly. Boris Karloff, eat your heart out. Trust Alicia Descourt to live somewhere so Gothic. Her PR people had probably picked it out for her.

Hoisting her bag over her shoulder, she went out past the ticket office. There turned out to be one taxi on the forecourt – an ancient and slightly battered car which was beginning to show signs of rust. Susanna had a quick look over her shoulder at the station's reception, but there were no phones. It looked like it was the rust-bucket or nothing.

She walked over to the car; the burly taxi-driver was sitting reading the sports pages of a newspaper, oblivious to his surroundings. She rapped on the window, and he started, opening the window with a smile of apology.

'Sorry, love, I was miles away. To be honest, I wasn't really expecting the train to be in this early.'

'Right.' She smiled at him. 'Do you have any passengers booked?'

'Not today, love. I usually meet the train, though, on the off-chance.'

'Good. Could you take me to Castle Pentremain, please?'

'Castle Pentremain?' His florid face paled, and he shook his head. 'Sorry, love. I can't take you there, tonight.'

She frowned. 'Why not?'

He shook his again. 'I just can't.'

'I see.' Susanna bit her lip. 'Is there another taxi in Pentremain?'

'No, just me. Mike the Taxi.' His voice dropped so that she could barely hear him. 'And if there were other drivers, they wouldn't take you to that castle tonight.'

'But why not?'

'Because no one goes there at night,' the taxi-driver informed her. 'No one.'

'Look, the woman who lives there—' Susanna was shocked to see the driver cross himself '—she's just a writer of horror stories.'

'Vampires. She writes about *vampires*.' His face had actually drained of blood; Susanna's eyes widened. Why was he so frightened? It was only fiction.

'Look, they're just stories.' She sighed. 'My boyfriend's decorating the castle for her, and I need to see him.'

He stubbornly shook his head. 'Not tonight. I can't take you.'

She shrugged, and picked up her bag. 'It looks like I'll have to walk there, then.'

'Not at night.'

'Look, Cornwall's not like London, full of muggers and rapists. And it doesn't seem that far.' She peered at the steep hill leading up to the castle. Her twice-weekly step aerobics class had left her reasonably fit, but it would still be a bit of a haul. 'About half an hour, I'd say.' She lifted her chin, her eyes glittering with determination. She'd come this far: she wasn't going to be baulked of seeing Brandon now.'

'I'll take you to the local inn,' the taxi-driver said. 'You can stay there, tonight, and I'll take you up to that place tomorrow morning. Nine o'clock sharp, if you like.'

The train journey had made her tired, hungry and thirsty; all Susanna really wanted to do was have a bath, a meal, and go to bed. Mike the Taxi was so stubborn that she'd never argue him into taking her to the castle. If she walked, it would take maybe half an hour; though distances were deceptive. She and Brandon had gone walking before, thinking that a gentle slope lay before them, and discovered that it was actually a hell of a lot steeper than it looked. The road up to the castle was probably just as deceptive: and, even after all that effort, there was no guarantee that Alicia would let her in.

In the end, she decided to take his advice and stay in the village. In the morning, she'd be fresh, she could take a taxi to the castle and arrive without wanting to collapse in a heap – and she'd be in the right frame of mind to tackle Brandon. And Alicia.

Three

The local inn turned out to be a seventeenth-century building, with tiny mullioned windows, lots of beams, and a huge inglenook fireplace in the bar area. Susanna loved it on sight. Her bedroom contained a double bed with a wrought iron bedstead, a small antique pine chest of drawers, a large matching wardrobe, and a small bedside table. The room smelled of pot-pourri – some seventeenth-century blend, to go with the house, she thought – and there was a large blue-and-white pitcher and ewer on top of the chest of drawers. It was the sort of quaint place that she and Brandon would have chosen to stay in, had they been touring round Cornwall.

She unpacked, shaking the creases out of her clothes, then had a long and sybaritic bath in the tiny en-suite. The landlord had thoughtfully provided a bottle of rose-scented foaming bath oil, as well as a bottle of shampoo, the usual tiny bar of white soap, and thick fluffy bath-towels. Susanna washed the grime of the journey from her body, then lay back in the bath, half-drowsing.

It had been a weird day, she thought. First, her encounter with Paul on the train – she still couldn't quite believe that she'd been so wanton, and only the slight stickiness between her thighs convinced her of the truth – and then Mike the taxi-driver's stubborn refusal to take her to the castle at night.

The fact that he'd crossed himself made her feel slightly

uneasy. Cornwall was meant to be full of mysterious things, she knew that: Tintagel, the Arthur myths, pixies and fairies. Was he just an over-superstitious villager – or was there something really creepy about Alicia Descourt and Castle Pentremain?

She shook herself. Ridiculous. Alicia was merely a Gothic horror writer, in her late thirties. She had become famous about five years before, for her Vampire Queen series, and the way she dressed was obviously to please her PR people. Alicia's dark hair was worn long and she kept out of the sun so that her skin was pale – or maybe she added a little make-up, to make herself look paler. She always dressed in black, and wore burgundy or deep red lipstick and black nail-varnish: her Gothic look, Susanna thought, was nothing more than a PR stunt, to make her seem more like the 'vampire queen' she wrote about.

Maybe the villagers were in on it, too, and Alicia paid them to scare tourists. There was probably a shop in the middle of Pentremain which was dedicated to her work, selling books, audio-cassettes, postcards, T-shirts and baseball caps: the usual marketing merchandise. If the tourists were given the right atmosphere, they'd be more likely to buy Alicia's wares. It was standard sales tactics, nothing more than that. And she was too media-wise to fall for it.

Soberly, Susanna got out of the bath, and dried herself; she dressed swiftly, choosing a pair of loose-fitting jeans and a dark green cotton shirt. She wasn't in the mood for dressing up; besides, she didn't want to attract attention. All she wanted was a good meal, and then to hit the sack, getting a decent night's sleep before she went to Alicia's spooky castle and faced Brandon.

She went down to the bar. It didn't seem particularly busy, but Susanna guessed that it was probably livelier at weekends. The thing that did disconcert her was the fact that she was the only woman in the bar. Still, she was dressed demurely enough: her outfit wouldn't exactly offend the locals.

The barman smiled at her. 'Yes, love, what can I get you?'

'A mineral water, please – and can I see the menu?'

'Of course.' He handed her a small red leatherette folder; while he sorted out her drink, adding the ice and lemon that she asked for, she ran her gaze down the menu. There were some traditional Cornish dishes, plus the usual bar-menu offerings of basket meals, lasagne and chili. She had a dim recollection of star-gazy pie being something with fishes' heads poking out of the crust, and she couldn't face that; eventually, she plumped for the beef in red wine with seasonal vegetables, and handed the menu back to him with a smile.

'On holiday, are you?' the barman asked.

It was a trivial conversation, meaning nothing to either of them, but Susanna appreciated it. 'Sort of. I've come to see my boyfriend – he's working in the area.'

'What does he do?'

'Brandon's an interior designer,' Susanna said. 'Alicia Descourt's asked him to do her castle.'

There was a noticeable drop in the level of conversation in the bar, and Susanna was uncomfortably aware that everyone was staring at her. It felt like the temperature had dropped a couple of degrees, too – though that was probably her imagination.

She shifted in her seat, and took a sip of mineral water. 'Would you mind telling me what's wrong with the place, please?'

'How do you mean?' The barman's face, which had previously been friendly, was now like a wax mask, hard and cold.

'Well, when I arrived today on the train, I asked Mike the taxi-driver to take me up to the castle, and he wouldn't – he said he couldn't do it at night, and *nobody* ever went up there at night. And the minute I mention the place here, the whole bar goes silent and everyone looks daggers at me.' She spread her hands. 'So what's going on?'

'You'd best stay away from that place,' an elderly, slightly cracked voice informed her; Susanna turned round to face the old man standing behind her. He was slightly shorter than she was, and very very thin. His eyes were pale blue, and slightly watery; his skin was florid, as though he spent most of his time in the pub.

She frowned. 'How do you mean, stay away from it?'

'It's not a good place,' he said. 'It's an evil place.'

'An evil place?' The logical part of Susanna's brain told her that this was just a stunt to scare her. Like she'd thought earlier, all the locals were in on it. Alicia paid them a little, every so often, and they were happy to tell spooky tales in the pub. It just added spice to the tourists' holidays, encouraging them to read more of Alicia's vampire books.

The less detached part of her shivered at the look on the old man's face. He had the air about him of a man who'd seen untold horrors – a man who drank a lot, but still couldn't forget them.

'An evil place?' she repeated, tipping her head to one side. 'How do you mean?'

'It's a wicked place, with wicked folk who live there. Bad things have happened there, in the past, and it's worse at night. You won't find anyone on the hill after dark – not a man, woman or child. Nor a dog or a cat, neither. All you'll find there are screech owls and bats.'

Bats. They were a protected species, and couldn't be moved if they colonized your attic or a church. Trust Alicia Descourt to find a place with bats – an environment which would give the perfect atmosphere for her Gothic horror works. Susanna didn't know whether she wanted to spit or to admire the woman.

'Isn't it always like that, in the country?'

He shook his head, very slowly. 'The castle's an accursed place. I should know. I used to work there, years ago.'

'And you're still here.' It was out before she could stop it.

He recoiled, almost as though she'd slapped him. 'Laugh at me all you like, young lady. But don't say that I didn't warn you.'

Susanna felt ashamed of her rudeness. 'I'm sorry. I came on the train from London this morning. It's been a long journey, and I'm very tired. I didn't mean to laugh at you – I just . . .' She swallowed. 'Look, can I buy you a drink?'

He paused for a moment, watching her warily; then decided to accept her offer. 'All right.'

The barman poured him a pint of ale, and they went to sit down at a small table by the fire.

'I'm Susanna James, by the way.'

'Thomas Penford.' He held out his hand.

She took it, shaking it warmly. His skin felt like paper beneath her fingertips, thin and dry, as though it would crumble if she squeezed his hand too hard. 'Pleased to meet you, Thomas.'

'And this is your first time in Pentremain?'

She nodded.

'Forgive me for asking, but why did you come here? Why didn't you go to one of the coast villages, the usual sort of places that tourists stay?'

'Because I've come to see Brandon. My boyfriend. He's working for Alicia Descourt, at the moment. As I said, he's an interior designer. He's sorting the place out for her.'

Thomas's eyes narrowed. 'Does she know you're here?'

Susanna's smile was hard. 'Not yet. She will, tomorrow.'

'I'd go home, if I were you. Stay as far away as you can from that place.'

She lifted her chin. 'I'm not going until I've seen Brandon.'

He stared at her for a long time. 'I'm not sure if you're a very foolish young lady, or a very brave one.'

'Neither. I just want to know what's going on.'

'When you do, you'll wish that you didn't.'

Susanna frowned. 'Thomas – what is it about the place? No one will tell me.'

'It's evil. Like I said, I used to work there, years ago. I was a gardening boy.' His hands shook slightly. 'I was sixteen. She must have been eighteen or nineteen.'

'Who?'

'Alicia.' It was the first time he'd named her, and his voice cracked as though the name had been wrenched from his throat.

Susanna strove hard to hide her disbelief. Thomas Penford was in his seventies, and Alicia was in her thirties. How could she possibly have been eighteen when he was sixteen?

She must have spoken aloud, or he must have known what she was thinking, because he smiled. 'I know. The ramblings of an old man who drinks too much.'

She stared at the table. 'I'm sorry. But she's in her thirties. I don't see how . . .'

'You will.' He took another sip of his beer, savouring its taste. 'I worked in the gardens. Sometimes, she used to watch me. Her eyes were very green – greener than yours, and hard and cold as emeralds. I didn't like the way she looked at me, and I told the head gardener.' He shrugged. 'He laughed at me, and said that I'd better grow used to it. She was the mistress, so she could do whatever she wanted, whenever she wanted, and I'd better be careful to keep her happy.'

'She was the head of the house?'

He nodded. 'Her parents had died abroad. An aunt or someone brought her up, until she was eighteen. Then she came here, to Pentremain, to claim her inheritance. That's when it all started.'

'All?' Susanna prompted.

'Little things, at first. There'd been a litter of kittens, wild ones, in the potting shed. I looked after them. I was going to take one home to my sweetheart.' He swallowed hard. 'And then, one day, I went to feed them. They were all dead, their heads ripped off. She'd done it.'

'Torn their heads off?' Susanna was horrified.

'And not with her hands, either. She'd sucked their blood out, left them limp as rag dolls.'

Susanna shivered. 'No.'

'And then she started watching me. She was always there. I

could feel her – whether I was in the secret garden at the back, or doing the lawns, I could feel her eyes on me. Always looking.' He shivered. 'And then, one day, I was in the secret garden at the back, trimming the roses. She came in, and started talking to me. I tried to say as little as I could – just yes or no – and I refused to look at her. Eventually, she just said my name. *Thomas*. I looked up . . .'

He closed his eyes. 'She'd taken all her clothes off. Every last stitch. I looked away, but she stood in front of me, her hands holding my face so that I had to look at her. I closed my eyes. "Thomas," she said, "look at me. I know you've been looking at me, wondering what my body was like under those voluminous rags." I told her I hadn't, of course I hadn't presumed to think about the mistress of the castle like that, but she just laughed. She took my hand, and placed it on her breast, holding it to her with her own hand and pushing my fingers to rub her nipples. Her skin was white and cold, just like alabaster – even though it was a hot day, and I was sweating from my work.

' "Look, Thomas," she said again. And when I looked, she had her other hand between her legs. Rubbing and rubbing and rubbing, her head tipped back and her mouth open, moaning. I was horrified – women just didn't do that sort of thing, in my day – but I was a young man. What else could I do?'

'So you made love to her?'

He nodded. 'She took my clothes off, and she had me in the middle of the rose garden. She made me suck her fingers, where they were wet from her touching herself. I hated her for it, and I was spiteful, pushed her against the thorns. But they didn't even touch her. There wasn't a single scratch or mark on her body.

'I'd wanted to keep myself pure, for my sweetheart, but I had no chance. What the lady of the house wanted – though she's no lady, I can tell you – she got. And she got it the way she wanted, too: with her on top, riding me and pushing her breasts into my hands. I was about to come before she did, but she stopped me – let me out of her just long enough to pinch my cock between finger and thumb, holding me back – and then she slid over me again, pushing down on me and grinding herself against me until she came.'

He laughed bitterly. 'I left, that day, and I didn't go back. But I could still feel her watching me, in the village. Every time I was with my sweetheart, it was *her* I saw, *her* I could smell, *her* little sighs I could hear. I never told Cathy, but she knew that something was wrong.' His lips twisted.

'We married, and moved to another village, but *she* was still there. Watching me. She even came to me, once. I was working on my own on the farm, mending fences, and she came to me. She tried the same tricks – stripping off and flaunting herself at me, showing me everything she had – but I was older, stronger. I refused.' He took a deep, shuddering breath. 'I wish now that I hadn't. The next morning, our little girl had gone. The doctor said it was a fever, a virus, but it was her. I know it was her.'

'Alicia?'

He nodded. 'She killed my child. She's haunted me, every night since. In the end, I had to come back to Pentremain. There was no point in going anywhere else – she would still have found me, and it would have happened again. Though once I was back in the village, she left me alone. When it was all too late.'

So that was why he drank. Fantasizing over the woman – and knowing that she was out of his reach. She felt sorry for him; but something in his story didn't quite ring true. 'And all this happened over fifty years ago?' She frowned. 'Alicia wasn't even born then.'

His laugh had no humour in it. 'That's what she tells the world, yes. But we all know what she is, around here.'

'Which is?'

'Undead.'

Susanna shook her head. This had gone far enough. 'Look, she dresses like a character out of one of her books, but it's just a fantasy. Or a PR stunt, to sell more books. It's nothing more than that.'

'You don't live here, so how would you know?' he asked.

'Because vampires don't exist. They're just stories made up to scare people. Or to entertain them.'

His eyes glittered as he stared at her. 'You don't live here,' he repeated, 'so how would you know?'

Susanna's eyes narrowed. 'What makes you say it's not just a story?'

'Well, it's different in the country. There are things here . . .'

'What things?'

'Things like *her*.'

A chill ran down Susanna's spine. It was weird how he hadn't ever actually said Alicia's name, apart from that once. It was all part of the PR stunt, she knew that: the locals telling spooky tales to entertain the tourists. First the taxi-driver brought people to the inn, and then one of the local characters in the bar started spinning a yarn about the old days. On the other hand, the watery blue eyes really did look full of pain. 'Are you trying to tell me that Alicia Descourt is a vampire?'

He nodded.

She shook her head. 'No. I'm sorry, I don't believe you.'

'Go there tomorrow, and you'll find out. She won't see you in daylight – her housekeeper will tell you she's "indisposed".'

'Writers work funny hours. Maybe she works best at night, and sleeps in the day.'

The man before her gave a harsh laugh. 'Oh, she does that, all right.'

The same bitter smile was reflected on all the other faces in the bar. Susanna frowned. 'Look, if you're telling me that she's a vampire, how come no one's denounced her before?'

'No one ever listens.' The elderly man shrugged. 'And we – we can do nothing. If you take a stand against her, your family suffers.'

'How do you mean?'

'Maybe your cat or your dog goes missing. I told you what

happened to the kittens. That's the first warning. If you don't listen, it's your child, next.'

'She kills children?'

'The doctor always says it's a virus – but we know what it really is.' He paused. 'Then it's your wife or husband. And then, slowly, everyone you've ever loved. She takes them one by one, and watches you slowly die inside. It might look like a car accident, or an illness, but it's her. She's behind it all.'

Susanna swallowed.

'Stay away from her,' Thomas warned her gently.

'I can't. I have to see Brandon.'

'Then if I can't persuade you not to go – just be very, very careful. Please. She's all charm, on the surface, but it hides something very . . .' He swallowed. 'She's a terrible woman. Evil.' He reached behind his neck, unfastening the catch of the small silver chain he wore. A crucifix dangled from it, glittering in the light; he handed it to her. 'Wear this. You'll be protected then.'

'Thank you.' Susanna was touched; though she still thought that it was part of Alicia's publicity machine. The local jeweller was probably in on it, and bought the crosses in bulk so that they were dirt cheap.

'Wear it,' he insisted; Susanna gave in, and fastened the tiny chain round her neck.

The barman materialized beside them. 'Your meal's ready, Miss James.'

'Thank you.' She smiled at Thomas. 'I'll see you later.'

'I hope so. I hope so,' he said, his voice tortured with fear and longing.

Susanna followed the barman into the small restaurant; there were one or two others sitting at the candle-lit tables, but they were engrossed in each other's company, and didn't seem to notice Susanna's presence.

The beef in red wine was superb, but Susanna picked at it. She was glad that she'd asked for another glass of mineral water, and not red wine. The colour made her think of blood, and the fantastic story that Thomas Penford had tried to tell her. Kittens with their heads ripped off, children dying from a mysterious virus, the rest of the family slowly dying, one by one . . .

Part of her was annoyed. Either the villagers were a load of superstitious peasants, still set in the last century's ways; or they were in Alicia's employ – that much was obvious. She shouldn't pay any attention to their tales. And yet . . . An icy trickle went down her spine. If what Thomas had told her was true, and Alicia really was a vampire, her books were written from experience rather than imagination. That would explain why Brandon had been writing those curt postcards: because he was under the vampire's spell.

She laughed at herself. God. Nearly everyone she knew had read *Dracula*, and how the aged count had forced Jonathan Harker to write those curt letters to Mina. What next? Was she trying to convince herself that Alicia had told Brandon to write those postcards? No, it was just some stupid publicity stunt, that was all – no doubt Thomas told the same story to anyone who stayed in the village. He was probably the stalwart of the local amateur dramatics group, and Alicia supported all the plays on condition that the actors told a few tales on her behalf.

As for the way Alicia dressed – well, it was just her way of identifying with the character who'd made her fortune. Had she written something about outer space, no doubt she would have stalked around dressed in a silver space-suit and tried to convince everyone that her castle was a landing place for UFOs.

The barman came through to collect Susanna's plate, and raised his eyes at the virtually untouched food.

'I guess I wasn't as hungry as I thought I was,' Susanna said apologetically.

'So you wouldn't like to see the dessert list?'

She shook her head. 'Though I'd like some cheese and biscuits, if you have some, please. And some coffee.'

'Of course.'

He came back a few moments later, and Susanna demolished the plateful. She sat for a while over her coffee then at last, the combination of food, her long journey and the fresh country air made her eyes grow heavy. She couldn't face seeing Thomas Penford again – she knew that ghoulish stories before bedtime, when she was sleeping on her own, would give her nightmares. So she slipped silently through the bar, and went upstairs to her room.

She suddenly remembered that she'd promised to ring Kate as soon as she was in Cornwall; she sat on the edge of the bed and dialled Kate's number. On the fourth ring, the answerphone kicked in; she scowled, and waited for the message to end before she spoke. 'Kate, it's Susanna.'

There was a click, the other end. 'Hi! How's sunny Cornwall, then?'

Susanna groaned. 'I might have known that you were call screening again.'

'Well. I'm not in the mood for my boss ringing me up with yet another brief, outside office hours, and asking if I can have a little something ready for presentation at half-past eight the next morning. Don't get me wrong, I'm a Nineties woman and I'm committed to my career and the firm – but there is such a thing as a fair day's work for a fair day's pay. It works both ways, not just to my dear employer's benefit.'

Susanna grinned. 'Still on the soapbox, then? Anyway, you're preaching to the converted, so you're wasting it, rather.'

'Yeah, I know. Not to mention boring the hell out of you you've heard it so many times already. Sorry.' Kate paused. 'So how is he, then?'

'I don't know. I'm staying in the village inn tonight.'

'Why?'

'Because That Woman's got all the villagers to spook tourists with some cock-and-bull story about not going up to the castle after sunset, and that sort of crap.'

'Right.'

'Then someone told me this incredible story, in the bar. Basically, Alicia's a lot older than she tells people.'

'So? Lot's of women lie about their age.'

'Not by fifty-odd years.'

Kate gave a chuckle. 'Right. *That* sort of cock-and-bull story.'

'Yup. Alicia Descourt doesn't just write Gothic horror – she *is* the Vampire Queen, if you listen to the villagers. Anyway, I'm playing it her way, and staying at the village inn instead of stomping up to the castle. And I suppose it makes more sense to tackle her tomorrow, when I'm fresh, instead of being half-dozy from the train journey.'

Kate laughed. 'You sound like you mean business.'

'I do.'

'Well, take care. Give me a ring when you're coming back.'

'I will.' Susanna smiled. 'Good luck with your Italian, if I don't speak to you before Monday. And if it doesn't work out, I might just have found a nice man for you.'

'Oh?' Kate was interested. 'What have you been up to, Susanna James?'

'That's for me to know, and you to guess.' Susanna grinned. 'We'll have a girly night out, when I get back to London, and I'll tell you all.'

'I can't wait!'

'Well, you'll have to. Patience is a virtue, you know.'

'And a business asset – neither of which I happen to have,' Kate retorted, laughing. 'See you later, then. Good luck for tomorrow.'

'Thanks.'

Susanna felt better for talking to Kate: at least her friend wasn't full of superstitious nonsense, unlike the Pentremain villagers. Now, all she needed was a bit of rest before the morning. She stripped swiftly, put her watch and the little silver cross and chain on the bedside cabinet, and snuggled down beneath the cotton sheets. It wasn't long before she fell asleep – and then she began to dream.

An owl shrieked, an eerie high-pitched cry; she stirred, but didn't wake. She was too tired, and the bed too comfortable, to open her eyes. And then the casement banged open, so hard that she thought the glass would shatter. She opened her eyes, then, to see the thin cotton curtains billowing open, and a shaft of brilliant moonlight coming through the window.

He stood there, his head slightly to one side, watching her. He was, she thought, the most beautiful man she had ever seen. He was tall, his body perfectly sculptured – not thin, but not muscle-bound, either. Like a classical statue.

She normally preferred blond men, but his hair was dark, almost black, and straight, brushed back from his forehead. He had an aristocratic face: thin, with high cheekbones and a largish nose. His eyes were shadowed, but she had the feeling that they'd be green. Intensely and beautifully green. His skin was pale, and reminded her of marble.

'*Mansize in marble*,' she murmured, thinking of the Nesbit tale she'd once read.

He smiled at her, his mouth generous and inviting. 'So you're awake, then?'

She nodded.

'I've been waiting for you.' His voice was cultured, ageless: she had no idea how old he was. He could have been anything from twenty-five to forty-five. The way he was dressed didn't give her any clues, either: a pair of well-cut black trousers, and a black cotton polo-neck sweater. The proverbial tall, dark, handsome stranger. The man in black. And he was all hers.

She didn't speak: she simply reclined on the pillows and smiled.

He walked across the room towards her, light as a cat: his movements were graceful, almost balletic. The bed creaked lightly as he sat down; he smiled at her. 'So beautiful,' he said, stroking her face with the backs of his fingers.

His touch was cool, and yet she felt on fire: she wanted him to touch her more intimately. She knew that he would, in his own time. He always liked playing, first. He smiled again, his face soft and inviting. His gaze was almost hypnotic: and she'd been right about the eyes. They were intensely green. A rich green you could lose yourself in, almost drown in . . .

Gently, he fanned her hair out, so that her soft curls fell over the pillow. 'Mm. That's nice,' he said softly. And then, with one lightning movement, he pulled the sheets from her body.

She lay perfectly still, waiting. His eyes raked up and down her body, taking in the curve of her narrow waist, her generous breasts. Slowly, very slowly, he trailed one finger in the valley between her breasts, stopping by her ribcage; he drew his finger up again, and she tipped her head back, offering her throat to him. He laughed softly: it was a sound full of sensuality and delight, and it made her shiver with anticipated pleasure.

The he drew his finger down over her body again, brushing lightly over her abdomen. In an almost reflex action, she parted her thighs; he moved to the foot of the bed, taking one ankle in each hand, and positioned her legs to give him a better view of her quim.

Her soft pink vaginal lips were fringed with pale fuzzy hair; he drew his tongue along his lower lip at the sight, and it was as though he'd actually licked her labia. Susanna shivered, and tilted her pelvis slightly.

He caressed the soles of her feet, relaxing her; and then said her name, very quietly. 'Susanna. Look at me.'

When she opened her eyes, he peeled off his sweater; his skin was very pale in the moonlight. She itched to run her fingers over his body, feeling the cool smooth texture of his skin, but she knew that she had to wait until he was ready. Until he commanded her.

He continued stripping, peeling off his trousers; it was only then that she noticed they were leather, and that he wore nothing beneath them. He stood there for a moment, naked, letting her watch him: his body was perfect, she thought. His long thick cock rose, erect, from the cloud of hair at his groin; it, too, was pale, but she thought that it was probably because of the moonlight.

Then he smiled, and crouched at the foot of the bed. He sucked her toes, one by one, until she was shivering with pleasure; and then he slowly kissed his way up her body. She closed her eyes and tipped her head back among the pillows as his cheeks brushed against her thighs. Her hands came up to clutch the wrought-iron bedstead, her knuckles whitening as at long, long last she felt the slow stroke of his tongue along her labia, searching her intimate folds and crevices.

'Oh,' she sighed; and then he began to lap in earnest, making his tongue into a hard point and flicking it rapidly over her clitoris until she bucked beneath him. He lifted her buttocks slightly, to give himself a better angle, and slid his tongue into her vaginal entrance, making her moan with pleasure.

When she was writhing beneath him, he changed tactic again, drawing his tongue along the complete length of her musky furrow in a slow, insistent rhythm. Susanna could feel her orgasm building, the pressure rising in her, and gripped the bedstead even harder: at last, as the tip of his tongue touched her clitoris, she cried out, her sex-flesh convulsing madly under his mouth.

He smiled again. 'Now,' he whispered softly, leaning over and fitting the tip of his cock at the entrance to her vagina. She was already wet from her first orgasm; he slid easily into her, filling her. She moaned, and wrapped her legs round his waist, pushing up hard against him as he began to thrust.

'Gently, gently,' he whispered, and she relaxed again, letting him break the urgency and set a new rhythm, a slow rocking which built her arousal slowly up to a peak.

She tipped her head back as she felt her climax exploding. 'Now,' he said again, and she felt the sharp sinking of his teeth into her flesh . . .

Four

The dream was so real that when Susanna woke up, the next morning, she went into the bathroom, pushed back her hair, and checked her neck for marks.

Of course, there was nothing there. No bruises, no little tiny red pin-pricks on her skin where the vampire had sucked her blood. Besides, she didn't look pale and ill, like the victims of cinema vampires: if anything, her face almost glowed with health, and she looked like she could run up the steep hill to Alicia's castle.

'You silly tart, James,' she told herself, laughing. 'You dreamed the whole thing. It was just a very erotic, and very realistic dream.' She ached slightly, as though she really had been pleasured and made to come again and again by her vampire lover; though that, she thought, was just her body reacting to her mind's suggestion.

And as for the dream itself: after the tale that Thomas had told her, and the book she'd read on the train, she was bound to have dreamed about vampires. Sexy vampires, because of what she'd done with Paul on the train and the fact that she missed Brandon. There was nothing more to it than that.

She had a bath, then dressed, choosing a pair of navy tailored trousers and a white silk shirt which showed off the voluptuousness of her figure and yet looked professional at the same time. Although she normally wore subtle colours, today she decided to make herself up in something brighter. 'A vamp to challenge a vampire,' she said with a grin, slicking on a coat of bright red lipstick. 'Anything you can do, Alicia Descourt, I can do better. Believe me. And that particularly includes making love with Brandon.'

She went downstairs to breakfast; the barman of the previous night was off duty, and a young girl in her late teens welcomed her. 'Good morning. Ready for breakfast?'

Susanna smiled. 'It must be something about the air round here – I'm absolutely starving!'

'That's what most of our visitors say. How about a full English breakfast, then?' the girl suggested. 'Bacon, eggs, sausages and mushrooms – and they're all local produce.'

'That'd be lovely. Thank you.' Susanna ordered some coffee to go with it, and sat down at a table by the window. The view was amazing – fields full of sheep, a clear, bright blue sky, and the craggy hill which towered above the village. It *was* steeper than Susanna had thought, the previous evening; she was suddenly glad that she hadn't been pig-headed, and had taken the taxi-driver's advice to stay here at the inn overnight. There was no way that she could have tackled the hill after such a long journey, and then tackled Alicia Descourt.

Her breakfast arrived; she was ravenous, and demolished the plate of bacon and eggs, followed by two lots of toast and local honey. She lingered over a final cup of coffee, then went upstairs to clean her teeth, reapply her lipstick, and finish packing. The little silver cross and chain lay on the bedroom table; Susanna looked at it. All this vampire stuff was superstitious nonsense. Of course she didn't need the cross and chain for protection. On the other hand . . . On sudden impulse, she put it on, tucking it out of sight under her shirt and took her bag down to the bar.

The taxi-driver arrived at nine o'clock precisely; Susanna smiled at him. 'Good morning.'

'Good morning.' He smiled back. 'To the castle, isn't it?'

She nodded.

He handed her a card. 'This is my number. Ring me when you're ready to come back again.'

'As long as it's before sunset, hm?' Susanna teased.

A flash of something that looked like terror passed over his face, but his voice was so calm when he spoke that Susanna thought she'd been mistaken. 'That's right. Before sunset. They're terrible roads around here, you know, and there isn't any street lighting, like you'd get in a town. One wrong move, and you're over the edge. There have been too many accidents like that – some of them very serious. Even fatal. I'd just rather not risk it.'

'Right.' That was a more likely reason, she thought, for not going to the castle after dark. She only wished he'd said that to her the previous night, instead of coming out with that spooky nonsense about nobody going to the castle at night and refusing to tell her why. Or maybe he was on commission from the village inn: if he could persuade people to go there instead of straight up to the castle, it was good for business – for both of them.

He took her bag, putting it in the boot; Susanna climbed into the front seat. It would have been a lot less hassle, she thought, if she'd driven herself. When she got back to London, maybe she'd arrange driving lessons. In the meantime, she hoped that the taxi-driver would stay smiling and cheerful, and not come out with any more of this vampire nonsense.

They set off; the road was steep, and Susanna wondered if the car was actually going to make it. The taxi-driver didn't speak to her; he was too busy coaxing the car up the hill. No wonder he didn't like the drive at night, she thought. It was hard enough in the daylight, when you could see where you were going. When it was dark, it must be murder.

And Castle Pentremain was definitely spooky. Even in daylight, it looked black and forbidding. It was smaller than most castles Susanna had seen – probably the remaining part of a larger building – and was built of local granite, she guessed, giving it a dark and brooding air. Most of the windows were narrow slits, designed for archers rather than for pleasant views.

Brandon would have fallen in love with the place at first sight, Susanna thought. No doubt he'd been designing the décor in a medieval style, the interior walls being painted pale colours and covered with richly-coloured tapestries, the floor carpeted in rush matting, and the lighting being mainly large wrought-iron chandeliers and candelabra. The furniture would be oak – antique, if he could find it, or else distressed reproduction pieces; there would be long oak settles covered in plump tapestried cushions, large tables with benches set by them, and an open fire roaring in the grate with a couple of wolfhounds sprawled in front of it . . .

She smiled to herself. Maybe it was worth doing a *Homefile* piece on the place, after all – if only to give their readers something a little different from the usual chocolate-box Victorian cottages. A castle in Cornwall: brooding, romantic and full of atmosphere. No wonder Alicia Descourt had decided to live and work in one. It suited the tone of her books perfectly. It had probably inspired most of the settings.

When they finally reached the top, Susanna looked back over the village. There was an incredible view; the castle had a wonderful defensive position. You could see for literally miles around. Marauding soldiers just wouldn't have had a chance to creep up to the castle and attack it by stealth.

'Well, this is the castle.' The taxi-driver helped her out of the car, then took her bags from the boot. 'Call me when you're ready to come back.'

Susanna smiled. 'I will. Thanks. How much do I owe you?'

He shook his head. 'Pay me on the return journey.'

'All right.' She smiled again. 'See you later, then.'

She walked over to the heavy oak door. Alicia Descourt obviously believed in keeping things authentic: rather than an electric push-button bell, there was a heavy iron bell-pull. Susanna tugged it hard; she couldn't hear a sound, but she assumed that the bell rang somewhere deep inside the castle, and the walls were so thick as to be virtually soundproof.

She waited for a few minutes, then tried again, in case she hadn't done it properly, the first time round. Still there was no answer. She left her bags by the front door, and walked round the castle peering up at it; there appeared to be no sign of life. No windows were open, no lights were on: the whole place looked as though it were deserted. She walked round the castle a second time, in case she'd missed something, but the place looked as though no one had been there for years.

Annoyed, Susanna returned to the front door, and gave the bell-pull a furious tug. Again, she waited: just when she was about to start hammering on the door and yelling, the door creaked open. A tall and gaunt woman stood in the doorway; she was wearing a black dress with an almost ankle-length full skirt and a high neck. Her dark grey hair was clipped tightly to the back of her head in a bun, she wore no make-up, and her face was cold and haughty.

'Yes?' Her voice was slightly clipped, and very aristocratic. This was obviously the housekeeper Thomas had told her about, the previous evening – the one who always told people that Madam was indisposed and couldn't see visitors.

Bloody hell, it's Mrs Danvers, Susanna thought, wanting to laugh hysterically. She forced herself to calm down, and smiled politely, disregarding the woman's cool and slightly ominous gaze. 'Good morning. My name's Susanna James. I'm here to see Alicia Descourt and Brandon Rodgers.'

'She has no appointments, today.'

'Oh, really?' She lifted her chin. 'Actually, it's Brandon I've come to see, not Alicia. I'm his girlfriend.'

The woman said nothing: simply stared at her. Susanna felt slightly unnerved at the pale grey stare, but held her ground. She'd come this far, and she wasn't going to be thwarted by some spiteful old biddy who liked playing games with people.

'May I come in?'

'Milady is indisposed. My instructions are that no visitors are allowed.'

'I see.' Susanna stared at her. 'No doubt her fans lap all this up, but I don't. Now, are you going to let me in, or do I have to call the police and tell them that you're being obstructive?'

The woman arched one well-shaped eyebrow. 'Indeed? This is private property.'

'I know.' Susanna gave her an acidic smile. 'But holding someone against their will is an offence. False imprisonment, it's called. I'm sure that Ms Descourt could do without the negative publicity – don't you think?'

The woman gave her a hostile glare. 'Milady is indisposed.'

Susanna's temper snapped. 'I told you, it's not your bloody "Milady" I want to see – it's Brandon. Now, are you going to let me in, or not?'

There was no answer.

Susanna tried to force down her anger. 'I'm staying here until you let me in,' she said quietly. 'And if need be, I'll ring your bell constantly until Alicia Descourt herself comes to the door, wanting to know what the problem is. So you've got two choices. Either you let me see Brandon, or I make enough noise to wake the dead.'

A flicker of macabre humour crossed the housekeeper's face. 'Indeed.'

'And I work in the media, so I'm not impressed with all your publicity stunts,' Susanna added, for good measure.

The housekeeper continued to block the doorway while she thought about it; eventually, she stepped aside. 'All right. Come in. Wait here while I talk to Milady.'

Susanna's eyes widened as she stepped into the castle. It looked like something from a Hammer Horror set. Very little light came in through the narrow windows, so the place was sombre and gloomy to start with. There was a thick layer of dust everywhere, and the air smelt musty, like old damp books or a run-down stately home with mildewed wallpaper.

It also, she thought, looked as if an interior designer had never been near the place. On the odd occasions when Brandon had fallen for a house he was working on and had taken her to see it, she'd seen swatches of material and books of carpet samples around the place, and little tell-tale squares of paint in different shades on the walls. Here, there was nothing.

There was a chance that maybe Brandon had kept all his work in one place, but she doubted it. He usually annexed a room to work in, if it was too far from London, and kept most of his samples there, but there were always signs of his work around the rest of the rooms. Something was definitely up.

He'd been here for three weeks, now – more than long enough to have agreed the designs with his client, and briefed local contractors to do the work. So what the hell had he been doing? Had he been so smitten with Alicia Descourt that he'd leaped between the sheets with her before starting work, and hadn't been out of her bed since?

Her eyes glittered with anger. *You bastard*, she thought, her temper rising again. *I've been worried sick about you – and all along, you've been lying to me.*

'Where's your employer?' she asked the housekeeper.

'She's indisposed.'

Susanna sighed. 'Look, spare me the melodrama, will you? I'm a journalist, and I know how annoying it is to be interrupted when you're in the middle of writing something. If she's busy with her latest book, fine – I'll wait until she has a break. Then I'd like to talk to her, please.'

'She's indisposed.'

'Oh, for God's sake!' Susanna grabbed the woman's arm. 'Just take me to Brandon. I don't care if he's in bed with her – I want to see him, *now*.'

The housekeeper said nothing: just gave Susanna another of her creepy smiles.

'Is it so much to ask?' Susanna glared back.

'I'll see if he's available. Wait here.'

Available indeed, you bloody cow, Susanna thought: but she knew that there was no point in antagonizing the woman. Instead, she contented herself with another steely glare at the housekeeper's retreating back. Then, as the door at the end of the corridor closed, Susanna turned to her surroundings.

She was waiting in a tall and narrow hallway. The flooring was old grey stone flags, which looked as though they were the original floor: and also looked as if they hadn't been scrubbed since the dark ages. There were no carpets to break up the monotony: had it been her place, Susanna would have scattered rugs everywhere, bright red and blue Turkish silk which would glitter in the light, changing colour when you looked at them from different angles.

The walls were a gloomy colour, a greeny-greyish dun which seemed to deaden the light; what it needed, Susanna thought, was virtually white walls, and lots of extra lighting. There were one or two prints on the walls, very dark, in narrow dark frames which could have been ancient mahogany or ebony; in the dim light, it was difficult to tell. She went over to look at one, and her eyes widened in shock. The man depicted on it wore courtly dress – she suspected it was late sixteenth century, or something similar – and looked exactly like the man she'd dreamed about the night before. Tall, aristocratic, with a sharp face and dark hair, and those stunning green eyes.

She shivered. It was coincidence, no more than that. She'd probably seen a copy of this painting somewhere or other before, and remembered it, deep in her subconscious. She shook herself, and moved on to the next painting. A woman was there, standing in what looked like an arched doorway – maybe one of the doors in Castle Pentremain.

There was a grey wolfhound at her feet, and the woman wore a black, low-cut dress in a late Elizabethan fashion which emphasized the paleness of her skin and the voluptuousness of her breasts. Her hair was dark, and her face was wreathed in a smile which made Susanna feel even more ill-at-ease than the man had, in the other picture. She suspected that it was actually Alicia Descourt, and the painting had been specially commissioned to be a 'matching' portrait to the man's. No doubt Alicia told everyone that the woman was her ancestress – or, even more outlandish, that it was a picture of herself before she became a vampire.

Susanna pulled a face, and moved away from the paintings. The thought of that woman enticing her boyfriend into bed made her furious. She could just imagine Alicia wearing that dress for Brandon, and using it to seduce him . . .

Alicia came into the room, holding a candle, and pouted prettily at Brandon. Then she set the candle to one side, and undid the dress swiftly, letting it fall to the floor and reveal her nakedness. Her skin gleamed in the candle-light – which also hid some of the wrinkles, Susanna thought bitchily – and she cupped her breasts in her hands, pushing them up slightly, almost in offering to him.

Brandon was in an awkward position. Refuse Alicia, however gently, and she'd take it badly. She'd threaten to make sure that he never worked again in this town, or any other: something corny like that. Her influence was certainly enough to do his business some serious damage.

On the other hand, to accept what she was offering was unprofessional. Brandon never mixed business with pleasure: it was a definite rule. You didn't sleep with your clients, your colleagues or your suppliers. He sat there by the fire, thinking about the best way to play it – and, while he was thinking, Alicia made the decision for him. She came over to where he was sitting by the fire, and took the notebook and pen from his hand. Then she slowly unbuttoned his shirt, sliding it off his shoulders and stroking his skin until he closed his eyes and tipped his head back, offering her his mouth.

Then she kissed him, very, very slowly, teasing his lips with hers until his mouth opened, allowing her to slide her tongue into his mouth and explore his sweetness properly. While she kissed him, she let her hands drift down to the waistband of his pale green chinos, undoing it and then undoing his fly.

Brandon gave a soft murmur as she freed his cock from his

underpants, stroking the hard column of flesh until he writhed beneath her, pushing his hips up and thrusting into her hand. Then she pushed him back against the rug, straddling him on all fours so that the tips of her breasts brushed against his chest. He felt her quim sliding against his cock, the warmth and heat of her flesh promising unbelievable pleasure.

Then she lifted herself slightly, curling her fingers round his cock and pressing it against her entrance. Then, achingly slowly, she lowered herself onto him until his cock sank deep inside her. She stayed there for a while, letting him get used to the pleasure of her quim wrapped round his cock like warm wet silk; then she began to lift and lower herself over him, slamming down so hard that her pubis ground against the root of his cock, and then pulling up slowly, slowly, so that his cock almost came out of her, before slamming down hard again.

As she moved, Brandon's hands came up to caress her breasts, his thumbs and forefingers playing with the hard peaks of her nipples. She tipped her head back, baring her teeth with the intensity of pleasure, and shifted slightly to increase the angle of his penetration. She continued to lift and lower herself on him until she felt his balls lift and tighten against her; and then she let herself go, pushing down on his cock until her own orgasm poured through her body . . .

No wonder Brandon had sent those curt postcards, Susanna thought, and stopped phoning her, if that sort of thing was happening every night. He wouldn't even need to think of his girlfriend in London. She glowered, and paced the hall again.

There was a couple of heavy oak doors in the hall, with wrought-iron hinges and large locks; although the housekeeper had told her to stay in the hall, Susanna couldn't help wondering what the rest of the castle was like. And whether she'd been right about the big room with the open fire.

Susanna Bluebeard, she thought with a grim and self-mocking smile, and headed for the first door. She tried twisting the heavy circular handle, but it was obviously locked.

Alicia obviously insisted on privacy, even when she had house-guests.

She tried the second door, and was sure that she felt the latch give. She twisted the handle harder, and eventually the door creaked open. She was just about to open the door properly and peek inside when she heard a cough behind her.

She jumped, and turned round. The housekeeper was standing behind her, looking even more dour and disapproving. 'What are you doing?'

Susanna decided to brazen it out. 'Looking to see what was behind the door. After all, I'm a journalist – maybe our readers would be interested in seeing this place. A before-and-after feature, perhaps, once Brandon's finished the job.'

'Milady would never allow it.'

'Now, why doesn't that surprise me?' Susanna lifted her chin, and drew herself up to her full height. 'So are you going to let me see him, or not?'

The woman gave her a steely glare. 'Follow me,' she said abruptly, and turned on her heel.

Susanna followed the housekeeper through a maze of corridors, up creaky wooden stairs; eventually, they stopped outside another of the heavy oak doors.

'He's in here,' the housekeeper said, a malicious smile crossing her face.

Susanna felt suddenly nervous, not sure quite what she was going to find. A hostile Brandon, furious with her for interrupting his work and being the clingy jealous girlfriend, or . . . She damped down her fears, and opened the door.

What lay behind it was completely unexpected. A naked Brandon, his cock buried deep in a laughing Alicia, had been one of the possibilities. Susanna could have coped with it, just about. But this?

She was shocked to see that the curtains were drawn, and Brandon was lying in bed, looking pale and weak, his eyes slightly bloodshot. He'd lost weight, too, and some of his muscle tone; even his hands looked thinner. He was obviously ill – but what was wrong? When had it started? Why hadn't anyone said anything to her – including Brandon, in those stupid postcards?

'Hello, Susanna,' he said, giving her a tired smile.

The housekeeper was forgotten; Susanna was at his side in a matter of seconds. 'Brandon – what's wrong?'

He looked faintly embarrassed. 'Would you believe, rheumatic fever?'

No, was the short answer. Brandon was disgustingly healthy, and she'd never known him have so much as a cold. When she'd been laid low with flu, once before, he'd nursed her uncomplainingly – and hadn't had so much as a headache or a runny nose himself. 'But you're never ill,' she said, frowning.

He shrugged. 'Maybe my luck just ran out.'

'No wonder you didn't ring me.' Relief rushed through her: thank God that this was the reason for his near-silence, not Alicia.

'I didn't have the energy. I sent you postcards, though, so you wouldn't worry about me.'

'Actually, they were what alerted me. They didn't sound like you.' She sat on the side of the bed, taking his hand and stroking his forehead. He felt hot and feverish. 'I rang your mobile phone, but it was switched off.'

He closed his eyes. 'The battery ran out. I recharged it – but I must have forgotten to switch it on again.'

That was also unlike Brandon. He was the most organized man that Susanna had ever met. He was even more efficient than Kate, who ran her life from a computer. A cold trickle of fear ran through her. What the hell was going on? And why hadn't Alicia Descourt's housekeeper told her that he was ill? 'Never mind,' she said softly. 'Have you seen a doctor?'

He nodded. 'The local quack came yesterday.' He managed the ghost of a smile. 'So much for the country air being good for me, eh?'

'Mm.' She squeezed his hand. 'Can I get you anything? A drink, or something to eat?'

He shook his head. 'It's OK. I don't feel like eating, at the moment, and Molly's been doing me hot milk.'

'Who's Molly?'

'The housekeeper.'

Susanna's lips twitched. 'She wasn't married to a Mr Danvers, by any chance?'

He picked up the reference immediately. 'No, of course not! She's fine, once she gets to know you.' He smiled. 'She's just very protective of Alicia's privacy. Which is just as well – she gets all kind of cranks ringing and calling, wanting to see her.'

'I'm not a crank. I'm your girlfriend,' she said quietly.

'I know. Sometimes Molly overdoes it.'

'So I noticed.' Susanna rolled her eyes. 'They're not much better in the village. They're full of spooky stories about this place.' *And about Alicia* – but something warned her not to say that to Brandon. Not yet. Not until she'd found out for definite what was going on between them.

'I wasn't expecting you to come down.' He was still holding her hand tightly.

'It was a spur-of-the-moment decision. I couldn't get hold of you, so I couldn't exactly give you any warning. Though I did try.' She gave him a slightly fierce look. 'Maybe you should try keeping your mobile switched on. Or at least set up a mailbox, so people can leave you messages.'

'Point taken.' He smiled at her. 'What about the office? Don't they mind you not being in?'

'Yvonne says they'll cope without me. Besides, I could always do a feature on this place, while I'm here. A "before-and-after" piece.' She shrugged. 'If Alicia Descourt gives permission, of course.'

'I'll ask her for you, if you like.'

'Thanks.'

His eyes seemed to be growing heavier and heavier; within a couple of minutes, he was asleep. Susanna looked at him, concerned. Brandon's skin was much paler than usual, and his hair looked thinner, almost lank, as it flopped over his forehead. There were dark shadows under his eyes, as though he hadn't slept properly for days, and his face looked gaunt. Though he was also clean-shaven. Her face tightened. Maybe it was something Alicia did for him – along with the odd blanket bath.

She sighed heavily. This was ridiculous. She should be more concerned with Brandon's health than this stupid jealousy over a woman she'd not even met. *Grow up, Susanna*, she told herself silently. *Stop being so bloody childish and melodramatic*.

Brandon moved his head, and the neck of his pyjamas – another first, as far as she was concerned, because Brandon always slept naked: maybe he'd borrowed them – fell open. Susanna frowned as she saw marks on his neck. She peered at them more closely; the marks were small punctures, an inch and a half or so apart, and they were surrounded by bruises. Judging by the colour, the bruises had been there for a couple of days.

She rubbed her jaw thoughtfully. The bruises were exactly where she had looked for marks on her own neck, that morning, after her vampire dream. Maybe Thomas Penford had been telling the truth after all: maybe Alicia Descourt really was a vampire, and she had the perfect disguise. Who would suspect a horror writer, a woman who was famous for her 'Queen of the Vampires' series, of being a vampire? The more she behaved like one of the undead, the more people would think it a PR stunt – as Susanna had, herself.

Susanna struggled to remember what she knew about vampires. They didn't like the crucifix – thank God she'd remembered to put that cross on this morning. They also didn't like garlic or sunlight. They slept during the day, they could change themselves into a bat or mist or a wolf, and they could also tame any wild animal, no matter how savage. They were seductive – and very deadly, because once they'd got you under their spell, they punctured your jugular vein and drank your blood until you died. Or else they made you a vampire, by making you drink their blood.

They slept in a coffin, lined with earth from their home, and the only way you could kill a vampire was to thrust a stake – preferably ash wood – through the heart, or shoot them with a silver bullet. Then you took the head off and filled it with garlic, and the vampire's spirit could rest.

Where did Alicia Descourt fit in with this? Susanna wondered. Firstly, she wasn't seen in daylight – so maybe she couldn't bear the sun. Secondly, she was seductive: Susanna knew that from her reputation, as well as from the picture she'd seen of the woman. Thirdly, the disgustingly fit and healthy Brandon had been drained during his stay at her castle – and he had marks on his neck which could quite easily be the marks of a vampire's teeth.

And on the other hand, they could be love-bites. The photos Susanna had seen of Alicia Descourt made her think that Alicia was the type of woman who'd want to leave her mark on a man – whether he was hers or someone else's. Susanna could imagine just how Brandon had got those marks. Lying there in the large oak bed, leaning back against the pillows, while a laughing Alicia straddled him. Maybe she had him bound to the corners of her four-poster bed with black silk scarves, so that he was totally at her mercy . . .

Susanna shivered. This was ridiculous. Alicia Descourt was *not* a vampire. She just liked to act as if she were one, and the whole thing was part of her publicity machine. Brandon really had picked up some virus or other, and that was all there was to it.

Five

Brandon woke, a couple of hours later, and smiled as he opened his eyes and saw Susanna at his side. 'Hallo.'

'Hallo.' She returned his smile. 'Do you want some water?'

He nodded weakly, and she helped him sit up, plumping the pillows behind him, then pouring him a glass of water.

He sipped at it gratefully, then handed it back to her; Susanna took a sip, too, and replaced the water on the bedside table. 'Are you hungry?' she asked.

He shook his head. 'Not really.'

I am, she thought: *but no way will the Housekeeper from Hell offer me anything for a late lunch. Except, maybe, for an arsenic sandwich*. She forced a smile to her face. 'It's a lovely day, outside,' she said. 'Why don't I open the curtains?'

'Well, the doctor did say that I should rest in a darkened room.'

Susanna wrinkled her nose. 'It must make you feel even worse, waking up in shadows. A couple of minutes of sunshine and a bit of fresh air will do you good.'

His lips twitched. 'Yes, nurse.'

If he was well enough to tease her, she thought, then he was definitely on the mend. And if he could stand sunlight, it would prove once and for all that the stories about Alicia being a vampire – and her own fears about Brandon being turned into one of Alicia's kind – were complete rubbish.

She walked over to the window, hauling the musty velvet drapes aside; the window-latch was stiff, but eventually she managed to open it. The narrow frosted glass had diffused the bright light outside; she rested her forearms on the windowsill for a moment, enjoying the brightness, before turning back to Brandon.

In the light, he didn't look quite so bad: his eyes seemed less dull, and his skin less pallid. 'How's that?' she asked.

'Fine.' He smiled at her. 'I've missed you, you know.'

She smiled back. 'And there was I, thinking that you'd forgotten me.'

'Never.' He patted the bed beside him. 'Come and give me a cuddle.'

'What sort of cuddle?' The words were out before she could stop them.

He grinned. 'I haven't seen you for a couple of weeks – or talked to you on the phone.'

'I thought you had rheumatic fever?'

'Whatever it is, it isn't catching. Molly and Alicia haven't caught it, and they've both been in the same room as me.'

She felt faintly guilty. She wanted to make love as much as Brandon did – and yet he'd been ill. She didn't want to overtax his strength and give him a relapse. 'Even so, shouldn't you be resting?'

He spread his hands. 'They say that a little of what you fancy does you good . . .'

'Right.' She walked over to the door, sliding the bolt across. 'Just in case we have visitors, at an inopportune moment,' she explained, at his surprised glance.

'We won't. Alicia always sleeps during the day.'

'Don't tell me, in a velvet-lined coffin?'

Brandon frowned. 'She's dramatic, I know, but she doesn't go quite that far.'

'I'm glad to hear it. Anyway, I didn't mean her.'

He was surprised. 'You mean Molly?'

'Mm.'

'But why would she interrupt us?'

Susanna scowled. 'She probably thinks I'm upsetting her patient, and making him have a relapse.'

He grinned. 'Talk about grumpy! I know what'll cure your bad mood, Susanna James. The same thing that'll help cure me.'

'Oh, yes?'

'Yes. Come here.'

She sashayed across the room towards him.

He looked approvingly at her clothes. 'I like that shirt. It's beautifully demure.' His voice grew husky, and his eyes darkened slightly. 'And I bet you're wearing something amazing, underneath.'

'There's only one way to find out, isn't there?' She tipped her head slightly on one side. 'That's if you really *are* well enough.'

Brandon gave a deep chuckle. 'Surely playing doctors and nurses will help me get better?'

She rolled her eyes. 'Oh, honestly!'

'I've missed you, Susanna. I've lain here awake at nights, thinking about you, and thinking how it would be if you were here with me. We'd have a four-poster, and I could play the vampire count with you.'

'Are you telling me that you're a vampire?'

'No, just that this is the perfect place to be one. It'd make a great setting for a film. One of Alicia's novels is going to be made into a film, but she won't let them use this place as a setting. She must be crazy – it's perfect.'

'It's dark, dingy, and the place looks like it hasn't been decorated since it was built. Or dusted, for that matter.'

'Actually, castles used to be decorated in very bright colours. Unfortunately, one of Alicia's Victorian forebears went a bit over the top in making this place look completely Gothic.'

'Otranto, mark two?'

'Something like that.' Brandon moistened his lower lip with the tip of his tongue. 'Anyway, I didn't think a lecture on décor was part of our plans.'

'You get side-tracked so easily,' she teased.

'Susanna.'

'Yes?'

'Just shut up, and come here.'

'You're supposed to be an invalid – and invalids aren't bossy.'

'This one is. He needs to be kissed better.'

'Indeed?'

'Like here.' He pushed the covers down, and undulated his hips.

She coughed. 'You're wearing pyjamas, darling.'

'I'm sure you can do something about that.'

'I *could*,' she agreed. 'Provided you ask me nicely.'

He grinned. 'Susanna, my love, would you kindly stop talking and come and fuck me senseless?'

She smiled, then, and came over to the bed – staying just far enough away to be out of his reach, and in his sight. Then she undid her trousers, pushing the material over her hips and swaying out of them.

'I'd forgotten just how bloody gorgeous your legs are,' Brandon muttered, undoing his pyjama jacket.

She said nothing, but undid her shirt, very, very slowly. Eventually, she let the silk slide over her shoulders to reveal a white lace stretch teddy.

'I *knew* you were wearing something nice,' he said huskily.

She smiled. 'Remember when you bought this for me?'

He nodded. 'You were having a really bad time at work – endless deadlines, and the Bitch Queen on your back nagging about everything from your writing style to your cross-heads. You were living on chocolate and junk food, and drinking enough coffee to make a zombie hyperactive – and I thought you could do with something to cheer you up and take your mind off it.'

'So you went shopping, and left me a note on the door, telling me to follow the instructions.'

'Mm. Having a nice long scented bath, changing into the clothes I'd left on the bed for you—'

'Just this, and a pair of high-heeled shoes,' she remembered with a smile.

'Black patent stilettos. And then you came into the dining room.'

'To find you sitting at the table, wearing nothing but a black bow tie: with candles everywhere, a bottle of champagne on ice, and a feast – strawberries, smoked salmon, blue cheese and black grapes.'

'You sat on my lap, and I fed you.'

Susanna's eyes were very green. 'And then you ate yours off me.'

'It makes me hard just thinking about it.' He wriggled out of the pyjama bottoms. 'See?'

'Mm.' Her voice was husky, and her erect nipples showed clearly through the white lace. 'Then you took this off me, very, very slowly. And we made love for hours.'

'Tantric sex. I'm going to take it up properly, when I come back to London.'

'And I'm going to take up driving.'

'I thought you said you couldn't be bothered?'

'After changing trains three times to get here, then the taxi refusing to bring me here until this morning . . . Let's just say I'd rather travel independently, in future.'

'Was it worth it?'

'What?'

'The journey.'

She spread her hands wide. 'That's what I'm just about to find out . . .'

'Don't take it off,' he said softly, as she hooked her thumbs into the narrow shoulder straps.

She smiled at him. 'You're definitely feeling better, then.'

'Mm.' He held out his hands, and she joined him on the bed.

Brandon pulled down the front of the lace teddy, just enough to release her breasts; the teddy acted almost as a push-up bra, lifting her breasts. 'Mm,' he said again, cupping her breasts in his hands and pushing them together to deepen her cleavage. 'Mm. Beautiful.'

He rubbed the tip of his nose in the valley between her breasts, then took one nipple into his mouth. 'God, you taste so good,' he informed her.

'It's rude to speak with your mouth full.'

'I don't care.'

Susanna smiled. She definitely had her man back. 'Indeed, Mr Rodgers,' she said softly.

Brandon lifted his head. 'I've missed you. The way you feel, the way you smell, the way you taste. And now I have some catching up to do.' He returned to his previous position, sucking first one nipple and then the other until the dark flesh was erect and Susanna was breathing hard, leaning back on her elbows and tipping her head back to expose her throat to him.

'I need this,' Brandon whispered, tracing her areolae with the tip of his tongue.

Susanna gave a small moan of pleasure, and lay back on the bed. Brandon rolled her teddy down further, and she arched her back, making it easier for him, then lifted her buttocks from the bed so that he could finish stripping her.

'You ought to be wearing black lace-topped stockings,' he said.

'Not with navy trousers.'

'I love seeing you walk around in just stockings and high-heeled shoes.'

'That's because you're kinky.'

'Oh? And who was it that suggested it, in the first place?'

Her laugh turned to a groan as he knelt by her feet and began licking his way up her legs, concentrating on the hollows of her ankle-bones and the soft skin behind her knees. She closed her eyes, tipping her head back against the pillows, as his mouth travelled slowly north, lingering on her inner thighs.

'Don't tease me,' she muttered pushing her pelvis up to meet him.

'Tease you?' He deftly bypassed her quim, and began nuzzling her abdomen.

Susanna almost cried out in frustration. 'That's not fair, Brandon.'

'I just want to refresh my memory.' He drew in a deep breath, filling his nostrils with her scent. 'Mm.'

Susanna decided to take matters into her own hands – literally. She slid her fingers in his hair, and pushed him unceremoniously downwards, tilting her pelvis at the same time.

Brandon laughed. 'Talk about impatient!'

'No, I want the patient in *me*,' she quipped.

'Any bit of him in particular?'

'He can start with his mouth.'

'Right.' Brandon breathed on her quim, keeping his mouth just close enough to tempt her, but far enough away so that he wasn't actually touching her. He teased her until the scent of her arousal was strong, and he could see her quim glistening with need: and then he drew his tongue along her labia, parting them to explore the folds and ridges of her quim.

'Ambrosia,' he said softly. 'That's how you taste. Honey and seashore and musk.' Then he began to lap her in earnest, making his tongue into a hard point as he flicked it across her clitoris, and then softening it again as he licked along her musky furrow.

Susanna murmured with pleasure as he inserted his tongue into her; she widened the gap between her thighs still further, and the pads of her fingers dug into his scalp, urging him on. As he continued to lick, she felt the familiar rush of pleasure running through her veins, pooling in her solar plexus and then exploding.

'Better?' he asked, raising his head.

'Mm.'

'Good.' He shifted up the bed, his lips still glistening with her juices, and kissed her so that she could taste herself in his mouth. 'But I haven't finished yet.'

'No?'

'I told you, I missed you. It seemed too— well, I just didn't feel like masturbating.'

'Maybe that's because you didn't phone me.' The conversations they'd had while Brandon had been on previous business trips had led them both to pleasure themselves madly.

'I know, and I'm sorry.' He stroked her face. 'Forgive me?'

She smiled. 'Of course.'

'I could always show you how sorry I am.'

She rubbed her nose against his. 'What a good idea . . .'

He knelt between her thighs. 'I've dreamed about this, night after night. Sinking my cock up to the hilt in you, feeling you moving against me.'

'What about Alicia?' She couldn't help asking.

Brandon smiled. 'You've got nothing to worry about, believe me. She's attractive enough, in her own way, but you're the woman I live with. You're the one I want to share my life with. And you're the one I want to carry off to the Cotswolds, sometime.'

She nodded. 'Everyone gets paranoid, at some point.'

'Well, we're together now. So just forget it, hm?'

'OK.'

He positioned the tip of his cock against her sex, then gently eased into her. 'God, you feel so good. Like warm, wet silk.'

Susanna laughed. 'What a terrible cliché, Brandon.'

'But it's true. It's exactly how you feel. Soft and smooth and wet and clingy.'

She wrapped her legs round his waist. 'Are you sure that you're really up to the exertion?'

'Even if I'm not, this is what I want,' he told her. 'Now shut up, and make love with me.'

It was an offer she couldn't refuse; the way he thrust into her made her spine tingle. She pushed up to meet him, and his movements took on a new and more urgent rhythm; at last, she felt his balls lifting and tightening against her, and finally his cock throbbing inside her – just as she reached her own climax.

He rubbed his cheek against her. 'I've just remembered,' he said softly, 'how much I love you. And how much I love fucking you.'

'Well, I'm glad the amnesia's gone,' she said wryly.

'Oh, it has.' He stayed inside her for a while longer, unwilling to withdraw; finally, he shifted onto his back, curling Susanna into his side.

Almost automatically, her fingers curved round his penis; he chuckled. 'Not had enough of me, yet?'

'In a word – no. I've missed the way you feel. The way you taste.'

'Well, I'm in your hands entirely.'

It was an offer too good to refuse. Susanna ran her hand over his abdomen, his chest; he'd definitely lost muscle tone, since his illness. It worried her: the Brandon she was used to would have suggested running down the hill and back up again before breakfast, finishing up with a few press-ups and some curl-ups. The fact that he'd been too ill even for an approximation of his usual exercise routine made her very uncomfortable.

Gently, she pushed the covers back. 'You're not cold, are you?'

'Not with you to warm me up.'

Susanna laughed, and moved to straddle him. She kissed him deeply, her tongue probing his mouth; then she gradually worked her way down his body, nipping gently at his throat – though avoiding the bruises on his neck.

She licked the flat hard buttons of his nipples; then her mouth wandered lower, across his abdomen. The expectation of what she was going to do next had made Brandon hard again; she smiled to herself. It had been far too long since they'd last done what he was thinking of.

He made a small murmur of pleasure as she curled her fingers round his erect cock and made her tongue into a sharp point, licking the sensitive spot just below his glans. He slid his fingers into her hair, massaging her scalp and urging her on. She smiled, and opened her mouth, letting the tip of his cock slide between her lips.

The she pushed her tongue against the eye, licking the tiny drop of clear moisture which had gathered there and revelling in its slightly acrid taste. Brandon groaned, and she let her lips slide further down his shaft, relaxing the muscles in her throat until the head of his cock was almost touching the back of it; then she began to suck, setting up a rapid and sharp rhythm which had him writhing underneath her and clenching his hands in bliss. She continued to fellate him, increasing the pressure on his cock until he cried out her name and her mouth was filled with the thick salty tang of his semen.

She swallowed every last drop, and shifted back up the bed; Brandon kissed her hard, enfolding her in his arms and cradling her against his chest. Susanna lay there, deep in thought, her fingertips moving in small circles against his skin. The sex they'd just shared had been good – very good – but something had been missing. She couldn't quite put her finger on it, but she was sure that the castle had something to do with it.

'Let's go back to London, tonight,' she said softly.

'I can't. I've got a job to do here, remember?'

'Yes, but you're ill. You can't work when you're ill – and I'd rather have you at home, so I can look after you properly. You can come back to Cornwall when you're better. Or subcontract the job. You've been here long enough to know what you want to do with the place. You can do the drawings and the report for Alicia just as easily in London as you can here, and let someone else get on with actually doing the painting or whatever.' She stroked his face. 'Come home, Brandon.'

He swallowed hard. 'Susanna – I have to finish the job.'

'I know. What I'm saying is that if you come home with me now, you'll get better, faster, and you'll be able to come back here and do the job then.'

He nodded. 'I suppose you're right. I don't know if I'm up to the train journey, though.'

'It isn't that bad. And if it's a choice between me driving your car, when my last driving lesson was a good ten years ago, or taking the train . . .'

He groaned. 'I'll drive.'

'You're not fit to drive, Brandon. Look, if you're that worried about it, I'll ring Kate and ask her to come and pick us up.'

'All the way to Cornwall, from London? You can't.'

'She's my best friend. I'd do the same for her.'

He shook his head. 'Don't ring her, Susanna. We'll take the train.'

'Good.' She slid out of bed, completely unconcerned by her nakedness. 'Where are your bags?'

'In the wardrobe.'

'Right.' The doors creaked as they opened; Susanna pulled a face at them, and hauled Brandon's small suitcase from the shelf at the top. It didn't take her long to pack his clothes; when she'd finished, she turned to him again. 'What about the bathroom? I could do with a shower, and I suppose the rest of your stuff's in there, too.'

He nodded. 'It's an en-suite. The door opposite the bed.'

She smiled at him, and went into the bathroom. It was as antiquated and uncomfortable as she'd expected, from what she'd already seen of the castle, but she made the best of it. At least the water was hot. She showered quickly, dried herself, and brought Brandon's things out into the bedroom, putting them in the suitcase.

'And now it's your turn,' she told him.

'How do you mean?'

'Wakey wakey, rise and shine, ups-a-daisy.' She indicated the bathroom. 'The quicker you are, the quicker we leave this place – and the quicker you get better.'

'I'd forgotten what a bossyboots you are,' he grumbled. He suddenly noticed the cross-and-chain. 'What's that?'

'What?'

'Around your neck.' He nodded at the crucifix.

She wrinkled her nose. 'One of the villagers gave it to me when I said I was coming up here. It's probably a village tradition, or something.'

'Protection against vampires, hm?'

'Well, you never know,' Susanna said, equally lightly. 'There are supposed to be bats here. Who knows what else?' She began dressing. 'Come on, hurry up. We don't want to miss our train.'

Six

Just as Susanna took the bags, ready to stride out of the castle and give Alicia Descourt a metaphorical V-sign, the door-handle rattled. She rolled her eyes. 'Mrs Danvers, methinks.'

Brandon frowned. 'Susanna, I wish you wouldn't keep calling Molly that. She's been very kind to me, especially since I've been ill.'

Susanna didn't trust herself to answer civilly, so she kept quiet and simply unbolted the door, opening it abruptly so that the housekeeper nearly fell into the room.

'Yes?' she said icily. Served the bitch right for trying to peep through the keyhole. It must have been fairly obvious that they'd celebrate their reunion in bed. Was the woman some sort of voyeuse, as well as the most awkward cow Susanna had ever met?

Molly recovered her composure within seconds. 'Milady would like you to stay for dinner.'

Susanna shook her head. 'Tell Milady that it's very sweet of her to offer, but unfortunately we don't have time for dinner.' She gave her sweetest smile, knowing that she was being so polite that she was actually being rude. 'We have a train to catch.'

'A train?' Mild shock passed over the housekeeper's face, as though she hadn't been expecting something like this.

Susanna nodded. 'I'm taking Brandon back to London, to see a proper doctor.'

'But Doctor Fellowes is very good. And the fresh air in Cornwall—'

'Probably caused Brandon's illness in the first place,' Susanna interrupted. 'We're returning to London. As soon as he's better, he'll come back to finish the plans for the castle.'

The housekeeper shook her head. 'You can't.'

Susanna's eyes were like ice. 'Oh, really? Just watch.'

'You can't,' the housekeeper repeated. 'It's too late. No one will come here after sunset.'

'Because of Milady's publicity machine? Well, tough. I'll call a cab from Truro, if I have to, and to hell with the expense.'

'They still won't come. Not with these roads.'

'Then we'll walk to the village.' Susanna was furious. First, the woman had refused to let her in; now, she was refusing to let her leave. This was ridiculous.

'It's dark. You'll lose your way – and besides, Brandon isn't well enough to walk all that way. It's too far.'

Susanna thought about it. What Molly was saying was true; but Susanna didn't want to spend a night in the castle. On the other hand, she wasn't going to walk back to the village alone and leave Brandon in the castle on his own, at the mercy of Alicia Descourt and her Mrs Danvers. There was only one choice. 'All right,' she said finally. 'But we're leaving first thing in the morning.'

Molly gave her a knowing smile, as if to imply that Susanna and Brandon wouldn't be doing anything of the sort. 'As you wish.'

Susanna dampened down her anger. The woman was doing it on purpose, and she wasn't going to rise to the bait.

'Milady is looking forward to meeting you. Dinner will be at seven-thirty.'

'Right.' When the housekeeper had left, Susanna closed the door behind her. 'Well, I do hope that Milady doesn't expect me to dress for dinner. I don't have anything suitable. Perhaps I should just borrow her broomstick, nip down to the village, and buy myself a little black antique velvet number. Preferably one running with mould. And maybe pop into the undertaker's for a bar of embalming soap, to perfume myself properly.'

Brandon winced at her tone. 'Susanna, I don't know why you've got such a downer on her. You've never even met her.'

'I haven't needed to! Let's face it, you've been ill, and she didn't bother to contact me to let me know. She's got the whole village in her employ, to tell the tourists creepy tales and scare them into believing that her books are real; and then there's this ridiculous business about no one coming here after dark.'

'You heard what Molly said. The roads are bad.'

'That's not the impression they gave me in the village last night. They tried making out that it was because it was so spooky here, and terrible things would happen after dark.' Susanna grimaced. 'It wouldn't surprise me if she believes her own publicity now, and thinks that she actually *is* a vampire!'

'Now you're being *really* ridiculous.'

'There's more than one type of vampire, Brandon. The worst ones don't suck your blood – they suck out your emotions. Which is a hundred per cent fouller, in my opinion.'

Brandon sighed, putting a hand on her arm. 'Calm down, Susanna, will you? We'll be out of here tomorrow.'

'Good. I've got the taxi's number – I'll ring him tonight, after dinner, and arrange for him to meet us at seven.'

'Seven?'

'It's after sunrise. And we have a train to catch, remember?'

'OK.'

'Right.' Susanna looked through her bag; she didn't have anything that would impress Alicia Descourt. Her black business-suit was too obviously just that – business wear – and leggings were equally inappropriate. The palazzo pants she'd worn on the train were crumpled; anyway she didn't want to wear the clothes she'd travelled in. Which left her with the white silk shirt and navy trousers she was wearing.

Well, it's meant to be 'manners maketh man', she thought, *not clothes*. She had no intention of letting Alicia Descourt faze her or make her feel uncomfortable, simply because she wasn't dressed for a sophisticated dinner.

She lifted her chin, and looked at Brandon. 'Well, are you going to give me the low-down on this woman, or what?'

'How do you mean?'

'I want to know what she's like. Looks, personality, taste: and if there's anything I should know before I meet her. You know, like what subjects to avoid.'

Brandon grinned. 'Telling you that would be more or less like telling you to raise them!'

'No, it won't.' Susanna's face tightened. 'Look, I don't want to antagonize the woman. I just want to get out of here. And since we can't go until tomorrow, we might as well enjoy this evening.'

Brandon smiled to himself. What Susanna meant was that she was actually very curious about Alicia, but didn't want to admit it. 'Well, she's taller than I expected. I suppose she's about the same height as you.'

'Five eight.'

'Mm. Same sort of build, too. Her hair's dark—'

'Dyed black,' Susanna interrupted.

Brandon shook his head. 'I don't think so. It's very long – she usually wears it brushed back from her face.'

'A bit like a medieval princess,' Susanna said, remembering the painting.

'I suppose so, yes. Anyway, her skin's quite pale. Her eyes are green.'

Green and hard, Susanna thought, remembering what Thomas had said. 'Like mine?'

He shook his head. 'No. They're – more intense, I suppose.' *And less kind*, though he decided not to tell Susanna that. She already had a bad opinion of the writer, and he didn't want to make it worse. 'She usually dresses in black.'

'Red lipstick, as well?'

He smiled. 'Yes, but it's a bit darker than your favourite battle-paint. And you know she usually wears black nail-varnish.'

'Right. So what's her personality like?'

Brandon shrugged. 'Difficult to say. She's very – guarded.'

'Guarded.' *That could mean a multitude of things*, Susanna thought. 'Is that a result of being famous, or do you think she'd be like that anyway?'

'Probably a bit of both. But she can be quite entertaining.'

Beautiful *and* talented. Susanna couldn't help asking the question. 'And do you find her attractive?'

'If you're asking if I've slept with her, the answer's no. I haven't. You know I never sleep with my clients.'

'But she's offered?'

'I didn't say that.'

The careful evasion gave him away. So Alicia *had* tried it on with him. The question was, why had Brandon refused? Out of loyalty to his girlfriend – or because something about the woman repelled him, at heart? Susanna remembered her own behaviour on the train, with Paul Beetley. Yes, in part, it had been revenge for what she thought Brandon was doing with Alicia Descourt: but in part, it had also been because she'd found Paul attractive. Like Brandon, she was intensely sexual by nature. And if Alicia was as attractive as Brandon had said . . . why had he refused her?

'I didn't actually ask you if you'd slept with her. I asked you if you found her attractive.'

Brandon took a deep breath. 'You're prejudiced against her, anyway. I don't want to make it worse.'

'Stop pussy-footing. Do you, or do you not, find her attractive?'

'Yes and no.'

Susanna groaned. 'I'd forgotten how bloody infuriating you can be!'

He grinned. 'Serves you right, for asking awkward questions.'

'I want to know, though. I mean, I know you don't usually

mix business with pleasure, but you've been stuck here with her, in the middle of nowhere.'

'I've been ill,' he reminded her.

'Even so – you made love to *me*, this afternoon. Why did you turn her down?'

'I didn't say I'd turned her down.'

She laughed. 'I know you well enough, by now.'

'All right. I've been tempted, yes – she's attractive, in a weird sort of way. There's something magnetic about her. You can't help being drawn to her, like a moth to a flame. And then you start panicking, feeling like she'll consume you.'

'Consume you?'

'Moth goes to flame. Flame consumes moth.'

And vampire consumes human. She shook herself. 'I see.'

'You asked, so I told you.'

'Mm.' She took his hand. 'Well, thanks for being honest with me. Basically, you didn't bed her because you bottled out.'

'Yep. I told you I was ill.'

She kissed him lightly. 'So it had nothing to do with wanting to be faithful to your girlfriend?'

He raised an eyebrow. 'And are you telling me you haven't been tempted, while I've been away?'

'Usually, you ring me. That keeps me going.'

'And because I didn't, this time?'

She blew him a kiss. 'Isn't the weather nice.'

Brandon drew her back towards the bed, sitting down and pulling her down with him, so that she sat with her legs draped across his. 'So you *were* tempted, then.' It was a statement, not a question. His grey eyes were suddenly lively. 'What happened?'

'It was on the train, on the way here. I was reading one of Alicia's books.'

'Oh?' Brandon was surprised.

'It was a long journey. My laptop battery wouldn't last that long, so I needed something to read on the train. When I got to the station, there was this huge display of her books. So I decided to buy one.' She shrugged. 'Anyway, I found it quite erotic.'

'Where were you sitting?'

'In an ordinary carriage. You know, the sort where the seats are opposite each other, and there's a table in between.' She smiled. 'You know I can't bear the other sort, where you're crammed into about half the space and hemmed in by other seats.'

'Right.'

'Anyway, this man had been watching me. He came over to talk to me.'

'What was he like?'

'Tall, dark hair, nice-looking.'

'The usual Susanna James type?' Brandon teased.

She grinned. 'Not quite. He had blue eyes, not grey, and I usually go for blonds.' She ruffled his hair. 'The Brideshead type. Just like you,' she teased.

Brandon wasn't to be deflected. 'So what happened?'

'He talked to me, for a while. Then he slid his foot up my leg.'

'His foot?'

'Yes.'

'And what happened, then?'

'His foot slid between my thighs.'

'Like this?' Brandon slid his hand between her thighs, almost in a mirror action of Paul's foot.

'Mm.' Susanna arched her back.

'Then what?'

'He started rubbing me.'

'Like this?' Brandon expertly located her clitoris through the thin stuff of her trousers and knickers, and began rubbing her.

'Exactly like that, until I came.'

'He made you come, in the middle of the train?'

She nodded. 'I had to bite my lip hard, to stop myself crying out.'

Brandon's voice was husky. 'So he was good, then?'

'Yes.' She shivered as Brandon continued to massage her clitoris. If he decided to prove that he could have the same effect on her body as her tall dark handsome stranger had, she wouldn't be able to help coming. She had nothing else to wear, so when she met Alicia, she'd smell of sex . . . A smile crossed her face. And that, she thought, would serve Alicia right.

'What happened then?'

'We went into the corridor between the trains.'

'Not the toilets, surely?'

She grinned. 'Apart from anything else, a British Rail toilet is too small for comfort! Anyway, the train was virtually empty, at that point. No one was going to come past and see us.'

'I see.' With his free hand, Brandon began unbuttoning her shirt again. 'What were you wearing?'

'Trousers and a shirt.'

'And underneath?'

'Knickers and a bra.'

'Mm.' He removed her shirt, then burrowed under the top of her lace body, cupping one breast. 'So you went into the corridor together.'

'And then he kissed me,' Susanna informed him, in a parodied simper.

Brandon chuckled. 'I don't know if I dare ask where!'

'My mouth, actually.'

'Anywhere else?'

'My neck.'

Brandon gave her a sidelong glance. 'Anywhere else?'

'If you're asking me, did he drop to his knees and put his face between my legs, the answer's no. He didn't.'

'Disappointing for you.'

Susanna chuckled. 'Maybe you can make up for it, later.'

'Was he good?'

'Not as good as you, darling.'

He grinned. 'Seriously?'

'Actually, I *was* being serious. But I admit, he was good.'

'I see.'

'Well, I hadn't seen you for a couple of weeks. You hadn't phoned me, and I was bored with my own right hand.'

'Randy bitch,' he said huskily. 'So what then?'

'He put his hand under my shirt, pushing his hand under the cup of my bra, and stroked my nipples.'

'Like this,' Brandon said thoughtfully, doing the same.

She gasped as his forefinger and thumb manipulated the hard nubs of flesh. 'Oh, yes.'

He stopped immediately. 'You were supposed to be telling me what happened,' he reminded her. 'Don't drift off the subject.'

'Considering how much you're distracting me . . .'

'Nothing of the sort. I'm merely acting out what you're telling me he did to you.'

She grinned. 'I could tell you a complete pack of lies.'

He lifted her slightly, removing the trousers and tossing them to one side. 'You could.'

'And you're anticipating what happened next,' she said, running her tongue over her lower lip. 'I undid his jeans.' She undid Brandon's jeans, and was pleased to note that his cock was fully erect. 'He was in the same sort of state as you, actually.'

'Indeed.' He tipped his head to one side. 'And what about you?'

'I forgot to tell you – before he kissed me, he took my trousers off.'

'In the middle of the train.'

'In the middle of the train,' she confirmed.

'I bet your exhibitionist streak loved that!'

'Well – yes. Once I'd stopped panicking that we'd be arrested for public indecency.'

'Anyway, you undid his jeans.'

'Then he lifted me up against the wall – like you did, that time in the office – and slid his cock into me.'

'How did he feel?'

'Good,' she admitted, burrowing into his underpants and stroking his cock. 'It was obscene, really. There I was, with a complete stranger, my trousers on the floor and my bra open and his cock deep inside me. Anyone could have seen us.'

'I bet you looked beautiful.' Brandon hooked the gusset of her knickers aside, and drew his finger along her quim. 'And it must have excited you.'

'How do you mean?'

'Because you're soaking wet. Remembering what happened is obviously turning you on.'

'Don't you think that might have a lot to do with what your hands have been doing to me?'

'Not to make you this wet.' He pushed one finger inside her, then removed his hand and licked the musky juices from his fingers. 'Mm. Very, very nice.' He slid the finger back inside her. 'So what happened then?'

'We both came. Then we got dressed and went back to our seats. I fell asleep against his shoulder for a while, then we reached his stop, and he left. He gave me his card.'

'Oh, yes? And what were you going to do with that?'

'That,' Susanna said carefully, 'rather depended on you.'

'How do you mean?'

'I thought you and Alicia were – you know.'

'Fucking each other?' Brandon shook his head. 'No, we weren't, and we're not.'

'Well, if you had been – I'd have probably thrown all your clothes out of the window, then stomped back to London and phoned him.'

'And as I'm not?'

Susanna's lips twitched. 'I think he might like to meet Kate.'

He grinned. 'You're a schemer, do you know that?'

'Mm-hm. So what are you going to do about it?'

'Well . . .' He rolled down her lace body. 'I thought I could do this.' He removed the garment from her, then gently moved her so that she was lying back against the pillows. Then he stripped swiftly, and knelt between her thighs. 'And this.' He positioned the tip of his cock at her entrance, and pushed until he was sheathed by the warm wet velvet of her flesh. 'And this.' He started to thrust, then, long slow strokes which made her shiver, then short rapid strokes which had her twining her legs round his waist and pushing up to meet him.'

At last, she cried out, her internal muscles flexing wildly; as Brandon reached his own orgasm, he held her closer, resting his forehead against her shoulder.

'Better?' he asked softly.

'Yes.' She nuzzled the curve of his neck.

'Good.' He withdrew, and kissed her gently. 'Better have another shower and get dressed again, sweetheart – Alicia doesn't like people being late.'

Susanna was very tempted to linger over a shower, and be deliberately late . . . but it wasn't worth it. Besides, she had other ideas. She smiled at him. 'If it's that crucial, I'll skip the shower.'

Brandon said nothing, but she knew that he knew what was in her mind. They both dressed quickly; then she turned to face him. 'Brandon.'

'Yes?'

'There was one thing you didn't tell me. Are there any things she hates talking about?'

'So you can bring them up?'

'So I can avoid them, actually.'

He thought for a moment. 'I don't think so.'

'Anything else I should know, before I meet her?'

He grinned. 'You sound like a woman about to meet her prospective in-laws for the first time. Or a new boss.'

'Neither. Maybe a prospective *Homefile* subject, but that's about it.' She took his hand. 'Come on, then. Let's brave the dragon.' A sudden thought struck her: didn't 'Dracula' actually mean 'dragon'? Her off-the-cuff remark was a little too appropriate.

Brandon led her through the dingy corridors; Molly met them at the foot of the stairs.

'Milady is not down yet. Perhaps you would wait in the dining room?'

'Thanks, Molly, we'll do that. We'll make our own way there – I know my way around now.'

Brandon was completely at ease with the woman, Susanna noticed; and Molly didn't seem at all put out at his familiarity. Whereas she didn't speak to Susanna at all, merely contenting herself with one of her icy stares.

'I really ought to call you Maxim,' Susanna murmured as Molly left them.

'Sh! She'll hear you.'

'Well. She gives me the creeps. She's just what I imagined Mrs Danvers to be.'

'And I suppose that makes you poor, timid little Mrs de Winter?'

'The woman with no name.' Susanna shrugged. 'In her eyes . . . I think, yes, I am.'

'She's very nice, once she gets to know you.'

I'm not sure if I want to get to know her. Or Alicia bloody Descourt, for that matter, Susanna thought; but she smiled gamely.

Brandon led her down a few more of the dingy corridors; eventually, he paused by one of the heavy oak doors. 'This is it,' he said.

The room turned out to be exactly as she'd expected. A heavy oak table in the middle of the room, surrounded by twelve leather-seated chairs; three heavy silver candelabra, each containing five blood-red candles, sat in the middle of the table. They were the only lighting in the room, with the exception of the fire which crackled in the grate.

Very Gothic, Susanna said silently. Either Alicia preferred to 'live' the settings for her books, because it helped her to write, or she was showing off. At that precise moment, Susanna wasn't quite sure which.

Three places were laid at one end of the table, and the silver and lead crystal glittered in the candlelight. If she's going to eat with us, Susanna thought, then she can't be a vampire. Vampires don't eat 'normal' food. They exist on blood alone.

'Might as well sit down,' Brandon said.

'OK.' Susanna followed him to the table; they sat facing each other. 'This room's really dingy,' she said. 'What are your plans for it?'

'Paler walls, a bit of subtle lighting on them, and stripped floorboards with lots of rugs,' Brandon answered promptly.

'Nice.' She looked at him through lowered lashes. 'I was surprised not to see fabric swatches and paint samples everywhere.'

'I'm keeping everything in one room.'

'Not even testing the colours on the walls?'

Brandon shook his head. 'I don't need to.'

'If you say so.' He was the expert; but it wasn't his usual way of working. She paused. 'Is she always late for dinner?'

'Alicia? I don't know. She didn't often eat with me. I was busy, first of all, not really taking proper breaks; and then I caught that virus. I suppose it was my own fault for trying to rush the job and not looking after myself properly. Anyway, Molly's brought my meals up to me, since I've been ill.'

'So this is the first time you've been up?'

'Well – yes.' He took her hand. 'Actually, having you around seems to have helped my energy levels.'

'Glad to hear it.'

He smiled at her; just as he was about to say something else, the door opened. Susanna stayed where she was, not even turning round to see who it was. If it was Molly, there was no point, and if it was Alicia . . . Well, if Alicia Descourt was expecting her to stand up, as though greeting royalty, she was going to be very disappointed.

A couple of moments later, the Gothic writer herself swept over to them, and sat in the chair at the head of the table.

'Hello, Brandon. I'm pleased to see that you're looking better,' she said. Then she turned to Susanna. 'And you must be Susanna. It's nice to meet you.'

'And you,' Susanna said stiffly.

Neither of them proffered a hand to be shaken nor a cheek to be kissed; the atmosphere was such, Susanna thought, that you could cut it with the proverbial knife. She was almost tempted to pick up a knife from the table and try it, but managed to stop herself.

Alicia nodded at the champagne. 'Perhaps you could do the honours, Brandon?'

He smiled at her. 'Of course.' He uncorked the bottle, then filled their glasses.

'Well, a toast, I think,' Alicia said. 'To Castle Pentremain – may you both enjoy your stay here.'

'Castle Pentremain,' Brandon echoed dutifully; Susanna muttered something unintelligible, and hoped that it would do. She didn't feel like giving a toast to Alicia's lousy castle.

Molly came in, a moment later, bringing plates of smoked salmon. *You might be a bitch*, Susanna thought, *and you might be affected, but I like your taste in food.*

Alicia monopolized the conversation during the hors d'oeuvres, talking about her plans for the castle. When the main course arrived – beef in a spicy sauce, with new potatoes, baby carrots and mangetout – she turned the conversation round to Susanna.

'Brandon tells me that you're a journalist.'

'That's right.'

'For a woman's magazine – one of the better ones.'

Susanna nodded. 'I like to think it is, yes.'

'Do you ever write fiction?'

Susanna smiled broadly. 'Definitely not.'

'But you read a lot.'

'Yes.'

'Do you ever review books?'

Was the woman actually angling for a review? Susanna

wondered. 'Occasionally, yes. But they tend to be ones that our readers would choose – Aga sagas, the occasional literary novel.'

'Not my work, then?'

'No.' Susanna had no intention of pandering to her and admitting that she'd read – and enjoyed – one of her books on the train.

'Susanna was wondering whether she could do a feature on the castle. You know, a "before-and-after" scenario,' Brandon added.

'Hm. I'll have to think about that. I don't like photographers hanging around me.'

'Fair enough. It was only an idea,' Susanna said.

They fell silent again, concentrating on their food; Susanna surreptitiously watched Alicia. She was as glamorous as Susanna had been expecting, with that beautiful jet-black hair, a perfect foil for her alabaster skin. Her eyes were a brilliant green – and Thomas Penford was right, they *were* hard, Susanna decided. But the most interesting thing about the writer was, whatever her pose, she was obviously not sexually interested in Brandon. So what the hell was going on?

Eventually, after the strawberries Romanoff, Brandon leaned back in his chair. 'I'm sorry, you'll have to excuse me. It's not the company, but I just don't think I can stay awake too much longer.'

'Well, it is your first day up,' Alicia said, her voice solicitous.

'Perhaps I should take you back to the inn with me tonight,' Susanna said. 'Our bags are ready, so all we need to do is call a taxi.'

There was the faintest glimmer of malice in Alicia's smile. 'You can ring Mike the Taxi, but he won't come. No one comes here after dark. And it's too far for either of you to walk. So you'll stay here tonight, as my guests, won't you?'

It didn't look as though they had any choice, Susanna thought. Alicia's question had been completely rhetorical. 'Thank you,' she said, through gritted teeth.

'Molly will see you upstairs,' Alicia told Brandon. 'And Susanna and I will have coffee.'

And what if I don't drink coffee? Susanna thought, cross at Alicia's imperious manner.

Brandon smiled wearily at them both. 'Fine. Don't wake me up when you come to bed, Susanna.'

'Of course not, darling. Though I really think I ought to go with you now.' The thought of being alone with Alicia made her nervous, for some reason. If only she hadn't listened to the old man in the pub. She could so easily imagine a younger Alicia flaunting herself sexually in front of the unsophisticated and naïve gardening boy . . .

'Molly will see that he's all right,' Alicia said, interrupting Susanna's thoughts.

Susanna's smile grew brittle. 'Then I think the choice is made for me, isn't it?'

Seven

Molly brought in the coffee on a silver tray, which she placed on the table between Alicia and Susanna. As Susanna had half-expected, the coffee was in an antique silver pot. Two white porcelain demitasses sat on the tray next to it, with a matching jug of cream and a small sugar-bowl containing demerara lump sugar and silver sugar-tongs.

Alicia poured two cups of coffee and looked at Susanna, her head slightly on one side. 'Cream and sugar?'

'Neither, thank you.'

Alicia smiled, and passed one cup to Susanna; she added two lumps of sugar to the other, and stirred hard. Susanna found herself willing Alicia to spill her coffee, and was cross with herself: she was being childish. The woman hadn't done anything to her, after all. Brandon was right – she shouldn't have such a downer on Alicia.

She took a sip of coffee, and was pleasantly surprised. 'It's very good,' she said.

Alicia nodded. 'Blue Mountain. It's ridiculously expensive, but I think it's worth every penny.' She smiled. 'And I'm old enough to indulge my vices; don't you think?'

'Mm.' Susanna felt uncomfortable, not sure what to say; she dropped her gaze, staring at the coffee cup.

Alicia's next words were a complete surprise. 'Why don't you just spit it out?'

Susanna looked up, frowning. 'What?'

'What you've been dying to say since I walked in.'

'That I'm worried about Brandon, you mean?'

Alicia nodded. 'I called the doctor out for him. Dr Fellowes said that it was rheumatic fever.'

Susanna's lip curled. 'Forgive me for sounding cynical, but Brandon's never ill. He's the only person I know who never catches a cold – not so much as a sniffle or a sore throat or headache, when everyone else around him is either sneezing their head off or dropping with flu. I just find it strange that he suddenly falls ill here.'

'And you thought that maybe it was something to do with me.'

A shiver ran down Susanna's spine. 'Is it?'

'What do you think?'

'I think,' Susanna said slowly, 'that you're playing games with me.'

Alicia smiled, and took another sip of coffee. 'Maybe I am.'

'There are marks on his neck.'

'The marks of vampire's teeth, perhaps?'

Susanna smiled thinly. 'You might have the villagers all ready and willing to tell the tourists that you're a vampire, to help your sales. You might like living up to your own PR hype. But I work in the media, remember. I'm not impressed.'

'But Old Tom's story got to you, didn't it?'

So Alicia knew about that: which meant that it had all been part of the hype, Susanna thought crossly. 'How long did it take you to write it? And how quickly could one of the leading lights of the local amateur dramatic group learn it?' Susanna fenced.

'You can believe what you like.'

'Those marks on Brandon's neck could be a love-bite.'

'And you think I did it?'

'Did you?'

Alicia threw her head back, revealing her beautiful white throat to its best advantage, and laughed. 'Believe what you like, child.'

'Child?' Susanna was incensed. How dare the woman

patronize her like this. 'There's probably ten years between us, that's all. Unless your PR people lie about your age, too.'

'Maybe they do.'

'Perhaps you'd do me the courtesy of dropping the act?' Susanna said.

Alicia smiled. 'I'm very tempted to say, "What act?"'

Susanna stood up. 'I've had enough. I'm not in the mood for playing your silly little games. Now, I'm going to join Brandon. Good night.'

To her surprise, Alicia, too, stood up, and took her hand. 'Susanna. I'm sorry. I just can't resist playing, with some people. You bring out . . . well, a certain something in me.'

'Am I supposed to feel flattered?' Susanna asked coldly.

'No. Though you've been just as rude and difficult as I have,' Alicia pointed out. 'So why don't we bury the hatchet?'

Susanna's eyes glittered. 'In each other's back, you mean?'

Alicia smiled. 'Sit down and finish your coffee, Susanna. Brandon's probably asleep, and it's too early for bed.'

'Don't you sleep all day and stay up all night?'

'When I'm working on a book, yes. I find that I work better at night. There are fewer distractions.' She dropped Susanna's hand, and sat down again. 'Would you like a brandy?'

Susanna shook her head. 'Thank you, but I'm not much of a spirits person.'

'Neither am I. But I thought I'd offer.'

'Mm.' Slowly, Susanna sat down. 'There *is* something you could do for me.'

'What's that?'

'Tell me the truth. Are you having an affair with Brandon?'

'No.'

'Or a one-night stand, causing those marks on his neck?'

'No.'

Susanna's eyes narrowed. 'So what are those marks, then? Who caused them?'

'Do you believe in vampires?' Alicia asked suddenly.

'Vampires?' Susanna shook her head. 'No. It's just a story –

folklore. Like Old Shuck, the black dog who haunts parts of Norfolk, or headless people running up and down Richmond Court.'

'There are stranger things in heaven and earth, Horatio.'

'I wrote a ten-thousand-word dissertation on Shakespeare and ghosts, as part of my degree,' Susanna said sweetly.

'I wasn't talking just about ghosts.' Alicia's eyes flickered. 'So you don't believe in them?'

'Ghosts? No they're figments of the imagination.' Susanna spread her hands. 'Or the psyche, delivered in a more acceptable format.'

Alicia's voice became husky. 'It's strange that someone who looks like you should have such a stolid imagination.'

'I'm a trained journalist. I work with facts, not fiction.' Something in Alicia's voice made Susanna nervous – and equally determined not to let her know it. She had a feeling that Alicia was the sort of person who thrived on other people's fear.

'Sometimes people disguise facts as fiction.'

'Yes.' Susanna drained her coffee.

'And sometimes we'd rather believe that things are fiction, not fact – because it's easier, and we don't have to confront something that worries us.' Alicia paused. 'Is that why you deny the existence of ghosts?'

Susanna sighed. 'Look, I've never seen a ghost, and I've never met anyone who's seen a ghost, either. I'm not denying that they exist – I'm simply saying that some people think they've seen a ghost because it's easier to believe that than try and find out the truth. I don't happen to believe in them, personally.'

'Supposing I tell you that I've seen a ghost?'

'Don't tell me – a suit of armour walking around the corridors of your castle at the first stroke of midnight, clanking chains and carrying his head under his arm?'

Alicia shook her head. 'Not all ghosts are like that.'

'A grey lady, then?' *It could be Molly herself – she was cheerless enough to be a ghost*, Susanna thought.

Alicia smiled. 'Let me tell you about the castle.'

'The castle?' Susanna was surprised at the sudden change of subject.

'It has a very interesting history.'

Susanna couldn't help a cynical smile. She had a feeling that Alicia was about to spin her a yarn. Did the woman really crave an audience that much, even such a hostile one?

Alicia ignored the smile, and began her tale. 'Many years ago – in the early sixteen hundreds, just after James the First came to the throne – a man called Ambrose lived here. He was the younger son and, as such, he was indulged by both his mother and his father, Lord Pentremain.

'He was a beautiful man. He was tall, with dark hair and the sort of fine sharp features you usually see in people with an ancient lineage. His eyes were as blue as cornflowers, and he had a ready smile which made him popular with the servants and the villagers alike. He was full of energy, full of zest for life: always laughing, always the one who'd attempt the impossible hedge when hunting, always the one who excelled at fencing. He was a good scholar, too, learned in all the arts. Mathematics, languages, law – nothing was beyond him.

'And yet his elder brother couldn't be jealous of him: Ambrose wasn't the type to crow about his abilities or be mean to those who weren't as good. And he didn't care about being the younger son. He wasn't plagued with jealousy that he would never be lord of the castle and own all the land he could see; or a plotter, working out how to get rid of his brother and inherit the lot himself. He simply enjoyed living. He was a man with sheer lust for life. Everyone loved him.

'One day, when he was about twenty, he took it into his head that he wanted to travel. With his knowledge of languages and law, he would make the perfect diplomat, and so his father arranged a meeting with the King. The King was pleased with Ambrose, and sent him to Orleans, on State business.

'Ambrose took to French society in a big way. He was popular with the men, for his prowess in fencing and hunting, and popular with the women, for his ready smile and easy charm. The younger ones tried to get him into their bed – men as well as women.' Alicia spread her hands. 'As I said, Ambrose was an attractive man. The older ones appreciated his courtesy and wit, and favoured him above all others; had they been younger, they, too, would have tried to get him into their bed.

'He was a scholar, but he had no monkish tendencies. Ambrose was a sensualist. His mouth had the sort of curve that made you shiver, wondering what it would feel like against your skin. And yet, at the same time, he never forgot that he was on State business. Gossip travelled fast in courtly circles, and to sleep with one woman would be to make an enemy of another. He knew that he couldn't afford to do that, so he smiled at everyone, was charming to everyone – and slept in his own bed, alone.'

Alicia's face became dreamy; Susanna was surprised to note that the writer's eyes had softened as she spoke about Ambrose. It was almost as though Alicia had known him, and loved him – although that was impossible. Ambrose had lived nearly four hundred years before: if he'd even lived at all. He could simply be a character in Alicia's next novel. Didn't novelists always fall in love with their lead characters?

'And then he met – let's just call her "A". Very little was known about her, other than the fact that she was Russian, of noble birth, and entertained lavishly. She was never seen in the daytime—' Alicia permitted herself the ghost of a smile '— though no doubt that was because the parties she threw never finished until almost dawn, and she needed to sleep at some time. The daytime suited her better. Hers was a *night* beauty.'

'Of cloudless climes and starry skies.' Susanna couldn't help the quote; Byron had always been one of her favourites.

Alicia acknowledged her with a smile. 'Something like that. She was the most beautiful woman in Orleans. She was tall and slender – a man's hands could easily span her waist – with masses of gleaming hair, black as a raven's wing. Her eyes were green, her face was as pale as the snow, and her lips were as red as ripe cherries.'

And her name was Snow White, Susanna thought bitchily.

'Her name,' Alicia said, as though she'd read Susanna's mind, 'was Russian, and difficult to pronounce. As I said, she was known as "A", or "The Countess".'

A shiver ran down Susanna's spine. Had Alicia *really* been able to tell what she'd been thinking, or had it been a lucky chance? She laced her fingers together beneath the table, hoping that Alicia would finish her tale soon, and let her go to join Brandon.

'Many courted her, many wanted to see if her skin was as soft as her velvet gowns. Women as well as men were attracted by her – she was like no one they'd ever met before. She wasn't the first Russian noblewoman seen in Orleans, but . . .' Alicia shrugged. 'She was unique.

'Ambrose saw her at a party. From then on, he had eyes for no one else. Yet none of the women who'd courted him felt scorned: if anything, they pitied him, because he was so obviously in love with the Russian countess. He pined for her – he couldn't eat, he couldn't sleep, he couldn't concentrate on anything. All he could do was think about her, and write poems that she never read – or, at least, never acknowledged.

'And then one day, a messenger called at his house. He had a note from *her*, summoning Ambrose to her house, that evening. Alone. He was distracted all day, wondering if she was going to tell him never to come near her again, or whether she was going to relent and let him woo her properly, ask her to be his wife. The minutes, the seconds, seemed to drag by.

'Then, at last, it was time. He arrived promptly at her house, and was shown into a small sitting room by the maid. The whole room was full of candles, giving the air a soft glow; someone far off was playing a spinet, a gentle tune which reminded him of the way she spoke.

'He sat down on one of the chairs, waiting for her to join him. It seemed like hours, though it could only have been a few minutes. And then she was in the doorway, holding out one hand to him. She was dressed in a deep emerald velvet gown, which matched her eyes and contrasted sharply with her pale skin and dark hair; the gown was low-cut, revealing the curves of her soft white breasts. She wore a simple necklace, an emerald pendant which rested in the shadowed vee of her cleavage; Ambrose's eyes were drawn to it, and he couldn't help wondering what it would be like to touch her there, taste her.

'He went towards her. What they said wasn't important – because, within moments, his mouth was on hers. Somehow, the door closed behind them, but Ambrose was in no state to care whether he had an audience. The only thing he knew about or cared about was the scent of her hair, the feel of her body next to his, the taste of her mouth.

'His hands went automatically to the back of her dress, undoing it and letting it slide to the floor. Beneath it, she was completely naked. She helped him strip, too, and drew him over to the silk Turkish rug by the fireplace.

'She lay down on the rug, stretching out; her skin glowed in the firelight, white and gold. Ambrose thought he'd never seen anyone so beautiful. He sat down next to her, then stretched out on his side, propping his head on his elbow, so that he could watch her. Then he drew his hand over her body, tracing her curves.

'He loved the way her breasts flattened out as she lay down: and yet they were still generous, and so very responsive to his touch. As his fingers brushed lightly over her flesh, her nipples grew dark and erect; he couldn't resist rolling first one, then the other, between finger and thumb. The contrast of the hardness of her nipples, the puckered skin of her areolae, and the soft warmth of her white skin delighted him.

'As he continued to caress her breasts, she arched towards him, parting her thighs. Ambrose, although he had always been careful in Orleans, was far from being a virgin. He'd been seduced by one of the bolder village girls when he was fifteen, and certain noblemen's daughters around Pentremain had made no secret of their feelings for him, when they were staying at the castle. Had he not come to their chambers, they would have gone to his. Ambrose was therefore skilled in the arts of love.

'And so, when the Russian countess parted her thighs for him, he knew exactly what she wanted. He teased her for a little, simply stroking her belly; but at last, he let his hands drift down to her thighs, stroking the soft skin until she shivered, and pushed her thighs further apart.

'Her knees were bent slightly, and he let his fingers walk up over her thighs. He could feel the heat of her quim, and he could smell her arousal – a warm, musky scent which made him itch to taste her. As soon as he touched her, she cried out; Ambrose, fearing that the servants would think he was hurting her and would rush in to disturb them, immediately kissed her, swallowing her moans of pleasure.

'And then he slid his finger over her quim, parting her labia and dabbling in her warm musky juices. Unable to resist it, he smeared the fluids over her nipples, then took his mouth from her, rubbing his fingers over her lower lip so that she could taste her own arousal.

'The countess sucked his fingers while he sucked her nipples, both of then tasting the same salty-sweetness; then he shifted to kneel between her thighs, and kissed his way down her body. He nuzzled her, the tip of his nose rubbing against her belly, breathing in her scent. He didn't recognize the perfume, but it was a heady and exotic mixture, and he loved it.

'She pushed her pelvis up towards him, needing release; he continued to tease her for a while longer, rubbing his cheeks against her thighs and breathing softly on her quim. And then, at long, long last, he drew his tongue down the musky furrow in one slow movement.

'She shuddered with delight, and he began to lick her in earnest, flicking his tongue across the hard nub of her clitoris in a way which made her whole body jerk. He continued lapping at her until she came; and then, only then, did he press the tip of his cock against her.

'He closed his eyes in bliss as he slid into her; she felt warm and tight round him, like liquid silk. He didn't think she was a virgin, but he had no less respect for her: this was the woman who'd haunted his sleep since the moment he'd met her. He could hardly believe that it was really happening, that he was really lying there, inside her, on the rug in front of the fire. And yet she felt so good under him . . . it had to be true.

'She drew her legs up, crossing her ankles around his waist so that he could penetrate her more deeply. He began to thrust, long and slow at first, and then speeding up as his excitement grew.' Alicia glanced at her audience of one, and was pleased to notice the flush along Susanna's cheekbones. As she'd suspected, Susanna was very receptive to erotic tales. She drew her tongue along her lower lip, and continued.

'Every time he thrust into her, he felt her heels on his buttocks, urging him deeper. And every time he withdrew, until the head of his cock was almost out of her, her internal muscles tightened round him, as if she couldn't bear to lose him. He'd never made love with a woman so responsive, a woman who matched exactly the same rhythm, and it drove him wild.

'It was a heady mixture, lust and love and passion. When he reached his climax, he felt as though his whole body was exploding and pouring into hers: and the way her vagina fluttered round him as she came, too, made him feel that if he died at that moment, he'd die in Paradise.

'He couldn't bear to pull out of her, and so he stayed where he was, taking his weight on his elbows. He stroked her hair back from her face, and thought that she was the most beautiful woman he'd ever seen. Her skin glowed from the after-effects of her orgasm, and her eyes – he could have drowned in her eyes. And then he knew that he couldn't live without her. He told her so – and she told him that she felt the same.

'They married in Orleans, and lived in her house. They continued to entertain as lavishly as when she had been single, and Ambrose indulged his bride's preference to sleep in the day and entertain at night. Though the best entertainment was always after their guests had gone, when they were alone to make love until they were sated.

'They were happy together, until a messenger came, one day, saying that Ambrose's father was desperately ill. Ambrose set off for England immediately, his bride promising to follow.

'He reached the castle the day after his father died. His mother was almost prostrate with grief, and his brother had barely the heart to take over as the new Lord Pentremain. He told Ambrose that he should bring his bride home: he was needed at the castle far more than he was needed in the King's service at Orleans. He was stern with his brother, disapproving of Ambrose's new lifestyle of sleeping through the day and waking at night, and said that France was doing him no good.

'Duty was still strong in Ambrose. He sent for his wife, and by the time that she arrived in Pentremain, he had settled back into his family's ways.

'The countess tried her best to fit in, but she found the lifestyle alien, particularly after Orleans. Everything was so formal in England. Everyone and everything had its place; there was none of the flexibility she was used to. The villagers thought her beautiful, but found her manners strange: they were suspicious of her, and never really took her to their hearts. Ambrose's mother, too, didn't warm to her or make her feel like a true daughter of the house.

'Ambrose's brother avoided her, whenever possible: she assumed that it was because he thought she was a bad influence on his younger brother.' Alicia smiled. 'Of course, there was another reason – one which she, in her modesty, could never have guessed. Ambrose's brother was in love with her. He was smitten by her beauty, and tormented nightly by dreams of her, naked, in his arms. The thought of her making love with his brother drove him almost insane – he tried not to think about it, but he couldn't help himself. He just needed to know how she felt, how she tasted, her scent when she was aroused.

'One day, it was too much for him. He found her alone on the castle battlements, looking out across the countryside, and took her in his arms. She struggled and pushed him away – but not before he'd stolen a kiss. And not before Ambrose, who'd come in search of his wife, had seen him.

'Ambrose challenged his brother to a duel, over his wife's honour, at dawn. In vain, she tried to persuade him not to do it – saying that it was of little consequence, and they could just leave Pentremain and go back to Orleans, forgetting what had happened. But Ambrose's blood had been fired with jealousy, and he refused to listen to her.

'She tried pleading with his brother, too – but he, like Ambrose, refused to listen to her. She dared not say anything to their mother – firstly, the old woman was ill, and the countess doubted if she could stand the burden of knowing that her sons were fighting. Secondly, she knew the old lady disliked her. And thirdly, the brothers were so stubborn that they would listen to no one's counsel, even their mother's.

'The duel was fought, the next morning. Ambrose and his brother were both skilled swordsmen, and the fight seemed to go on for ever. Harder and harder they fought, the only sounds being the clash of steel upon steel, and the Russian countess's sobbing – because Ambrose had insisted that she be present, to ensure a fair fight.

'In the end, Ambrose won – just. He had lost a lot of blood in the fight, and was very near death, but she nursed him back to health. She sat with him day and night, putting cool cloths on his head when he was hot, and making him nourishing broths and potions from her native land, until he was well again.

'The mother, of course, died not long after the brother: the double blow of losing her husband and her son was too much for her. The whole village mourned her. And although they loved Ambrose, they were still suspicious of his wife. They started to talk about what had happened to the family.

'First, Lord Pentremain had died. Then the brothers, who had always been so close, had fought a duel to the death. Then

Lady Pentremain had died. It was almost as though the family was cursed – and it had all started when Ambrose had met his strange Russian bride.

'The muttering had just about died down – not forgotten, merely buried under the surface – when there was an epidemic in the village. Several children died, and the doctor couldn't say what was wrong with them. They all seemed pale and sickly – and, being Cornwall, the talk in the village turned to the supernatural. Some thought it was the pixies, taking the children's spirits. Some thought it was witches, bearing a grudge against certain families.

'And some thought of vampires. The children had all been weak, as though they'd lost blood. Vampires slept all day, and prowled around the village at night – and there was only one person they knew like that. Ambrose's wife.' Alicia bit her lip. 'Because once the old lady and the new Lord Pentremain had died, Ambrose and his wife had fallen back to their old habits from Orleans, sleeping in the day and being up all night.

'After one more child had died – Elizabeth, the most beautiful child in the village, with flaxen hair and a face like an angel – it was too much for the villagers. One night, when Ambrose was away on business, they stormed the castle. The servants, who had never taken that much to Ambrose's wife, and blamed her for the quarrel between the brothers, did nothing to stop them.

'She wasn't strong – she was pregnant with their first child – so she didn't put up much of a struggle. The villagers took her up to the battlements, and threw her into the ravine. When Ambrose came home and found what had happened, he swore that he would be avenged in hell for the death of his bride. He destroyed half the village, in his madness, then threw himself off the battlements.

'Ambrose was buried with his wife in the family vault, the last of the Pentremains. No grass will ever grow in the area where his wife fell, and it's said that he haunts the castle on moonlit nights, still weeping for his bride.'

Susanna smiled. 'Very good.' She paused. 'But also very Bram Stoker, don't you think?'

Alicia tipped her head forward slightly in acknowledgement. 'Perhaps. But there's also another version of the story. The tale of a beautiful Russian countess who slept in the day and entertained at night was known in more than one city in France – and over an impossibly long period of time. It seemed that when the countess grew bored, she moved on.' Alicia's smile was faintly malicious. 'And I don't mean bored with society – I mean bored with the blood of the city's inhabitants. Whenever the Russian countess was in a city, a mysterious wasting disease seemed to strike local children.

'She was known as the *broucolaque* – the vampire – by certain areas of the city. She always dismissed it, saying that because she was not a native Frenchwoman, people would naturally blame her for anything they couldn't understand. And yet it fitted in. The sleeping in the daytime, being so active at night – and no one ever saw her eat or drink anything.

'Because vampires cannot be hurt by usual means, therefore she did not die when the villagers threw her from the battlements of Castle Pentremain. And neither did Ambrose – because when he became Lord Pentremain, she made him drink her blood so that he, too, was a vampire . . .'

'That would explain some of Old Tom's stories, then,' Susanna said, feeling a shiver run down her spine and trying to ignore it. There was a look on Alicia's face which she couldn't place, and which made her feel extremely nervous.

'Maybe. Maybe not.'

'Well.' Susanna stood up. 'Thanks for the story, but I really ought to check on Brandon.'

'As you wish.'

'Goodnight.'

'Goodnight.' Alicia smiled: Susanna wasn't sure if it was just her imagination, fired by the story Alicia had just told, but her canine teeth seemed slightly longer than normal, a little sharper . . .

Eight

Alicia didn't offer Molly's services to guide Susanna back to the bedroom she was to share with Brandon; Susanna wasn't sure whether she was more relieved or disappointed. Molly wouldn't exactly have been her favoured choice of companion – but on the other hand, any company would have been preferable to walking around a dimly-lit and warren-like Gothic castle on her own, particularly after hearing that very creepy story about its early history . . .

She drew herself up to her full height. Maybe Alicia had intended to scare her. Well, she wasn't going to give the woman that much satisfaction. She stalked through the corridors, ignoring the shadows, until she finally reached the bedroom.

She opened the door gingerly; to her relief, it didn't creak. Brandon had fallen asleep with the bedside light on, the Dickens paperback he'd filched from her bag lying on the bed beside him. Gently, she closed the door behind her, then walked over to the bed, taking the book from beside him and placing it on the bedside cabinet.

A lock of hair was in his eyes; she couldn't resist smoothing it back. He looked absolutely exhausted, his face white: she felt faintly guilty for inciting him to make love to her, when he really wasn't well. Then she noticed the marks on his neck; if anything, they looked slightly darker.

She frowned. She'd been expecting them to fade, not grow darker. It wasn't anything to do with Alicia – she'd been with the woman, ever since Brandon had gone to bed. Molly was just about the last person she'd expect to be the cause of the marks. Which left . . .

A shiver ran down her spine, and she was cross with herself. Alicia's spooky story about Ambrose and his bride was just that, a spooky story – probably the basis of her next novel. That, combined with the atmosphere of Castle Pentremain itself, was enough to give anyone the creeps. Even so, she couldn't help drawing a crucifix on a piece of paper from the A4 pad she always carried in her case, and pinning it to the door.

Reasoning that if she had a shower, she'd probably wake Brandon, and he could do with an unbroken night's sleep, she stripped and slid into bed beside him. She settled down against the pillows, and was soon asleep.

She woke the next morning, feeling refreshed; Brandon was still asleep, and she crept out of bed so as not to wake him. The crucifix was still pinned to the door; feeling slightly ashamed of herself, she removed the piece of paper and hid it in the back of her pad.

It was still early – not quite seven o'clock – so she went back to bed, picking up a book and soon losing herself in it. Some time later, she felt a movement beside her in the bed and looked up. Brandon was stretching.

'Morning,' she said softly. 'How are you feeling?'

'Like hell,' he admitted.

She put her hand on his forehead; it was dry, and very hot. 'I think we'd better get a doctor out to you.'

'I'll be all right.'

'Don't be so macho,' she chided gently. 'Your temperature's well up, and you just said that you feel like hell. I'll go and find Alicia, and ask her to call the doctor.'

'You had a good evening with her, then?'

'Sort of. She told me a spooky tale about this place which should have given me nightmares,' Susanna said drily.

'But you liked her?'

'Sort of. Anyway, it's the doctor for you, Mr Rodgers.' Susanna slid out of bed, and put on Brandon's dressing gown. 'Do you want a glass of water or something, before I go?'

He shook his head. 'It's all right.'

She kissed him gently on the forehead. 'I'll see you in a minute, then.' Barefoot, she padded out through the corridors. How Molly managed to keep the place even semi-clean, she had no idea – it was huge. She supposed that it was easier, in some ways, because there were fewer carpets to trap the dust, and she'd already noticed that Alicia wasn't one for ornaments. Even so, the idea of having to do that much housework wasn't one which Susanna relished.

The whole place seemed deserted. Susanna opened door after door, and no one was there – most of the rooms didn't even have furniture in. At last, she reached the kitchen; Molly was there, washing up.

'Good morning,' Susanna said.

Molly gave her a surly look.

'I need to see Alicia, please.'

'Milady can't be disturbed.'

No surprises there, Susanna thought crossly. 'Look, Molly, I know you and I don't see eye to eye, but this really is important.'

'Milady needs her sleep.'

'I wouldn't ask, if it wasn't important. She didn't go to bed that much later than me, did she?'

'Milady always sleeps in the daytime, and works at night.'

Susanna sighed. Brandon had told her that, and even if he hadn't, she should have known it. 'Molly, Brandon's really ill. He needs a doctor. His forehead's burning. Can you tell me the doctor's number, please?'

For one horrible moment, Susanna thought that the housekeeper was going to refuse; then, with a scowl, Molly dried her hands and stalked out of the kitchen. Susanna followed her into what turned out to be the sitting room; Molly indicated the small mahogany telephone table and handed her a small telephone book open at 'D', with the doctor's number written on the first line.

As Susanna had half expected, Alicia had an old-fashioned telephone: it was probably an antique, she thought, dialling the number.

'Pentremain surgery is closed until half-past eight. If you need to see the doctor urgently, please call us on Pentremain six eight nine four.' Susanna frowned, cleared the line, and dialled the other number. It rang four times, five, and then at last an elderly voice answered. 'Hallo?'

'Is that the doctor, please?' Susanna asked.

'Yes. Dr Fellowes speaking.' Wearily, as though he wished that it wasn't.

'I'm sorry to bother you, but my boyfriend's ill. I believe you've already seen him – Brandon Rodgers?'

There was a pause, as though the doctor were trying to remember; then, eventually, he said, 'Yes.'

'Brandon's a lot worse, this morning. Could you come to see him, please?'

'And who might you be, young lady?'

'I'm Susanna James. And I'm ringing from the castle, with Molly's permission.'

'I see. And what are his symptoms?'

'I'm not a nurse, but his temperature's definitely higher than it should be. His forehead's burning. He's pale, he aches all over, and he's very tired. I'm really worried about him.'

'It's probably nothing that a little rest won't cure.'

'I think it's more than that.' Susanna strove to keep her temper under control. What was it with the villagers, that they hated coming up to the castle? Was it just because they didn't like being put out for strangers? She'd always heard that Cornish folk were friendly: so far, she hadn't seen that much of the fabled hospitality and kindness.

'I've already seen him, and I told Molly that he just needed rest, and good plain food. A spot of beef tea will pep him up.'

'He's getting worse. Surely he needs something more than rest and beef tea?' Susanna's temper finally snapped. 'Look, if you don't want to come out, fine. I'll simply call an ambulance.'

'There's no need for that, young lady.'

'So are you coming to see him, Doctor, or not?'

There was a sigh. 'All right. I'll be over in half an hour.'

'Thank you.' Susanna put the phone down. 'He's coming over in half an hour,' she said to Molly. 'Perhaps you'd be good enough to call me when he's here? I'll be with Brandon.'

Molly said nothing; Susanna glanced at her watch, noting the time; and turned on her heel. Bitch. Even if Molly didn't like her, surely she could call a truce with her, for Brandon's sake? She stalked back upstairs to the bedroom; her temper immediately cooled down when she saw Brandon. He looked absolutely terrible.

'Dr Fellowes will be here in about half an hour,' she said softly. 'Can I get you anything? Water? A hot drink?'

He shook his head. 'Nothing. But I'm so cold, Susanna.'

'I'll ask Molly for a hot-water bottle, or something?'

'It's all right. I don't want to bother anyone.'

'You won't be.' Susanna stroked his face, and kissed him gently. 'I'll see you in a minute.'

Molly was still in the kitchen when Susanna arrived there. She said nothing when Susanna walked in; Susanna took a deep breath. Much as she would have liked to slap the woman, it would do no good whatsoever. If she antagonized Molly, she would have no chance of getting a hot-water bottle for Brandon – and Brandon was more important than female pride. 'Do you have a hot-water bottle, please? Brandon says he feels freezing.'

There was a stony silence; Susanna was just about to yell at the woman that she'd look for one herself, when Molly went to a cupboard, pulled out an ancient rubber bottle, and handed it to Susanna in silence.

'Thank you.' Susanna didn't bother trying to make polite conversation; she simply filled the kettle, let it boil, and made the hot-water bottle. She left the kitchen without another word; by the time she reached the bedroom, Brandon had pushed all the bedclothes back, complaining that he felt boiling.

'So much for your hot-water bottle, hm?'

He smiled wryly. 'Sorry to mess you about.'

'No problem.' She squeezed his hand. 'All I'm worried about is getting you better again.'

'Yeah, I know.'

She went into the bathroom, coming back with a damp flannel to wipe his face. 'That feels good,' he said.

She returned the flannel to the bathroom, then came to sit on the bed next to him. He drowsed against the pillows; Susanna had never seen him look so ill, and it worried her. She only hoped that Dr Fellowes would be more use, this time round.

She showered quickly and dressed, resuming her place by Brandon's side. The next half-hour dragged, but at last Molly opened the door and ushered the doctor into Brandon's bedroom. Dr Fellowes turned out to be a thin, almost gaunt man in his late fifties, with thinning hair, small gold round-rimmed glasses, and a nervous habit of rubbing his chin. He covered his mouth when he spoke, as though afraid, and tended to mumble: Susanna wanted to shake him, tell him to stop being silly and buck his ideas up.

He sounded a lot less feeble on the phone, she thought. Maybe it was the castle that unnerved him. The Gothic creepiness was enough to unnerve anyone. Though she wished he wouldn't keep looking over his shoulder, as if he expected something to creep up on him and grab him from behind. It made the back of her neck prickle.

He examined Brandon, and finally turned to Susanna. 'It's rheumatic fever,' he said.

Susanna frowned. 'That's what you said before – but he's worse, now.'

'It's a relapse.'

'What causes it?'

'A virus.'

In other words, Susanna thought, *he didn't know*. 'I see. Well, can I take him back to London with me?'

The doctor shook his head. 'It's dangerous to move him, at this stage. You'll have to wait until he's better.'

'Which is likely to be when?' she prompted.

'I'm not sure. I'll come back in a couple of days, and see how he is,' the doctor replied. 'In the meantime . . .' He handed her a small bottle of tablets. 'Antibiotics. They should help.'

'Thank you.' *For being virtually useless*, she added silently.

'Well, I must be off. Patients to see, you know,' he said brightly.

In other words, you can't wait to get a million miles away from Alicia's creepy castle, Susanna translated to herself. But why should someone like a village doctor – someone who should by his very nature be unaffected by superstition – be so afraid of the place? Or was he, too, in Alicia's pay, putting on a performance for anyone outside the village.

There wasn't much she could do about it. She could either go home, and leave Brandon to the less than tender mercies of Molly – or she could stay, and nurse him herself. Put like that, she had only one choice.

'Do you mind if I borrow your phone?' she asked Brandon.

'No – it's charged up. At least, it should be.'

She smiled at him. 'I'll be staying here for a couple more days than I thought I would, so I need to let Kate and Yvonne know.'

'What about work?'

'I can work from here. Anyway, I'll do more work here than I will if I'm miles away in London, worrying about you.' She ruffled his hair. 'I'll nip into the village this afternoon, to get you some magazines. Maybe Alicia could order extra papers, too.'

'I don't think she has them delivered.'

No. Not if paperboys had to deliver them in the dark. 'I'll get some papers as well, then.'

'Thanks.'

She smiled at him, and took the mobile phone from his bags. She switched it on, and frowned. 'The signal isn't brilliant, even for a digital.'

'Why don't you take it up on the battlements? If you go to the end of this corridor, there's a door to some stairs. They lead up to the battlements – and there's a fantastic view.'

'Do you think I ought to ask first?'

Brandon shook his head. 'Alicia said you were her guest. She knows you're a journalist, and she knows you want to do a *Homefile* piece on the place. She'll probably be more surprised if you don't do any exploring.'

'I suppose so.' She kissed him lightly. 'See you in a minute, then.'

She left their bedroom, and walked down to the end of the corridor. As Brandon had told her, there was a door leading to a narrow spiral staircase. The air smelt faintly musty, and Susanna suspected that the castle's bats probably lived somewhere nearby; she shivered slightly, then lifted her chin and walked up the stairs.

There was another heavy oak door, at the top; it creaked slightly, but opened easily enough when she tried it. And then she was on the battlements.

The view was incredible. It had been stunning enough from Brandon's bedroom window, but this was something else. If she'd been Alicia, Susanna thought, she'd have put a glass roof over the battlements, and either slept up here or used it as a workroom

She took a deep breath of air, and rang Kate's number. There was a fifty-fifty chance that Kate would have gone out already; she crossed her fingers hard, and was relieved when Kate answered on the third ring.

'Hallo?'

'You sound like you're still half-asleep,' Susanna said, amused.

'Not far off it.' Kate yawned. 'So how are you? How's Brandon? And what's going on?'

'One at a time,' Susanna said, laughing. 'I'm fine. Brandon's ill, though.'

'Brandon? Mr I-never-get-a-cold? Never.'

'The local quack say's he's got rheumatic fever, would you believe? Apparently, it's a viral infection.'

'That's doctor-speak for not knowing what caused it.'

'Mm. I want to get Brandon back to London, but the doctor says he's too ill to travel.'

'Look, if you want me to drive down and pick you both up, it's no problem.'

'Thanks, Kate. I really appreciate it. But I suppose the doctor's right – I'd better not move him, just yet.'

'Hm,' Kate said. 'What about the Vampire Queen? Or can't you talk?'

'Considering that I'm talking on a digital mobile phone, which can't be tapped, and I'm standing in the middle of the castle battlements, what do you think?'

'I think you should tell me everything!'

'Right. Well, she's got this real Mrs Danvers of a house-keeper, called Molly. Talk about surly! But I have to stay on Molly's good side, in case she takes it out on Brandon and poisons him, or something.'

'And Alicia herself?'

'Very Gothic. More or less what I'd expected. This place is incredibly creepy – it's dark, full of corridors, and hasn't been decorated in centuries – and she likes telling her guests creepy tales after dinner.'

'Well, she does write about vampires. What did you expect her to do, tell you some sweetness-and-light bedtime story about fluffy-wuffy bunny-rabbits?'

Susanna laughed. 'Hardly. Anyway, I'm staying here for a

few days, until Brandon's well enough to travel.'

'If you need a lift, just ring me.'

'Thanks. Though I'll make sure it isn't Monday night.'

Kate chuckled. 'Good. Well, take care. Is there anything you want me to do? You know, nip in to your flat and check the mail, or anything?' Kate had Susanna's spare key.

'Thanks for the offer, but there's no need. I expect we'll be back in a couple of days. I'm not expecting anything *that* urgent.'

'Right. Well, ring me when you hit London, then.'

'I will. See you soon!'

Susanna returned from the battlements with regret. The dank, dingy atmosphere in the castle was oppressive, especially after the bright sunlight and the view from the battlements.

When she reached their bedroom, Brandon was asleep. She laid a hand on his forehead; he still felt burning. The marks on his neck, too, still seemed livid. Then she remembered the cross and chain.

She was half annoyed with herself, for playing along with Alicia's little game. On the other hand, it might not be a game – and this was one of the few weapons which, according to legend, would work. She reached behind her neck, undid the clasp, then put the little chain round Brandon's neck. It might be superstition – but it might also protect him, in her absence.

She kissed him gently on the forehead, then headed for the kitchen. As she'd hoped, Molly was there.

'I'm just going to the village, to get Brandon some magazines and some papers. Do you want me to bring anything back for you?'

Molly stared at her in surprise. 'Such as?'

'Look, Molly, we don't like each other – but we're going to have to put up with each other for the next few days, until Brandon's well enough to travel and we can leave here. It seems stupid for both of us to go into Pentremain, and that's why I asked you if you wanted anything.'

Molly thought about it. 'I can't think of anything.'

'Well, the offer was there. I'm walking to the village – I suppose that'll take about half an hour?'

'Something like that.' Molly was still guarded – but at least, Susanna thought, the woman was talking to her.

'I'll be back at around lunchtime, then.' Susanna paused. 'Would you prefer me to ring the bell, or borrow a key?'

Molly shrugged. 'There is no spare key.'

'I'll ring, then. See you later, Molly. Have a nice morning.' Susanna gave her an approximation of a friendly smile, and left the kitchen.

The walk down to the village was longer than she'd expected; the slope of the road, too, was steeper than she'd remembered. She made a mental note to buy a bottle of water in the village: she'd need it, coming back to the castle. And Brandon certainly wasn't strong enough to handle the walk, she thought with resignation. They'd definitely need a taxi to leave the place.

She bought half a dozen magazines and a couple of newspapers, then headed for the tiny village shop which doubled as the post office, supermarket and butcher's. To her relief, they sold bottled water. She also bought Brandon some grapes, the ingredients for her mother's chicken soup, some fish, and some flowers for Molly. Maybe the gesture would make the old bat realize that Susanna was serious about a truce – and might make her more likely to let Susanna cook Brandon a few meals herself. Starting with the soup.

She was just about to leave the shop when a familiar voice said in her ear, 'So you've survived, too. Believe me now, do you? Or hasn't she made herself known to you yet?'

Susanna turned round to face Thomas Penford. 'Oh. It's you.' She looked coldly at him.

'You've met her now then?'

'Yes. And I also know that you're one of the village players, and she wrote that little story for you. It was very effective – you almost had me believing you, for a while.'

'That's what she told you, is it? That she wrote the story, and I'm one of the village players?'

Susanna rolled her eyes. 'I'm only surprised that you don't all walk around wearing "I love Alicia" T-shirts.'

'I beg your pardon?'

'Oh, come on, Thomas! All this fuss about not going to the castle at night, and the way you all cross yourselves when her name's mentioned, and giving people silver crosses and chains – it's just too Bram Stoker. I'm only surprised that you don't try pretending you're all gypsies, too.'

'What?'

'Wasn't it a gypsy woman who gave Jonathan Harker the cross, in the carriage on the way to Dracula's castle?' Susanna gave him a contemptuous look. 'Try being a bit more subtle, next time you speak to someone who isn't one of Alicia's adoring fans.'

'I don't know what you mean,' Thomas said stiffly.

'Come on. Why don't you admit that you're all in on it? Her publicity hype, that is.'

He stared at her for a moment. 'That's what *she* told you?'

Susanna rolled her eyes. 'She didn't have too. It stands out a mile. Her creepy housekeeper's just as bad. I bet the tourists leave her huge tips. They'll lap it up.'

'No tourists go to Castle Pentremain,' Thomas informed her. 'No one goes there without *her* say-so. The last few people who went there . . . Well, they went at night. The next morning, they were found dead, completely drained of blood.'

'And of course, the papers didn't say anything, because Alicia used her special powers to hide the evidence?'

'That's right.'

She smiled thinly. 'Then good day to you, Mr Penford. I don't think that you and I have anything more to say to each other – besides, I want to get back to Brandon, to see if he's better.'

'That depends on whom she chooses,' Thomas said mysteriously.

'How very, very interesting.' Susanna laced her words with pure sarcasm.

'They get lonely, you know. Vampires. That's why they choose someone to stay with them. Her last companion died a year or so ago. He's buried in the churchyard – and if you don't believe me, his name was Edward Langham. You'll see her initials on the grave – "beloved of AD", it says.'

Susanna shook her head. 'I really don't want to hear any of this.'

'No.' He smiled thinly. 'Because you're going to be the next one.'

'What?'

'It's obviously not your boyfriend. If she'd wanted him, she would have done something by now. She would have given out that he was dead, so you'd mourn him in London and stay away from Pentremain. But no – she let you come here. And her housekeeper admitted you to the castle.' His smile was far from comforting. 'You're her chosen one.'

'That's a load of rubbish, and you know it.' Susanna had had enough. 'You've had your fun, Mr Penford. Now, go away, and leave me alone.'

'As you wish. But don't say I didn't warn you.'

Susanna said nothing, and began to walk away. When she was sure that Thomas wasn't following her, she slowed her pace. She only realized that she was walking in the wrong direction when she came to the church.

She smiled to herself, forgetting the ugly incident with Thomas. She'd always liked pottering round old country churches. If there was anything interesting – some special brass, a pretty rood-screen – she might be able to use it for a *Homefile* feature.

The church turned out to be just like any other little country church, with no special features; even so, it *was* pretty, and Susanna lingered there for a while, tracing the carving of the pews and reading the names on the brasses and the stone flags in the aisle.

When she came out, she wandered through the churchyard. Some of the graves were ancient indeed, dating from the early eighteenth century; others were newer. Including that of an Edward Langham, who'd died the previous year. *Beloved of AD.*

A shiver ran down her spine. Thomas had probably been spinning her another yarn. The initials 'AD' weren't exactly uncommon. Of course the man had had nothing to do with Alicia . . .

'I knew you'd come. I knew you'd have to see it for yourself.'

She jumped at the sound of his voice behind her, then turned to face him and scowled. 'Thomas, just leave me alone. I'm tired of all this stupid play-acting. I'm waiting for Brandon to get well enough to travel, and them I'm leaving. Both of us are.'

'If she lets you.'

'Don't be ridiculous. This is England, not Transylvania. She's not Dracula, refusing to let me leave her castle and giving me to some harpies to keep me quiet.'

He leaned against the grave. 'She likes women, as well as men. And I should know – I've seen her.'

'Spying on her, were you?' Susanna's tone was waspish.

'No. I was doing my job, trimming back the roses from the side of the house, and I happened to look through the window. She was there, with Ellen, in the sitting room.' A smile curved his lips. 'She was pretty, was Ellen. A bit like you, with lots of golden hair, except her eyes were blue. She had a beautiful smile, and lips like a rosebud. Had I not been with my sweetheart, I could have fallen in love with Ellen, quite easily, and married her. Well, if I'd been of her station, of course.'

Despite herself, Susanna was curious. 'Who was Ellen?'

'She was the daughter of one of the farmers around here. They had a lot of land, her family. Her father was planning to marry her off to some gentleman or other. But then Ellen took up with *her*. They used to go horse-riding together, and Ellen would come to stay at Castle Pentremain as much as she could.

'She gave out that they were like cousins – sisters, even –

but it wasn't like that, between them. That day I trimmed back the roses . . . Well, they were dancing together. There was no music, but she was singing, and they were dancing to her song. Ellen was spellbound by her voice, that much was obvious.'

'Why didn't you leave the roses until they'd gone?'

'I couldn't.' Thomas's face was grim. 'Because she saw me at the window.'

'And she put a spell on you, I suppose, to make you stay there and watch?'

'You may laugh, young lady, but I swear to you that I couldn't move. I couldn't have left my place by the window if my life had depended on it. And that's how I know that she likes women – because I saw what she did to Ellen.'

Susanna knew that she was being stupid to encourage him, but there was something in his voice that she couldn't resist. 'Don't tell me – she sank her fangs into Ellen's neck and drank her blood?'

'Something far more shocking than that. Knowing her, I wouldn't have been surprised had she drained Ellen's blood – but no. She undressed the girl like a lover. First her silk dress, rustling to the floor: then her underthings, smoothing them from her skin until Ellen was naked. And still she was singing, almost as though she were hypnotizing the girl.

'Then she undressed, just like she had with me. Only this time, she didn't rub herself. She took *Ellen*'s hand, and drew it between her legs, making *Ellen* touch her and give her pleasure. She threw her head back, howling like a wolf when she came.'

Typical of a vampire, to howl like a wolf, Susanna thought. And as for the lesbian scene – Thomas wasn't being original there, either. Bram Stoker had been there before him. The more Thomas told her, the more convinced Susanna was that Alicia had written the story for him, as a blatant rip-off of *Dracula*.

'And then Ellen took her hand away, glistening with *her* juices, and licked every last drop of it from her fingers.'

Susanna was tempted to ask if Thomas had masturbated at the sight, or thought about joining them. It would have been a pretty scene: one woman sliding down on the young man's cock while the other sat on his face, letting him pleasure her with his mouth – and maybe caressing each other's breasts as Thomas brought them both to a shattering orgasm.

'Then Ellen dropped down on her knees, burying her face in *her* crotch. She slid her fingers in Ellen's hair, urging her on – making her lick her as though Ellen were a man.'

Susanna smiled to herself. Yes, Thomas had definitely wanted to join them. Obviously, he hadn't dared.

'Ellen lapped and lapped and lapped until *she* came again. Then it was her turn. Ellen lay down on the floor, and *she* moved her legs so that her knees were bent and wide apart. Then *she* lapped at Ellen, making Ellen writhe beneath her and cry out in her crisis. Then she kissed her, like a lover, before standing up and going over to the mantelpiece. There was a silver candelabrum there, with creamy beeswax candles in it. She took one, and went back over to Ellen, who was still lying on the floor.

'Then, very slowly, she stroked Ellen's thighs apart, and pressed the end of the candle to her sex. It slid into her, and Ellen opened her mouth in pleasure, tipping her head back and baring her throat.

'I saw *her* open her mouth, her teeth becoming long – but she didn't rip Ellen's throat out. Instead, she drew her tongue along it, and began to suck on her breasts – all the while pushing the candle back and forth inside Ellen.

'When Ellen came, she took the candle out. It glistened in the light – and she licked every last drop of Ellen's juices from it, before putting it back in the candelabrum.' He smiled thinly. 'And that's how I know, young lady, that she likes women as much as she likes men.'

'So what happened to Ellen?'

'She married and moved away. That's when *she* got her claws into Edward. He kept her going, until he died last year.

And now she's lonely, looking for his replacement.'

'How come no one ever says anything about Edward in interviews and what-have-you?'

Thomas shrugged. 'Maybe they think he was her father, her grandfather. Though we know different, around here.'

'But you never say anything, in case she revenges herself on your family,' Susanna finished, remembering his previous tale. 'Though I'm a journalist, and you're telling me. I have plenty of friends in London. What makes you think I wouldn't tell them, or write the scoop myself?'

Thomas simply smiled. 'You won't. Because you know what's good for you.'

Nine

Susanna had virtually forgotten Thomas's story when she reached the castle again. The hike from the village had been every bit as tough as she'd expected, but she thought that the exercise would do her good. She missed her twice-weekly step class, and tackling the hill on which Alicia's castle was built was more or less the next best thing to a workout. Susanna decided that she'd walk to the village and back every day, for as long as she had to stay in Pentremain.

Molly answered the bell first time, and was surprised when Susanna gave her the flowers.

'These are for you,' Susanna said with a smile.

'What are they for?' Molly asked, her eyes narrowing suspiciously.

'Because you've looked after Brandon, while he's been ill. I just wanted to say thanks, from both of us. I appreciate what you've done for him.'

'Oh.'

Susanna watched carefully for any signs of softening in Molly's face. There wasn't a single one. Still, at least she'd tried. She summoned a smile as she followed Molly back into the castle. 'I wondered if you'd mind if I made Brandon something for lunch. It's my mother's chicken soup – it always worked for me, when I was a child, and made me feel heaps better.'

Molly was silent.

'I promise I won't make a mess in your kitchen, and I'll clear up after myself. Besides, it'll give you a bit of a break, won't it?'

Still silence. *Well, don't they say that silence means consent*? Susanna asked herself. She followed Molly into the kitchen. 'I'll just pop up to see Brandon, and take him his newspapers, before I make the soup. I bought him some grapes – could I borrow a bowl to put them in, please?'

Molly banged about in a cupboard, and handed Susanna a bowl.

Susanna smiled. 'Thank you. And would you mind if I put this little lot in the fridge? I wouldn't like it to go off.'

Molly waved one hand in the direction of the fridge, then turned her back. Susanna put the chicken, the fish and the milk she'd bought in the fridge, then went back upstairs to see Brandon. He was sleeping peacefully, so she let him be, simply putting the armful of papers and magazines on the bedside cabinet, and placing the bowl of grapes on the top.

The castle felt dingy and constricting; she decided to go onto the battlements again, and ring Yvonne. She found a corner of the battlements where she could sit comfortably and in relative safety, and dialled Yvonne's number. It rang and rang; she was about to give up when Yvonne answered. 'Hallo?'

'Yvonne? It's Susanna.'

'Hi, how are you? Did you have a good trip?'

'I'm fine. It took ages, though, so I'm definitely taking driving lessons when I get back to London. Right now, I wouldn't care if I didn't see another train again until next year!'

'How's Brandon, or shouldn't I ask?'

'He's ill – the doctor says it's rheumatic fever, but I get the impression that he'd say that about anything.'

'Local quack, huh?'

'Something like that. Anyway, I'm going to stay here for a

few days, to look after Brandon. Obviously I'll do some work, while I'm here – I'll fax some copy through to you, from Truro station. The phones are hard-wired here, and I forgot to bring the modem anyway.'

'So much for you being the office techie.' Yvonne's voice was warm with amusement. 'Dare I ask how you're getting along with Alicia Descourt?'

'She's OK. In small doses – she's a bit too intense for comfort, to be honest. All the villagers delight in telling you creepy stories about her, or about the castle.'

'And I bet that goes down well with you.'

'Not,' Susanna finished, laughing. 'How's everything in the office?'

'Fine. I've a list of messages for you as long as your arm, but there's nothing that won't keep. Madam's due back on Monday, but I'll tell her that you've had a personal problem and you're taking holiday to sort it out.'

'You can tell her that Brandon's ill, if you like. She approves of him – on a purely professional basis, of course.' Susanna smiled. 'She might be less of a cow about it, if you tell her the truth.'

'Right.'

'Anyway, I'd better go. I'll call in, later in the week. If you need me, ring me on Brandon's mobile.' She gave Yvonne the number. 'And I'm getting a mailbox set up, so if the phone's switched off, you can still leave a message.'

Yvonne groaned. 'You'll turn the poor man into as much of a techie as you are!'

'It'll do him good,' Susanna said, laughing. 'Well, take care.'

'And you. Give my love to Brandon, and say I hope he feels better soon.'

'Thanks, I will.'

Susanna felt oddly bereft when she hung up – even more so than she had when talking to Kate. It was as though she'd cut herself off from contact with the outside world . . . She shook herself. That was ridiculous. Of course she hadn't: at the very least, she had the mobile phone, and she could always go into the village if she wanted to see a face more friendly than Molly's. Anyway, she had things to do – like setting up a mailbox for Brandon's phone, and making him some chicken soup.

As she'd half-suspected, Brandon had brought the instructions for the mobile phone with him. Unlike herself and Kate, he wasn't comfortable with modern technology, seeing it as something he had to do for his business rather than enjoying it. He was well-organized, thanks to his paper diary, and could lay his hands on any file within seconds – unlike Susanna, who was fine with computer files, and messy with paper ones.

She took the book out to the battlements, flicked through the pages until she found the section on setting up a mailbox, then deftly went through the process to set it up.

'That's the first bit sorted, then,' she said. She rang Kate's number again, expecting the answerphone; after the fourth ring, Kate's voice cut in. 'It's Kate and Bill – you know the drill – leave your number after the tone.' Bill was actually Kate's cat: but the idea of a resident male had the effect of putting off any heavy-breathers. Susanna smiled. 'Hi, Kate, it's Susanna. I've set up a mailbox on the mobile, so if you need to get hold of me and the phone's switched off, you can leave a message.' She gave Kate the number. 'See you later – and have fun with your Italian.'

Brandon was awake when she went back into the bedroom.

'Hi, how are you feeling?'

'Not wonderful,' he admitted.

'Well, all you need to do is lie there and rest. I brought you plenty of papers and magazines, and some grapes; and you'll be having Mrs James's chicken soup for lunch.'

'Molly's cooking something from your mother's recipe?' Brandon was surprised.

Susanna shook her head. 'Better than that. *I* am.'

He chuckled. 'Considering how much you hate cooking . . .'

She smiled sweetly at him. 'I can do it, if I really have to. I just choose not to, most of the time.'

'Why have you decided to do it now?'

'Because Mrs Danvers will probably refuse to cook you the sort of food my mother always cooked when I was ill as a child. Chicken soup, poached fish, that sort of thing.'

'So what makes you think that you'll be able to do it, without a recipe book?'

'Put it this way – it'll either be good enough to help you feel better, or bad enough to force you to get well quicker, to avoid having to eat too much of it!'

Brandon hugged her. 'Oh, Susanna. I do appreciate this, you know.'

'I know.'

He pulled a face. 'I hate chicken soup.'

'Me, too – though it's the only thing I feel like eating when I'm ill.'

'Weird woman.'

Susanna shook her head. 'As a matter of fact, it's scientifically proven that chicken soup is one of the best things you can eat, when you're ill. It's not just an old wives' tale, before you say it.' She rubbed her nose against his. 'I'm not that bad a cook, you know. Clare's given me a few tips, when I happen to have walked into a testing session at the *Homefile* offices. The only reason I let you do all the cooking at home is because you love doing it.'

'You'd live on fruit, cheese and biscuits, if I didn't.'

'For a while, yes. Then, once I'd settled into a routine, I'd probably get round to feeding myself properly.'

'So you could do without me, then?'

'In the kitchen, yes.' She kissed him lightly. 'In the bedroom is a totally different matter.'

'I see.' He cupped her breasts. 'Need some attention, do you?'

'After yesterday, when you gave yourself a relapse – I think I'd better be patient.'

'No, you're the nurse. *I'm* the patient.'

'Ha, ha.' She removed his hands, her fingers gentle. 'Anyway, how about some lunch?'

'You'll do nicely.'

She laughed. 'Oh, Brandon. When you're better, I'll take you up on that, with pleasure. But for now, you're supposed to be resting.'

'Shouldn't nurses wear dinky little skirts, and black stockings?'

'Not this one. Apart from the fact that she doesn't have any stockings with her, and her skirt belongs to a business suit, she doesn't want the patient's temperature to go up any more.' She plumped up his pillows. 'Now, I'll bring you up some soup, and a jug of blackcurrant – you could do with the vitamin C.'

He smiled back at her. 'I wish that all the people who told me that you were a hard-living workaholic journo could see you now.'

'Well, they can't.' She smiled at him. 'But you can have great fun denting my image when we get back to London.'

'Doesn't that give you a good motive to keep me here longer?'

Susanna shook her head. 'Surprisingly – no.' She wanted to be out of Castle Pentremain as soon as possible. 'Now shut up, and rest.'

'Yes, ma'am.'

Molly wasn't in the kitchen when Susanna returned: so much the better, Susanna thought. She poked around in the cupboards until she found a chopping board, a couple of knives, a jug and a saucepan, and began making the soup. One of her mother's 'secret' ingredients had been garlic – an ingredient which had been missing from the meal, the previous evening.

Reasoning that it was good for the blood, and had nothing to do with warding off any so-called vampires, Susanna crushed the garlic on a plate, and added it to the soup. She tasted it: it wasn't quite how she remembered it, but it wasn't too bad.

She wished that she'd thought of buying some granary bread to go with it; still, Brandon probably wasn't up to eating much. The soup would do, for now. She poured a helping into a bowl, put it on the tray she'd found in another cupboard, and left the saucepan with the rest of the soup at the back of the stove. She'd already cleared up everything else; depending on whether Brandon wanted a second helping, or wanted to leave the rest of it until the next day, she'd clean the saucepan later.

Humming to herself, she carried the soup up to Brandon.

His face showed surprise at the first taste. 'I never thought I'd say it, but this is actually rather good.'

'I told you that I could cook, if I had to.'

'Wow. Molly's got a definite rival in you.'

Susanna rolled her eyes. 'I don't see myself as a rival to anyone. I just want you to get better, that's all.'

'Mm. Is there any more of this?'

'If you want it, yes. If not, I'll ask Molly if I can put it in the fridge for tomorrow.'

'What's in it?'

Susanna grinned. 'That's a James family secret. Uh-uh.'

'So unless I marry you, I have to just guess?'

'That's about the strength of it. Anyway, it's handed down from mother to daughter.'

'So that makes it marriage and a kid, before I get the secret.'

'Yup. And that's assuming that our daughter would actually tell you.'

Brandon grinned. 'I love fencing with you. Nobody does it quite like you.'

'I did a term's seminars on logic, when we did Victorian lit. You've no idea how much difference that makes to *Alice in Wonderland*.'

'I can guess.' Brandon finished his soup. 'That was excellent. Thanks.'

'More now, or tomorrow?'

'Tomorrow, I think. It was nice – but I really don't think I could eat any more.'

'Then I suggest you have a little nap.'

He grinned. 'I think I've sussed one of the ingredients. Sleeping pills.'

'Wrong. How about chicken?'

'If I was up to it, I'd throw this pillow at you.'

She laughed. 'Well. Get some rest.'

'What are you going to do?'

'Sit on the battlements and do some work.' It was an answer he could cope with. What she actually intended to do was a little exploring. She could start with the library – and maybe the castle would yield a few of its secrets to her. Enough for her to be sure that Thomas Penford was spinning her a yarn, not telling her the truth . . .

She picked up her laptop. 'See you in a bit.'

'OK.' He blew her a kiss as she left the room.

The laptop had been an excellent idea, Susanna thought. If Molly found her in the library and disapproved, she could always claim that she'd needed to do some work, and wanted somewhere quiet where she wasn't disturbing Brandon or Alicia.

Smiling to herself, she descended to the hall. Molly didn't come rushing out to meet her and demand where she was going, so Susanna wandered through the hall at her leisure.

She came across the pictures she'd seen the previous day: the dark-haired man still reminded her of the man she'd seen in her dream. She wondered idly if this was the man Alicia had told her about, after dinner: or maybe he'd been the inspiration for it. He was certainly good-looking, and had the fine sharp features of an ancient race – though his eyes were green, not blue.

The other picture, Susanna thought with a smile, was definitely Alicia. She knew that now, having actually met the woman. No doubt Alicia had had it done as a whim. Maybe she'd been pretending to be the Russian countess of her tale, when she sat for the portrait. And then she'd seduced the artist, letting her dress drop to the floor to reveal that she wore nothing underneath it, before walking over to him and taking the brush from his hand . . .

She grinned to herself. If she kept this up, she, not Kate, would be the one with an erotic novel hidden in the bottom of her desk! Shifting her laptop to her other arm, she walked through the hall and tried the first door on the left. It still refused to give; rather than tug harder at it and risk rousing Molly, she went to the next door.

It opened easily; this time, it didn't creak, as though someone had oiled the hinges. Maybe it had been Molly – Susanna certainly hadn't seen a handyman around the place. She pushed it fully open, and was pleased to discover herself in the library. 'Brilliant. You couldn't have done it better if you'd tried,' she said under her breath.

She went into the room, and closed the door behind her. It was an incredible room: long and narrow, with the walls covered entirely in made-to-measure oak bookshelves. One set of shelves, at the far end of the room, had a glass door set in front of them; Susanna guessed that the cabinet was locked, and wondered what was so precious that it had to be kept under lock and key.

The other question was why Alicia hadn't offered to lend Brandon a few books, to keep him occupied. Had Susanna been in Alicia's position, the first thing she would have done was to ask Brandon what sort of things he liked reading, and to bring him up a selection of novels and short stories.

Still wondering just what made Alicia Descourt tick, Susanna went into the middle of the room, putting her laptop on the low table. There were a couple of big old-fashioned red-leather armchairs set either side of the fireplace, each with a small table next to it. Susanna smiled when she noticed the silver trays set with lead crystal decanters and matching glasses: sherry, whisky and brandy. Alicia had said that she didn't drink, so maybe they were more for effect than for use.

Then she noticed the window-seat at the other end of the room. She walked over to it, and drew a sharp intake of breath at the view. It was the secret garden that Thomas had talked about – the one full of roses, where he'd made love to Alicia when he was a young man. Did that mean that the sitting room where he'd seen Alicia with Ellen was next door? And if so, was it the room that was locked? Why had Alicia locked it?

She couldn't think of any answers, so she started looking along the shelves. The glass case was locked, as she'd suspected, and the books inside it seemed to be very old leather-bound books about witchcraft and the supernatural. No doubt these were Alicia's primary sources for the background to her books. Why they were locked away, Susanna had no idea – particularly when she came across a section of leather-bound first-edition Victorian novels. They were worth at least as much as Alicia's supernatural collection, so why weren't they, too, locked away?

Eventually, she chose a copy of *Tess of the d'Urbervilles*, an old favourite, and curled up in one of the big leather armchairs. This was the sort of room she'd definitely have, she thought, if she ever won the lottery or was left a huge fortune by an unknown great-aunt in Australia.

She settled down to read and, at length, fell asleep, the book dropping into her lap. She was woken by someone shaking her shoulder.

'Huh?' she said, forcing her eyelids apart.

'What are you doing in here?' Molly demanded, her voice harsh.

'Reading a Hardy novel. Look, Brandon needed some rest, and you can't rest with someone else prowling around the room. I thought I'd do some work, and imagined that Alicia had a library, which would probably be a good place for me to work, without disturbing anyone.'

'So you prowled around until you found it.'

'Actually, it was the first door I tried.' Susanna lifted her chin. 'I don't make a habit of prowling around, thank you very much. If you'd been available, I would have asked you first.'

Molly said nothing.

'And as for this – I suppose I got side-tracked by the books.' She placed the novel carefully on the table next to her, and uncurled from the chair. She stood, drawing herself up to her full height. 'I love books, and I'd never do any damage to them. I'm sure Alicia won't mind – and as you said she wasn't to be disturbed, I decided not to try *prowling around* to find her.'

'Milady doesn't like people in her library.'

'Fair enough. I know, now, and I won't trespass again. OK?'

Back to hostilities, Susanna thought with a sigh.

'And you said you wouldn't leave my kitchen in a mess.'

'One saucepan. You weren't around, so I couldn't ask you if I could put the soup in a covered bowl in the fridge.'

'The kitchen stinks.'

'Of chicken soup? I put some garlic in it, but not that much.' Susanna sighed. 'Look, Molly, I don't want to fight with you. I don't want to be here any more than you want me cluttering up the place, but until Brandon's better, I'm staying. Alicia doesn't have a problem with it, so why should you?'

There was no answer.

'And I'm intending to cook some fish for Brandon, tonight. He doesn't feel well enough for anything heavy. I assume that isn't a problem?'

Molly shrugged. 'I'll have to ask Milady.'

'You do that.' Susanna replaced the Hardy on the shelves, and collected her laptop. 'Now, is there anywhere I can work without upsetting you or Alicia, and without disturbing Brandon?'

'As you are here now, I suppose you might as well stay here. Just don't touch anything.'

Susanna was tempted to offer to let Molly search her for stolen contraband, when she was ready to leave the room, but decided that it would only make matters worse. Instead, she gave Molly her sweetest smile, sat back in the leather chair, and switched on the little machine.

Some time later, when she'd finished sketching out an article about country churches, she stretched, turned off the machine, and left the library. She was half-expecting Molly to be standing at the door, demanding to check that she hadn't secreted some important volume about her person, but the way was unbarred.

She went back to Brandon's room, and discovered that he was awake and reading one of the papers she'd bought in the village.

'Hi. How are you feeling?'

'Not so bad. But I don't think I'm up to dinner, tonight.'

'That's what I thought. So you get Mrs James's special poached fish – otherwise known as sole bonne femme.'

He grinned. 'I wish I had a camera, to prove to everyone that you're actually cooking this stuff for me. Gourmet food – I mean, it just isn't you. TV dinners have been your limit ever since I've known you. Are you sure you haven't enlisted Molly's help?'

'Since when did Mrs Danvers let Mrs de Winter do anything?' Susanna fenced. She suddenly noticed that he'd taken off the cross and chain. 'Brandon – what did you do with the crucifix?'

'The one you were wearing last night, you mean?'

'Mm.'

'It's in the bedside cabinet. Did you put it round my neck?'

She nodded. 'Just a whim. Humour me, will you?'

'What?'

'Just wear it, Brandon.'

He smiled. 'You don't really think that there are vampires around here, do you?'

She refused to answer that one. 'Just humour me, Brandon. Please?'

'OK. Though the chain's a bit too small, for my liking.'

'Even so.'

He shrugged, and reached over to the drawer of the bedside cabinet. He took the chain out, and replaced it round his neck. 'Happy now, are you?'

'Yup. And as your reward, you'll have a nice gourmet meal, prepared by my own fair hands.'

'Hm. I'm not sure if that's a threat, or a promise.'

'Both.' She plumped his pillows. 'Can I get you anything, in the meantime?'

He grinned. 'There's an answer to that.'

'If it involves sex, then forget it. You're not well enough.'

'Don't you think I'm the best judge of that?'

'You weren't, yesterday,' she reminded him. 'Now, behave.' She kissed him, and went down to the kitchen. Molly hadn't said anything about dinner for that evening, so she had no idea whether she should cook for herself as well as for Brandon. Though she'd only bought enough fish for onc. Well, if she wasn't to eat with Alicia, maybe she could make herself a sandwich or something.

She hummed to herself as she cooked the sole bonne femme; then she took it up to Brandon, deciding to do all the clearing up together.

Brandon ate it appreciatively. 'It's almost worth being ill, to be fed like this.'

She grinned. 'Considering how much you love cooking, and how you always shoo me out of the kitchen, I don't quite believe you.'

'Are you eating with Alicia tonight?'

'I'm not sure.' Susanna eyed his empty plate. 'Though I think I'd better take that downstairs and clear up in the kitchen – otherwise Molly will most definitely not be pleased with me.'

'Right.'

Molly returned to the kitchen just as Susanna put the last pan away. She surveyed the kitchen, then gave a curt nod. As Susanna was about to leave the kitchen, she said, 'Milady will dine with you at eight, tonight.'

'If it's the same room as last night, I'll find my own way there.'

Molly said nothing, so Susanna left the room. Clothes were

definitely becoming a problem, she thought. She had nothing else with her apart from the business suit she'd dismissed, the previous night; the rest of her clothing needed washing, and she was loath to ask Molly if there was a washing machine.

When she got back to the room, Brandon was sleeping; she went into the bathroom, closing the door behind her, and washed out most of her clothes, leaving them to drain over the bath. Then she changed into her business suit and her one remaining shirt, and went downstairs to dinner.

Alicia was already waiting for her in the dining room. 'Good evening. How's Brandon?'

'Sleeping. He looks a bit better. I think the antibiotics are helping.'

'Good.'

Alicia was dressed in a rather low-cut evening gown; Susanna felt considerably under-dressed. 'Look, I wasn't expecting to be here for very long. I didn't bring any formal clothes with me, unless you count this—' she tugged at the sleeve of her jacket '—and the rest of my clothes are drying over the bath.'

'You could always borrow something from me.'

Something in the glitter of those hard green eyes made Susanna wish that she'd kept her mouth shut. The idea of going into Alicia's bedroom and trying on things from her wardrobe, with Alicia watching every move she made, wasn't one she wanted to entertain. 'It's kind of you to offer, but I don't think we have the same taste.'

'Ah, well. If you change your mind.'

Molly brought in a plate of oysters. Alicia smiled. 'I love these – don't you?'

What are you up to? Susanna wondered. 'Yes.'

'Then help yourself.' Alicia opened an oyster, tipping it down her throat and swallowing with a small cat-like sound of appreciation.

Susanna followed suit.

'Molly said you were in the library today.'

Susanna nodded. 'I wanted to do some work, and I didn't want to wake Brandon. I didn't think you'd mind if I worked in one of the other rooms, and a library's the obvious place.'

'I rarely use it.'

'Molly said you didn't like other people using it, either.'

Alicia laughed. 'I'll tell her to back off. She can be a little too zealous about guarding my privacy. If you want to work in there, go ahead.'

'Do you mind if I borrow a novel or two, to read while Brandon's sleeping?'

'Be my guest.' Alicia spread her hands. 'Ha. Well, you already are.'

'I was reading *Tess*. Molly was a bit twitchy about it.' Susanna sighed. 'I told her, I love books, so I won't harm anything – and I certainly wouldn't think of stealing your books.'

'Of course not. Like I said, I'll tell her to back off.' Alicia paused. 'What were you working on?'

'Something about village churches. It's just an outline, at the moment.' Susanna took another oyster. 'Pentremain church is very pretty.'

'Isn't it just?' Alicia poured two glasses of Chablis. 'I take it that you do drink white, as well as red?'

Susanna nodded. 'I do. Thanks.'

'Well – *salut*.' Alicia sipped the wine. 'Mm. Gorgeous. Bone-dry. I detest sweet wines.'

'Me, too,' Susanna admitted.

'We have a lot in common, you know.'

Susanna's smile was mirthless. 'Like Brandon, you mean?'

Alicia laughed. 'Believe me, you don't need to worry about any competition from me, where Brandon's concerned.'

'No?'

'I told you last night. I'm not having an affair with him.' She ate another oyster. 'So you went to the village today?'

Susanna nodded. The way that Alicia ate her oysters, licking her lower lip with such obvious relish . . . If it wasn't so utterly ridiculous, she'd think that Alicia was making a play for her.

Then she remembered Thomas Penford's story about Alicia and Ellen, and shivered.

'Cold?' Alicia asked solicitously.

Susanna shook her head. 'I'm fine.'

'Good.' Alicia sipped her wine. 'So what do you think of Pentremain?'

'Pretty. And very quiet.'

'Which is precisely why I live here. It's quiet, and I can do a lot of work without being interrupted all the time.'

Molly came in as they finished the oysters, and cleared the table. 'Molly – I've told Susanna that it's all right to use the library, and to borrow the books, if she wants to,' Alicia said, smiling sweetly. 'After all, she is our guest.'

'Very well, Milady.'

Susanna had drunk enough wine on a near-empty stomach to make her reckless. She smiled at Alicia when Molly left them alone again. 'Is it mandatory to have a Mrs Danvers, if you live in Cornwall?'

Alicia laughed. 'Is that how you see my poor Molly? She's a sweetheart, really. Like I said, she's just over-protective. She's worked for my family all her life.'

'Known you since you were knee-high to a grasshopper?'

'That sort of thing, I suppose.' Alicia sipped her wine.

'Right.' Susanna smiled. 'I do like your library. There's a beautiful view. Not to mention all the books – leather-bound first editions, most of them.'

Alicia nodded. 'I inherited some of them, but – well, in my line of work, I suppose it's as natural to read a lot as it is to write.'

'Why do you keep some of them under lock and key?'

'Which ones?'

'The ones about vampires and witches and superstitions.'

Alicia shrugged. 'Habit, I suppose. They're my main source material. I like to keep them together. It's convenient.'

Molly came in with the next course, putting the tureens on the table and leaving them to it. Alicia topped up their glasses, and opened another bottle.

'I really don't think I should have any more,' Susanna said.

'Nonsense. It's good for you. All the latest medical research says that you should drink a couple of glasses of wine a day.'

'I think I've already had mine, today.'

Alicia smiled. 'Just keep me company, then.' She spooned rice on to a plate, adding a generous portion of seafood mornay, then handed the plate to Susanna. 'Help yourself to vegetables.'

'Thanks.' *Molly might be a surly old bat*, Susanna thought, *but she cooks well*. Maybe that was why Alicia put up with her housekeeper's moods.

They ate in silence for a while; all the time, Susanna was aware of Alicia's eyes on her. It was as though the older woman was undressing her mentally, and it made her feel uncomfortable.

'I saw Thomas Penford again, today,' she said, breaking the silence.

'Oh?'

'He was full of tales about you. As usual.'

Alicia smiled. 'What is it this time? That I eat babies for breakfast?'

Susanna shook her head. 'Not quite. He was telling me about someone called Ellen.'

'Ellen?'

'Mm. He said he watched you seduce her in the sitting room.'

Alicia laughed. 'Oh, really?'

'So he was spinning me another yarn?'

'Yes and no.'

'One you told him to learn?'

Alicia laid down her fork. 'What are you trying to ask me, Susanna? If I'm attracted to women?'

'Yes.'

She smiled. 'I am. Men, too. Donne hit the nail right on the head when he talked about *Love's sweetest part, variety*. It gives you so much more to choose from, if you play with both sexes.'

'I see.'

Alicia's eyes glittered. 'Why do you want to know, Susanna? Don't you believe me, that I'm not attracted to Brandon? He's nice enough, but he's not my type. I like my men dark.'

Susanna knew that she was on dangerous ground, and she was furious with herself for saying it, but the wine had loosened her tongue. 'And your women?'

'Blonde. I like golden hair – masses of it, tumbling down in ringlets.' Alicia ate another forkful of seafood mornay. 'And usually, I prefer them smaller than me. I like little blonde women, Susanna.' She didn't look at Susanna, but it was obvious what was on her mind when she added, 'Sometimes, I forget the "little".'

Ten

Susanna wasn't sure whether Alicia had just thrown down the gauntlet or not. She wasn't sure whether she wanted to find out, either. Instead, she ate another mouthful of the seafood. 'This is very good, isn't it?'

Alicia smiled, as though acknowledging her cowardice, and allowed the conversation to settle back to more anodyne topics. Fresh fruit followed the seafood, and Susanna was both fascinated and appalled by the way that Alicia opened a ripe fig and sucked the flesh out. Was it her imagination, or was Alicia drawing her attention to the famed association between figs and a woman's genitals?

'Lawrence, *Women in Love*,' Alicia said.

Susanna's eyes widened. Yet again, it seemed that Alicia had read her mind. It unnerved her – and excited her, at the same time. Alicia had an aura of danger about her. Maybe it was all part of her act as the Gothic author; maybe not. Susanna was torn between fascination and unease.

'Fresh fruit needs good wine,' Alicia announced, opening another bottle and topping up their glasses.

'I really don't think that I need any more,' Susanna protested. 'I'm not a great drinker. I don't live up to the alcoholic-journalist stereotype.'

'Like I said, keep me company. Good food and an audience always makes me want to talk, tell stories: and my throat gets dry.'

'Ever tried water?'

Alicia grinned. 'It doesn't have quite the same effect.'

'Right.' Susanna ate a couple of grapes. 'Do you always tell people stories, before you actually write the book?'

'Is this an interview?'

Susanna shook her head. 'I'm merely curious.'

'A habit which killed the proverbial cat.'

Susanna raised an eyebrow. 'Is that a warning?'

Alicia smiled. 'That's what M R James called one of his collections. *A warning to the curious.*'

'If people weren't curious, men wouldn't have walked on the moon. We wouldn't know that Venus was covered in gas, and that Jupiter has many moons.' Susanna lifted her chin. 'Penicillin would never have been discovered. Or radium.'

'Or the atom bomb. My point exactly.'

'Alicia, I'm not in the mood for a sparring match.'

'That's a pity.' Alicia's voice was almost a purr. 'I think I'd like to spar with you, Susanna.'

'Not right now.' Susanna sliced up a banana.

Alicia laughed.

'What's so funny?'

'I expected you to eat it the earthy way, straight from the skin. You've got the kind of mouth that would drive a man into a cold shower, if he watched you eating a banana properly.'

'Well, I happen to like my fruit in slices. Apples, bananas, peaches – whatever. It's more convenient to eat, and less waste, that way.'

'I bet you do that with Mars Bars, too.'

Her good humour was infectious; Susanna couldn't help smiling back. 'I don't know if I want to know what you think people should do with them!'

Alicia grinned, catching Susanna's inference. 'Nah – they're the wrong shape. I prefer Flakes. The texture's exquisite, if someone eats one out of your cunt. And the taste is exquisite, if you eat one out of someone else's cunt.'

Susanna's smile broadened. Alicia was the last person she'd

imagined having this kind of conversation with. Kate, yes – Kate loved bawdy stories. But the hyped-up Gothic writer? It didn't seem her style. 'That's terribly clichéd.'

'But immense fun. Believe me.'

'Is that what you would have done with Ellen?'

Alicia frowned. 'That's a funny use of tenses.'

'No. Thomas's story was of a time nearly sixty years ago.' Susanna spread her hands. 'I'm not sure if Flakes were made then.'

'And you believe Thomas?'

'That it all happened nearly sixty years ago, you mean? Well, you haven't corrected me.'

'Touché.'

Susanna smiled. 'So am I to believe that you're really several hundred years old? First of all, Thomas tells me some ridiculous tale about you seducing him when he was about fourteen – and he's obviously now in his seventies. Then you tell me about a Russian countess, whose name begins with "A" – just like yours – and who lived around four hundred years ago. Then Thomas tells me that you're bisexual, and took up with a bloke called Edward when Ellen went away to marry someone. And you've hinted that maybe he was telling the truth.'

'I like having sex with women as well as with men, yes.'

'And how old are you, precisely?'

'As old as my tongue, and a little older than my teeth.'

'Alicia – do you always play games with people?'

Alicia smiled. 'Yes.'

'Why? Are you so afraid that people won't like you if they know who you really are? A woman in her late thirties, who writes Gothic tales and who's really rather lonely, at heart?'

'Is that how you see me?'

'Isn't that how you are?' Susanna fenced. 'Thomas says that you're lonely.'

'And you think I was planning to persuade Brandon to fill the gap?'

'No.' Susanna was definite. 'That's what I thought, before I came here.'

'And now?'

Susanna sighed. 'I don't know. Every time I think I've worked you out, you seem to change. Are you chameleon or lamia, I wonder?'

Alicia smiled. 'It's refreshing, talking to someone who's well-read.'

'Brandon's well-read. Probably more so than I am.'

Alicia spread her hands. 'Brandon has rheumatic fever, and I don't think he's quite up to this.'

'What about Molly?'

Alicia shook her head. 'Molly's devoted to me – but in a maternal sort of way.'

'And you need a different sort of devotion.'

Alicia nodded. 'I do. As, indeed, did the Russian countess.'

'Are you writing a novel about her?'

'Perhaps.' Alicia smiled.

'You said she was a *broucolaque*. So what happened, after she was thrown from the battlements?'

'She survived. As did Ambrose. They lay low, for a while, until people forgot about them; and then they travelled. They went to Europe: they could not go back to France, for obvious reasons, so they turned to the East. They travelled through the Slavic countries, then to Russia.'

'Visiting the countess's family, there?'

Alicia shook her head. 'She had no family. She was a *broucolaque*, remember? As far as her family were concerned, she was dead. Which I suppose she was, in some respects. They stayed in Russia for a while, but Ambrose had the wanderlust. He wanted to experience new places, new things. So they went to India.'

'India.' Susanna didn't know whether to be disbelieving or fascinated. Brandon was right in his assessment of Alicia – there *was* something about her which attracted your attention, even though you knew that it would bring about your downfall.

She shivered, forcing her thoughts back to Alicia's story. 'India.'

'Yes. It's a dark sub-continent, full of many myths. Vampire flowers, vampire trees. Vines which suck your blood.'

'There *are* vampire flowers,' Susanna interrupted. 'I've seen them, at Kew. Big red trumpets which attract insects – but the insides are slippery, and the insects drown inside. Then they dissolve, and the plant sucks them up.'

'Exactly. These plants are on a larger scale.'

'I thought they were from Africa, or from the rain forests of South America?'

Alicia spread her hands. 'I am no botanist. I am no geographer, either. All I know is that they went to India. Land of the princes, filled with gold and ivory and rubies beyond compare. The countess looked better in emeralds, to match her eyes; but Ambrose had a fancy that he wanted her in gold and rubies.

'They travelled until they found a man who said he could carve her likeness in ivory, and make it so lifelike that Ambrose could imagine that he had two wives. The countess smiled at this, and said that if he could have two wives, she could have two husbands.

'Ambrose smiled at this, and said that maybe the craftsman could carve a likeness of him, too. But she said no, she didn't want a second fair-skinned husband. She wanted someone darker.

'He knew immediately that the countess had her eye on someone – and what she wanted, she usually had. She fantasized about her intended lover at night, and sometimes murmured his name while Ambrose was making love to her. Ambrose knew that the countess had passion enough to satisfy another man as well as himself, so he wasn't too bothered. Ambrose wasn't the jealous type, either.'

Susanna frowned. 'And yet he had a duel with his brother, over the countess.'

'Sibling rivalry. That's different.'

'You said they were never jealous of each other, before.'

Alicia groaned. 'You ought to be a detective, not a journalist.'

Susanna grinned. 'I warned you – I notice things.'

'Right. Well, let's just say that the longer Ambrose was with the countess, the less jealous he became – because he knew that he was the one she loved, the one she shared her life with. OK?'

'OK.'

'He was just curious to know who the man was, and what it was about the man that attracted his wife so much.'

Alicia smiled. 'Have you ever noticed just how beautiful Indian men are?'

Susanna thought about it. 'Well – there was the lead actor in *Kismet*, though I can't remember who he was.'

Alicia didn't enlighten her. 'So you see what I mean? Dark soulful eyes, a good bone structure, a generous mouth, hair so black it has blue lights in it . . . and that beautiful clear skin, the colour of *café-au-lait*.' She smiled. 'Our countess had fallen in lust with an Indian prince, from the nearby village. She'd seen him swimming in the river at sunset – naked – and she liked the look of his body. He was lean, and yet not scrawny or skinny. His muscles were perfectly toned, as though he were a Classical statue. And – most importantly, in her eyes – he had a very promising cock, long and thick. It didn't matter if he didn't know how to use it; she could always teach him. If he was a virgin, so much the better – she could train him in her ways.

'The countess could imagine stretching out on billowing layers of blue and purple silk, their brightness accentuating the paleness of her skin, as she waited for the prince to join her. Half the time when Ambrose made love to her, she was thinking of her prince, smelling his exotic scent, tasting his flesh.

'Ambrose decided to find out a little more about the prince, and see how the land lay. So he arranged a meeting with him, one evening – without the countess, of course.

'The prince's name was Sunil. He was young – far younger than Ambrose, and younger still than our countess – and he was ambitious. He knew that he would have to make most of his own fortune, because he had elder brothers, but he was bright enough to be able to do it. He'd already arranged deals with the explorers who were beginning to filter through to India. Ambrose, he thought, was just another.

'Sunil was expecting to barter for gold, for jewels and spices: he was disappointed when Ambrose walked in, bringing nothing with him to trade. Part of him wondered if it was some trick; part of him wondered if what Ambrose wanted to trade was too precious to be carried around. And if it was . . . The possibilities were very bright, indeed.

'It was his curiosity that was his undoing.' Alicia gave Susanna a meaningful look. 'His people brought food and drink; Ambrose took his fill, still without saying why he had come to see Sunil. And then, at last, he came to the point. He spoke of his dearest treasure – not naming it, of course – and how he would be willing to bargain.

'He said just enough to whet Sunil's appetite, without giving anything of his plans away. Sunil agreed immediately to come to the place where Ambrose was staying, the following evening. Their agreement was that the price would be sealed when Sunil had viewed the goods.

'And then Ambrose returned to the countess. He said nothing of what he had been doing, ignoring her questions and changing the subject whenever her guesses were too close.

'The following evening, Ambrose set out a room in their apartments. The bed was covered with glowing silks, and the room was scented with nutmeg and cinnamon.'

'Like a fruit cake,' Susanna said with a grin.

'Nutmeg and cinnamon are both very potent aphrodisiacs. Don't knock them.' There was a flash of impatience in Alicia's voice. 'Do you want to hear the rest of the story, or not?'

Susanna shrugged, and sipped her wine. 'You're the storyteller. Isn't it your choice?'

Alicia's eyes became icy, for a moment, then softened again. 'As I said, Ambrose prepared this particular room for the reception of Sunil. When the countess saw what he had done, she knew immediately what his plans were, and smiled. He'd arranged it all as a treat for her, of course.

'Sunil arrived, and was shown into the room. The countess was lying on the bed, hidden by a thin layer of purple silk; underneath, she was entirely naked, except for a ruby in her navel and a thin collar of emeralds. The important thing was that she could hear everything that was going on.

'Ambrose and Sunil began talking. Wine flowed freely and, eventually, the conversation turned to trade. Ambrose began to speak of his greatest treasure, and described the countess to Sunil. He told Sunil that his treasure was mainly ivory, and yet soft to the touch. That his treasure was decked with emeralds, rubies and gold. And that its secret was eternal life.

'Sunil's eyes glowed – and then he saw the carving of the countess. "That?" he asked, nodding to the statue. It was mainly ivory; it had an emerald collar and ruby in its navel, and its nails were painted gold.

' "Better," Ambrose told him.

'Sunil went up to the statue: as the craftsmen had promised, it was lifelike, almost a living representation of the countess herself. All it needed was someone to breath that one spark into it, and the statue could have moved. Sunil was fascinated by it, and couldn't resist touching its arm. It felt cool as marble – and yet somehow soft.

'He thought that maybe it was his imagination. Then Ambrose laughed, and explained that the carpenter had promised him a second wife, the almost-living image of his own. His dearest treasure, he added.

'Sunil frowned, then. Was Ambrose's wife dead?

'Ambrose smiled at this. In a sense, yes – she was a *broucolaque* – but Sunil didn't need to know this. He simply said, "Look," and removed the green silk covering.

'The countess lay there, still as her statue. Sunil frowned, wondering if it was another of the statues, and Ambrose was some kind of madman, unhinged by his wife's death. And then the countess opened her eyes, turned her head towards him, and smiled.

'It was then that Sunil noticed her complete nakedness – with the exception of her jewels, of course. She caught the spark of interest in his eyes, and knew that she had won. With another smile, she brought her knees up and parted her legs.

'Ambrose knew immediately what she was going to do. They'd been together so long, by then, that they could read each other's minds, most of the time. He ushered Sunil to the bottom of the bed, to give him a better view, and guided him down onto the cushions.

'As the countess slid her palms down the inside of her thighs, Sunil swallowed hard – he could barely believe what he was seeing. A living version of the beautiful statue . . . and she was pleasuring herself. He caught a flash of gold, and realized that her fingernails were painted gold – as, too, were her toenails. All her bodily hair had been shaved off, to match the statue: all that remained were the glorious raven locks on her head, which glittered in the candlelight.

'She wore a thin gold bangle around one ankle, and three or four matching bangles on each wrist; as she parted her labia with one hand and slid a finger deep inside herself, the bracelets jangled together. Sunil opened his mouth, and Ambrose smiled to himself. The prince was hooked, and his wife would have her "second husband" – the dark-skinned man who'd caught her eye, days before. He only hoped that Sunil would be worth the wait, for her. But then again, knowing the countess's powers . . .

'She continued to rub herself, pistoning her finger in and out – first slow, then fast, varying the pace and pressure to give herself the most pleasure, while her thumb massaged her clitoris. Her nipples were erect and dark against her ivory skin, and the furrow she was rubbing was a rich deep crimson, laced with purple.

'Sunil could smell her arousal, even over the spices; it made him want to touch himself, to touch her, give her even more pleasure. Ambrose anticipated his next move, and sat down next to the prince, laying a warning hand on his arm. "It's her show," he said simply.

'Sunil didn't like the idea of not being the one in control – but he couldn't resist the beautiful woman on the bed. Had he left, then, his dreams would have been haunted for ever by the woman he'd so nearly possessed . . .

' "How much?" he whispered hoarsely.

' "She sets her own price," Ambrose said. "Watch, and wait."

'Sunil watched until the countess tipped her head back and cried out in orgasm; a rosy mottling appeared over her breasts. Then she stretched out her legs, propped herself up on her elbows, and lifted her right hand, beckoning him with one finger.

'Sunil looked at Ambrose, who nodded.

' "What's the price?" Sunil asked.

'Ambrose smiled. "If you have to ask, you can't afford it."

'At that, Sunil's pride inflated as much as his already hard cock; he wriggled quickly out of his clothes, and joined her on the bed. Ambrose settled himself down on the cushion, and smiled to himself. She had made a good choice – the Indian prince had a good body. Firm, smooth and well-sculptured; his buttocks hadn't quite yet started to run to fat, and his cock was long and thick. *Nice*, he thought, and sat back to enjoy the show.

'Sunil drew the flat of his hand down the countess's body. His skin contrasted perfectly with hers, *café-au-lait* and ivory. His fingers were long and sensitive, and the countess tipped her head back against the pillows, willing him to touch her properly.

'The blue silk she'd chosen for the bed was a perfect foil for their bodies, Ambrose thought; he smiled as Sunil cupped her breasts, licking first one hard nipple and then the other. The countess wriggled slightly under him, and he began to suckle her breasts. She gave a small sigh of pleasure, and arched her back as he kissed his way down her body.

'This was what she'd imagined: feeling him nuzzle her breasts and belly, and finally the soft skin of her inner thighs. She closed her eyes in bliss as Sunil, drawn by the musky scent of her arousal, drew his tongue down her cleft.

'As she'd hoped, Sunil was skilled in cunnilingus – he lapped at her, making his tongue into a point while he teased her clitoris, then letting his tongue slide the whole way along her furrow, from top to bottom. She clenched her hands, squeezing her fingers into her palms as Sunil continued to please her. Then she felt the heat of orgasm swirling through her, coiling in her loins and suddenly exploding.

'Sunil rocked back on his heels, smiling at her and waiting for her to recover.

'When her breathing slowed, she didn't say a word: just sat up and kissed him deeply, nibbling at his bottom lip until he opened his mouth and let her tongue explore him. She pushed him gently backwards; losing his balance, he sat down properly. Then he felt the warmth of her quim rubbing against his cock, and smiled, sliding one hand between them.

'He positioned his cock at the entrance to her vagina; she smiled, and sank down on him, curling her legs round him and pressing her heels hard against his buttocks. Then she lifted and lowered herself on him, closing her eyes and tipping her head back.

'Sunil bit gently at her throat, sensitizing her skin; she nearly laughed with the pleasure of it all, and the pleasure that was to come, but still said nothing. She wrapped her arms round his neck, and he massaged her clitoris, rubbing gently at first, and then harder as her movements over him grew more frantic.

'At last, they came; she felt his seed spurt deep inside her. All the time, Ambrose had been watching them. Part of him gloried in his wife's beauty and the spectacle he'd witnessed;

part of him was jealous, and wanted to murder Sunil, because he'd given the countess so much pleasure.

'Yet his love for the countess overcame all – particularly when she rested her chin on Sunil's shoulder, and gave Ambrose a large wink and a smile. They were conspirators, bound together by a nameless secret. A secret which Sunil might – or might not – share, depending on what she decided.

'At last, the countess moved, letting Sunil's penis out of her. She kissed him lightly, then took a long thin piece of blue silk, binding his eyes with it. Sunil was nervous – this was outside his experience – but she stilled his protests with a kiss.

'Gently, she guided him to lie face down on the bed, then beckoned to Ambrose. She removed the loose clothing which Ambrose had adopted in India, stroking his body and feeling her fingers tingle at the familiar feel of his skin. Even after all these years, he still excited her.

'It was entirely mutual; Ambrose's cock was hard, and a small drop of fluid appeared in the eye as his wife stroked him. She dropped to her knees, touching her tongue to the drop of fluid and savouring its taste.

'Then she stood up again, smiling. She took a bowl of oil, which had been hidden by the silks on the bed, and anointed her hands with it. Then she rubbed her hands over Ambrose's, transferring some of the oil to his skin.

'The oil was scented with vanilla; she breathed in the scent, smiling, then began to smooth her hands down Sunil's back. At her nod, Ambrose joined in, running his hands over the beautiful flesh, digging his fingers into the muscles, until Sunil began to relax.

'Sunil thought that he was in paradise. Ambrose's hands were sensitive and gentle, and Sunil was almost convinced that the four hands caressing his body belonged to the countess and her beautiful statue.

'The countess caressed his buttocks, unable to resist oiling her hands again and sliding her fingers in the crease between his buttocks. Sunil tensed, and the countess stopped what she was doing, just long enough to stroke his face and reassure him wordlessly that she wasn't going to hurt him. Then she resumed her former posture, caressing his buttocks and gently splaying his legs.

'She pressed her finger into the puckered rosy hole between his buttocks, so very gently; at last, it gave, and she began to move her finger back and forth, very slowly. Sunil moaned with pleasure, his cock stiffening beneath him, and the countess smiled.

'She nodded at Ambrose, who turned Sunil onto his back. Sunil's penis was magnificently erect. The countess touched it lightly, teasing him, and then moved to massage his chest and his belly, her fingers mingling with Ambrose's. Sunil couldn't help tipping his hips towards her, his need for release was so great; the countess smiled, and added some ginger to the oil before she slid her hands round the hard column of flesh. The effect was immediate: Sunil cried out in pleasure, his cock seeming to grow even more.

'The countess widened her eyes at Ambrose, indicating Sunil's cock. Ambrose frowned, not sure that he read her meaning aright. She slid one finger into her mouth, sucking it, then nodded at Sunil again.

'Ambrose shrugged, and knelt by the bed. It wasn't something that turned him on, particularly, but he always indulged his wife. He cupped Sunil's penis in his hands, as the countess raked Sunil's thighs lightly with her nails, then bent his head.

'Sunil murmured in pleasure as a mouth slid over his cock; he imagined it to be the countess, and wished that he could see what she was doing to him. He, too, had been captivated by the contrast in their skin.

'He lifted his hands to the blindfold, but the countess had tied it too cunningly. He couldn't remove it. She noticed what he was doing, and smiled to herself. Swiftly, she moved up to undo the blindfold; Sunil smiled at her, imagining that is was the statue – or the countess herself – fellating him.

'Then he looked down – and saw Ambrose. Before he could make a protest, the countess kissed him, hard, then let her lips travel down his body. While Ambrose continued to suck Sunil's penis, the countess licked his balls, taking them into her mouth and nipping gently at his sac.

'Sunil gave himself up to pleasure, and finally he came, his semen spurting into Ambrose's mouth. Ambrose didn't swallow the warm salty liquid – he waited until the countess kissed him, letting her taste Sunil's essence.

'The countess's eyes gleamed with sensual fire. This was a night she'd dreamed about – and both men were doing exactly what she wanted them to do. They were enjoying it as much as she was, and the thought made her wet. She flexed her internal muscles, torn between wanting to be filled and wanting to suck Ambrose's cock. But then again, she thought, she could quite easily do both.

'She ran her tongue along her lower lip as the idea came to her. Unbeknown to Ambrose, when he had gone to visit Sunil, the countess had gone to visit the women of the palace. She had learned a few tricks from them: although she had thought of saving this particular one for Ambrose, she itched to try it out.

'She took Ambrose's hand, leading him to the top of the bed and guiding him to kneel by Sunil's shoulders. Then she took a bowl of honey, mixed with powdered anise. Ambrose frowned, not understanding what she was doing; *later*, her eyes told him. Later, she would repeat it with him. But for now . . . She began to smear the mixture over Sunil's cock, which stiffened immediately and seemed to grow even larger.

'He knew exactly what she was doing, and smiled in approval. The countess grinned back, and straddled him, curling her fingers round his cock so that she could position him where she wanted, and lowered herself gently onto him.

'The combination of the size of his cock and the tingling sensation of the honey-and-anise mixture made her draw a sharp intake of breath. Then she lowered her body so that she could kiss Sunil and stroke Ambrose's thighs at the same time.

'She lifted herself again, stretching forward; Ambrose, too, leaned forward, and the countess eased her mouth along his cock. He closed his eyes in pleasure, sliding his hands into her hair and massaging her scalp with the tips of his fingers.

'Sunil, looking upwards, had the beautiful view of Ambrose's cock disappearing into his wife's mouth: it excited him even more. He reached out to touch the countess's generous breasts, rolling her nipples between thumb and forefinger, pinching them slightly to give her greater pleasure.

'The countess was almost delirious with pleasure as she raised and lowered herself onto Sunil's cock, grinding her pubis into his, and sucking Ambrose's cock at the same time. She soon found the rhythm she wanted, sliding Ambrose's cock deep into her mouth as she raised herself, the Indian prince's penis almost out of her; then slowly withdrawing from Ambrose as she pushed herself down again.

'It seemed to go on for ever, a perfect triangle of bliss. Then her internal muscles went into spasm, clutching Sunil's cock; at the same time, she felt both men's balls lift and tighten, and suddenly Ambrose was coming into her mouth, and Sunil was pushing hard into her, as if pouring his whole body into her.

'The countess, who knew how hard it was for two people to climax at once, was stunned at the force of three people coming at the same time. It was perfect.

'Eventually, the three of them lay on the bed, the countess on her back in the middle and the two men lying on their sides next to her, stroking her skin. The countess turned her head towards Ambrose, widening her eyes; he nodded, almost imperceptibly. He was ready when she was.

'They remained in silence for a while; then Sunil spoke. "I see, now, about your dearest treasure. But the secret of eternal life?"

'The countess smiled. "Oh, it's very simple."

' "Remember," Ambrose warned him, "she names her own price."

'Sunil wasn't put off. "Name it."

'The countess smiled again; only this time, her canine teeth had grown longer . . .' Alicia shrugged. 'And that's it, for now.'

Susanna frowned. 'Oh, come on! Did she kill him, or not?'

'Killing isn't the same as making someone into a vampire.'

'All right. Did she give Sunil what he wanted – the price, I take it, being his earthly life?'

Alicia smiled. 'What do you think?'

'I think it's very mean of you to tease your audience.'

Alicia's voice grew husky. 'Then what, Susanna, do you want me to do?'

'Tell me the rest of your story. The proper ending.'

'Now?'

'Or tomorrow, if you like.' Susanna winced. 'Though I'm going to have the mother of a hangover, tomorrow.'

Alicia smiled. 'Molly has a few remedies. None of them poisonous, I hasten to add – though they taste like it, at the time.'

'Do you always drink this much?'

'It depends. Sometimes, I drink more than others. We didn't have that much, really. Three or four bottles.'

A great deal more than Susanna usually drank – and she felt as though she'd been drinking something far more potent than wine. She stood up, swaying unsteadily. 'Right. Well, I'll see you tomorrow, then. Thanks for the story. I look forward to the next part.'

Alicia smiled. 'In good time. See you tomorrow.'

Eleven

Susanna had no idea how she got upstairs to bed. The wine seemed to kick in as soon as she left the relative warmth of the dining room; the cold air in the draughty corridors of Alicia's castle had the same sort of effect as winter night air after a party, and she reeled against the wall.

'Oh, hell,' Susanna murmured. She must have drunk more than a bottle or so. A lot, lot more. Unless . . . she shivered. No. Of course Alicia hadn't drugged the wine. She didn't have any reason to do that sort of thing – did she?

The next thing Susanna knew, she was lying between cool cotton sheets. She had no idea how she'd undressed – her clothes were probably lying in a tangled heap on the floor, or trailing from the door to the bed. Whatever, at least she was in bed.

She closed her eyes, wishing that the room would stop spinning; then she felt a weight on the other side of the bed. Brandon. She smiled. Obviously he'd been in the bathroom when she'd staggered in. Just as well he'd been awake, really, or she'd have woken him, the way she was stumbling around like an elephant.

An Indian elephant, rather than an African one, she thought, laughing to herself. An Indian one like the prince in Alicia's story. What had his name been? Sun something. Sunil. She'd tell Brandon about it in the morning. He'd appreciate it. Maybe he'd appreciate a ginger massage, too. Ginger and vanilla and honey. She could lick every last drop of it off his skin. Mm.

Without opening her eyes, she curled into Brandon's arms. She smiled to herself. Thank God, he wasn't wearing those ridiculous pyjamas – whoever they'd belonged to. Molly's husband? No. The old bat didn't look the married sort: or the widowed sort, for that matter. Alicia's friend? What had his name been? She screwed her eyes tight, trying to remember, but failed. Too much wine. She'd remember, tomorrow night, to drink lots of water before dinner, and leave her wine glass untouched.

He drew his hand down the side of her body, smoothing his palm over her soft curves, cupping her buttocks; Susanna smiled, and cuddled closer. 'Are you really up to this?' she murmured.

'What makes you think I'm not?'

He pushed his hips against hers, and she felt his erect cock pressing against her. 'Mm. You're supposed to be convalescing.'

'Maybe making love is good for you.' His voice was rich with amusement.

'So you keep telling me. But doesn't that depend on what your doctor says?' The erotic tale which Alicia had told her had made Susanna feel aroused; she couldn't help curling her fingers round Brandon's cock. 'Mm.'

'So you're in the mood for it, too? I don't know if I dare ask what you and Alicia have been up to.'

'Talking. What else do you think?'

'I don't know. I wasn't there, was I?'

'She fed me some wine – too much, I think – and told me this story about the vampire countess, her husband, and an Indian prince.'

'Indeed. A threesome.'

'But with the right proportions,' Susanna corrected.

He chuckled. 'Greedy girl. So what happened?'

'They had an interesting evening. The countess gave the prince a ginger massage.'

'A what?'

'A ginger massage,' Susanna repeated. 'It's meant to be very erotic. You know, mixing oil with ginger and rubbing it into your man's cock. It makes the blood vessels dilate and gives him a mammoth erection.' She giggled. 'Though I'm not going to try it out on you just right now.'

'I should hope not. You're not in any state to give anyone a massage.'

'No.' She shifted onto her back, propping one leg over his; then she took his hand, placing it over her quim before settling back with her hands behind her head.

'Mm. You feel as warm as ginger,' he said.

'You're cold,' she complained, shivering and pushing his hand away. 'Freezing.'

'Warm me up, then.'

'I thought you'd never ask.' She placed her hand over his again, drawing it back to her quim. The coolness of his skin was surprisingly arousing. 'How about like this?' She began to move his hand back and forth, guiding his middle finger to rub her clitoris in the way she liked, a gentle figure-of-eight motion.

'That's very nice.'

'Better keep it quiet. We don't want to wake Alicia or Molly, do we?'

'No.' Again, his voice was filled with amusement. There was obviously a reason why he was laughing at her, she thought: maybe she was slurring her words, or something.

She continued guiding his hand until she felt the familiar pleasure pooling in her veins, concentrating in her solar plexus and exploding there.

'Better?' he asked.

She lay back against the pillows, her quim contracting deliciously. Far from sating her arousal, he'd amplified it. 'For starters, yes.'

'So what, now?'

'I'd like you to fuck me. A long, slow session.' She laughed.

'Lots and lots and lots of sex. That's what I'd like.'

'I hoped you were going to say that.' He shifted between her thighs, pushing the sheets back. As he pushed into her, Susanna frowned. The weight was wrong. She'd been drinking – but she knew Brandon's body anywhere, and the body against hers didn't feel like his. She wrapped her legs round his waist, pulling him more deeply inside her, and knew for definite then that it wasn't her lover. Brandon was big, but he wasn't *that* well-endowed.

She opened her eyes, and nearly screamed as she saw his face.

He laid a finger over her lips. 'Hush, little one.'

She swallowed. 'I thought you were Brandon.'

The man from the portrait – the man she'd dreamed about in the village inn – smiled back at her. 'Well, I'm not.'

'You could have said, before we – you know.'

'Before I fingered you to the orgasm you obviously needed?'

She flushed. Did he have to put it so bluntly? 'Yes.'

'And are you in any fit state to go to bed with Brandon? You said yourself that he's convalescing, and he needs his rest. If you'd lumbered into his room like you did mine, he'd be wide awake, by now.'

'Oh. Sorry.' What he'd said suddenly registered with her. *His* room. 'You mean that you're staying here?'

'You could say that, yes.'

She frowned. 'Then why haven't I seen you here before? Why haven't you dined with Alicia and me? Why hasn't Molly told me not to disturb you or whatever?'

'Because Molly doesn't say any more than she has to, and Alicia likes to have all the attention focused on her.' He grinned. 'Let's just say that she sparkles more with an audience of one.'

Susanna could understand that. Alicia had been much livelier when she'd been on her own with Susanna than when Brandon had been there. 'Right.'

He pulled back so that the head of his cock was almost out of her. 'So what now? Do you want me to stop, and take you back to your own room – or shall we continue?'

Susanna knew that she was playing with fire. She didn't know this man from Adam, and she'd dreamed about him as a vampire. She'd seen his picture on a wall – someone who'd lived years and years before. Or was he Alicia's secret lover, and she'd had that painting done of him on a whim?

Then again, maybe he was just a continuation of her dream. Susanna had always had realistic dreams. This one just happened to be erotic – fuelled by Alicia's tale of Ambrose, the countess and Sunil.

What the hell, she thought, and smiled. 'What makes you think you're up to it?'

He grinned, and thrust back into her. 'This.'

'Oh, yesss.' As he pulled out of her, Susanna flexed her internal muscles, pulling against him; as he pushed back in, she opened herself to the full, letting the tip of his cock rub against her cervix.

God, he felt good, she thought. Long and thick, just like the prince's cock that Alicia had described. And he knew how to use it, too, pivoting his hips and moving in small circles, to change the angle between their joined bodies and increase the pressure.

She suddenly realized that she didn't know his name. Or who he was, where he'd come from, what he was doing in the castle. 'Who are you?' she asked.

'Whoever you want me to be,' was the annoying reply.

She knew someone else who talked like that. Alicia. And they had exactly the same colour eyes, too, the same pale skin and dark hair. Their faces weren't that dissimilar, really, when she thought about it. She groaned. 'God, I should have guessed it straight off. You're Alicia's brother, aren't you?'

He stilled for a moment. 'Why do you say that? Does that make fucking me the next best thing to fucking Alicia?'

She glowered at him. 'Who says I want to fuck Alicia?'

He smiled, stroking her face. 'You shouldn't answer questions with questions. Anyway, it's obvious.'

'Is it?' Susanna frowned.

'Yes.' He was very definite.

'How can you tell?'

'Because it's written all over your beautiful face that you would like to tumble between the sheets with her.' He dipped his head to kiss her.

'I've never made love with another woman. I've never been attracted to one, either.'

'Before now, that is.' He smiled at her. 'Alicia's a good enough place to start.'

She scowled at him. 'How would you know?'

His smile said it all: first-hand experience.

'So you're not her brother, then?'

'We didn't share the same parents, no. Either of them.' He shrugged. 'But there are many definitions of brother. Not just the genetic one.'

Susanna couldn't quite get her head round that. She felt too muzzy. 'Are you related to her?'

'Does it matter?'

'Now you're the one answering a question with a question.'

He bent his head to suck one nipple, drawing his teeth gently against the sensitive flesh so that she moaned. 'I'll take that as your answer,' he said, laughing.

'I know your face from somewhere,' she said, stroking the dark hair back from his face. 'I saw you in a dream, once.'

'Only once?'

She grinned. 'Dear me. Delusions of grandeur setting in, are they?'

'Just take me at face value, Susanna,' he said softly, his voice sending a shiver down her spine. 'What you see is exactly what you get.'

'So you're not even going to tell me your name?'

'Just think of me as your lover in a dream.'

'Dream. Woman wailing for her demon lover,' she murmured.

He grinned. 'You've been reading too much Coleridge. Or was it Elizabeth Bowen, who had the demon lover carrying the woman off in a carriage?'

'I can't remember. Alicia would know. Maybe she's got it in her library. We could go down and have a look.'

'Not right now. I've got more important things in mind.' He grinned. 'Now, shut up will you?'

Susanna acquiesced, and gave herself up to the pleasure of the way his body moved inside hers. He brought her to the point of coming, then stayed perfectly still inside her, letting her body calm down again before continuing to make love to her. On the third time he did it, Susanna whimpered, and locked her legs hard round his waist, using her heels to push his buttocks towards her.

'All right, little one, we'll play it your way.' He thrust into her, right up to the hilt; she gave a muffled cry against his shoulder, and then her quim shivered round him.

She lay back against the pillows, drowsy and sated at last. 'Thank you. I enjoyed that.'

'Good.' He stroked her breasts, teasing the rosy tips between his thumb and forefinger until they were firmly erect. 'Though I haven't finished, yet.'

'Oh?'

He withdrew from her, stroking her face. 'I think you're going to like this, little one.'

'Time for pudding,' a soft voice said by her ear.

Susanna's eyes widened as she turned her head and saw who sat beside the bed. Someone who'd obviously been watching everything that had just happened . . . 'Alicia!'

'I thought you'd put on a good show.' She smiled. 'Remember, Susanna, I told you that I like blondes.'

Susanna's eyes narrowed. 'Little ones, you said.'

'The exception proves the rule.' She smiled sweetly. 'And he's right. I do perform better, with an audience of one.'

'So that means I don't get to play, too?' he asked, looking disappointed and amused at the same time.

'Definitely not. This time, I want her to myself.'

Susanna shook her head, her eyes widening. 'I don't think so.'

'I'm not going to hurt you, if that's what you're worried about.'

Susanna was tempted to say, 'You wouldn't dare', but knew that to challenge Alicia would be a huge mistake. Instead, she swallowed. 'It wasn't that.'

'Then what? Worried that you're some kind of pervert, for wanting to make love with another woman?'

'Who says I want to?'

Alicia smiled, and lightly touched Susanna's nipples. 'These do.' She let her hand drift slowly downwards, across Susanna's abdomen, and drew one finger along Susanna's quim. She touched the same finger to her mouth, licking off the glistening juices. 'Mm. That does, too. And there's a little pulse down there—' she gestured to Susanna's quim '—which gives you away completely, it's hammering so hard.'

'I've never done this sort of thing before.'

'I know.' Alicia smiled again, and Susanna felt a slight flicker of fear. 'But I have. Like I said, I'm not going to hurt you. I believe in pleasure. In the whole of life's richness.'

Without warning, she dipped her head, and kissed Susanna, hard. Susanna wanted to struggle; at the same time, the way that Alicia nibbled her lower lip made her want to give in, let Alicia do exactly what she wanted.

She closed her eyes, concentrating only on the way that Alicia's soft hands explored her body. Caressing her breasts, lifting them slightly and pushing them together – and was it her imagination, or were there two pairs of hands caressing her? No. Of course not. He was watching, this time. The archetypal man's dream, to watch two women making love.

Alicia, too, was enjoying herself; Susanna could tell from the deliberate way Alicia touched her, arousing her and scrutinizing her response. She couldn't suppress a soft moan as Alicia played with her nipples, pinching them just hard enough to be arousing without hurting her.

Susanna pushed her head back against the pillows, arching up towards Alicia; there was a low chuckle, then she felt Alicia's long hair drifting over her skin, caressing her lightly. And then, at last, she felt Alicia's mouth close over one nipple, suckling the hard peak of flesh.

'Is this how Sunil felt?' she couldn't help asking.

Alicia paused. 'How do you mean?'

'When the countess started making love to him?'

'I dunno.' Alicia's voice was suddenly amused. 'Having never been male, I can't actually tell what they feel from the inside.'

'Have you ever fancied being male?'

'Maybe just for a day. I'd like to know how it feels when a man comes.'

'Lovely,' a male voice informed her.

'And you can shut up. You always say that,' Alicia retorted, laughing. 'Which tells me nothing, really.'

'Men just don't like talking,' Susanna said. 'Brandon does, sometimes – but I suppose men just prefer action.'

'Well, I like both.' Alicia's voice was a purr. 'Tell me how you're feeling, Susanna. Tell me how you like what I do to you.' She kissed her way across Susanna's abdomen. 'How's that?'

'Nice.'

Alicia caught the slightly nervous tone. 'You don't sound too convincing.'

'I told you, I haven't done this sort of thing before.'

'How sweet. A virgin.' She chuckled, a rich earthy laugh which had a thread of danger running through it. 'The countess would enjoy this. The idea of being the first . . .'

Susanna coughed. 'Not exactly.'

'Your first woman. It's a kind of virginity, Susanna – if you're talking technicalities, of course.'

Susanna shivered as Alicia's fingertips brushed her thighs.

'Don't tense up,' Alicia advised. 'I think you're going to like it. It's not so very different from what Brandon would do with you – or what you've already done tonight, with Miladdo here.'

'No.' Susanna's voice was very small.

'Relax. Go with the flow.' Alicia cupped Susanna's Venus mound. 'Mm. You're lovely and warm.' She slid one finger along Susanna's labia. 'Wet, too.'

'That might have something to do with me,' the man beside her remarked.

'True.' Alicia rubbed her cheeks against Susanna's thighs. 'There's only one way to find out.' She breathed on Susanna's quim. 'Talk to me. Tell me how it feels.'

Susanna shivered with anticipation. 'I can feel your breath against me. Any minute now, you're going to lick me. I'll feel your tongue slide down my labia; maybe you'll suck my clitoris, or maybe you'll just slide your tongue deep inside me.'

'Both, I think,' Alicia mused, doing exactly what Susanna had described.

Susanna arched against the bed as Alicia began to lap at her, the speed and pressure of her tongue calculated to bring Susanna to a raging orgasm.

'Tell me how it feels,' Alicia commanded through a mouthful of Susanna's flesh.

Susanna couldn't resist the retort. 'Lovely.'

She was rewarded with an appreciative male chuckle – and by Alicia nipping her. 'Don't tease!'

'I don't feel comfortable, describing things to a writer—'

'You're a writer as well, but you deal in facts, not fiction. So stop stalling,' Alicia demanded. 'Tell me like it is. The facts.'

'All right, all right. I feel like I'm lying on the bottom of the sea bed, and there are waves just drifting over me. It's very gentle, at first, a tiny pressure running over my skin, from my toes right up to the top of my head. The more you lick me, the more the waves start to swell, growing deeper and harder.'

'Funny, that,' Alicia mused. 'You taste like seashore and honey.'

'Also due to me.'

There was the sound of flesh sharply against flesh, followed by a muffled 'Ow!'; Susanna, who didn't bother to open her eyes, imagined that Alicia had delivered a very well-aimed and stinging slap to his inner thigh.

'Now, shut up,' Alicia said. 'I'm talking to Susanna, not to you.'

'Yes, my lady. Whatever you say.'

Alicia ignored him and continued to lap at Susanna, drawing her nearer and nearer to orgasm until Susanna felt that she was drowning in the middle of a whirlpool, and said as much. Alicia merely smiled against her skin, and carried on until Susanna cried out and her quim flexed madly beneath Alicia's mouth.

'Not so bad, was it?' Alicia said, shifting to sit beside Susanna and stroking the hair from her face.

'No,' Susanna admitted. 'Er – I take it that you want me to repay the compliment?'

To her surprise, the writer leaned over and kissed her, very lightly. 'I think you've had enough for tonight. But soon. Very soon.'

Her voice was full of promise, sending a shiver of anticipation through Susanna. Alicia was leading her into a new world, a world which scared her and fascinated her at the same time.

'Of course, you could have a surrogate,' a male voice said. 'Tell me what you were going to do with her, and I'll do it for you.'

Alicia's voice was full of laughter – and triumph. 'You're just sex-mad. Any excuse, isn't it?'

'Alicia. You're the one who initiated me, remember?'

Susanna's eyes narrowed. 'Isn't either of you going to tell me who he is? Or even his name?'

He grinned. 'Let's just say I'm the man with no name.'

Susanna was cross and amused at the same time. Amusement won. 'In that case, shouldn't you wear a poncho, have stubble and a ten-gallon hat, and chew a cheroot?'

'And smell of horse,' Alicia added, joining in the game.

He spread his hands. 'That's the Wild West. If I were American, I think I'd be more like Quincey Morris.'

Susanna groaned. 'Why does everyone around here bring everything back to *Dracula*?'

'That's Pentremain for you,' he told her, stroking her face. 'And with Alicia's day job being writing about vampires . . .'

'Isn't that a night job?'

'She's a quick learner,' he informed Alicia. 'And a good memory.'

'Journalist training,' Susanna said. 'Nothing more than that.'

He smiled. 'Which brings us back very nicely to the subject in hand.'

Both women stared at him, uncomprehending. 'What do you mean?' Susanna said, finally.

'I mean, that as you're a quick learner with a good memory, one of the best ways to teach you something is to show you. Alicia said she'd like you to make love to her, very soon; so if I show you what she likes . . .'

Susanna giggled. 'Bit difficult.'

'Oh?' He tipped his head to one side, giving her a sensual smile.

'Because you're male and I'm female.'

He smiled. 'Some things, it doesn't matter what sex you are.'

'I suppose not.'

'So.' He stroked her face, then lifted her to a sitting position, plumping up the pillows behind her. 'Get yourself comfortable.'

Part of Susanna didn't really believe that this was happening. She was sitting on a king-size bed in a Gothic castle, watching a beautiful woman and an even more beautiful man make love . . . no, this had to be a dream. It couldn't possibly be real. It was all because of Alicia's story about

Sunil, the countess and Ambrose . . . She pinched herself surreptitiously, and had to bite her lip to stop a small cry of pain. So it *was* real. She drew her knees up, crossing her ankles and wrapping her arms round her legs, and settled back against the pillows.

He pushed the bedcovers back, then positioned Alicia on the bed so that her arms were above her head. With a smile, he took a green silk scarf from a drawer of the small chest beside the bed, and fastened her wrists to the bedstead. Susanna was surprised. She'd expected Alicia to want to be the dominant one, all the time. At the same time, she was intrigued. Was this part of a deeper game, where Alicia was still in control?

Slowly, he began to kiss his way down Alicia's body. He started with her mouth, running his tongue along her lower lip and nibbling at her lip until her mouth opened; then he thrust his tongue inside her mouth, exploring her. Then he moved to kiss her throat; she tipped her head back against the pillows, exposing the alabaster flesh to him.

For a moment, Susanna thought that she saw his canine teeth suddenly grow longer; then she blinked, and the vision dissolved. He was no vampire, sucking Alicia's blood: he was simply kissing her, nibbling at her flesh in a way that made her groan softly and push against him, wanting more intimate contact.

He stroked her breasts, pushing them up and together before playing with her nipples, rolling them between thumb and forefinger. Alicia had generous breasts; Susanna thought that, in many ways, Alicia was simply an older and dark-haired version of herself. She had the same generous curves and narrow waist, long well-shaped legs, and the same habit of stretching, cat-like, when she was aroused.

He bent his head to suckle one breast, and Alicia arched her back again, pushing up towards him. He laughed against her skin. 'Don't be impatient. We have all the time in the world, remember?'

Alicia laughed, too; Susanna frowned, sure that she'd

missed something important, and not understanding what. As if sensing her unease, he looked up at her, and smiled, blowing her a kiss to reassure her.

Susanna smiled back, and he nodded in approval before kissing his way over Alicia's belly. Alicia parted her legs, tipping her pelvis up almost in command that he should lick her; he merely smiled, and kissed his way down one leg, sucking each toe in turn when he reached her feet. He moved over to the other foot, licking the instep and the hollows of her ankles, before nibbling his way up her leg.

Alicia wriggled impatiently; with a smile, he stretched out his tongue and drew it the full length of her quim. She gave a sigh of pleasure, parting her legs wider to give him easier access. He continued lapping at her, alternatively sucking at her clitoris and plunging his tongue deep inside her, until a tell-tale rosy mottling appeared on her breasts and neck. She gave a small cry, and Susanna saw the flesh of her belly leap as she came.

He leaned over to kiss Susanna, rubbing Alicia's juices over her lips in a way that shocked and aroused Susanna at the same time. She touched the tip of her tongue experimentally to her bottom lip, and discovered that the taste of Alicia's arousal was very similar to her own. He gave her a broad wink, then untied Alicia, who stretched, and rubbed her wrists. 'Not bad, for starters,' she said, her voice still husky with arousal.

'Did I say that I'd finished?'

She spread her hands, and he laughed. 'Well, I haven't.' He kissed her again. 'I think it's time you returned the compliment, don't you?'

Alicia laughed. 'I was waiting for that.'

With a broad smile, he sat on the bed, facing Susanna, leaning back with his hands supporting his weight and his legs wide apart. Alicia knelt between his thighs, tossed her hair back, and bent her head.

By the look on his face, Susanna thought, she'd just slid his cock into her mouth, and was beginning to swirl her tongue over the head of his penis. Alicia seemed to remain perfectly still, and yet Susanna could see the effects of the way she sucked him, on his face: the dilated pupils, the way he tipped his head back, opening his mouth in a soundless moan of ecstasy, and then licked his lower lip, wanting more.

Then Alicia began to move, dipping her head up and down; as she eased his cock into the back of her throat, her lips and teeth exerting a tight pressure on his shaft, he couldn't suppress a cry of pleasure. Susanna couldn't see the look on Alicia's face, but she had a feeling that Alicia was enjoying it just as much. No way would a woman like Alicia do anything that she didn't want to do.

Alicia continued to fellate him until he sank back onto his elbows; he clenched his fists, and Susanna knew that he was coming. Alicia sat up, a few moments later, swallowed, then turned to face Susanna; suddenly, she pulled Susanna towards her and kissed her hard so that Susanna, too, could taste the salty fluid, in an erotic echo of the way that he'd kissed her.

He remained still for a moment, his eyes still closed in bliss; eventually, Alicia prodded him. 'Wake up,' she said softly.

'I am.' He opened his eyes, heavy-lidded. 'Don't be so demanding.'

'We had a deal.'

'I know.' He shifted to his knees. 'How do you want it, tonight?'

'Hard. Fast and furious.' She stroked his cock until it stiffened again. 'And I want it now.'

He kissed her, then guided her onto her knees. He turned her so that she was facing the bedstead; she leaned forward slightly, pushing her bottom out and grasping the rail of the bedstead. He smiled, and knelt between her thighs. Susanna watched, spell-bound, as he positioned the tip of his cock against Alicia's vaginal entrance, then pushed hard until he was sheathed up to the hilt.

He stayed there for a moment, then began to thrust; Alicia,

too, began to move, pushing back against him as he slid into her, then pulling away from him until he withdrew. He slid one hand around her waist, stroking upwards and brushing the soft undersides of her breasts until she closed her eyes, making small murmurs of pleasure; then he let his hand slide down again, dipping between her thighs so he could seek her clitoris.

As their bodies thrust together, Susanna could hear the slap of his balls against Alicia's quim; almost without realizing that she was doing it, she had let her hand slip between her legs, and began to rub herself, very quietly. He turned his head to look at her, as though sensing what she was doing, and smiled encouragingly at her; Susanna began to rub herself harder, abandoning herself to the highly-charged erotic atmosphere in the room. As Alicia reached her climax, almost wailing in delight, he came, too; and Susanna felt her internal muscles go into a familiar spasm, almost as if in sympathy with the two lovers.

Finally, he slipped from Alicia, and slid off the bed, pulling the covers back. Alicia shifted to lie in the middle of the bed, urging Susanna to cuddle into her; he joined them on the other side of Alicia, cuddling into her and twining his fingers through Susanna's

'There's a time for play,' Alicia said softly, 'and a time for rest. And now, I think, sleep.'

To Susanna's surprise, her eyelids immediately felt heavy, and she fell asleep.

Twelve

When Susanna woke, the next morning, she wished that she hadn't. She felt like hell, and even the dim light in the room made her eyes hurt and the back of her head throb as if someone had hit her with a sledge-hammer. She moaned softly, and turned her face back into the pillow.

Brandon was reading; as she stirred, he put his book down and smiled at her. 'Good morning.'

'Uh,' she said, her voice muffled by the pillow.

He grinned, stroking her arm. 'Heavy night, was it?'

Susanna shifted to face him, screwing her eyes tightly shut. 'Yes.'

'So what happened?'

Susanna wasn't sure. She was in bed with Brandon, not in some other room in the castle with Alicia and the man from the picture in the hall. So had she dreamed it, or had it happened and they'd carried her back to Brandon's bed? And if it was the latter, how come he hadn't woken when they'd put her to bed?

She tried sitting up, and a wave of nausea hit her. 'Uh. Alicia and I – let's just say that we got through a lot of wine, last night. A lot more than I usually drink.' Luckily her mouth didn't taste awful, sour like gone-off wine. Though in a way, it surprised her: on the rare occasions when she'd had a hangover, every sense had been affected by it. Her fingers had felt fuzzy, her hearing dulled, and she had only been able to smell sour wine.

'Did she tell you any more spooky stories about the castle?'

Susanna shook her head – and immediately regretted it. 'No. She told me something about the same characters, but it was set in India. It was more erotic than spooky – though the ending was a bit iffy. I wasn't sure if the Indian prince was going to be turned into another vampire, or just drained. Alicia just left it hanging.'

Brandon was intrigued. 'How do you mean, erotic?'

The words seemed to blur in her mind. She squeezed her eyes shut, to block out the light. 'Haven't we already had this conversation? Last night, when I told you about the ginger massage?'

'No.' Brandon couldn't help laughing. 'Most people get amnesia, when they've had too much to drink. Trust you to go the other way, and remember things that didn't happen!'

Oh, but they had happened, Susanna thought. Just not with you. Or had they? 'I suppose it was just a dream. You know the sort of dreams I get.'

'Yes, like waking up on a Tuesday, convinced that it's Wednesday, because you dreamed about work and meetings.' He stroked her forehead. 'How bad do you feel, on a scale of one to ten?'

'With ten as hell – about eight, I think.' She sighed. 'It serves me right. I don't deserve any sympathy. I should have stopped drinking a lot earlier than I did.'

'But you were enjoying yourself?'

'Well – yes. Maybe I'll ask for some water, next time, or coffee.' She swallowed hard. 'I feel disgusting.'

'It's dehydration. Go and clean your teeth. That'll make you feel better. And in the meantime, I'll brave Molly in the kitchen and scrounge some fresh orange juice and a bottle of mineral water. That'll put you back to rights.'

She frowned. 'Hang on, you're ill. You shouldn't be wandering around a draughty old castle. I'll go, myself, in a minute.'

He smiled at her. 'I feel a lot better today. Anyway, I'm sick of lying around in bed. I could do with stretching my legs.'

'Yesterday you were at death's door.'

He didn't bother denying it. 'Well, today I'm not.'

She sighed. 'Brandon, you've got a virus. You'll probably feel like hell in an hour or so.'

'So I'll make the most of it now, while I don't.' He vaulted out of bed. 'And when I get back, you can tell me all about Alicia's horny story – if you can remember it.'

'I can remember everything perfectly, thank you very much.'

He grinned. 'Even your dreams, afterwards.'

'Yup.' Not that she was going to tell him about the handsome stranger, and making love with Alicia. And then watching them together.

She lay back against the pillows. Had it been a dream, or hadn't it? As soon as Brandon left the room, she kicked the sheet back, and checked her body for marks. She narrowed her eyes. There wasn't a single one. No physical proof, then. The stickiness between her thighs could be anything from her own arousal through the dream, to having made love with Brandon in her sleep. It wouldn't be the first time that *that* had happened.

Pulling the sheet back up again, she closed her eyes. God, why had she let Alicia fill her glass up like that? She'd been weak, feeble, and thoroughly pathetic.

'What you need, Susanna James,' she told herself, 'is some fresh air, and walking into the village will make you feel a lot better.' But not just yet. Not until her head had stopped throbbing and her stomach had stopped threatening to deposit its contents everywhere.

Brandon reappeared, carrying a bottle of mineral water, a jug of orange juice, and two glasses. 'Right. Let's play doctors and nurses.'

Susanna groaned. 'I'm not up to that!'

He grinned. 'I didn't mean having sex with you, actually.'

He poured her a glass of orange juice. 'Come on, drink up. Molly did offer to make you a hangover remedy, but I didn't think you'd drink one.'

Susanna pulled a face. 'You never know what's in those things. Anyway, I told you, it's my own stupid fault. I deserve to suffer.'

'Yeah, you probably do. Sloshing back the wine and having a girly natter with Alicia, while I was lying here, ill and lonely . . .'

'You were asleep,' Susanna reminded him waspishly, 'and Alicia isn't the sort for a "girly natter", as you put it.' She drained the orange juice.

'Better?'

'It will be.'

He smiled at her. 'I thought I might get up today.'

'You'll do nothing of the sort. I don't want you having a relapse.'

'I feel a lot better.'

He looked a lot better, too – and much better than Susanna felt. She smiled ruefully at him. 'Yeah, well. We're a right pair, aren't we?'

'Mm.' He climbed back into bed. 'How do you fancy spending the morning in bed with me, then?'

'As long as you let me sleep, fine.'

'You really do feel rough, then?'

'Yup.' She stroked his face. 'Now, will you shut up and let me go back to sleep?'

A couple of hours later, she woke again, feeling a lot better, and cuddled into Brandon.

'Welcome back to the land of the living,' he remarked drily, putting his book down. 'And, by the way, you snore.'

'I do not.'

'If you'd brought your dictaphone with you, I would have taped you, to prove it,' he teased.

'Huh.' She stretched. 'So what have you been doing, while I slept off my hangover?'

'Reading. Though I've virtually finished the books you brought with you, and the magazines.'

'Bored?'

He nodded. 'A bit. Maybe I could do some work, in bed?'

'Definitely not.' She sat up. 'Tell you what, I'll go into the village. I could do with some fresh air – and I'll buy you a pack of cards, or something. Together with most of the papers.'

'You're on.' He looked at her. 'Are you up to the walk?'

'It'll probably help clear my head,' Susanna insisted. She showered quickly, and changed into leggings and the shirt she'd rinsed out the previous night. It was creased, but she didn't feel like asking Molly for an iron. She wasn't in the mood for doing battle.

'Right. I'll see you later, then.'

'OK.'

'I'll bring you some barley sugar. And I'll make you eggy bread, for lunch.'

Brandon chuckled. 'Now that's what I call nursery food!'

'It's light, nourishing and good for you.' Susanna kissed him. 'And don't you dare do any work, while I'm gone. If I find you anywhere near your computer – or mine – I'll wipe all the files. And that's a promise.'

He nodded. 'Point taken. See you later, then.'

Susanna bumped into Molly in the hall. 'I'm just going out for some fresh air, and to get a few bits and pieces for Brandon. Is there anything you want?'

'No.' There was a faint edge to Molly's voice; Susanna wasn't quite sure why, but wasn't particularly interested in finding out.

'I'll ring the doorbell when I get back. Unless you feel like lending me the only key, to save you running round after me?'

Molly's stony silence said it all. Susanna shrugged, and left the castle.

By the time she reached the village, she was feeling a lot better. The fresh air worked marvels on the remains of her hangover, and she felt more her usual self.

She hummed to herself in the paper shop while she chose some papers, a couple of puzzle books, and a pack of playing cards. There was a surprisingly wide range of sweets next to the counter; she picked up some barley sugar, butterscotch and humbugs. She thought about buying Molly a box of chocolates, but decided against it. Molly probably wouldn't appreciate it, and she'd probably end up buying just the sort of chocolates that Molly didn't like. Sod's Law. She smiled at the shopkeeper, paid, and left the shop.

'She doesn't normally let them out, you know, once they're in her lair.'

The words were so unexpected that she jumped, dropping the bags of sweets. She glowered crossly as she picked them up again. 'Thomas. You startled me.'

'Sorry.' He eyed her, shaking his head. 'You know, her victims always remind me of roses. Bright and colourful, until she picks them – then they loose their bloom. Just like you. Pale, losing weight, looking haunted.'

Susanna rolled her eyes. 'Oh, for God's sake, Thomas. Do you have to spout all that garbage? I told you, I'm not a tourist, and I'm not part of Alicia's fan-club. You don't have to give me the spooky treatment.'

He smiled thinly. 'If only I was.'

'Ha, bloody ha. It's stopped being funny, Thomas. If you can't be straight with me, then leave me alone.'

'I am being straight with you.'

Susanna made a sound of exasperation, and turned on her heel.

'You're not wearing the cross and chain I gave you,' Thomas said suddenly.

She turned back to face him. 'That's because I don't need to.'

'And that attitude, child, puts you in even greater danger. You won't win against her, you know. She gets what she wants, in the end. She always has, and she always will.'

Susanna gave him a saccharine smile. 'For your

nformation, Brandon's a lot better today, and we'll be leaving n a couple of days. And the reason I look pale, as you put it, ıs though I've lost my bloom, is because I have the tail-end of ı hangover, caused by drinking too much wine with Alicia, last ıight. White wine, before you start trying to be spooky and :laiming that she made me drink blood. Very good white wine. She's been the perfect hostess, which is more than I can say for ıer housekeeper. So thank you very much for your concern, ɔut it's not needed.'

'You're playing a very dangerous game.'

Susanna scowled at him. 'You get a real kick out of this, lon't you? Feeding on people's fears. I'm beginning to think :hat you're the vampire around here, not her.'

Thomas recoiled. 'I'm not a vampire.'

'You are. You don't feed on blood – you feed on emotions. And that's the worst sort, in my view. Now, goodbye.'

She walked away from him, back towards the castle; she :ould have sworn she heard him say, 'Then God be with you, :hild,' but she refused to turn round and argue with him again.

Bloody man. Why couldn't he just leave her alone? None of the other villagers behaved like he did. Even Mike the Taxi ıad just waved to her, when he'd seen her. Since that first ıight, when he'd tried to scare her, he'd been perfectly pleasant o her – no warnings of doom and gloom. Thomas just took the vhole thing too far.

By the time that she reached the castle again, she was horoughly revitalized, and virtually bounced up to the door. She pulled the bell-handle, and Molly made her wait for ten ninutes before deigning to answer.

'Isn't it lovely outside?' Susanna said, smiling at her.

'If you like that sort of thing.'

Miserable old bat, Susanna thought, her smile still fixed. Would you like a sweet?'

'I don't eat sweets.'

How about just saying 'No, thank you'? Susanna thought. Oh well, never mind. I'd like to make Brandon something nice for lunch. I promise not to use garlic this time, and I'll clean up after myself. I take it that you don't mind?'

Molly said nothing; obviously Alicia had kept her word and told her housekeeper to back off.

'Right, then. I'll just pop up to Brandon with these, and I'll get cracking. It's eggy bread – if you'd like to join us?'

Molly simply curled her lip, and walked away.

Susanna pulled a face at her back, and went upstairs to Brandon.

'Buy the whole shop, did you?' he asked, amused, as she laid her goodies on the bed.

'I thought this lot might keep you going.' She ruffled his hair.

'Sweets are incredibly bad for you.'

'I know. But how often are you ill?'

'Point taken.' He smiled as he saw the pack of cards. 'Oh, so you're on for strip poker, this afternoon?'

She shook her head, laughing. 'I can't play poker, and you know it.'

'Strip rummy, then?'

She grinned. 'You're on. I'll make a start on lunch, then. I don't know about you, but I'm starving.'

'You're definitely over your hangover, then.'

'Definitely.' She kissed him. 'See you in a minute.'

Molly was nowhere to be seen, to Susanna's relief; she made their lunch, then carried the tray up to Brandon.

'This is real nursery food. Wonderful,' he said, tasting it. 'You know, I never would have believed you capable of this.'

She winked at him. 'Obviously I have hidden depths.'

He grinned. 'It'll be interesting to find out what else I don't know about you.'

'After two years of living with me?' She spread her hands. 'Not a lot.'

'You kept your culinary talents well hidden.'

'That's because you're a better cook than me, and I like being waited on.'

'Right.'

When they'd finished lunch, Susanna took the tray downstairs and cleared up in the kitchen. Molly still wasn't around; hoping that the housekeeper wouldn't be annoyed with her for taking liberties, Susanna opened another carton of fruit juice, poured it into a jug, and took it up to Brandon.

'Are you still on for that game of strip rummy?' he asked.

She frowned. 'I don't know if it's such a good idea, Brandon. I don't want you getting a chill.'

'Who say's I'm going to be the one to end up naked?' He raised an eyebrow. 'And before you say that you're hopeless at cards, I'm giving you an advantage. A large advantage – I mean, I'm wearing two items of clothing, compared to God knows how many you've got on.'

Susanna spread her hands. 'All right, then. You're on. I suppose it'll be more fun for you than playing patience.'

'And don't tell me you're going to do loads of work. Not with the tail-end of a hangover!'

Susanna grinned. 'I didn't think you'd swallow that one, somehow.'

'Right, then.' He picked up the cards.

Susanna coughed, and held out her hand.

'What?'

'I'll shuffle them myself, thanks all the same.'

'I haven't fixed the pack. I wouldn't do that to you.'

'No?' Susanna gave him an arch look. 'What about when you tried teaching me to play strip poker?'

He had the grace to flush. 'Once. That was all – once.'

'So I'll shuffle them. How are we scoring?'

'Usual – first to a hundred points wins that game. And can choose an item of clothing for the other one to remove.'

'Except that I don't get a lot of choice, in your case.'

'If you want to strip down to your bra and knickers, to make it even, be my guest.'

Susanna laughed back. 'You must be joking! I need all the help I can get, playing against the Demon Card King.'

'Fair enough.'

'And before we start, I'd better lock the door.'

'Why?'

'Because if Molly decides to come and bring you a drink, when I'm losing badly, it's going to be bloody embarrassing, that's why.' Susanna locked the door, and returned to the bed. 'Right, then. Are you keeping score?'

'Does that mean that your brain doesn't feel up to it, Susanna, my love?' he teased.

'Got it in one, Sherlock.' She passed him a pad of paper and a pen. 'And no cheating, either.'

He grinned. 'I don't think I need to, somehow.'

Brandon won the first three games, meaning that Susanna had to remove her socks and her leggings. Susanna won the next game, stripping off Brandon's pyjama bottoms; and then Brandon had a run of luck which left Susanna wearing only a very brief pair of knickers.

'Well. Once we've finished the clothes, we're onto forfeits,' he said with a grin.

'Oh, yes? Don't forget, *you've* only got one piece of clothing left, too.'

He smiled, and promptly won the next game. 'You were saying, Susanna my love?'

'I hate you,' she said, removing her knickers. 'What do you mean by forfeits?'

'We'll play in minutes, I think.'

She frowned. 'Minutes?'

'Each time you lose, you give me a minute of oral sex.'

'A minute at a time or all at once?'

'It's up to you. I suppose it depends on how much you lose, doesn't it?'

'For someone who was mega-ill yesterday, you recover pretty quickly,' Susanna grumbled.

'I do indeed.'

She won the next game. 'We're quits, now.'

'Don't be such a chicken.'

'All right, all right. We'll play on. And I'll keep the scores.'

'Anyone would think that you didn't trust me.'

Susanna grinned. 'I don't!'

By the time they'd finished playing, Brandon owed Susanna two minutes, and Susanna owed Brandon ten minutes.

'I think I'll claim mine, right now,' Brandon said, stretching.

'I don't think you're well enough.'

'Ah-ah. Losers always have to pay their bets.'

'What about my two minutes?'

'Later. Winners' forfeits, first.' He lay back, and closed his eyes. 'I'm going to enjoy this.'

Susanna looked at him, and shivered. She could still remember the beautiful man from last night, and the way she'd watched him as Alicia fellated him; her vision blurred until she wasn't sure just who was lying on the bed, waiting for her to indulge him.

She shook herself. It had been a weird dream, the night before, not reality. For some reason, the picture of the man in the hall had made enough of an impression on her to make him appear in her dreams. Too much wine, listening to sexy stories, and lying in bed with an extremely attractive man was enough to make anyone have dreams like that, she told herself crossly.

Brandon opened his eyes. 'Are you OK?'

'I'm fine,' Susanna lied.

'Not your hangover getting its second wind, or anything?'

'I was just watching you, and thinking how gorgeous your body is. That's all.'

He sat up, and kissed her. 'Susanna. You're such a flatterer.'

'I mean it.' She drew one hand down his body, the flat of her palm travelling across his sculpted muscles. 'You feel fantastic.'

He lay back against the pillows, closing his eyes again. 'Don't stop,' he said softly.

She smoothed his flat belly, then let her hand drift lower – missing his erect cock by a few teasing millimetres. Brandon gave a mock growl, and she chuckled, stroking his thighs. 'Dear, dear. Impatient, aren't we?'

'Just a patient, who'd like to be indulged,' he quipped, propping himself on his elbows and looking meaningfully at her.

'All right, all right.' She rubbed her face against his stomach, then breathed against his cock. He sighed happily, and closed his eyes, lying back against the pillows again.

Susanna stretched out her tongue, making it into a hard point, and flicking it over the sensitive spot at the base of his glans; Brandon gave a soft murmur of pleasure, and slid one hand into her hair, urging her on. He gripped the bedstead with the other, his knuckles turning white as his grip became tighter, an immediate reaction to the way Susanna slid his cock into her mouth.

She began to suck, just on the very tip of his cock, licking the head and exerting a very gentle pressure. Then she slid her lips along his shaft, setting up a slow easy rhythm which had Brandon moaning and caressing her hair, encouraging her to move faster, harder.

Her thumb and forefinger ringed the base of his shaft; as she lowered her mouth, she raised her hand, and as she raised her mouth again, she drew her hand back down to the root of his cock, increasing the pleasure for him.

At last, he cried out, and her mouth filled with warm salty liquid. She swallowed every last drop, and sat up again, smiling at him. 'Better?'

'Much.' He took her hand, kissing the tips of her fingers. 'And now, I'll return the compliment.'

'Only if you're up to it.'

'Of course I am.'

'I'm not casting aspersions on your masculinity.' She stroked the hair back from his face. 'God knows, you're the most virile man I've ever met. But you're supposed to be convalescing. I don't want you doing too much, too soon, and making yourself ill again.'

He grinned. 'I never knew you were such a fusspot. Susanna James, the cool and hip journalist . . .'

She laughed. 'Oh, come on. There's nothing cool about what I do. I don't think *Homefile* would rate too highly with the style police.'

'Whereas your body would. Very highly indeed.' He pulled her towards him.

'Thanks for the compliment – but I get the impression that you engineered this conversation to get back to the subject of sex.'

'Would I?' he teased, his grey eyes glittering.

'I think so,' she said, arching against him as he began to stroke her breasts. 'Mm. This feels nice.'

'Doesn't it just?' He kissed her, lightly at first, and then sliding his tongue into her mouth as she parted her lips. He shifted position so that she was lying underneath him, then kissed his way down her body, licking the hollows of her ankles and the sensitive skin behind her knees.

Susanna closed her eyes, giving herself up to the waves of pleasure which swept through her as he drew his tongue along her labia, seeking the hard nub of her clitoris and teasing it with his tongue-tip until she wriggled beneath him. Then he began to suck it, very gently, until Susanna moaned and pushed against him, her hands reaching down his body and silently telling him that she wanted to feel his cock filling her.

He shifted back up her body, rubbing his nose against hers; then he positioned his cock at her entrance, and slowly slid inside her. Susanna made a small noise of pleasure, and wrapped her legs round his waist, pulling him in more deeply.

Visions of what had happened the night before – the handsome stranger from the picture – flashed through her mind, and she frowned.

'It's all right,' Brandon said softly, mistaking the look on her face. 'I wouldn't do this if I didn't feel up to it. Believe me.'

'I know.' Susanna forced the thoughts of the stranger from her mind, and smiled at her lover. 'I know.'

Brandon made love to her slowly and tenderly, his thrusts in a slow and gentle rhythm; her climax started equally softly, feeling like a gentle wind blowing over her, and then suddenly turning into a hurricane which swept all thoughts of Alicia, the stranger, and their connection with the castle, from her mind.

Her internal muscles flexed wildly round the hardness of his cock, and she cried out; the way her quim shivered round him tipped him into his own orgasm, and he buried his head in her shoulder as he came.

'I love you,' he said softly.

'Me too.' She stroked his face. 'Promise me it'll always be this good between us?'

He smiled. 'Ask me that again when we're geriatrics in our bath chairs, wittering on about the old days.'

'Yeah.' She rubbed her nose against his. 'You know, I could curl up and go to sleep, right now.'

'That exciting, was it?'

'Actually, yes. Making love's probably the best relaxant there is.'

He grinned. 'So much for "Not tonight, darling, I've got a headache?" '

Susanna laughed back. 'Exactly. It should be "Yes please, it's the best cure there is!" '

He withdrew from her, turning onto his back so that she could cuddle into him, resting her head on his shoulder. 'Actually, I think you have a point. I could do with a sleep myself.'

'Then shut up,' Susanna said drowsily, closing her eyes.

What seemed like a few minutes later, she woke.

'I wondered if you were turning into one of the Seven Sleepers, for a minute!' Brandon said as she stirred.

She smiled. Considering they'd closed their eyes for, what, twenty minutes? 'Just call me "Rip".' She stretched. 'Mm. I don't know if I can be bothered to get up.'

'Don't, then,'

She glanced at the clock, and her eyes widened. 'Bloody hell! It's half past six!' She'd slept for four hours.

'So?'

'So, I'm supposed to be cooking dinner for you. Molly'll want the kitchen, and she'll be furious if I get under her feet.'

'Why don't I come down to dinner tonight? That would solve the problem,' Brandon suggested.

Susanna shook her head. 'You're having at least one more evening's bed rest, and that's that.' She kissed him and got out of bed. 'I need a shower – then I'll do you some food.'

'I'm not that hungry.'

'Even so, you have to eat, to make sure you get all the right vitamins and protein.'

Brandon rolled his eyes. 'Yes, boss.'

'I'll see you in a bit, then.' She blew him a kiss, and headed for the shower.

Luckily, Molly wasn't in the kitchen; Susanna deftly made a large fluffy mushroom omelette, adding cheese for extra protein, and cooked some mangetout to go with it. She'd grown used to the castle, now, so she found her way back to their bedroom before the meal grew cold.

Brandon ate every last scrap, and put the plate away from him with a sigh. 'That was lovely. Thanks.'

'Now, get some rest,' Susanna directed. 'I'd better clear up the kitchen, before Molly goes on the war-path.'

'Right.'

Molly still wasn't in the kitchen; Susanna quickly cleared up, and headed back upstairs. She opened the door quietly; Brandon was sleeping again, so she decided not to wake him, and went back downstairs to the library.

She spent the next half-hour or so curled up in the big leather armchair, reading the first edition of the M R James she'd found on one of the shelves; the castle was the perfect setting for James's creepy tales, and she could almost imagine one of the curtains suddenly metamorphosing into a nameless horror with a face of crumpled linen, at the sound of a whistle . . .

She shivered, and closed the book. It had grown dark outside; dinner would be soon. She thought about the previous evening again. If she hadn't been dreaming, then who had the mysterious stranger been? Why wouldn't Alicia introduce them properly? And – her skin prickled in a mixture of anticipation, excitement and fear – would he be joining them at the table, that evening?

Thirteen

There were indeed three places set at the table when Susanna went into the dining room; Alicia was already there, although there was no sign of the handsome stranger.

'Good evening.'

'Good evening,' Susanna replied, sitting down and unable to resist looking at the empty place, wondering where the stranger was.

Alicia looked at her, her head slightly on one side. 'Molly said that Brandon's better, today. I though that he might be joining us tonight.'

Susanna shook her head. 'I'm afraid not. He's better than he was – but not that much better. I don't want him to overdo things and give himself another relapse. I thought another evening in bed would do him good.'

'That's sensible.' Alicia spread her hands. 'Maybe we'll see him tomorrow night, then. I'll tell Molly to clear his place, when she comes in.'

'I made him an omelette earlier, so he won't starve. And Molly won't have to go rushing up to him with a tray.' Susanna fought to hide her disappointment that the stranger wasn't going to join them. Maybe it had been a dream, after all.

'Good.' Alicia paused. 'How's your hangover?'

'Gone, now.' Susanna smiled ruefully. 'But I'm not drinking any more than one glass of wine tonight.'

'Yes, hangovers are awful, aren't they. They throw you out for the whole day.'

The way Alicia was acting towards her . . . it was the final proof, Susanna thought, that she'd been dreaming, the previous night. No way could Alicia have made love to her one night – then act like the cool and charming hostess the following evening, as though nothing had happened between them.

Molly brought in avocado and prawns, and gave the table a cursory glance. 'Just the two of you tonight, is it, Milady?'

'Yes.' Alicia smiled at her housekeeper. 'Susanna's already cooked Brandon something.'

'And I cleared the kitchen up afterwards,' Susanna added.

Molly said nothing: merely gave her a hostile stare and left the room.

'She's a bit territorial about her kitchen, I'm afraid,' Alicia said ruefully.

'Mm.' Susanna looked at the hors d'oeuvres. 'This has to be one of my favourite dishes. I adore avocados.'

'So do I.' Alicia's lips quirked. 'I told you, we have a lot in common.'

To Susanna's horror, she actually blushed; in order to cover her confusion, she took a gulp of wine. 'How's the book going?' she said, desperately steering the conversation onto something more neutral.

'Fine.'

Susanna winced at the flatness of Alicia's tone. 'Sorry, that was tactless of me. I imagine you don't like talking about your current book, when you're writing it.'

'Something like that. It's superstition, I suppose. I once told a friend about a book I was writing, when it was in the early stages, and he thought the idea was useless. He mocked me; and every time I sat down to write, I heard his voice echoing through my head. I just sat there, in front of my typewriter, unable to write a word; in the end, I junked the book.'

'Ouch.'

Alicia shrugged. 'As a matter of fact, he was right. I found the draft at the back of a drawer, a few months ago, and I read it through. It was terrible. So he did me a favour, in a way.'

'But now, you prefer to keep your work to yourself until it's finished.' Susanna was oddly disappointed. She'd been sure that the tale of Ambrose and the Russian countess had been part of Alicia's latest book, and she'd been the privileged audience . . . Obviously not.

'Something like that.' Alicia raised her glass. 'Well, cheers.'

'Cheers,' Susanna echoed, taking a very small sip of wine.

Alicia didn't speak much during the main course or the pudding; Susanna decided not to press her. Everyone had days when they just didn't feel like entertaining others. Maybe she should excuse herself before coffee, let Alicia have some time to herself.

As if Alicia had read Susanna's mind, she smiled. 'Sorry. I'm being terrible company, tonight.'

'I gate-crashed in the first place; there's no need to apologize. I'm the one who's intruding.'

' "Who am intruding", actually, if you're saying it.'

Susanna didn't take offence. 'Grammatically, I agree. Colloquially, I don't.'

The small exchange seemed to have tipped the balance of Alicia's mood; she poured herself another glass of wine, and offered the bottle to Susanna – who, remembering the morning's hangover, refused. 'Thanks, but not tonight. I can't handle a second hangover like this morning's one in a row!'

'Fair enough. Coffee?'

'Well, I was thinking about going to bed.'

'Why? It's early.'

Susanna flushed. 'I feel like I'm imposing. Being a demanding guest, and what have you.'

'Well, you're not. Stay here for a while. I promised you the rest of the story last night, did I not?'

'Sunil, Ambrose and the countess, you mean?'

Alicia nodded. 'If you'd like to hear it.'

'Yes.' Susanna's face became scarlet again. God, she

sounded like a teenybopper, eager to hear her idol speak. She was furious with herself for being so childish. And yet she couldn't help it. As Brandon had said, there was something compelling about Alicia. Something which drew you – and, Susanna acknowledged as a tiny *frisson* ran down her spine, something which terrified you as well.

Molly brought in the coffee, together with white chocolate mints. 'One of my fetishes, you might say,' Alicia said, with a meaningful look at Susanna.

Susanna's eyes narrowed. Was Alicia trying to tell her that last night had really happened? Refusing to meet the writer's eyes, she poured two cups of coffee, adding sugar to Alicia's.

'You remembered how I like it, then.'

'Yes. I'm a journalist, remember; I'm supposed to notice those sort of things.' Susanna's tone was flippant, covering the mass of confusion she felt.

'True.' Alicia stirred her coffee, and took a sip. 'Mm.' She bit into one of the mints, savouring it, and then started on her story.

'Well, the countess didn't kill Sunil. She simply took enough blood for her needs, sharing it with Ambrose. The next morning, Sunil woke in his own quarters, thinking that he'd had a weird and wonderful dream – and when he travelled to see Ambrose, the next morning, he discovered that the Westerners had already left, and no one knew where they were going.'

Susanna frowned. 'I thought Ambrose promised him the secret of eternal life?'

'Life-in-death is what he meant.' Alicia smiled. 'Vampires don't always make other vampires when they kill – otherwise the whole planet would be populated with vampires. Hungry ones, with nothing left to feed on.'

'Yeah, I suppose so.' Susanna felt embarrassed at her own naïveté.

'Anyway, the countess didn't want another companion. Ambrose was her heart's desire. Sunil had been – a whim.' She smiled. 'The countess had merely wished to indulge some of her other appetites.'

'Right.' Susanna paused. 'And why did Sunil think it had only been a dream?'

'Hypnotism. The countess had told him that he wouldn't remember her properly, that he'd think of the night's events as a dream – and also that the mark on his neck had been made by some sort of insect.' Alicia shrugged. 'It was very simple, and very effective. Sunil really did believe that it had all been a dream – though the countess had a profound effect on his life. He never married. He always thought of the woman from his dreams, and no other could match up to her beauty.'

'That's awful.'

Alicia shrugged. 'There are worse things. What's the point of marrying someone just for the sake of it?'

'What about heirs, and whatever? Wasn't he part of some dynasty?'

'He was the younger brother, remember. It wasn't important that he should have heirs.' Alicia smiled at her. 'Don't be too upset on his behalf. For that one night, he tasted true bliss – and not that many people have experienced it.'

'I suppose not.'

'Ambrose and the countess travelled around India for a while. They met many people and saw many things, but eventually, Europe drew them back. They went to Vienna, for a while, and Salzburg.'

Susanna's lips twitched. 'Don't tell me. The countess took a fancy to Mozart, but went a little too far and ended up draining him, just as he finished writing his *Requiem*?'

Alicia grinned back. 'Nothing of the kind. You've been reading too many hack vampire stories. And she wasn't Shakespeare's Dark Lady, either, before you start on that one.'

Susanna flushed. It had been one of her other ideas. 'Sorry. It's your story.'

'As I was saying, the countess and Ambrose went to Austria, to Hungary. They spent their time travelling from city to city, careful not to arouse suspicions as to their true nature. They kept themselves to themselves, not entertaining much; everyone thought that they were honeymooners, not wanting the company of others, and so they were left alone.

'But in the end, Ambrose grew homesick. He needed to breathe English air, hear English people around him – and not just those doing the Grand Tour or whatever. He tried to keep his longings from the countess, but she could read his thoughts. She'd seen the yearning in his eyes, and she knew what he wanted. So they came back to England – to London, where they could be as anonymous as they pleased.

'It was the 1890s, and the Decadents held sway. In arty circles, the poets and artists liked absinthe – and the whip. They didn't mind which end they were, either: putting stripes on someone else's skin was as exciting for them as feeling the sting of leather against their own buttocks.

'The countess was in her element. It meant that she could virtually drug her victims with absinthe, before drinking their blood: and know that she was giving them what they wanted, at the same time. She could have sex with as many pretty boys as she liked, whip them, and lick the blood from their wounds without them even beginning to guess her true nature. To them, she was simply a beautiful woman who would indulge their kinkier desires; and for the countess, it was a novelty, not having to pierce their skin with her teeth to taste their blood.'

'How did Ambrose react to her being unfaithful to him?'

Alicia shook her head. 'She wasn't unfaithful to him. There's a big difference between having sex and making love – and an even bigger difference between physical and emotional gratification. The countess needed a lot of physical stimulation, and she indulged herself with whoever took her fancy – mainly men, but sometimes women as well.

'Whatever she did, Ambrose was the one she loved. He was the one she shared her heart with, and he was the one who shared her life. Being unfaithful to him would mean that she was planning to take herself another companion, and gradually push him out of her life. He was her great love, and she had no intention of doing that, believe me.'

Susanna nodded. 'Right. So he wasn't at all jealous?'

'No. He had his own diversions. Ambrose didn't like the poets, finding them too pretentious and far too self-absorbed. He also didn't like the absinthe habit, or their need for what they called "the English vice" – it wasn't a taste he shared. So Ambrose began to mix with the theatrical set.

'Remember, he was a scholar; he'd always loved words, and their power. He spent his evenings at the theatre, watching anything from Shakespeare to Wilde. Revenge tragedy, Restoration comedy, Victorian satire – he saw it all. He loved the atmosphere, the way that actors could be anyone or anything they liked. So while the countess indulged herself with her poets and her artists, driving them to madder excesses, he spent his evenings watching plays and talking with the arty set afterwards.

'He had the occasional snack on the way home to the countess, but this was London of the 1890s, remember. Since the Ripper, the papers had become virtually immune to murdered prostitutes and what-have-you. Nobody noticed the odd person slumped in a gutter looking pale and drained. They simply thought it was an excess of gin. Besides, even if they had probed further, and seen marks on the victim's neck – who would suspect the young English gentleman and his beautiful Russian wife as being the cause?

'One night, at the theatre, Ambrose got chatting to a young man. This young man was interested in the occult, in new scientific breakthroughs – and Ambrose was enchanted by his mind. He knew that the countess would appreciate him, too, so he couldn't resist taking the young man home to meet the countess.

'She had had a quiet evening, for once – some of her poets had cried off, saying that they had to write, that she'd inspired them and they would be back to see her just as soon as they'd finished their great works – so she was pleased to have the company. Ambrose explained about the young man's interest in the supernatural, and that he wrote the odd short story; the countess knew exactly what he was thinking. That maybe this young man could bring them both . . . a certain satisfaction, in hearing their story told.

'She had cognac brought, for Ambrose and the young man. Then, when the young man had grown comfortable with them, she told him that she, too, wrote stories. He asked if he might read them – she said no, she'd never written them down. They were all in her head.

'Then he asked her if she would tell the stories to him. She smiled, and said that she might bore him. He was very gallant, and said no, of course not. He pleaded with her, and eventually she agreed to tell her tales – on condition that he did not interrupt her. The young man agreed eagerly to her terms, and he settled down in the big leather chair by the fire.

'Ambrose sat on a low stool at the countess's feet, as was his habit; she played with his hair, unable to resist touching him when he sat so close to her. And eventually she told her tale – a tale about a Russian noblewoman, a woman she called Anoushka.

'Anoushka lived in a very remote part of Russia. It was a land filled with snows and wolves and bears, a hard land where the men were strong – and so were the women. Anoushka was extremely beautiful: she had the typical Slavic high cheekbones, pale skin and dark hair. But her eyes were her best feature – they were like liquid emeralds.

'She was blessed with more than just beauty: she was wise, she was kind, and everybody loved her. And yet on the day of her birth, an old hag at the far side of the village predicted that the child was doomed. The crone was ignored, of course. No one could possibly believe that sort of thing about a noble child. As the baby became a toddler, and then a happy little child, the old hag's warning was forgotten.

'One day, when Anoushka was nearly eighteen, a stranger came to the village. There was something different about him

– something strange that no one could identify. The old hag, had she still lived, would have known immediately: but she had died, the winter before, and no one had taken her place as the village wise-woman.

'Anoushka met him while she was out riding, one evening: she'd been to visit friends of the family in another village, and had forgotten the time. She was riding back, careful not to overtax her horse – but something frightened the horse, he shied, and Anoushka fell off.

'She wasn't badly hurt – luckily, the ground where she'd fallen was covered in fresh soft snow – and she was just dusting herself down and preparing to remount her horse, who was grazing nearby, when the stranger galloped up. He'd seen her fall, and he'd come to her rescue.

'Anoushka thought he was the most beautiful man she'd ever met. She assumed that he was a nobleman from another part of Russia – certainly, no peasant farmer could have afforded that kind of horse or could dress in that kind of way – and she wondered what he was doing in her village.

'He avoided all questions, simply helping her back onto her horse and travelling back to her father's castle with her: and he left her at the gate. Anoushka sang her rescuer's praises, and the old count, who doted on his daughter, determined to reward the young man in some way.

'Eventually, he managed to find out where the young man was staying, and invited him to the castle. He thanked the stranger for rescuing his daughter, and asked if he could do anything in return. The stranger smiled, and said yes: the count could give him his daughter.

'The count had already been thinking of marriage for Anoushka – some alliance with a strong dynasty, to someone who could protect her. This young man, with no past and no family (for he refused to tell anyone where he came from) was not what he had in mind. He smiled, and said no, he could not: his daughter was too precious to him.

'The young man persisted, gradually letting the old count

know that he was from a noble family, and had the sort of wealth that the count could appreciate. And in the end, the count agreed – provided that it was acceptable to his daughter, because he loved her dearly and would not force her to do anything she did not want to do.' Alicia smiled. 'Very enlightened, for fifteenth-century Russia, I know, but that's how it happened.

'Anoushka was summoned, and the count told her what the young man had proposed. She had dreamed about him since the moment she'd first met him – strange dreams which left her feeling hot and aching when she woke, longing for something to . . .' Alicia spread her hands. 'Anoushka couldn't explain what she wanted, what she needed, but she knew that she needed some kind of release – and that it was connected with the strange young man.

'She agreed to the proposal, and she was married to him, a few weeks later. The whole village came to the wedding, and the dancing and singing went on all day and all night. But eventually, it was time for Anoushka to join her husband in the marital bed.

'He had agreed to stay at the castle for the first week of their marriage, and then he would take her home to his own people. The count wasn't keen on the idea of his daughter going so far from home, but he could hardly demand that she and her new husband stayed at his castle. Besides, it was only fair that her new family should meet her, too. None of them had attended the wedding. The count thought that they must be curious to know what the new bride was like – and was proud father enough to want to show off his daughter's grace and beauty.

'At last, the newlyweds were alone. The young man asked Anoushka to dance for him; he hummed a song for her to dance to, a sad melody which he said was from his part of the world, a special song. She danced; and when the song ended he took her in his arms.

'He undressed her, very slowly; the white dress of silk and

lace fell to the floor, leaving Anoushka naked. She was a modest girl, but she did not bow her head, or blush in shame. This, she knew, was what she had been waiting for. She simply held out her arms, and the young man picked her up and carried her to the bed.

'She lay on the feather mattress, watching him while he stripped. She had never seen a man naked before, and she was curious. And because she loved her new husband, she was not afraid when she saw his erect sex rearing towards her.

'Anoushka, of course, was a virgin. The young man knew this, and he made sure that she was as aroused as he was, kissing her body all over. When he kissed down her body to the parts Anoushka had always been taught were private, she tensed, not sure what he was going to do; but as she felt the long slow stroke of his tongue against her, and the sudden feeling as though she were melting beneath his mouth, she relaxed again.

'Finally when he judged that she was ready, he entered her. He covered her mouth with his own, swallowing her cry of mingled pain and pleasure; and as he kissed her, the pain dissolved, becoming a sea of pleasure. And then she climaxed, her body clutching at his as he thrust deep inside her, pushing him into his own release.

'Anoushka's love for her husband grew each day; and although she could hardly bear to be parted from her family, she knew that she could not live without him. And so she went with him, in a large black coach pulled by strong black horses, across to the other side of Russia.

'The old hag, had she still lived, would have said that her prediction was just about to come true. Anoushka was doomed. And so it proved, for her husband had hidden his true nature from her. When they had travelled a certain distance from her family, he made himself known to her for what he really was.' Alicia smiled. 'In France, they would call him *broucolaque*.'

'He told her that she had a choice. She could go back to her family, and forget that she'd ever met him – or she could go with him. If she chose to walk the same path as he did, she could never see her family again. They would have to believe her dead – as she would be, in some respects. She would be part of the Undead, living life-in-death, and she would live as he did, feeding off the living.

'Anoushka felt as though she'd been ripped in two. She loved her family, and she had been brought up as a religious girl. What he was proposing was ungodly, against everything she had ever believed in: and yet she could not live without him. She knew that no one else could ease the ache and the deep longing in her heart – the longing for his body joined to hers. And so she chose.

'That night, the young man made love to his bride more tenderly than ever before. And as she climaxed, her body fluid and relaxed, he sank his teeth into her neck, draining her blood. She was almost fainting away when he stopped, and drew his teeth over his own wrist, letting a thin trickle of blood seep over his skin. He let the drips of blood fall onto her lips, then gently set his wrist to her mouth, urging her to drink from him as he had drunk from her.

'She did. And the next day, he wrote a letter to her family, saying that there had been a terrible accident, and Anoushka had been killed while out riding with him. He blamed himself for the accident, and said that he would never darken their home again. He would live a life of penance for what had happened to Anoushka.

'In some respects, it was true: he felt guilty at taking her so far from her old life. And yet he loved her, and could not live without her. She was the one who made his life whole, the one he had been born to marry; and Anoushka felt the same about him. The old crone would have agreed with them; he was Anoushka's destiny and her doom.

'They travelled on through Russia, through to Europe.' Alicia smiled ruefully. 'Europe was their undoing. They had gone to Paris, thinking themselves safe in a large city. But he grew careless, forgot to hide his tracks. He'd taken blood from some young women, and hadn't bothered hypnotizing them afterwards, saying that they'd never remember who he was: all they'd remember would be his black cloak and a shadowed face. Unfortunately, when the young women recovered from their fever, they spoke to their nurses, their priests, about the beautiful young man who had drunk their blood.

'Eventually, he was traced. The mob came for him – luckily, Anoushka was out somewhere at the time, or they would have killed her, too.' Alicia's face tightened. 'She came home to discover their house in flames. She knew immediately that he was inside, and there was nothing she could do to save him. She felt as though someone had ripped her heart out, and stood there almost prostrate with grief: being a *broucolaque*, her senses were greater than when she was human, and so she could hear his screams as the flames consumed his body. She could feel everything he felt, the way his skin crackled and his blood boiled in his veins.

'He perished with her name on his lips. She swore vengeance on those who had killed him, saying that she would extinguish their bloodline, no matter how long it took.

'And she did. She spent the next few weeks destroying the people who'd killed him, starting with the youngest. Babies sickened and died from an unknown fever. Young women were overcome by lethargy and fainting, eventually passing away. Young men found themselves fighting duels over a beautiful woman they'd just met whose honour had been compromised, in their view – and every one of them died against a better opponent.' Alicia spread her hands. 'As a *broucolaque*, she could change shape. Traditionally it was a bat or a wolf, or mist – but she changed into a man, one who fought duels and won.

'When she'd wiped out the youngest ones, the ones who could bear children and carry on the bloodline, she started on the oldest ones. The men she visited and used her sexual power over them, turning them impotent; and the women, she visited with dreams. She hypnotized them so that they would never remember her visit, but she told them of the way her husband had suffered. The nightmares they suffered afterwards led most of them to be committed to the asylum.

'Once she'd cleansed Paris, her anger diminished. Part of her wanted to leave France, the place where the love of her life had suffered such a cruel fate, but part of her needed to stay, be as near to him as she could. Paris was out of the question, so she travelled through the other cities. She was more careful, this time, taking only small amounts of blood from each victim.

'Years and years later, she came to Orleans. Her nature meant that she would never grow old – not in human terms. She always looked young; not a single grey strand would touch her raven hair. By the time she reached Orleans, she had grown lonely. The only way she could cope with the loss of her husband was to hold parties, fill every hour of the night with glittering entertainment, talking and laughing and drinking. In the day, she slept; and the next night would be another party.

'It went on for – oh, who can say how long? And then a young man was brought to one of her parties. A young Englishman, who had become an ambassador for the King. The first time that Anoushka saw him, she nearly fainted: he was the living image of her dead husband. He had the same dark hair, the same beautiful aristocratic face. Only his eyes were a different colour – cornflower blue, instead of green.

'She ignored him for a time, thinking that maybe she was mad – maybe she missed her love so much that she was hallucinating. She made discreet enquiries about him, and discovered that he was a scholar and a courtier. He knew languages, law and mathematics. He rode, he fenced, and everyone loved him.

'That was when she became convinced that he was her dead love, returned to her. And so she summoned him to meet her, one evening – a *rendezvous à deux*.' Alicia smiled. 'His name was Ambrose. You know the rest, so I won't bother telling you again. Let's just say that the countess told the young man the ale of how she met Ambrose, and what happened when he rought his bride home to England. She finished her tale with he Russian countess being thrown from the battlements, and he young man lapped up every single word.'

Alicia laughed. 'He did exactly what they'd hoped. He went ome and wrote the story. A publisher accepted it, and he was reatly excited – the first time that he'd had the literary uccess he'd craved all his life. He knew that it was going to e the book of his dreams.

'He went home to see Ambrose and his wife with the news. Ie was honest enough to admit to them what he'd done, and aid that he'd put her name on the manuscript, if she liked – ut the countess merely smiled and said no, he was the one vho had written it, and he should have the credit.

'It was printed, and it was very popular. The young man rought them a signed copy, bound in leather; Ambrose read it o the countess, one evening.' Alicia's lips twitched. 'They iscovered that the young man had changed a few telling etails. For a start, the main character wasn't the countess – it ras a count. A count named after a fire-breathing dragon. The ount lost his bride in a district of Russia, and he was the one vho wreaked his revenge.

'When the countess asked him why he had changed her tory, he explained that it was because no one would believe a voman could be that powerful, to wipe out the bloodline of everal families in Paris.'

Susanna scoffed. 'That's rubbish. Come on, there was a ueen on the throne!'

'Women still couldn't vote,' Alicia reminded her. 'As for heir property – it was only very recently that women were llowed to keep the right to their own property, on marriage. here wasn't that much power.'

'I suppose not.' Susanna frowned. 'So are you telling me hat this young man was an Irishman, and his first name was braham?'

Alicia smiled. 'Work it out for yourself.'

Susanna grinned. 'Well, like you say, it makes a change from Mozart or Shakespeare's Dark Lady.'

'It does.'

'Though Anoushka's story isn't quite like *Dracula*.'

'Like I said, he changed a few details – muddled it up in a dream.'

'Right.' Susanna glanced at her watch, and her eyes widened as she realized the time. 'God, is it really that late? Sorry, I shouldn't have kept you talking. Not when you want to work.'

'I don't work *every* night.'

Susanna stifled a yawn. 'No.'

'But you're tired. Go to bed.' Alicia smiled. 'Pleasant dreams.'

Fourteen

Susanna didn't dream, that night; she was almost disappointed, when she woke, to realize that she hadn't had another dreamlike encounter with the beautiful man from the picture.

It had definitely been caused by having too much to drink, the previous night, she thought. It was almost worth the hangover to have another dream like that . . . or maybe not.

She turned over in bed, and discovered that Brandon was still asleep. He looked better; the shadows beneath his eyes had disappeared, and his colour was more or less back to normal. If he was feeling as good as he looked, Susanna thought, she'd have trouble with him – he'd want to get up, do some work, or just do anything rather than lie in bed for another day.

When he woke, Susanna's suspicions were confirmed. Brandon informed her that he felt a lot better, and he was getting up. It took all her powers of persuasion, plus the promise of letting him get up for dinner, to make him agree to spend the day in bed.

She walked into the village again, to fetch the daily papers and some more grapes for Brandon; this time, to her relief, she didn't see Thomas Penford. She hummed happily to herself as she tackled the steep hill back to the castle; she could get used to this. A daily walk, to give her some fresh air and some exercise, and then living a life of leisure . . .

Molly let her in with bad grace; Susanna simply smiled, and went back upstairs to Brandon. They spent the day playing cards; as the sun set, Susanna told Brandon about Alicia's tale, the previous night and how Alicia had woven it all together by talking about how Anoushka, the Russian countess, had become a vampire in the first place.

'No ginger massage, this time?'

Susanna laughed. 'Not in the middle of a Russian snowdrift! Anyway, Alicia ended last night's instalment in the 1890s – in London. She might bring it up to the present day tonight, so I thought I'd better bring you up to date, or you'll lose the plot completely.'

'Right.' Brandon looked interested. 'So is this her latest book, then?'

'I'm not sure. I thought it was, but then she said that she never lets anyone read it until she's finished.'

'Maybe she's finished it, and she's trying it out on you for audience reaction,' he suggested.

'Maybe.' Susanna stretched. 'Anyway, you need a shave if you're to be presentable tonight.'

'Hint taken.' Brandon let Susanna have the shower first; when she emerged from the bathroom, wrapped in a towel, he smiled at her. 'The problem with recuperating, it makes you feel so weak.'

She narrowed her eyes. 'Oh, yes? And what might you be after, Brandon Rodgers?'

'How about washing my back for me?'

She grinned. '*Just* your back?'

'Well, if you feel like washing other parts of me . . .' He rubbed his jaw. 'If you wanted to really indulge me, and shave me as well, I wouldn't protest.'

Susanna tipped her head on one side, giving him a mischievous look. 'Shave you where, precisely?'

He grinned back. 'My face, darling. No way am I letting a razor go anywhere near my cock!'

'Funny, that,' she mused. 'Men rabbit on about how erotic

it is if a woman shaves off her pubic hair, but the minute you suggest returning the compliment, they back off.'

'Women's bodies are more attractive than men's, anyway.'

She laughed. 'Now you're trying to justify yourself.'

'So will you wash my back for me, or not?'

She thought about it for a moment. 'All right. I'll indulge you – as you're recuperating from an illness. Just don't expect it every day, from now on.'

'Just birthdays, Christmas, anniversaries—'

'—and any day with a "y" in it?' Susanna finished, laughing.

Brandon ran the bath, and stripped swiftly, testing the water before stepping in. He sat down and leaned forward slightly, closing his eyes. 'Right, then. I'm ready when you are.'

Susanna knelt beside him, and lathered her hands, smoothing her fingers over his shoulders. 'How's that?' she whispered in his ear.

'Lovely.'

She nibbled his earlobe. 'I'm not rubbing you too hard?'

'No.'

She continued to rub his back with the soap, then sluiced the foam from his skin. 'There you are. That's your back done.'

He leaned back against the bath. 'What about my front?'

'A shave, I believe you said.' Susanna raised her eyebrows. 'I still can't quite believe that you're going to let me shave you.'

'If it had been a cut-throat razor, I wouldn't.'

'Why? Don't you trust me?'

'It's not that – just that it'd be too easy for you to cut me accidentally. At least these things aren't so dangerous.' He indicated the disposable razors on the bathroom shelf.

'True. Well, lie back and enjoy it, as they say.' Susanna lathered his face, and carefully shaved him. 'Feel more pampered now, do you?' she asked, when she'd finished.

'Almost. Just one more thing . . .'

Susanna grinned as she realized that his cock was erect, and he was making it nod at her. 'Something else wants washing, hm?'

His broad smile said it all for him; she laughed, and soaped her hands again. She made her hands into a tube, sliding it down over his cock; Brandon closed his eyes in bliss. 'Mm. I'd almost forgotten just how good you are at this.'

'It's about time I jogged your memory, then.' She began to masturbate him gently with her right hand, her soapy fingers slippery against his skin.

As her hand moved up and down his shaft, her fingers working his foreskin back and forth, he gave a small moan of pleasure, and gripped the side of the bath. Susanna smiled to herself as she saw how white his knuckles had become: he was holding himself back, and having difficulty in doing so.

She let her left hand drift down to cup his balls, massaging them gently; as Brandon gave a sharp intake of breath, she began to stroke his perineum. When she reached the puckered rosy hole of his anus, she pressed one finger against it. He swallowed, and splayed his legs wider apart, giving her the access she wanted.

She continued to rub his shaft with one hand, while she slid one finger inside him, pushing it slowly in and out in a way calculated to drive him wild. At last he cried out, and she saw his balls lift and tighten; and then his cock throbbed in her hand, the creamy white fluid jetting up.

'Better?' she asked.

'Mm.' He leaned over and kissed her lingeringly. 'Much better.'

'Now I suggest you finish having your bath on your own.'

'Spoilsport.'

She grinned, knowing exactly what he'd had in mind. The bath was one of Brandon's favourite places for making love. 'If I stay here, you know what'll happen – and we'll be late for dinner.'

'So?'

'So, we're guests, and it'd be rude to make Alicia wait for

us. Besides, it's your first evening up. Don't overdo things, hm?'

He thought about it. 'I suppose you're right – though I still feel deprived.' His eyes danced. 'What are the chances of you making it up to me later?'

She grinned. 'That's for me to know, and you to guess.' She stood up, gave him an exaggerated pout, and sashayed out of the bathroom, dropping her towel as she reached the bathroom door.

Brandon groaned, and she heard the sound of very energetic splashing as she dressed. A few minutes later, he came out of the bathroom; as soon as he'd finished dressing, they walked down to the dining room together.

Alicia was already waiting for them. 'Good evening.'

Susanna smiled, and sat down. 'Hi. Sorry we're a bit late.'

Alicia shrugged. 'You're not. I'm early.' She turned to Brandon. 'It's nice to see you up and about. So you're feeling better tonight, then?'

'A lot better than madam did, yesterday morning.' He sat opposite Susanna, and slipped his shoes off. If Alicia decided to tell them both an erotic story, that evening, he had every intention of adding a few ad libs of his own – for Susanna's attention only.

'I learned my lesson,' Susanna muttered. 'So I'll stick to mainly water again, tonight.'

'We didn't have *that* much, the other night.'

'You're probably more used to it than I am.'

Alicia smiled. 'Well. Maybe.'

Susanna searched her hostess's face. She could find no trace of lust in Alicia's eyes, no tiny betraying twinkle in her eyes which would mean that her dream, two nights before, had been reality. It had just been a dream induced by Alicia's story and the face of the man in the hall.

Molly came in, and silently dished up melon and prawns; when she'd left the room again, Susanna turned to Alicia. 'I've been telling Brandon about the story you've been telling me.

About Anoushka, the Russian countess, and how she met Ambrose, and what happened to them when they went to India.'

'It all sounds very interesting,' Brandon said. 'Susanna was wondering if you were going to bring the story up to date, tonight.'

'From London in the 1890s to the present day?' Alicia shrugged. 'I could, yes. If you wouldn't be bored, that is.'

'No chance of that.' Susanna smiled at her. 'Whatever I thought of you before I came here, you're a damn good storyteller. I read one of your books on the train – the first one.'

Alicia's eyes narrowed. 'You didn't say anything, before.'

'No.' Susanna avoided Alicia's gaze. 'Well, I enjoyed it; but the tale you've told me about the Russian countess and Ambrose is even better. I want to know what happened to her.'

'Well, after that book was published, they travelled for a bit. Scotland, Wales – all the wilder parts of the country. The countess knew that what Ambrose really wanted was to go home, to see what had happened to Pentremain. So, eventually, they came back. The castle had been bought by some awful people – new money, the sort who wanted to impress people with how much they could buy. Needless to say, their taste was appalling. The sort who have gold-plated taps in the loo and think that it makes them posh.' Alicia pulled a face.

'Nobody in the village really liked them. Anyway, the countess managed to wangle an invitation to the castle. It was a mistake – the place wasn't how Ambrose remembered it, and the countess could see how upset he was at the way these people had "renovated" the place. They'd thrown money at it, and yes, they'd saved the roof from falling in and the walls from falling down – but their so-called renovations just weren't in keeping with the castle. Ambrose wanted to leave, as quickly as possible, but she had other ideas. She hatched a scheme to get the castle back for him, to return it to its rightful owner.

'She told the owners that Ambrose had originally come

from this part of the world, and they'd been researching the history of his family. She said that his family had once lived in the castle – which was true – and that there were some very tragic and very spooky tales about it.

'They lapped it up, thinking that they'd bought themselves a nice piece of heritage. The countess was a born story-teller, and this time, she intended to have a very precise effect on her audience. She was going to scare them shitless, so they'd want to leave.

'She told them about the duel between Ambrose and his brother, and how the villagers had decided that Ambrose's wife was a vampire and flung her from the battlements. She made things sound far gorier than they actually had been – the women in the audience looked green by the time she'd finished, and even the men looked a little worried.

'When she'd finished her tale, she was silent: then, before they had a chance to clap or speak, she added that the castle was supposed to be haunted. The father of the household – a portly man with a face like a squashed weasel and horrible piggy eyes – said that they'd never seen any headless warriors walking around the castle, or heard chains rattling, or heard weird wailing at midnight, so he didn't believe a word of it.

'The countess simply smiled, and exchanged a glance with Ambrose. That evening, the family saw the castle ghosts for the first time. They saw Ambrose, bloody and almost dead from his wounds, returning from the duel; and they heard his bride's wails as she was thrown from the battlements. No one admitted it in the morning, but the countess saw their pale faces over breakfast, and knew that her plan was working.

'Every night after that, the ghosts reappeared, at exactly the same time – until eventually the people who lived there could stand it no more, and sold up.'

Alicia smiled. 'You can guess who bought the castle. They settled in, and were happy: Ambrose felt that he'd come home, at last. The villagers accepted them, too, because Ambrose's family had originally come from the area – needless to say, he didn't say who he really was. They wouldn't have been able to handle that.'

'What about Anoushka? I mean, didn't she want to return to Russia, to her own homeland?'

Alicia shook her head. 'She was happy wherever Ambrose was. There was nothing for her to return to, in Russia; the graves of her family had long since crumbled to dust, as had the castle where she'd lived. Whereas Ambrose still had Pentremain.' She smiled. 'And that's it. Full circle.'

'Very good.' Brandon smiled at her. 'Though I wasn't expecting that.'

'How do you mean?'

'From what Susanna's told me, the rest of the story's been more . . . well . . .'

'Erotic?'

He nodded.

Alicia smiled. 'Maybe later. I think better after coffee.'

Susanna watched Alicia throughout the meal. Her behaviour towards Brandon was impeccable; the concerned hostess worried about her guest's recent illness. She was perfectly polite to Susanna, too – but there wasn't that sparkle Susanna had seen on recent evenings.

Her eyes narrowed. What had the stranger said, in her 'dream'? Something about Alicia preferring an audience of one – performing better when she could concentrate her energies on one person. She frowned. So had it been a dream, or hadn't it?

She was suddenly aware that Alicia had asked her a question, and flushed. 'Sorry. I was miles away.'

'So I see.' Alicia topped up her glass. 'I was saying, do you miss London when you've been away for a while?'

'Yes and no. Sometimes, it's nice to be away from the rat-race. Other times . . . well, I'd miss my friends. Besides, I like the energy of London, the way that something's always happening.'

'It's definitely a rat-race,' Alicia said. 'I've lived in London, and I don't think I could do it again. Not after here.'

The conversation remained on neutral ground until Molly brought in the coffee. Then Brandon turned to Alicia. 'So what started you writing about vampires, in the first place?'

She shrugged. 'Who knows where your dreams, your ideas, come from? I started doing some research, and found it interesting.'

'So do vampires really exist? Or is it all just imagination, as Susanna thinks?' Brandon persisted.

'It's like anything else – if you believe in them, they exist; if you don't, they don't. Like UFOs or ghosts or whether men really went to the moon or if it was all an elaborate hoax.'

'Do you believe in vampires?' Brandon asked softly.

In response, Alicia simply smiled. She topped up their glasses, and leaned back against her chair. 'In vampires, or the legends surrounding them?'

'Both,' Susanna said.

Alicia took a deep breath. 'Vampires – well, they're real enough, in my books. I've researched it, and there are a few cases which can't be explained in any other way. I'm not talking about Elizabeth de Bathory taking a bath in the blood of a virgin, in the hope that it would make her young – I'm talking about graves which were exhumed, and the body was still fresh, long after it should have started to decay.' She shrugged. 'It could be mass hallucination, of course, or some bacteria that science hasn't identified yet.'

'But you don't think so?'

'No,' Alicia said softly. 'As to the legends . . . Well, some of them are ridiculous. Can you imagine a vampire being repelled by garlic? A herb? It's like the superstitions about witches being repelled by yew trees. The smell's unpleasant, but that's all. It's an irritation, not a deterrent. Think of eating food which has been too heavily laced with garlic.' She spread her hands. 'If you're hungry enough, you just numb yourself to the taste, and eat.'

Susanna grimaced, visualizing what Alicia meant: a vampire,

starving, and sucking blood – regardless of whether the body was covered with garlic. 'That's a bit gruesome.'

'But true.'

'What about warding off vampires by the sign of the cross?' Brandon asked.

'It only works if the person wearing it believes in it – like holy water, or just about any other symbol of faith. It you don't believe in it, it becomes an empty symbol, with no power to move your spirit or to encourage you.'

'So you're saying it's a mental thing, not the cross itself?' Susanna asked.

Alicia nodded. 'Like the myth about vampires having power over wild animals. Think about it – wild animals attack if they smell fear. Vampires have no fear, so wild animals won't attack them. I suppose some people see that as "having power" over wild animals.'

'And what about having power over humans?'

Alicia thought about it. 'Well, like I said, it's a mental thing. Most vampires are well-read, and I don't mean just literature – scientific theory, history, anything they can get their hands on. Vampires thirst for knowledge.'

'As well as blood, you mean?' Brandon asked.

Alicia smiled. 'Yes, as well as blood. They have enquiring minds. They like to know things. And let's face it, what's more seductive than someone promising to teach you things you've never seen before, things that other people don't know? If you feel you're being initiated into something special, that you've been chosen – a mixture of human vanity, pride and inquisitiveness means that you're hooked. And the person promising you all these things therefore has power over you.'

'What about vampires having to sleep in coffins, lined with earth from their birthplace?' Susanna asked.

Alicia laughed. 'Folklore. It's not true at all.'

'And all that stuff about vampires being killed with a stake through the heart, or a silver bullet, is all just a load of rubbish too?'

'It's based in folk tales – but yes. Basically, it's rubbish. The only thing that can kill a vampire is direct sunlight – and it has to be strong. That's because it causes a chemical reaction in a vampire's blood which is invariably fatal.'

Susanna smiled. 'Oh dear. It sounds like we're cross-examining you, doesn't it?'

'I feel like I've got my interviewing face on,' Alicia admitted, smiling back.

'It wasn't meant to be like that,' Brandon said. 'I was just curious.'

Susanna and Alicia exchanged a glance, and burst into giggles.

'What's so funny?' Brandon demanded.

'Susanna said something like that to me, the other night. We were quibbling about M. R. James and how curiosity killed the cat,' Alicia explained.

'He wrote a couple of vampire tales,' Susanna said thoughtfully. 'I borrowed your copy in the library, the other day, and one of them was in there.'

'Are you thinking of the one about the vampire children, or the one about the wailing well?' Brandon asked.

'Both.' Susanna was thoughtful. 'Vampires don't seem to age. Why's that, Alicia?'

'The moment you become one of the undead, your physical appearance stops changing. You stop ageing. So if you're made into a vampire child, you stay a child – even though your emotions and needs and desires become more sophisticated, you're still a child, in appearance.'

'So the advantages of being a vampire are that you never grow old, and you don't worry about not having time to do things. Sounds a good life to me,' Susanna said.

'There's more to it than that. The first thing you find is that your perceptions change. You hear things that were out of your hearing range before. Your vision's sharper, too. And as for touch, smell and taste . . .' Alicia shivered, closing her eyes. 'It's like inhabiting a sensual new world.'

'O brave new world, that has such people in it?' Susanna quipped.

'Yes.' Alicia was definite. 'The pads of your fingertips become much more sensitive. Every time you touch someone, you can actually feel the blood beating though their body, the way their muscles move. Every sinew, nerve and tendon – you can feel it. Areas of your body which were sensitive to touch will become even more sensitive: kissing's much more fun, for starters. The taste, touch and smell of your lover is much more intense. You can virtually taste his arousal by licking the inside of his wrist.'

'So making love, as a vampire, is more fun?'

'Oh, yes.' Alicia smiled at Brandon. 'Though if you're thinking about the ginger massage – a vampire would find it almost unbearably pleasurable. There's a thin line between pain and pleasure, and that would definitely cross it.'

Brandon winced as he thought about it. 'Better make sure that I'm not a vampire before I persuade Susanna to try it out on me, then!'

They were still laughing as Molly brought in the coffee – and a further supply of the white chocolate mints.

Brandon tasted one. 'Mm. These are gorgeous.'

'One of my little weaknesses – as Susanna discovered earlier.'

Susanna narrowed her eyes. Was Alicia hinting at something more than just the chocolate? The older woman's face gave nothing away; she simply smiled, and poured them all some coffee.

They lapsed into a comfortable silence while they drank their coffee; then Alicia stretched. 'So you want to know more about Ambrose and Anoushka?'

'Yes.' Brandon looked rueful. 'It sounds like I missed most of it – Susanna told me a potted version, but it isn't quite the same.'

'I'll tell you the rest some other time, perhaps,' Alicia said, her voice suddenly smooth and seductive.

Susanna tensed. What was going on? Was Alicia bored with her and, now that Brandon was better, was she transferring her attentions back to him? She was silent as Alicia continued, 'But for now, I'll tell you about what happened in Pentremain.

'Ambrose and Anoushka celebrated their return to the castle in the old way – with their bodies, under the stars. The battlements were safe enough, and the night sky here is incredible – not least because you don't have the same light pollution around here as you do in the city.

'That first night, they ripped out all the tacky horrible things the previous owners had done to the castle. It didn't take them long – because, of course, a *broucolaque* has greater strength than average people. Though it did make them dusty; one of the few things they didn't rip out, because Anoushka liked it, was the shower in the main bathroom. It came in useful, that evening, to rid them of the dust and dirt of their evening's work.'

Alicia smiled. 'And, of course, it served another purpose. Some years before, on their travels, they'd made love in a waterfall, by moonlight. Showering together reminded Ambrose of that night – and he couldn't resist making love to his beautiful wife in the shower.

'He soaped her down, sluicing all the dirt from her body; then he used the powerful spray-jet to arouse her, playing it over her breasts and her belly and her buttocks. Her nipples soon became hard and reddened; Ambrose smiled, and parted her thighs, directing a jet of water between her legs to massage her clitoris.'

Brandon suddenly remembered the times he'd done something very similar with Susanna, and smiled. The look on her face as she listened to Alicia showed that the tale was arousing her – whether it was Alicia's words, anticipation of what was coming next, or anticipation of what she and Brandon would do when they were on their own again, he wasn't sure. Probably a combination of all three.

He smiled to himself again. That tale Susanna had told him about Paul Beetley, and how he had aroused her with his foot, under the table . . . Well, it was about to be repeated. With pleasurable consequences for both of them. He nudged one foot between Susanna's; she glanced at him, startled, and flushed bright red as she saw the look in his eyes.

Alicia continued her story, apparently oblivious to what was going on under the table. Brandon's foot crept higher and higher, finally arriving between Susanna's thighs, and he began to rub his toes back and forth across her quim. He could feel the heat of her arousal through the thin stuff of her trousers, and smiled; it was going to be an effort for Susanna not to come. Or to come quietly, without making Alicia aware of what was going on . . .

'Anoushka came again and again as Ambrose played the shower on her; and then, finally, he lifted her, balancing her weight against the wall as he slid his cock deep inside her. It was a celebration of everything: being together, being alive—' Alicia permitted herself a wry smile, '—in a sense, and being back at Pentremain.'

'She closed her eyes, burying her face in his neck as he continued to thrust deep inside her; her whole body tingled, and she wanted the moment to go on for ever. Eventually, she felt pleasure rushing through her veins, and she climaxed, her internal muscles contracting hard around Ambrose's cock in a way that tipped him into his own orgasm.

'They clung together, the water still beating down on them; and then Ambrose withdrew gently from her, setting her down on her feet. He smiled, then, and took her hand, switching off the shower and leading her out of the bathroom.

'Neither of them cared that it was an October night, crisp with frost, and they were damp and naked – after all, a *broucolaque* cannot catch a cold. They were in love with each other, with the night, and with the intensity of their existence, a feeling which burned in them like a brilliant flame.'

Susanna swallowed hard and dug her fingernails into her

palm, hard, to stop herself moaning; the combination of Alicia's erotic tale and Brandon's gentle yet insistent caressing of her quim was almost too much for her.

Alicia carried on with her tale; Susanna was sure that those intense green eyes could see exactly what was happening under the table, but Alicia made no comments, gave no inkling in her tale that she knew what was going on.

'Ambrose led her through the dark corridors of the castle, up steep staircases which creaked as they trod on the boards, and finally up a narrow stone spiral staircase to the battlements. Anoushka froze, for a moment, remembering what had happened there before, but Ambrose led her on, telling her that it was all right. They were going to exorcize the ghosts of the past, and celebrate their reunion.

'It was a full moon, and the air was cold and crisp round them; Anoushka's body gleamed silver by moonlight, and the droplets of water in her hair glittered like the stars. Ambrose held her at arm's length, just looking at her and drinking in her beauty; with a smile, she did a small pirouette, letting him see all of her.

'Ambrose's body, too, was like molten silver; the countess couldn't resist touching him, sliding her hands over his cool damp skin. She loved the clean hard lines of his body, the way he felt against her fingertips. Touch wasn't enough: she wanted to taste him, taste the cold of the October night air mingling with his skin.

'She dropped to her knees before him, bowing down to kiss his feet – not as a servant, you understand, but as an equal, indulging herself as much as she was going to indulge him. She worked her way slowly up his legs; as she reached his thighs, Ambrose tangled his hands in her long dark hair, urging her on.

'His cock reared up at her from the dark cloud of hair at his groin; she sat back on her haunches, looking at Ambrose, her eyes glittering. Then she drew her tongue very slowly along her lower lip; Ambrose shivered in anticipation, knowing what she was going to do next, and longing for the feel of her mouth round his cock.

'She smiled and opened her mouth, curling her fingers round his cock. She drew just the tip of it into her mouth, licking and sucking the engorged head until Ambrose cried out with pleasure. Then she slowly worked her way down his shaft, taking all of him into her mouth so that the tip of his cock touched her soft palate; he almost came, but she held him back.

'She continued to suck and lick him until he almost passed out with pleasure; then she let him climax, and he cried out her name for the whole world to hear.' Alicia smiled. 'Though there were some in Pentremain who wondered if wolves had suddenly reappeared in Cornwall, because they could have sworn that they heard a long drawn-out howling . . .'

Susanna couldn't hold out any longer; with a small sigh of pleasure, she came, her quim flexing madly. Brandon gave her a mischievous smile, and turned to Alicia. 'Very good. If I'd known that I'd been missing this sort of thing, I'd have got better sooner!'

Alicia gave Susanna an amused glance, and Susanna flushed beetroot: the author had known everything that was going on. And she'd deliberately told them a story that would turn Brandon on, and make Brandon pleasure Susanna under the table . . .

Fifteen

t took Susanna a long time to open her eyes, the next morning. ›he felt as though she were hungover, although she'd drunk no nore than half a glass of wine the previous night. All she vanted to do was curl up and go to sleep – preferably for the ext week.

Maybe I'm coming down with Brandon's bloody virus, she hought. That would be the worst thing that could happen: lthough she'd begun to enjoy her stay at Pentremain, and even ɔ like Alicia, she wanted to go back to London. She wanted ife to be normal again. It was like being at the end of a holiday hat's just a couple of days too long – you just want it to be ver, and to be back home again.

'Morning, sleepy head,' Brandon said cheerfully as Susanna orced her eyelids open and sat up. 'I wondered if you were lanning to sleep all morning.'

'No.' Susanna eyed him with a mixture of irritation and elief. Relief, because he was rapidly becoming more and nore like his old self, and that mark on his neck had faded; nd irritation, because Brandon was always disgustingly heerful in the mornings, whereas Susanna needed at least one nd a half cups of coffee before she felt human enough to talk anyone.

'So what's the plan for today? Are you going to let me get p?'

'Provided you don't do any work, maybe. And you're not walking into the village with me, either – it's quite a hike, and you're not really up to it, yet.'

'Mrs Bossy-boots,' he teased, laughing. 'I feel like I could walk to the top of the world today.'

'Well, you're not.' Susanna dragged herself out of bed. 'You can get up after lunch, if you like – but not before. I'll go and get some papers.'

'You don't look too well, yourself, this morning.'

'I'm all right,' she lied.

He stroked her face. 'That was quite a tale, last night.'

'Mm.' She shifted to face him. 'And you were bloody mean, making me come like that!'

'I thought you might enjoy it.' He grinned. 'Let's face it, it was no different from what you did on the train.'

'There's a huge difference between a virtually empty train and a private dining room with someone else sitting between you!'

'Oh, really?' Brandon's hand slipped down to cup one breast. Her nipple was already erect, and he toyed with it between finger and thumb. 'Well, this particular part of you doesn't seem too angry with me . . .'

Susanna couldn't help laughing. 'Oh, Brandon! You're so . . . so . . . well.'

'Words fail you?' he quipped, laughing back.

'Yeah.'

'Makes a nice change.' He nuzzled her shoulder. 'Mm. You're lovely when you've just woken up. You're all warm and cosy.' He pulled her on top of him. 'Like a little dormouse.'

'Little, hm?'

'You know what I mean.' He reached up to rub his nose against hers.

'Aren't dormice supposed to have blue eyes?'

Brandon tipped his head to one side. 'Susanna?'

'Mm?'

'Shut up.' He opened his mouth over hers, kissing her

deeply; when he took his mouth from her again, Susanna's face was flushed and her pupils had expanded.

'I want you,' he said softly. 'I want to be inside you.'

'Then do something about it.' Susanna's voice had grown deeper, slightly husky.

He smiled, lifting her slightly and sliding his hand round his cock, positioning its tip at the entrance to her vagina. 'You feel like a furnace.'

'Indeed, Mr Rodgers?' She sank down onto his cock, rubbing her pubis against his. 'How's that?'

'Lovely. Like being wrapped in warm wet silk.'

She pulled a face. 'Oh, Brandon! Can't you think of anything more original?'

'Not when my cock's buried deep inside you, no. And when your breasts are only inches away from my face . . .' He cupped her breasts in both hands, pushing them together. 'God, you're lovely,' he breathed, and lifted his upper body so that he could bury his face in her breasts. 'I love the way you smell, the way you taste, the softness of your skin . . .'

She slid her hands round the back of his neck, massaging it gently, then lifting his head so that she could kiss him. Then she began to move, raising herself slowly so that he slipped out of her, millimetre by millimetre, until the head of his cock was almost out of her, then slamming back down hard, grinding her pubis against the root of his cock.

She flexed her internal muscles against him, squeezing him as she raised herself, then letting herself go fluid as she sank back down on him. She leaned back slightly, changing the angle of his penetration to give them both more pleasure; Brandon continued playing with her breasts as she moved, stroking the soft undersides in the way she liked, and then teasing her nipples, pulling them gently and rolling them between his fingers and thumbs.

Her head fell back as her pleasure grew; Brandon took advantage of the position to kiss her neck, tiny nibbling kisses on the sensitive spots at the side of her neck and the hollows of her collar-bone. His teeth grazed her skin, and Susanna gave a small moan of pleasure.

At last, he felt her quivering round him, gently at first, and then suddenly harder as orgasm splintered through her. He felt a rush of pleasure, and then his own climax poured into her. He wrapped his arms round her, pulling her close to him; she lay with her cheek against his, her eyes closed.

'OK?' he asked softly.

'Mm.' Making love had relaxed her so that she felt like curling up beside him and going to sleep again; though she didn't say as much.

'Are you sure you won't let me go with you to the village? Even if we take it slowly?'

'Absolutely sure. You're staying right here, in bed.' With an effort, she lifted herself from him. 'Maybe you can come with me tomorrow. Though if you're well enough to hike round the hills, you're well enough to handle the train.'

'Or drive.'

She shook her head. 'No. Not that sort of distance. We'll get the train.'

'Yes, Madam.'

She grinned. 'Any more of your cheek, and I'll tie you up in the castle dungeons – and give you a good spanking, as well.'

'That's a promise, is it?'

She laughed. 'No. I think you'd enjoy it too much!'

He wrinkled his nose at her. 'Apart from the fact that neither of us is into those sorts of games, I don't think there are any dungeons here.'

'Really? And there was I, thinking that maybe there was a secret passage from the castle to the village, which would be less steep than that bloody hill.'

' 'Fraid not.'

She kissed him, and climbed out of the bed. 'Right. Shower, first, then the daily hike . . .'

She felt more awake after she'd washed her hair, and had a cold shower, turning the water on full so that the jets were like little needles hitting her skin. As she dried herself, she caught sight of herself in the mirror, and frowned. There was a mark on her neck – just like the mark Brandon had had, and in the same place. No doubt that had been caused by their recent love-making.

And no doubt that had been the cause of the marks on Brandon's neck, too. Love-bites – and they could only have been from Alicia. The tales Alicia had told her made it obvious that the woman was highly-sexed, and an attractive man like Brandon was an obvious target for her desires. Despite Alicia's insistence that she hadn't had a fling with Brandon, there wasn't any other explanation. It couldn't possibly be Molly. There wasn't a warm bone in the housekeeper's body.

She was still thinking about it while she walked down to the village. Why should Alicia lie to her? Or Brandon? And yet . . . something nagged at her. Something wasn't right. She just couldn't put her finger on it – yet.

It was a pleasant day, and she found herself wandering through the pretty little churchyard again, after buying the papers. She was lost in thought when a familiar voice said beside her, 'Still here?'

She squeezed her eyes tightly shut. Thomas Penford. 'Look, just go away and leave me alone, will you? I'm not in the mood for your stories today.'

'She's really got you hooked, hasn't she? You won't hear a word said against her. Just like the last one.'

Susanna sighed. 'Look, I admit that I didn't like her before I met her, but I think I understand her more, now. She's treated me well, especially when you consider that I came here uninvited, and I really think you're taking this "She's an evil vampire" story a bit too far.'

Thomas's eyes were watery. 'I knew she'd trap you. I told you, she always gets what she wants in the end.'

Susanna lifted her chin, and gave him a contemptuous stare. 'I really don't care what you have to say, Mr Penford. Now, will you please leave me alone?'

'As you wish. But ask her about Margaret. Ask her what happened to Margaret, last year.'

Susanna knew that it was a mistake to ask, but the words were out before she could stop them. 'Who's Margaret?'

'*She* said that Margaret was her new secretary. Used to come down to the village and post letters, she did. And the longer she stayed there, the paler and thinner she got. Just like you are – all the bloom gone from her cheeks. It was obvious why. *She* sucked her blood. And then Margaret stopped coming, one day. We never saw her again.'

'Maybe she was ill, and went home.' Susanna was irritated by him. He always had to give a spooky interpretation to anything that happened. 'People do leave jobs because of illness, you know.'

Thomas shook his head. 'Oh, no. The day after Margaret stopped coming to the village, there was fresh ground dug up in that castle. In the gardens, at the back, by the rose bushes. I know. That's where she used to put all her victims. By the rose bushes. Just you look.'

Susanna's patience gave out. 'I don't think that will be necessary. Now, good day to you, Mr Penford.' She turned on her heel and walked at speed out of the churchyard, knowing that the old man wouldn't be able to keep up with her. She didn't stop until she was halfway back to the castle; then, feeling slightly giddy, she sat down, leaning against a tree.

She felt as though she'd run a marathon, and it worried her slightly. She was fit, and she'd been doing this walk every day since she'd been to the castle; even allowing for the fact that she'd taken it faster, this time, she still shouldn't feel that bad. Maybe she *was* coming down with Brandon's virus – in which case, she'd rather be back in London. The idea of Molly looking after her wasn't a pleasant one.

After a couple of minutes, she felt better, and went back to the castle; Molly made her wait at the door for nearly a quarter of an hour before letting her in with a surly look.

Brandon gave a guilty start as Susanna opened thei

edroom door; she smiled at him. 'Would you mind putting my aptop back where you found it?'

He brought it out from under the covers. 'How did you know?'

'Because I know you. You're a workaholic.' She sat down on he bed, and handed him the papers.

'You look as if you're fuming about something. What's appened? A row with Molly?'

'No. It's just that bloody little man in the village – Thomas enford. Every time I see him, he comes out with some tale or ther about Alicia. He knows I don't believe a word of it, so hy doesn't he just shut up and leave me alone?'

Brandon gave a low whistle. 'He's really rattled you, hasn't e? What's he said?'

Susanna scowled. 'He keeps wittering on as if Alicia itends me to be her next sacrificial victim. I mean, first of all, e says that she seduced him when he was a young man – and e's at least seventy, now. Then he rabbits on about all these eople Alicia's supposed to have sucked dry, including her last ecretary . . .' She shivered. 'I just wish he'd leave me alone nd go and bother someone else.'

'Next time, *I'll* get the papers.'

She shook her head. 'It's OK. I'll just ignore him. I don't sually let him rattle me – it's probably because I'm a bit tired. nyway, we'll be back in London in a couple of days, won't e? So we won't ever have to see him again.'

'Yes.' He stroked her face. 'Susanna, you're burning hot. I ope you're not going down with this thing.'

'I'm fine. It's probably just temper,' she lied.

'Right. Well, are you going to let me get up this afternoon?'

She nodded. 'It's a nice day. If you can wheedle lunch out f Molly – or if she'll let me make us both a sandwich – we ould sit in the gardens.'

'Deal.' Brandon handed her the laptop, and vaulted out of ed. 'Yeehah! Out at last!'

Susanna chuckled. 'Oh, really. It's been for your own good, nd you know it!'

Brandon persuaded Molly to let them make som sandwiches, and they spent the afternoon lazing around th gardens. Susanna felt much better by the time they went bac into the castle, and also hungry.

Molly surpassed herself that evening, with crab-fille cannelloni, fillet steak in a brandy and cream sauce, and summe pudding. Susanna was careful to drink no more than a coupl of sips of wine, and stuck mainly to water, ignoring Brandon' slightly amused glances and Alicia's raised eyebrows.

Alicia didn't tell them another story over coffee: the tal was light and inconsequential, and Susanna found hersel growing impatient. She wanted to tell Alicia to stop pussy footing around and – what?

She was annoyed with herself. Honestly. First of all, she ha gate-crashed the castle, demanding to see her lover an virtually accusing Alicia of having an affair with him. The she'd stayed on to nurse Brandon, and kept Alicia away fror her work every evening, listening to her stories of Ambros and the countess. And now she was expecting to be ente tained, like a spoiled child. There was nothing wrong wit light chat. Most dinner parties thrived on them.

Except any party which included Alicia Descourt wouldn be like most parties. There was something about Alicia something that Susanna couldn't quite pin down, but whic made her feel restless and nervous and excited, all at the sam time.

Eventually, Brandon stretched. 'Would you mind if I had a early night? I feel a bit tired. I suppose it's all the fresh air.'

'Probably. It's best not to overdo it too soon,' Alicia sai solicitously.

'Do you want me to come up with you?' Susanna asked.

Brandon shook his head. 'No, it's all right. I'll be fine.'

'Why don't you stay and talk for a bit, Susanna?' Alic invited.

'Are you sure I'm not interrupting your work?'

Alicia laughed. 'No, you're not. I'm not in the mood f

working yet, anyway.' She smiled at Brandon. 'Goodnight.'

'Goodnight.' He smiled at them both, and left the room.

Alicia topped up their coffee cups. 'You've been quiet, tonight.'

'I'm a bit tired,' Susanna said.

'That's not all, though, is it?'

Susanna frowned. 'How do you mean?'

'You're tense. I can sense it. Someone's made you angry, haven't they?'

Susanna sighed. 'Your pal from the village amateur dramatic society. I mean, it's fine for the tourists, and if you hear him just once, it's deliciously creepy. But when he keeps going on and on and on . . . I swear, I'll strangle him, next time!'

Alicia smiled at her. 'Just ignore him. He's an old fool.'

'I know,' Susanna said feelingly.

'Even so, you're tense. Maybe you should have another glass of wine, to help you relax.'

Susanna shook her head. 'I'll be fine.'

'Or I could give you a massage.'

Susanna was very still. Thoughts of what she'd dreamed – or maybe what had actually happened, she still wasn't sure which – came back into her mind. Alicia kissing her way down her body, parting her legs, and . . . She shivered.

'What's the matter, Susanna? Afraid of what I'll do to you?' Alicia's voice was husky. 'Afraid of me touching you?'

Susanna took a deep breath. 'Look – Alicia, will you be honest with me?'

'About what?'

'What happened the other night. The night you told me about Sunil and Ambrose and the countess.'

Alicia shrugged. 'We talked; then you went to bed.'

'On my own?'

'You left the room on your own, yes.'

Susanna sighed. 'Don't play with me, Alicia. What I want to know is – did I end up in the wrong room?'

'Whose room?'

'I don't know his name. And his face . . .' Susanna closed her eyes. 'Christ, this sounds stupid. All right. Cards on the table. I had this dream – at least, I think it was a dream – that I went into the wrong room, and I ended up making love with the man in your painting in the hall. Then you were there, too. Only, the next thing I knew, I was waking up next to Brandon, in our room. So did I dream it all, or did it happen?'

'What do you think?'

'That's just it. I don't know.' Susanna opened her eyes, and stared at Alicia. 'What did happen, Alicia? Did I dream – or was it all real?'

'Why are you so afraid, Susanna?'

Susanna's eyes narrowed. Why wouldn't Alicia answer her question?

Alicia took her hand. 'Why are you so afraid?' she repeated, tracing a tiny complex pattern on Susanna's palm with her fingertip.

Susanna's face set. 'I'm not afraid of anything.'

'You're shaking.' Alicia held her arm up, and Susanna's fingers trembled in the light. 'Trembling as though you're afraid.' Her voice became soft, coaxing. 'There's nothing wrong with being sexually attracted to the same sex, as well as the opposite sex. Nothing wrong at all.'

Susanna swallowed. 'I'm strictly hetero.'

Alicia continued to stroke Susanna's palm. 'Are you?'

'Except in that dream,' Susanna admitted.

'And what happened in your dream?'

'I made love with him. Then I found out that you were watching. You made love to me, while he watched. Then you made love to him.'

'Sounds like quite a night.'

'Mm.' Susanna swallowed hard. 'You said that you like women.'

'And men. Though Brandon – attractive as he is – isn't my type. I like my men dark.'

'As in *café-au-lait* skin?'

Alicia nodded. 'Or just dark hair and Celtic pale skin.'

'The Gothic type.'

'Stop trying to change the subject, Susanna,' Alicia commanded, her voice soft and sensual.

Susanna swallowed. 'Tell me about Ellen.'

'Ellen?'

'Is what Thomas says about you true? Or is it complete fiction?'

'That's two questions.'

Susanna looked Alicia in the eyes. 'Tell me about Ellen. Please.'

'All right. I had a friend, called Ellen, when I was younger. I suppose I was in my early twenties, at the time. We were just friends – then, oh, I don't know. You know how these things happen. We were fooling around together one day – then it got serious, and we started kissing each other. One thing led to another, and we ended up in bed together.' Alicia was still holding Susanna's hand; though instead of tracing the little complex pattern on her palm, she was stroking Susanna's wrist, feeling the little pulse-point beat more and more rapidly.

'The first time, neither of us was really sure what we were doing . . . but we experimented a bit, tried doing things to each other we would have liked someone to do to us . . . and it worked.' She shrugged. 'It got better. We could barely keep our hands off each other. Then I suppose we got a bit careless, took a few too many risks.'

'Like stripping off in the dining room and using a candle on each other?' Susanna's voice was slightly wobbly.

'Oh, that.' Alicia laughed shortly. 'Yes. Yes, I can remember sliding a candle into Ellen's beautiful cunt, and making her beg me to do it harder, faster. And making love with her outside, on a new-mown springy lawn, in the rain. Things like that. All the things you read about in books, we did. Licking cream off each other's bodies, using a dildo on each other, and spending hours with our faces in each other's groins. I loved every minute of it.'

'So what happened?'

'Her family thought I was a bad influence on her. She was rich, you see, an heiress. They wanted her to marry, and carry on the dynasty.' Alicia shrugged. 'She gave in to them, in the end. I suppose her new husband was all right. He was a bit dim, a bit dull and boring, but at least he treated her well. He didn't hit her, or bully her, or humiliate her by screwing around.'

Susanna could fill in the rest of the story. 'So you found it easier not to see her, after she married?'

Alicia nodded. 'I had a couple of affairs, afterwards.' She smiled wryly. 'Actually, I fucked my way round London, to try and forget her. Anyone with a good cock would do.' She sighed. 'You wouldn't do that sort of thing now, of course. Not without protection. But back then – anything went.'

'Sex and drugs and rock and roll?' Susanna quipped.

'Just sex. Lots of it.' Alicia shrugged. 'There were a few women mixed in, as well. Threesomes, group sex. That sort of thing. I suppose we probably smoked a few joints, come to think of it, though we didn't bother with hard drugs. The sex was the important thing.'

'Right.'

'I'm shocking you, aren't I?'

Susanna shook her head. 'No. But it's not my scene – I like having my man to myself – but I know people who are into that sort of thing. It's their life, and if it makes them happy, then so what?'

Alicia stroked her face. 'So are you a rebel at heart Susanna?'

Susanna shook her head. 'I'm very plain and boring. I suppose you'd say that I was into vanilla sex. Brandon and I – well, we've messed around with silk scarves, a little light bondage. Though nothing like spanking or whipping or enemas. I'm not into pain, and neither's he.'

'It depends on the type of pain.' Alicia drew her tongue

along her lower lip. 'And, of course, on how it's done.'

'Maybe. Though it doesn't really interest me. I'm more into the mental side of things. Sex in dangerous places – like in my office.' She flushed. 'And I did have a brief encounter on the train, on the way here.'

'Eat your heart out, Celia Johnson?' Alicia quipped.

'Something like that.'

'And sex under the table, at dinner parties.'

Susanna flushed. So Alicia *had* known what was happening.

'It was pretty obvious. You colour beautifully when you come, and Brandon's face was full of mischief. It wasn't too hard to work out what was going on under the table.'

'Sorry.'

Alicia smiled. 'Actually, it was quite entertaining. You were trying so hard not to show that anything was happening. And all the time, you were dying to call out. You're a noisy lover, at heart.'

Susanna's face turned an even deeper shade of beetroot. 'Oops.'

'I don't mind. And as for your "vanilla sex" – well, there's nothing wrong with it.'

'Or ginger,' Susanna said, before she could stop herself.

Alicia chuckled. 'I wondered if that might interest you.'

Susanna frowned. 'So your story, about Ambrose and Anoushka – it was all for my benefit? To soften me up, make me more receptive to you?'

Alicia spread her free hand in answer, and continued stroking Susanna's wrist.

'What about Margaret?'

'Margaret?'

'Last year. Thomas said she used to post your letters. She looked pale and sickly. Then he didn't see her any more.'

Alicia laughed shortly. 'Oh, that. I got bored doing my own typing. I thought maybe if I dictated into a machine, and got someone else to do the bits I hate – like typing, and filing – then maybe I'd be more productive. Only Margaret was a bit sickly. She caught every cold going – and then some. In the end, I thought it best if we parted company.'

'So you didn't have an affair with her?'

'No.' Alicia's voice deepened. 'I told you, I like little blondes. Margaret was dark – and she was built like an Amazon. That's why it surprised me that she was so sickly.'

'Right.' Susanna swallowed. 'So what now?'

'That's entirely up to you.' Alicia raised her hand to her lips, and kissed it. 'You can leave now, alone – or you can stay here with me for a while longer. We could talk, or . . .' She didn't have to spell it out: Susanna knew what the rest of the sentence would be. Talk, or make love.

Her mouth was suddenly dry. 'Alicia . . .'

'Think of it as a good-bye present. You'll be leaving in a couple of days.'

'Separate worlds, separate lifestyles.'

'Exactly.' Alicia ran the backs of her fingers down the skin of Susanna's neck. Automatically, Susanna tipped back her head, and Alicia stroked the curve of her collar bones. 'There's a mark on your neck,' she said softly.

'Brandon. This morning,' Susanna whispered.

Susanna couldn't see Alicia's smile, but she knew it was there. 'Susanna. You're not drunk, and you won't be forced into anything you don't want to do. If you want me to stop, just say so now.'

Susanna couldn't have said a word, even if she'd tried; she merely closed her eyes. Slowly, Alicia unbuttoned Susanna's shirt; Susanna shivered as her skin was exposed to cool air, and again as Alicia eased the material over her shoulders, letting the garment fall behind her.

'It's all right,' Alicia said softly. 'I'm not going to hurt you. It's just for pleasure, and there are no strings attached for either of us.'

'I know.'

'Then open your eyes. See what I do to you. Watch me, watch my mouth and my hands.'

Alicia's voice was commanding, yet persuasive; slowly, Susanna opened her eyes.

'That's better. You have beautiful eyes. They go grey when you're worried, and brilliant jade when you come.'

Susanna flushed. 'So it wasn't a dream, then?'

Alicia smiled. 'Maybe I'm guessing.' She hooked her fingers into the straps of Susanna's bra, and drew them down slowly. 'I like your taste in underwear,' she breathed. 'I could imagine you in black, or navy – rich, dark colours. But white lace . . . it's so sensual. So much like your skin, pale and delicate . . .' She deftly undid the clasp, and let the lacy bra fall to the floor.

'Your breasts are perfect. Absolutely perfect. Generous, soft and smooth.' Alicia crouched down next to Susanna, leaning her weight on the chair, and cupped Susanna's breasts. 'So very beautiful.'

Alicia's hands felt cool, yet sensual, in the way they stroked Susanna's skin. Susanna ran her tongue along her lower lip.

'I'd like to kiss them,' Alicia said huskily. 'Would you mind?'

Susanna was silent.

'As the saying goes, silence indicates consent,' Alicia said, dipping her head and kissing the soft white globes, her lips cool and gentle. 'Mm. You smell gorgeous,' she said. 'Soft and sweet and powdery. It makes me want to taste you.' She drew her tongue along the undersides of Susanna's breasts, and then finally made her tongue into a hard point and flicked it across the hard buds of her nipples.

Susanna couldn't help a soft moan; Alicia smiled against her skin, and began to suckle one breast, rolling the other nipple between her thumb and forefinger.

Susanna felt her loins heat and grow liquid as Alicia continued caressing her breasts; when Alicia suggested that maybe they should leave the table and go somewhere more comfortable, Susanna was on her feet in seconds.

Alicia didn't make a big show of triumph; she merely led

Susanna to the rug in front of the fire. 'More comfortable for us both,' she said softly.

Susanna bit her lip. She was wearing only her trousers and her knickers – she'd kicked her shoes off, long before, and her bra and shirt were where Alicia had dropped them. Alicia herself was fully clothed. 'I feel like a whore,' she said.

'Why? We're equals.' Alicia looked down at her clothes, and smiled. 'Well, we will be, in a minute.' She turned round, lifting her hair and tipping her head forward. 'Unzip me,' she said softly.

Susanna unzipped the dress, and was suddenly aware that Alicia was completely naked beneath it. She wore no bra or knickers – merely a pair of lacy hold-up stockings.

'I think I'm the one in the whore's outfit, somehow,' Alicia said with a grin as she pushed her dress off her shoulders, stepped out of it, and kicked it to one side. 'And you're the one who's wearing too much.' She helped Susanna out of her trousers, then hooked her thumbs into Susanna's knickers. 'May I? Or would you prefer to do it yourself?'

Susanna flushed beetroot. 'I'm not used to this.'

'I know. That's why I'm taking it gently.' Alicia stroked her face. 'So relax. There's nothing to worry about. Nothing in the world.' Her voice was almost a purr. Slowly, she eased Susanna's knickers down over her hips, then crouched down and drew the material down to Susanna's ankles; gently, she lifted up one foot, then the other, tossing the garment to one side.

'Nearly there.' She smiled, and sat back on her haunches, rolling down her stockings and removing them slowly. Susanna was fascinated. Alicia had beautiful legs, long and shapely; her body was slim, and yet she had generous curves. Clothed, Alicia was striking enough; naked, she was breathtaking. And exactly as Susanna remembered her from the dream – which made Susanna sure, now, that it had all really happened.

Alicia patted the rug next to her. 'Don't stand on ceremony,' she said.

Susanna looked at her feet. 'I'm not. It's a rug, actually.'

Alicia laughed, and Susanna sat down. Alicia took her hand, kissing the palm lightly and folding her fingers over it. 'Friends?' she asked.

'I think so. I wasn't sure, when I first met you, but . . .' Susanna frowned. 'There's still something about you that makes me nervous.'

'Let it go,' Alicia advised softly. 'What you see is exactly what you get.' She cupped Susanna's face, and kissed her, lightly at first and then harder.

The next thing Susanna knew, she was lying on her back, and Alicia was stroking her inner thighs – never quite getting near enough to ease the ache in Susanna's quim. 'Please,' she said softly.

'Please what?' Alicia let her fingers drift nearer to Susanna's musky furrow – and yet still she didn't actually touch Susanna there.

'Make love to me.'

Alicia smiled. 'I thought you'd never ask.' She drew one finger between Susanna's labia, exploring her intimate folds and crevices, and then at last slid it deep inside. Susanna sighed, parting her legs wider and closing her eyes; Alicia began to move her hand back and forth in a slow and easy rhythm, building Susanna's excitement to fever pitch before pistoning rapidly in and out, rubbing her clitoris with her other hand.

When Susanna came, it was as though she were seeing stars, bright flashes of light; her whole body seemed to become liquid, and she cried out in bliss . . .

Sixteen

Susanna woke some hours later, to find herself in a strange bed. She wasn't alone, either – she could hear someone breathing next to her. Cautiously, Susanna turned her head to the side; her eyes widened as she recognized who was lying next to her. Alicia.

She frowned. Alicia had said that she usually worked at night, and slept in the day; how come she was asleep, now? And what the hell was Susanna doing in her bed?

Memories of the evening came back to her, suddenly: the way Alicia had made love to her on the rug in front of the fire. Susanna flushed. God, she'd behaved like a bitch on heat, almost begging for it. She felt guilty at having enjoyed herself so much, with Brandon feeling slightly rough again and lying in their bed alone; and she certainly shouldn't be sleeping here. Brandon needed her more. And as for Alicia's reaction . . . well, she'd have to deal with it in the morning.

She pushed the covers back, careful not to disturb Alicia. She had just about managed to sit up and swing her legs round to the floor when the door opened – and in walked the man she'd dreamed about, the other night. She froze, for a moment: she was completely naked, and she had no idea where her clothes were. Scattered about the castle anywhere between the dining room and Alicia's bedroom, she supposed.

On the other hand, she had nothing to hide. If this was a

dream, it didn't matter, anyway; and if it was reality, he'd already made love to her, and he knew what her body was like. She lifted her chin and stood up.

'Where are you going?' he asked softly, crossing the room and taking her wrist.

'Back to bed. My own bed,' she said, equally quietly.

'Running out on Alicia? She won't be very pleased if she wakes up and finds you gone.'

'I'll explain it to her later.'

He shook his head. 'You can't leave, not now.'

'Are you threatening me?'

'No.' He drew one finger through her cleavage, then curved his hand round to cup one beast. Her nipple peeped out between his thumb and forefinger.

Susanna swallowed. 'Look, I don't know who you are, but I want to go back to bed.'

'All in good time.' He smiled. 'And it also depends whose bed you're talking about.'

'Mine,' Susanna said crossly. 'Mine and Brandon's.'

'Are you sure about that?'

'Yes.'

'I can smell your arousal,' he said quietly. 'Musk and honey and seashore. Your quim's almost weeping in anticipation of what we're going to do together.'

Susanna flushed deeply. How the hell could he tell how aroused she was, when he'd barely touched her.

'If you go back to your own bed, Brandon will be asleep. He's ill – so it's unfair to wake him. Which means that you'll be lying there, your quim aching to be touched, and there will be nothing you can do about it. Except to use your own right hand, maybe – and isn't that a waste, when all you have to do is just ask me?'

'Ask you what?'

His eyes held hers. 'To give you what you need, Susanna, what your body's crying out for. To fill your lovely juicy cunt with my cock. To suck you and fuck you until you've lost count of how many times you've come, spilling your nectar into my mouth and milking my cock dry with the muscles of your beautiful cunt.'

She made a face. 'Now you're being coarse.'

He smiled, his eyes amused yet gentle. 'What would you prefer me to say?'

She turned her head away, refusing to look at him.

'Susanna.' His voice was filled with a heady mixture of promise and amusement and desire. 'You want to make love. Brandon's asleep. Alicia's asleep. I'm awake – and I feel the same way that you do. I want to make love with you. So why fight it?'

She lifted her chin as she turned back to look at him; her eyes glittered with scorn. 'For one thing, I still don't know your name. And don't come out with that crap about your name not mattering. It does.'

'Does it?' He grinned, suddenly. 'Isn't it more exciting, having sex with a stranger?'

Her lips twitched; his good humour was infectious. And he was right – it was a ridiculous situation. 'You should be dressed completely in black, then. And leave me a rose on my pillow, or something.'

He smiled. 'And chocolates?'

'And champagne.'

His voice grew husky. 'I'd like to drink champagne out of you.'

Susanna wrinkled her nose. 'In theory, it sounds nice; in practice, I'd imagine that it's unbelievably painful.'

'There's probably a bottle in the fridge. Alicia usually has some lying around.' He raised an eyebrow. 'Want to try it?'

She shook her head. 'No, thanks.'

'That's a shame. You don't know what you're missing.' He glanced at the bed. Alicia was still sleeping peacefully. 'And I think we'd better continue this elsewhere.'

'Continue what?'

'Our conversation – and whatever happens after.' He drew his tongue along his lower lip. 'When you come, you'll scream loud enough to wake the dead.' Noticing the look on her face, he added, 'And that's in pleasure, not pain.'

'How do you know?' she demanded, still in a whisper.

'I just do.' He took her hand and led her out of Alicia's bedroom. He closed the door behind them.

Susanna pulled her hand out of his. 'Look, I don't exactly relish walking around the castle stark naked. For one thing, it's bloody cold in these corridors; and secondly, what if we bump into someone else?'

'Someone else being Molly, you mean?' He shrugged. 'We won't. She's asleep. We're the only ones awake, right now.'

'How can you be so sure?'

'Trust me.' He grinned. 'I think I prefer you drunk. You're not so argumentative.'

'So it *did* happen.' Susanna's lips thinned. 'I was beginning to think that it had all been just a dream.'

'And Alicia let you think it.' He spread his hands. 'Well, she likes being mysterious. It suits her.' To Susanna's surprise, he unbuttoned his shirt and removed it, putting it on her. It was pure cotton, so soft that it felt almost like silk against her skin; it was still warm from his body, and she could smell his scent, a clean masculine smell which made her want to touch him.

'Better?' he asked.

'A bit,' she muttered, unwilling to let him know how much his scent turned her on.

'Good. Now, are you going to stand here arguing with me, or are you coming with me?'

She was silent; he smiled, and took her hand again. 'Come on, then.'

He led her down the corridor to another room, and opened the door. 'So, Susanna. Come into my parlour.'

'Said the spider to the fly.'

He grinned. 'Scared I might eat you?'

She coloured furiously at the *double entendre*. 'Do you mind?'

'No. I'd like to eat you. I'd like to taste the honey flowing from you,' he informed her, his voice low and sensuous. 'I'd like to lick you all over, like a cat.' He closed the door behind them. 'I want to kiss you and feel your body flower beneath my touch. I want to make you come, again and again and again. I want to pour my body into yours.'

'I get the message,' she said drily.

'So what's it to be? I'm not going to force you to do anything you don't want to do.'

Susanna narrowed her eyes. 'Why did you bring me here?'

'To my bed? Because Alicia's asleep, and I'd like you to myself. If I made love to you there, she'd wake up, and want part of the action – and I'm feeling selfish, right now.' He stroked her face. 'And I don't think your boyfriend's the type to enjoy sharing either. So as I see it, that leaves us with my bed, or my bed. What do you think?'

'I don't know whether to hate you for being arrogant, or to admire your nerve.'

He drew the backs of his fingers across her cheek. 'I'm not that arrogant, when you get to know me. I just want to make love to you, and I'm being very clumsy about asking you. Alicia said that you were full of hidden fire – and you certainly felt good, the other night. I'd like to repeat the experience, and maybe add a few frills.'

She suddenly remembered the way he'd tied Alicia to the bedstead. 'What sort of frills?' she asked suspiciously.

He smiled. 'There's only one way to find out, isn't there?' He kicked his shoes off, and unbuttoned his trousers, easing them over his hips and stepping out of them. He removed his socks at the same time; Susanna's eyes widened as she realized that he was wearing a pair of dark green silk boxer shorts, and the thin material did nothing to hide his erection.

If he noticed the look on her face, he made no comment: he merely stripped off his boxer shorts.

'You should have been a Chippendale,' Susanna said, her lips twitching.

He grinned. 'If that's what you fancy, there's a bow tie in my wardrobe. All you have to do is say, and I'll dress up for you. Anything you please.'

She shook her head. 'I was teasing you.'

'I see.' He paused. 'May I have my shirt back, please?'

Slowly, Susanna removed his shirt, and handed it to him.

'Thank you.' He dropped it on the floor. 'Now. Would you like to talk – or would you prefer to make love?' He pulled the covers off his bed, and lay down, folding his hands behind his head and drawing one knee up slightly. 'Or, even better, shall I make the decision for us?'

She stayed where she was. 'I still don't know your name.'

'Is it really that important?'

'To me, yes. I'm not in the habit of fucking total strangers I've never met before.'

He shrugged. 'We've already met. Twice.'

She shivered. So that night in the village inn hadn't been a dream, either . . .

'And as for what happened between us – we're hardly strangers, Susanna. We know each other very well, in the Biblical sense.'

She flushed. 'Don't twist my words. You know exactly what I mean.'

'All in good time. Come and sit with me.' He smiled appealingly at her.

She knew that she could just turn round and walk out of the door. Nothing was stopping her. And yet . . . there was something about him which compelled her to stay. She remembered Brandon's words about Alicia: she attracted people, but it was like the way a moth was drawn to a flame. Alicia's allure attracted you to something that could destroy you; this man had the same kind of atmosphere about him, a hidden and dangerous feeling that excited her and terrified her at the same time.

Attraction won. She walked slowly over to the bed.

He smiled, his eyes lighting up with pleasure. 'I'm so glad you chose it to be this way.'

She gave a short mirthless laugh. 'Did I have a choice?'

'Yes. Of course you did.' He took her hand, and sucked her ingers, one by one. 'Mm. You taste of Alicia. Mind you, that's ot surprising, considering what you've been doing with her.'

'Thanks a lot.' Her jaw set. 'You make me feel like a tart. A heap one, at that.'

He laughed. 'That's the last phrase I'd use to describe you. 'ou're not cheap, Susanna, and you're not a tart; you simply oze sensuality. Alicia couldn't resist you.' He spread one and. 'Neither can I, for that matter.'

Susanna's eyes narrowed. 'So what's your relationship to licia, exactly? You still haven't told me.'

He sighed. 'God, I wish you didn't want to *know* so much, ll the time. Look, it's complicated. Very complicated.'

Then let's make it simple, Susanna thought. Interview chnique. She was good at interviews – asking open questions hich drew her subjects to talk more. With this one, she'd have keep it to closed questions, probe gently until he gave in and ld her the truth. 'Are you her lover?'

'Yes, I am.'

'And you've been her lover for a long time?'

He nodded.

Susanna thought for a moment. 'You said something about eing her brother – though not in the genetic sense.'

'You remembered that?' He was impressed. 'She said you ad a razor mind. And a good memory, too.'

She shook her head, smiling ruefully. 'You're not going to ll me anything else, are you?'

'To be honest, I don't want to talk about Alicia and me, just ght now. I'm more interested in you.' He licked the inside of er wrist. 'And although you have a fabulous mind, I'm more terested in your fabulous body, at this precise moment.'

She threw her head back, laughing. 'That has to be the orst chat-up line I've ever heard!'

'Maybe – but you're still in my bed. That's the important ing.' He leaned over, rubbing his nose against hers. 'Now,

would you mind leaving the questions until later, an
indulging me in a little carnal relations?'

Slowly, he traced the curve of her shoulders, his fingertip
gliding along her collarbone and dipping into the hollow
beneath it, then across the other shoulder. His hand drifted u
to curve round her throat, his touch still very light an
sensitizing her skin; finally, he cupped her chin, and bent hi
head towards hers.

His kiss was gentle, his mouth nibbling softly at her lowe
lip until her mouth opened, allowing him to slide his tongu
against hers. His hand moved round to caress the nape of he
neck beneath her hair; Susanna's hands moved automaticall
to his back, stroking him and urging him on.

'Mm. I love the way you taste. Sweet and clean,' he sai
breaking the kiss and licking the hollow behind her ear. 'I wa
to kiss you everywhere.'

Susanna swallowed. He'd barely touched her, and yet he
whole body was tingling. He'd suddenly turned from autocr
to lover, and it was unnerving – instead of someone she wante
to fence with, to argue with, he'd become someone she wante
to make love with. Very badly.

'I feel a bitch,' she muttered.

'Hm?'

'Brandon's lying asleep in our bed. I've made love wi
Alicia – and now, here I am with you. I'm like some over-sexe
bitch, not caring where I take my pleasure, as long as someo
makes me come.'

He stroked her face. 'Actually, you do care. Too much.' H
sighed. 'Stop fighting yourself, Susanna. You're not committi
a crime.'

'It feels like it.'

He bit her earlobe. 'Then how about I kiss you until you fe
better? And I promise you, you will feel better.' He let the pal
of one hand rest against her breast, her erect nipple pushi
against him. 'All the places where you ache to be touched,
be licked and sucked and stroked – I'll do it. And you'll fe

so much better, afterwards. So very much better.' His voice was slightly hoarse, and very, very seductive . . .

Susanna still felt like a bitch; but at the same time, her body responded to his lightest touch. She needed to make love – she needed the release of orgasm to stop the ache she felt, deep inside. The way he spoke to her, looked at her, was hypnotic. It tempted her and commanded her at the same time.

She sighed. 'I'm in your hands.'

'Good.' He kissed her lightly, pushing her back against the pillows, and began to kiss his way down her body. He licked the ridge of her collar bone, until she tipped her head back, offering him her throat; he took tiny bites at her flesh, more to arouse than to hurt, and then travelled down to her breasts.

He licked her areolae, making his tongue-tip hard as it brushed against the tiny pimples; he breathed against her nipple, cool air which made the hard buds ache and hurt. Susanna opened her mouth in mute pleading, and he drew one nipple into his mouth, sucking fiercely on it and then paying attention to its twin. She felt his teeth graze her skin, very, very lightly; and then he moved lower, to nuzzle her ribcage, and then her abdomen.

Even before he moved, she knew that he wasn't going to put his mouth to the place where she ached for him to kiss – not yet. He knelt by her feet, picking up one leg and stroking her insteps. Rather than tickling her, it felt wonderful, and she sighed, tipping her head back against the pillows and willing him to move north again.

He nibbled the hollows of her ankle, licking his way up to the sensitive skin at the back of her knee; then he repeated the movements along her other leg. Susanna wriggled against the bed, aching with anticipation; he laughed softly, and kissed her thighs.

Unable to bear it any longer, she brought her hands down to tangle in his hair, and urged him up to her quim. She almost cried out at the first stroke of his tongue along her cleft, the tip of his tongue parting her labia so that he could explore the folds and crevices more easily. The way he licked her was different from the way Alicia had kissed her, less knowing – and yet more sensual.

She was already wet with anticipation, and the movements of his tongue brought her to a swift orgasm, her flesh expanding and contracting rapidly over his mouth. He let his tongue lie flat against her, until the aftershocks of her orgasm had finished, and then slowly eased himself back up her body, kissing and licking her skin as he moved.

'Now?' he asked softly.

Susanna couldn't speak; she merely nodded.

He smiled at her, sliding one hand between them and curling his fingers round his cock, guiding it to her entrance. Her sex felt hot and moist against his glans, and he gasped as she slid her legs round his waist, pressing down on his buttocks with her heels, and lifting her own buttocks at the same time so that he slipped easily into her.

'God, you feel good,' he said. 'Tight and hot and wet. I could melt into you, I really could,'

'So let us melt, and make no noise,' she quoted.

He rubbed his nose against hers. 'Donne. The only problem is, I don't think it's possible for us to make love quietly.'

'No?'

'No.'

The sensuality in his eyes sent a shiver through her body. He really meant it . . . Then he began to move, his lower body moving in tiny oval movements to increase the sensations for both of them.

'Let it go,' he said softly. 'Flow with it.'

Susanna did as he said. She stopped struggling against the riot in her loins and her head, and let it take over. Her reward was immediate, in a bubbling warmth that started at the soles of her feet and rolled upwards to her solar plexus. She cried out in pleasure as she reached her climax, and her legs tightened round his waist.

He stopped then, letting her quim ripple round his erect ock; as the contractions grew weaker, he slipped very gently rom her. 'I haven't finished, yet,' he said.

Susanna swallowed. This was a man with *real* staying ower, she thought. Brandon was good, but this man made him ook like an amateur . . .

Gently, he turned her over onto her stomach, guiding her nto her hands and knees. She tensed for a moment; he rubbed is cheek against her back. 'Don't worry, I'm not planning nything kinky. I know you like it with a dash of vanilla, as hey say.'

'Am I that obvious?'

In answer, he laughed softly, and knelt between her thighs. Ie slid gently back into her quim, then laced his fingers etween hers before beginning to thrust.

Susanna couldn't help crying out as the tip of his cock eemed to touch her cervix, sending wild sensations through er body; he nuzzled her ear. 'What was that you were saying bout making no noise?' he teased.

The only answer she could make was another groan of leasure as he changed the rhythm from slow and easy to hard nd fast, pulling almost out of her and then slamming back in. he began to pant, pushing back against him as he pushed into er; his balls slapped against the lips of her quim, sending xtra shockwaves through her.

He released one of her hands; she suddenly realized his tention when he curved his arm round her body, stroking her igh and then sliding his hand upwards towards her quim. She ied out again as he found her clitoris and began to rub it in a gure-of-eight motion which had her squirming beneath him. he pleasure seemed almost too much; when she came, it felt s though the spasms of pleasure were never going to stop.

She felt the hot rush of his seed inside her; and then the arp puncturing sensation of his teeth in her neck . . .

Seventeen

usanna came to, and found herself lying in Alicia's bed again. licia and the stranger were sitting next to her, looking oncerned. Both of them were naked – as was Susanna herself.

'What happened?' Susanna mumbled, trying to focus and iling.

'You passed out.' Alicia stroked Susanna's hair back from r forehead; her hands felt cool, and Susanna felt grateful for At the same time, Susanna knew that there was something rong. Something very badly wrong. She'd been in *his* room, aking love with him in his bed: so why was she back in licia's room now? How did she get there? Had he carried her?

'My mouth feels terrible,' Susanna said, pulling a face. 'Can have some water, please?'

Alicia helped her to sit up. 'I usually drink fruit juice, if I ake in the night and feel a bit off colour.' She reached over to r bedside cabinet and picked up a glass of red liquid. 'Why n't you try this?'

Susanna's eyes narrowed as she saw the rich ruby colour. uit juice? It looked more like good claret, to her. 'It isn't ine, is it?' she asked suspiciously.

Alicia laughed softly. 'No. It's not.'

'Right.' Susanna looked at it. The only red fruit juice she uld think of was cranberry juice, which she detested; still, ything would taste better than the horrible sourness in her

mouth. She took the glass, and sipped the liquid gingerly. I
wasn't cranberry juice; whatever it was, it tasted slightly rust
a little salty, and she nearly gagged on it.

'Drink it,' Alicia said quietly. 'All of it. It'll make you fe
much better.' She held Susanna's fingers over the glass, tippin
it up so that Susanna had to drink.

When the glass was empty, Alicia smiled. 'Now, that wasn
so bad, was it?'

'No, I suppose not.' Susanna's head began to spin. 'Wh
was it, anyway?' she asked.

'Blood,' the stranger told her, a tender smile on his lips.

'You what?' Susanna's eyes were going out of focus, and sh
wasn't sure what was going on – whether he'd really said wh
she thought he'd just said.

'Blood,' he repeated. 'Mine and Alicia's, mingled, if yo
want to know whose.'

She could hear a heavy throbbing sound. 'What the hell . .
She passed out again, only to wake a few moments late
feeling even worse.

'This isn't funny,' she slurred. 'I want to go home. Now. L
me call a taxi. I want to go home,'

'Shh, it's all right.' The stranger stroked her forehead. 'I
all right. Calm down.'

Something in his tone made her suspicious. 'What have y
done to me?'

He exchanged a glance with Alicia. 'Shall you tell her,
shall I?'

Alicia made a face. 'You, I think. I've done enough talkin

'Right.' He smiled, and took Susanna's palm, stroking h
hand.

She could feel every pulse in his fingertips, and shivere
'Don't. I feel so . . . so . . .' She stopped, not knowing how
describe how she felt. Dizzy, sick, exhilarated and confuse
all at the same time.

'You'll feel better soon. When you're used to it.' He smil
at her. 'I know what you're going through, believe me.'

'How?' she demanded, growing even more convinced that they'd done something to her, slipped her something in that horrible red liquid. What had it been? Some hallucinogenic drug or other, or even poison?

His voice was soft, and calm, and rhythmic; somehow, it soothed her. 'Because I felt like this, when she initiated me.'

Susanna squeezed her eyes tightly shut. What he was saying didn't make any sense. Yet, at the same time, she had a horrible feeling that she knew what he was going to say next. All she had to do was wait to hear him say it. 'Initiated you into what?'

'We're vampires, Susanna. Both of us. Alicia and I – and now you.' He leaned forward and kissed her, just above the temple. 'Alicia initiated me. Now it's my turn to initiate you.'

'Initiate me?' she repeated stupidly.

'Make you one of us. You've drunk our blood; it'll take a while before your body gets used to it. That's why you feel so woozy, right now.'

'As if I had a hundred doses of flu rolled into one.'

'Something like that,' he agreed. 'It won't be long before the blood cells multiply, and you'll become like I am. Like Alicia is.' His eyes glowed. '*Broucolaque*.'

She digested this. Vampires. She could believe it of Alicia, but – who the hell was he? He still hadn't even told her his name . . .

He smiled, as though reading her mind. 'My name,' he said, very softly, 'is Ambrose.'

Her eyes narrowed. 'As in the man in Alicia's story?'

'The very same.' He smiled at her again, his thumb stroking her wrist in a comforting rhythm.

Susanna didn't believe him. 'The man in her story had blue eyes. He lived nearly four hundred years ago.'

'I did,' he agreed smoothly. 'I was born while Elizabeth the First was on the throne – here, in Pentremain, in this castle. And I had blue eyes, before she made me one of her kind.' He smiled. 'Then, I changed. My eyes became green, and my skin became pale.'

'So you're telling me that you're a vampire, that she made you one, and now you're making me one.' Susanna felt light-headed, as though she'd been drinking on an empty stomach. She felt like she could fly – like a bat, a vampire bat. She laughed. 'You're telling me a complete load of bullshit. Vampires don't exist. They're just fiction. Bram Stoker, eat your heart out.'

Alicia came to sit beside her. 'Oh, but we *do* exist.' She picked up Susanna's other hand. 'I'm here. Right beside you. I exist, don't I?'

'So you're telling me that Old Tom was right all the time, and you're actually a vampire?'

Alicia nodded.

Susanna shook her head in disgust, and wished that she hadn't. It caused the blood to thunder in her veins, and the noise was appalling. All her senses seemed to have become magnified, and she wasn't sure that she could cope with it. 'I don't believe you.'

'It's true.'

'But you write vampire stories. You're a very famous Gothic horror writer.'

'Exactly. It's the best disguise,' Alicia said simply. 'I can be myself – and everyone thinks that it's just a publicity stunt, a way of selling more books. Let's face it, you did, when you came here.'

Susanna closed her eyes. 'Now you're teasing me.'

'Look at me.' Alicia cupped Susanna's chin, forcing her to open her eyes. 'Look at me, Susanna.' She opened her mouth, letting her canine teeth grow longer. 'You see?'

Susanna made a small sound of contempt in her throat. 'That could be any old film-maker's trick. Just special effects.'

'It could be – but it isn't. We're vampires, Susanna. And you're one of us, now that you've drunk our blood.'

Susanna shivered. 'How do I know that you're telling me the truth?'

'She is,' Ambrose told her. 'The only thing she hasn't told

you is her real name. Alicia Descourt's her *nom-de-plume*.' Susanna knew what he was going to say, even before he opened his mouth. 'Her real name's Anoushka.'

'Do you mean to tell me that the story you told me over the past few nights is all true? Ambrose, Anoushka and all their adventures?'

Alicia inclined her head. 'Every last word. That's why I said that it wasn't my latest novel.' She paused. 'It wasn't fiction, Susanna. It was the truth.'

Susanna digested this. 'You said that Ambrose was the love of your life, and you were the love of his.'

'True,' Alicia acknowledged, bowing her head slightly.

'Then I don't understand why you want someone else to join you.'

'Sometimes, you need others around you. Others of your kind,' Alicia said simply.

'Why me?'

Ambrose groaned. 'I thought that being like us might stop your questions. Obviously not.'

Susanna's eyes narrowed. 'Why me?' she repeated.

'I had originally intended to have Brandon,' Alicia admitted. 'I thought that he made a nice contrast to Ambrose. Then you turned up.' She shrugged. 'You're more strong-willed than he is. More difficult, asking more questions – and very, very sensual. So Ambrose agreed with me that you would suit our purpose better.'

'Which is?'

'She's already told you. To have another around us, another of our own kind.' Ambrose licked the inside of her wrist, and she shivered. It wasn't the first time he'd done it – but this time, the feelings were so much more intense . . .

'They will be.'

Her eyes widened. 'Did I speak aloud, or did you read my mind?'

'He read your mind,' Alicia said. 'It's part of being a vampire. You'll learn it, too, in time – now that you're one of us.'

'Supposing that I don't want to be a vampire?'

Alicia shrugged. 'It's a little late for that, now.'

'I didn't exactly have a choice, in the first place,' Susanna reminded her.

'It's not all bad, you know. Apart from having a slightly unusual diet and staying out of the sun – and scientists have proved that the sun's bad for you, in any case – it's an interesting life. All your senses are heightened – touch, scent, sound, taste, sight. Your perceptions, too, are deeper.' Ambrose smiled. 'And Alicia's already told you how much better it is, making love as a vampire. How everything's so much more intense, so much more pleasurable.'

'Why don't you show her?' Alicia suggested. 'Then, maybe, you'll convince her.'

Susanna shook her head. 'I don't want you to convince me. I want you both to tell me that this is some sick joke, and to stop playing games with me.'

'We're not playing, Susanna my sweet,' Ambrose said softly, stroking her cheek. 'It's all true. Every last word of it.'

'I don't believe you.' She narrowed her eyes. 'You've fed me some spiked drink, that's all. I feel like hell, right now, but I'll be fine in the morning – or the day after.'

There was a trace of pity in his smile. 'You drank our blood, Susanna. No drugs, no alcohol: just vampires' blood. There's no going back, now.'

She stared at him; he was completely serious. And the way he said it had been so matter-of-fact: no triumph, no gloating or hatred or emotion in his voice. To him, it was just a fact of life – or life-in-death.

'So what happens now?'

He traced her jawline with one finger; Susanna felt as though his flesh melted into her flesh, and they became as one. She could feel his pulse against hers, the dull insistent throbbing of his blood through his skin – and she was shockingly aware of how much it aroused her.

'What happens now—' his voice was whisper-soft

promising passion and lust and raw need '—is the next part of your initiation.'

He drew his tongue along his lower lip, and Susanna itched to touch the tip of her own tongue to it. The nausea and giddiness seemed to be disappearing, now, and she felt full of some weird kind of energy. She smiled, tipping her head back slightly, as though offering her throat to him. 'The next part?'

Very slowly, he ran one finger down the curve of her throat, letting it drift down through the valley between her breasts. Her nipples tightened with anticipation, the areolae darkening and the skin puckering as the tissues of her nipples hardened and grew erect. She drew a sharp intake of breath and closed her eyes, imagining what it would be like if his fingertips actually touched her breast. Or his mouth, sucking gently on the hard peaks, his tongue caressing her . . .

Alicia's eyes gleamed. 'I *knew* you'd be this responsive,' she said softly. 'I knew it.'

Susanna's eyes snapped open, and she glared at the other woman. 'This is all just entertainment to you, isn't it?'

'No.' Alicia spread her hands. 'If you would prefer me not to watch, I understand.'

'This time.' The words were out before Susanna could stop them.

Alicia laughed. 'I couldn't have chosen you better if I'd gone to London and found you myself! Next time, it'll be the three of us together, bound in pleasure . . .' She arched her back like a cat. 'Mm. I think you're a woman of my own heart, Susanna.'

'Your own blood, too,' Susanna said wryly. She turned to Ambrose. 'I know what you meant now, when you said that there's more than one sort of brother.'

He nodded slowly. 'We're not of the same parents, but we're of the same blood.'

Alicia slid off the bed. 'I'll leave you to it, then.'

Susanna had a sudden panic-stricken thought. 'Where are you going?'

Alicia smiled. 'Not to take it out on Brandon, if that's what you're thinking. I'm going to my study, to do some work.' She shrugged on a robe, walked over to the doorway, then turned round to look at Susanna, spreading her hands. 'I told you, I write at night. And I *do* have a novel to finish, in case either of you have forgotten what I'm supposed to do for a living.'

'Right.' Ambrose smiled at her. 'We'll come and get you, when we're ready.'

She blew them a kiss, and left the room; Ambrose moved to lie beside Susanna. 'So now it's just you and me. For a little while.'

Susanna felt strangely shy; and yet she couldn't bear to make herself a fool in his eyes by snatching up a sheet to cover her body.

Again, it was as though he read her mind. 'Susanna, there's nothing to worry about. You've gone through the pain of your body changing. And now, you're going to learn its pleasure.' He took her hand. 'Touch me.'

'Where?'

He grinned. 'Anywhere you like.'

'As long as it's your cock?'

'Eventually, yes.' He gave her a sensual pout, then appraised her body. 'It certainly suits you, being *broucolaque*.'

'Hm?'

'You look like an angel. A dark kind of angel. Your hair's like molten gold, and your skin's pure white. Luminous.'

Susanna looked at her body, and was shocked to discover that he was right. There wasn't a mark on her body; the slight tan she'd obtained from the summer had gone, as had the sprinkling of tiny moles on her arms. She looked as though she'd been made from marble or ivory, and her skin almost glowed. It was like some weird incandescence surrounded her.

'Like moonlight,' he suggested, reading her thoughts.

She looked at him, seeing him through different eyes. He had white skin, too, glowing with that same weird incandescence. His eyes gleamed with a similar light, a bright green which looked as if they could see to the depths of her soul. 'Like you,' she said softly.

He nodded. 'It's not just sight, either. It's sound – I can hear your heart beating, and hear when it speeds up or slows down. And scent.' He looked at her, his expression teasing and affectionate. 'Close your eyes and tell me what you can smell.'

She did so, frowning. 'Honey and seashore,' she said eventually. 'Something sharp, and something sweet, and something a bit musky.'

'That's you. And me. It's our arousal, our bodies telling us to melt into each other.' He smiled. 'Taste and touch, too, are different. Touch me, Susanna. Taste me. Feel what we can give each other.' He turned over onto his back, spreading his body in blatant invitation. Susanna was aware of a pulse beating strongly between her legs; if it was possible to orgasm just at the thought of what was going to happen, she was going to do it right then, she thought.

'No,' he corrected gently. 'This is just for starters. But believe me, the first time you come, as a vampire, it's like nothing on this earth.'

She shivered.

'Let me show you,' he said softly. 'Let me take you through the next stage, show you how much pleasure you can have . . .'

She nodded, deciding to trust him, and shifted to kneel beside him. She rested the fingertips of one hand on his chest; the light sprinkling of hair had an amazing texture, compared with the softness and smoothness of his skin. His body seemed to glow in the dim light, his skin radiant and the interplay of his muscles as he breathed fascinated her. God, he was beautiful, Susanna thought. Physically perfect, from his lean and muscular body to the slightly overlong hair to his beautifully sculpted cock.

She wasn't sure how long she stayed there, absolutely still, just watching him and feeling the way his skin pulsed under her fingertips. It could have been hours. Time no longer had any meaning for her, no longer mattered.

She let her hand drift down over his abdomen; he closed his eyes, holding his breath for a moment in expectation of the way she would curl her fingers round his cock. She smiled as she caught his thoughts: not yet. She wanted to know the rest of him, feel him and taste him, before they made love. She bent her head, resting her cheek against his chest; he felt so good. He smelt good, too: clean and masculine, and then the tang of his arousal, so sharp she could almost taste it.

'Pheromones,' he said softly. 'You can sense them more acutely, now.'

'Mm.' She turned her head slightly, and touched the tip of her tongue to his skin. God, he tasted good. She could even taste a hint of his blood through his skin, a rusty and sensual taste which made her want to lick him, use her teeth so that a thin trickle of blood flowed over her lips . . .

He laughed. 'No, Susanna, you won't need my blood again. Though it might amuse you to exchange a few cells with me, from time to time.'

Only an hour before, the idea would have been repugnant. Now . . . She smiled, and kissed his throat. Humouring her, he tipped his head back so that she could explore his throat properly, licking his skin and giving him tiny erotic nips on the sensitive spots at the side of his neck.

'You're a fast learner,' he breathed.

'Mm.' She rubbed her cheek against his, then brought her mouth down very gently over his. She licked his lower lip, delighting in the softness of his skin; then, when he opened his mouth, kissed him more deeply, exploring his mouth. The kiss seemed to go on for ever; when she lifted her head, they were both shaking.

'God. It's almost like *you're* the one initiating *me*,' he said huskily.

Susanna swallowed. 'I almost came just from kissing you.'

'I told you it was good.' His eyes glittered. 'And believe me, it gets better.'

She moved to straddle him, letting her quim rest on his

rect cock. She could feel every vein, every fold of skin, gainst her, and it made her shiver.

Ambrose cupped her breasts; she cried out as his thumbs ightly stroked her nipples. He was right: her senses were eightened, and the light caress made every nerve-ending cry ut for more. He raised his upper body and smiled at her, then, is eyes a deep and sensuous green. She knew what he was oing to do, and tipped her head back, sliding her hands in his air as he bent his head to one breast. He stayed millimetres way from her, just breathing on her nipple, and her whole skin ingled; the scent of honey and seashore became stronger.

God, she wanted him to touch her, so much! She almost roaned in the agony of waiting; and then, at last, he licked her reast, his tongue-tip circling her areola and then flicking apidly across her nipple. Her clitoris seemed to twitch in ympathy, and she cried out again, digging the pads of her ingertips into his scalp and pushing her breasts against him. he felt him laugh softly against her skin, and then he began o suck.

Susanna had always enjoyed having her breasts kissed and ouched, but this was something else. All her nerve-endings eemed to ripple, wave after wave of sensation concentrating ound her nipple, where Ambrose's mouth touched her skin, hen pushing outwards to arouse her whole body.

He slid one hand between their bodies, stroking her bdomen and then pushing his hand between her thighs; the econd that his questing finger touched her clitoris, she cried ut, the sensation was so good and so sharp. When he began o rub her, she shook, hardly able to bear the intensity; nowing how she felt, he straightened up, letting her sink her eeth into his shoulder to stifle her cries of pleasure.

When he'd brought her to the edge of orgasm, he lifted her lightly, pausing in his caresses to position the head of his cock t the entrance to her vagina. She lowered herself gently onto he rigid muscle, feeling her internal muscles contract sharply ound him. Her blood seemed to be fizzing in her veins, and every nerve-end was overloaded with sensation: it was th most incredible thing she had ever felt, and she wanted it to g on and on and on for ever.

He rubbed his cheek against her. 'I told you it was good,' h whispered, 'and this is just the start. Fuck me, Susanna. Rid me hard. Let it all go.'

He sank back onto the bed, his hands sliding down t support her; Susanna almost laughed with the sheer joy of i and began to move, lifting herself gently upwards and the slamming down hard, grinding her pubis against the root of hi cock. She moved her lower body in small circles, flexing he internal muscles round him; as she bore down on him, he tilte his pelvis, pushing up so that he was enveloped by her so flesh to the hilt.

All of a sudden, Susanna felt the familiar beginnings c orgasm: but this time, as Ambrose promised, it was far mor intense. The warm rolling pleasure in the soles of her fe made her skin tingle; as it slowly moved through her body, sh felt as if her whole being was concentrated on it, her enti body contracting and convulsing in pleasure. As it coiled u her spine and exploded, her body became a thousand sta imploding, a mass of pulsing energy, and she howled alou with the sheer joy of it.

'Woman wailing for her demon lover,' Ambrose said softl and cried out himself as the contractions of her intern muscles brought him to his own release.

She sank down, resting her head against his shoulders; h wrapped his arms round her. 'OK?' he asked softly, nuzzlin her ear.

'Mm. You were right. It was like nothing on earth.'

He chuckled. 'And indoors, too.'

She pulled back enough to meet his eyes. 'What's th supposed to mean?'

'The night is our element, Susanna.'

She suddenly caught his meaning. 'And tonight we celebra – as you and Anoushka did, when you got the castle back?'

'Something like that. Though only if you want to.'

Susanna felt more alive, more vibrant than she'd felt in years. She smiled. 'Oh, yes, I want to.'

'But?' he prompted.

'What makes you think there's a "but"?'

He grinned. 'Because you never stop asking questions.'

She grinned back. 'OK. What I want to know is – would Alicia mind?'

'I don't think so.' He stroked her face. 'Though I think she'll want our undivided attention, a little later – to make up for being left out of it this time.'

'Right.'

He smiled. 'And the rest of it?'

'I've been thinking. You, Alicia . . . I'm not the first person you've wanted to join you, am I? There was Sunil.'

Ambrose shrugged. 'He wasn't right for us.'

'What about Edward?'

'Neither was he.'

'But Alicia let him stay here, for years and years – according to Thomas. To make up for losing Ellen, that is.'

'Mm. She has whims. Edward was one of them, and I respected that.' His eyes glittered. 'Any more questions?'

'No.'

'For now,' he added wryly.

'For now,' she agreed. She stood up, stretching like a cat. He laughed. And she tipped her head on one side. 'What's so funny?'

'When I took you to my room, you were Ms Prim-and-Proper, worried about what Molly would think if she saw you walking down the corridor with me, naked. And now . . . you're not in the slightest bit self-conscious.'

'No.' Susanna paused. 'What about Molly, though?'

'She'll be fine. Now she knows that you're the one Milady wanted. Oh, and before you ask, the reason why we have separate rooms at the moment is because Alicia prefers it, when we have guests and we have plans for them.'

'Right.'

'Don't think,' he advised her quietly. 'Now's not the time for thinking. It's a time for sheer, mindless, hedonistic sex. Celebrating the loss of your virginity as a *broucolaque*.'

Susanna laughed; it was Ambrose's turn to tip his head on one side and ask, 'What?'

'It's just that you're very direct.'

He stroked his cock. 'Oh, yes.'

She grinned. 'Then lead on, Macduff.'

'Actually, it's "lay on". And that's rather more appropriate, for what I had in mind . . .'

Laughing, they left the room, and Ambrose led her down the corridors. They climbed the narrow stone staircase to the battlements, and Ambrose led her into the night.

It was a cold crisp night, although Susanna didn't feel chilly. She was more aware of the feel of the wind against her skin, the scent of the night. She closed her eyes, concentrating on one sense at a time: scent, breathing in the night air and feeling it fill her lungs. Taste, opening her mouth and tasting the crispness of the air. And finally, she looked up and saw the stars.

'That's the best part of living in the middle of nowhere. No light pollution, like you get in the cities. And this,' Ambrose said quietly, 'was how the sky looked when I was your age. And how Byron saw it.'

'It's beautiful.' Susanna swallowed. 'Breathtaking.'

'I know.' He stood behind her, wrapping his arms just around her rib-cage and letting her lean back into his body as she looked up at the stars.

Susanna remained there motionless, for a while, and then she realized that he was stroking the soft undersides of her breasts. She closed her eyes, letting her head sink back onto his shoulder. He shifted so that he could kiss the curve of her shoulders, running his tongue along her skin and following it up with tiny nibbly kisses which made her knees buckle.

Ambrose spun her round, taking her in his arms and kissing her properly, his tongue exploring her mouth and his hands running down over her back to cup her buttocks, squeezing gently before moving on, stroking her to fever pitch.

He sank to his knees, parting her thighs and licking her quim until she cried out, losing her balance; then he pulled her down to join him so that she straddled him, half sitting on his thighs, with her feet flat on the floor. He shifted slightly, letting his cock slide into her; she groaned, and buried her face in his shoulder. 'God, Ambrose, you feel so good,' she murmured against his ear.

'I should hope so, too,' he teased, thrusting into her; then, with one deft movement, he leaned forward, wrapping her legs round his waist and laying her onto the flagstones.

There was a time, once, when Susanna would have yelped at the touch of the freezing stone against her skin; this time, she merely laughed, and locked her legs tightly round him, urging his thrusts on with the pressure of her heels against his buttocks.

As they came, Susanna tipped her head back and let her cries ring out freely; Ambrose smiled his approval, then stopped her mouth with his own. He lay buried in her, still, until the aftershocks of her orgasm had dimmed, and her face was dreamy.

'Welcome to the night,' he said softly, rubbing his nose against her. 'And now – I believe Anoushka is expecting us.'

With regret, she untangled her limbs from him, letting him ease his way out of her; he stood up, helping her to her feet. 'OK?'

She nodded. 'OK. Better than I'd expected.'

He ruffled her hair. 'I told you so. Everything's going to be fine, now. You're with us.'

He led her back down to the castle corridors, and through to Alicia's study. He walked in without knocking, to Susanna's surprise; Alicia sat at the far end of the room, by a deep red velvet-curtained window. As she became aware of their presence, she closed the file she was working on, and turned round.

It was a room Susanna had never been in before; she couldn't help staring round it. There was a bookcase next to Alicia's desk – Susanna supposed that the books crammed in it were Alicia's most-used reference books, kept there to save her having to go all the way down to the library when she needed them – and her desk was simply a plain table, containing a state-of-the-art computer and printer. There was a filing cabinet on the other side of the desk, and that was it.

'Surprised?' Alicia asked.

Susanna nodded. 'I wasn't expecting you to have such a – well – such a minimalist study.'

Alicia smiled. 'I have to, I'm afraid. I'm distracted too easily. This is just enough for me to work with – and most of the time, I keep my modem disconnected. It's too easy to play with the Net, and waste good working time.'

'Right.'

Alicia looked at her lover, then at Susanna. 'Well?'

Ambrose nodded. 'Now, she's one of use.' His face suddenly darkened. 'Or she will be, when she's done one last thing.'

Susanna frowned. 'What's that?'

Ambrose shrugged. 'To be a vampire, Susanna, you need to learn to kill.'

Eighteen

Kill?' Susanna repeated stupidly.

'You have to kill,' Ambrose said, this time more gently. Otherwise you'll starve.'

'But Alicia ate normal food.'

Alicia smiled. 'You don't need fresh meat, all the time.)ccasionally we go vegetarian, just for the hell of it.'

'You're really teasing me, now.' She smiled back. 'Alicia. I now you're broad-minded, but I feel a bit guilty.'

'For fucking my lover?' Alicia shrugged. 'You did it with ıy blessing.'

Susanna nodded. Alicia really was the most outrageous 'oman she'd ever met. In some ways, she would have liked to et Kate and Alicia together. *That would be one hell of a meeting*, he thought, the two most outrageous women she knew, trying) outdo each other. She smiled. 'I don't know what the hell ou put in that red stuff, but it was absolutely dynamite. I ssume I'll be back to – er – normal, tomorrow?'

'This is tomorrow, Susanna,' Alicia said softly. 'Tomorrow nd tomorrow and tomorrow . . .'

Susanna's smile faded. Alicia sounded almost as jaded as ıe king she'd just quoted. 'You mean, you're not joking about ıis vampirism thing? You didn't just feed me some drug or ther in that drink?'

'It's all true, Susanna. You need to kill. Just every so often, when you're growing weak and need a fresh surge of life.' Ambrose's eyes held hers. 'It's your choice. You can kill your first human, and live like us – or you can starve, and die. It's entirely your choice.'

She knew almost before they stood up where they were going to take her. To Brandon's room.

'It's easy,' Ambrose said. 'All you do is put your mouth to the pulse in the neck. Let your teeth sink into the skin, so very slowly – then suck. Feel the warmth of his life flowing into your mouth, soothing the ache in your belly.'

Susanna shivered. His words made her feel nauseous. Kill the man she loved? And yet – it was true, she did have an ache in her belly, an indefinable hunger. 'I . . .' She swallowed. 'Look, don't laugh at me, but I don't think I could stand you watching me.'

'It's your first time. You need us there, for support and guidance,' Alicia said.

She shook her head. 'Please. I need to do this on my own

Ambrose put his hand on Alicia's arm. 'Leave her,' he sai softly. 'We'll know if she needs us.'

Slowly, Susanna opened the door, and went inside. Sh closed the door behind her, then bolted it, for goo measure, although she suspected that Ambrose and Alicia Susanna couldn't quite get used to the idea of calling he Anoushka – could open the door any time they chose, bolte or not.

She walked over to the curtains, opening them and the unlatching the window. The night air streamed in, cold an crisp; she closed her eyes, drinking in the scent and taste of th night, as she had on the battlements with Ambrose. He wa right. Everything was so much richer, as a vampire, so muc more sensual. Everything from tasting the night, to makin love, to breathing. She was aware of every muscle, every por every beat of blood in her veins.

She opened her eyes again, looking out at the stars. The were so bright, they almost hurt; and she could see pattern he'd never really noticed before, as well as her old favourites: Cassiopeia, the Pleiades and Orion.

Taking a deep breath, she dragged her eyes away from the tars and went over to the bed. Brandon lay there, sleeping; he was naked, and had obviously fallen asleep while waiting for er to come to bed. The covers were pushed partly back, and e was lying on his side, almost rolling onto his stomach, one rm curved up as though he were cuddling some invisible body ext to him.

God, he was beautiful, she thought. He was the man she'd roken every single one of her rules for. No mixing of business nd pleasure, she'd always said; then she'd gone to interview omeone for a feature, and he'd been there, working on the ouse. She'd fallen for him on the spot, and ended up going for drink with him – and then back to his flat.

No sex on a first date. And yet when Brandon had un-ressed her, that night, she'd made no protests. If anything, he'd helped him. She smiled wryly. In Brandon, she'd found a oul-mate. Someone so in tune with the way she thought, the ay she felt – and someone who felt the same. She'd moved in ith him, a week later, not caring that everyone frowned, ying she ought to get to know him a bit better first. She knew nough about him to know that she wanted to be with him.

They'd had such good times. Not just the sex: they'd shared lot of laughter, too. Like the time Brandon had taken her to a oetry reading – the work of a friend of a friend. They'd sat on e front row, and then the poet had come in – dressed ompletely in black, with a large black angora cardigan flung er the top. He'd worn a lot of silver and a lot of amber; his air had flopped over his forehead, and he'd worn little round asses. Susanna and Brandon hadn't been able to look at each her, knowing that they'd burst into giggles.

When the poet actually started speaking, Susanna had had feign a coughing fit. It wasn't just the way that he murdered s own work, emphasizing too many words and overdoing the bilants – it was the way he'd held the book at arm's length,

and rocked back and forth as he read, his groin coming close
and closer to Susanna's face.

Brandon had parodied it later that night, she remembered
At home, naked – though he at least had chosen decent poetr
to read. Some of Donne's most erotic works; and eventuall
he'd moved close enough for Susanna to lean forward and tak
his cock into her mouth. Brandon had continued declaimin
poetry, concentrating hard on the words and pretending t
ignore what Susanna was doing to him; in the end, he ha
groaned and dropped the book, twining his fingers int
Susanna's hair and urging her on as she fellated him.

Susanna sat on the edge of the bed, stroking his forehead. I
hadn't all been nights out, followed by wild sex. Sometime
they'd had an evening in, watching an old film and sharing
tub of ice-cream. Though inevitably, while they'd both bee
sprawled full-length on the sofa, Brandon's hand had sli
under her top to caress her stomach, then slowly inserted itse
into her bra, pulling the cups down so that he could stroke he
breasts. She'd felt his erection pressing against her buttock
and pushed back against him, rubbing herself against his bod

The film had been forgotten, then, and they'd ended u
undressing each other, caressing each other's bare skin an
finally making love, Brandon sitting on the sofa and Susann
kneeling over him, her breasts pushing into his face as sh
moved over his cock.

'Oh, Brandon,' she said softly. Making love with Ambros
had been good – but it wasn't quite the same as making lov
with Brandon. With Brandon, it had been as much a mental a
a physical thing; she couldn't bear to think that it would nev
happen again.

Kill him, or die herself. It was such a clear-cut choice. N
grey edges, no room for negotiation.

She leaned over, drinking in his scent. It was so aching
familiar, and so much more intense; she could have cried. Wh
was he the one she had to drain? Why couldn't she have
mortal lover for years and years, like Alicia had? Though at th

same time, it would be like watching him die slowly, over the years – all the time knowing that she was immortal.

He stirred, and turned over, opening his eyes. 'Susanna.' He smiled at her. 'I dunno, you're becoming as bad as Alicia – up all night.'

It was too close to the truth for comfort. She simply shrugged.

'I've kept the bed warm for you.' His voice was throaty, betraying his arousal; Susanna shivered. To make love with Brandon, one last time . . . surely Alicia and Ambrose wouldn't deny her that?

She reached out, stroking his cheek. The contours of his face were so familiar; and yet, at the same time, alien to her.

He took her hand, sucking her fingers one by one; she'd always found it erotic before, but now, as a *broucolaque*, she found it incredible. The way he sucked, the rhythm meeting the same pounding beat as her blood. The feel of his tongue against her fingers; and then against her palm . . .

She tipped her head back, closing her eyes and willing him to continue. Brandon laughed softly, and kissed her wrist, touching the tip of his tongue to her pulse; her breathing quickened, and he pulled her down onto the bed beside him.

She felt the bed move; then she realized that Brandon had shifted to kneel at her feet, and had pushed the bedclothes back completely.

'You'll get cold,' she protested.

'Then warm me,' was his laughing response.

'Brandon, I mean it . . . you've been ill.'

'Stop worrying. I'm fine.' He smiled at her. 'I want to make love to the woman of my dreams. Any objections?'

Only that I'm supposed to kill you instead, Susanna thought wryly. 'No.'

'Good.' He lifted one foot, massaging the sole; Susanna could have purred, it felt so good. He worked his way up her leg, stroking her skin in a way which would have aroused her in the past, and drove her completely wild now. Every nerve-end, every pore and muscle and millimetre of skin was more sensitive; and the pleasure of it made her want to laugh with sheer joy, or howl with triumph, she wasn't sure which.

He followed his hands with his mouth, covering her skin with kisses; she quivered with anticipation, scenting his arousal as well as feeling it, and desperately wanting him inside her.

'God, you feel so good,' he said, drawing his finger the length of her quim.

She shivered. 'So do you.' She wanted him badly – and yet, at the same time, she wanted to prolong this, to make it really good for both of them. She sat up, resting one hand on the nape of his neck and tangling the other in his hair, drawing his mouth down to hers.

He tasted as she remembered: clean, male and spicy. Again, it was more intense: the feel of his tongue pushing against her own, the way he nibbled at her lower lip. He made a trail of kisses across her cheek, and she tipped her head back; he kissed his way down the sensitive cord at the side of her neck, licking and nipping gently.

Her nipples ached so much to be touched, to be kissed, that she arched her back, pushing her breasts towards him. He chuckled. 'Three guesses as to what you want, hm?'

She smiled, blowing him a kiss. 'You know me so well, Brandon. You know exactly what I like.'

'Tell me anyway.'

'I'd like you to lick my breasts and suck my nipples. I'd like you to use your mouth on me, give me pleasure. I'd like you to suck my fingers and my palm, giving me a hint of what's to come. Then I'd like you to kiss your way down my body; then rub your face against my thighs: then breathe on my quim until I start wriggling and pushing towards you. Then I'd like you to draw your tongue along my quim, exploring the folds and crevices of my labia, before flicking your tongue rapidly across my clitoris. While you're working on my clitoris, I'd like your finger sliding into me – no, make that two fingers – and want you to keep going until I come, my juices running over our hands. Then I want you to lick my juices off your skin; nd kiss me, letting me taste myself on you.'

'Well, that's explicit enough.'

She grinned. 'Though I'm sure you can improvise on the cene.'

'I could indeed.'

She looked archly at him. 'Well, what are you waiting for, en?'

He smiled, and sat opposite her, taking her palm. Keeping is eyes fixed on hers, he kissed the soft flesh at the heel of er palm, biting it gently, before taking her thumb into his outh and sucking it, letting it slide back and forth between s lips. He gave each finger in turn the same treatment, irroring the suction of her sexflesh when his cock was buried eep inside her.

A shiver of anticipation ran down her spine, and he dropped kiss in the centre of her palm, curling her fingers over it, efore working his way up her arm. He lingered over the pulse her wrist and the soft skin at the crook of her elbow, before bbling his way over her upper arm to her shoulder.

He breathed in her sweet powdery scent; she tipped her ead to one side, and he buried his face in the curve of her eck, his lips playing lightly over her skin. She swallowed hard desire lanced through her: this was a game where she had be patient, letting him arouse her slowly to fever pitch. She d all the time in the world.

Though if she did what Alicia and Ambrose wanted her to , Brandon most definitely didn't. She squeezed her eyes ut, trying not to think of that, and forcing herself to ncentrate on what he was doing to her and how good it felt.

He licked the hollows of her collar bones, then slowly oved down over her breasts. He breathed on her nipples, not tually touching them with his lips or taking the hard peaks flesh into his mouth; she had to force herself not to tangle r fingers in his hair to pull his mouth down to her skin.

Gently, he eased her backwards, working a trail down he
body. He nuzzled against her abdomen, and she felt desire kic
sharply through her. Exactly as she'd asked him to, he rubbe
his face against her thighs, taking in the spicy musky scent o
her arousal, and brought his lips to within half an inch of he
quim. Susanna gasped as he breathed on her warm moist flesh
and wriggled slightly, pushing towards him.

He moved back, and she almost howled with frustratio
'Brandon . . .'

Hearing the note of urgency in her voice, he shifted positio
and slid his tongue gently along her quim, tasting the salt
tang of her. 'Mm. Seashore and honey,' he murmured, flickin
his tongue across her clitoris and teasing the little bud of fles
from its hood.

They'd done this so many times before, in so many differe
places, but it had never grown stale for Susanna: and now, wi
her senses heightened, it seemed even better. She reached u
to grip the headboard, her knuckles whitening as she clung
it. Exactly as she'd specified, Brandon slid first one then tw
fingers into her, moving gently at first, then varying the pac
and rhythm, working her up to a pitch then slowing down aga
before he brought her over the edge to orgasm. Again a
again, she was a hair's breadth away from coming, whe
Brandon stopped, stroked her hair, and let her calm dow
before starting again. Just when she could take no more, a
was about to beg him to let her come, pleasure explod
through her. She cried out, squeezing her eyes shut, and sa
back against the pillows.

Brandon tapped her gently on the cheek so that she open
her eyes again, then licked her glistening juices from h
fingers. He bent down to kiss her, nibbling her lower lip.

'You taste of me,' she said languidly.

'Mm. Good?' he asked, shifting to cuddle her.

'Mm.' How good, he'd never know: it felt like a thousa
tiny orgasms fizzing on her tongue. No wonder Alicia a
Ambrose enjoyed making love so much.

He tucked her into his shoulder, holding her close. She lay uietly beside him, one leg curled over his, her hands idly roking his skin.

'What are you thinking?' he asked.

How I can possibly bear to kill you? 'Nothing,' she said, uzzling against his chest.

'Nothing?'

'All right. If you must know, I have this overpowering urge —' *To suck your blood, to feed on you.* She swallowed hard, queezing her eyes shut.

He stroked her cheek. 'Shy? That's not like you.'

She laughed. 'No. I just don't want to overdo it, in case you ve another relapse.'

'But at the same time, you like good sex, and lots of it?'

'Something like that.' And blood. Feeling a life-force gainst her mouth, feeling it trickle down her throat and warm e ache in her belly. God, God, God, this was nothing like e'd expected. Ambrose hadn't warned her about this – and either had Alicia.

There was something else which might help, even if it was ly temporary... She smiled, and ran her hand over his est, tracing his muscles and then drifting down to caress his bcage. She could hear his heart racing, a rapid and strong unding, and forced herself to block it out: the sound of blood his veins would be too much for her to handle, as she felt ght then, and she wasn't sure how good her self-control was. She concentrated on touch and taste and scent instead, eathing in the scent of his arousal. It was so strong that she uld almost taste it; she touched the tip of her tongue to his idriff, and almost gasped at the sharp tang of his skin.

'Good enough to eat, hm?'

She flushed scarlet. Had he guessed? Were the changes in r so obvious that he could tell?

He mistook her blush for something else. 'Susanna, don't ll me you're becoming shy with me, after all this time?'

She shook her head. 'Just being stupid, that's all.'

He shifted so that he could kiss her. 'I love you.'

'You, too.' She rubbed her nose against his; the famili gesture of affection was somehow more erotic, to her ne senses.

'Make love to me, Susanna,' he suggested huskily.

She smiled, kissing her way back down his body. She ra her tongue along the length of his shaft, and was thrilled by th way that his cock quivered under her mouth. She had a feelin that another act she'd always enjoyed was about to be revelation to her. 'Like this, you mean?'

'Mm.' He closed his eyes in bliss, tangling his fingers in h hair and stroking her scalp as she lapped at his skin. H couldn't help a soft moan of pleasure as she slid her lips ov his glans, first concentrating on the sensitive groove at its ba with the tip of her tongue, and then letting her lips slide slow down the shaft.

He tasted good, of raw sex and clean masculinity. His sk was so thin on his cock that she could almost taste the bloo through it; she forced the thought out of her mind, licking a sucking him until Brandon was writhing underneath her, a crying out with pleasure. She continued fellating him, pushi her tongue-tip into the small eye at the top of his penis a relishing the tang of the clear fluid weeping from it.

Finally, she felt his balls lift and tighten, and then war salty fluid gushed into her mouth. The slightly acrid salty ta was near enough to Ambrose's blood to keep her bo satisfied; she swallowed every last drop.

She shifted up the bed to lie beside him, and was surpris to see tears in his eyes. 'What?' she asked gently.

'I don't know what it is about you, Susanna – it's somethi different, and whatever it is, it seems to have made everythi between us so much more . . .' He sighed. 'Oh, hell, I ca explain it. You're the one with the words. It's just more inten When I came, just then, I saw stars. It's always been go between us, but this . . . This is something else.'

It's called making love with a vampire, Susanna thought.

ampire who's supposed to kill you, and can't bear to. And yet, f I don't drink your blood, I'll die. I have to choose – and hoose the right thing. Both of them are wrong for me.

'You feel it too, don't you?'

She nodded. She did – but not for the same reason that he lid. 'Don't say anything,' she said quietly. It only made her lecision harder.

'OK. If you won't let me tell you how I feel, I'll let my body lo it for me.' He cupped her breasts, his thumbs rubbing gently gainst her skin; she gave a small murmur of pleasure, loving vhat he was doing to her, and lay back against the pillows.

He rubbed his face against her breasts, nuzzling them, efore taking one nipple into his mouth and sucking gently. As he arched her back, he sucked harder, then transferred his ttentions to its twin, rolling the first nipple between finger nd thumb until Susanna was writhing under him.

He slid one hand between her thighs, checking her arousal; he felt warm, and very wet, to the touch, and he smiled, neeling between her thighs and sitting back on his heels. 'We lid this the night before I came here,' he said with a grin. 'You eemed to like it then.'

Susanna licked her suddenly dry lips, remembering how ood it had been; he blew her a kiss, then positioned his cock t the entrance to her vagina, lifting her buttocks and bringing er body up to meet his. He draped her thighs over his so that er feet were flat against the mattress; then eased one hand etween their bodies and began to rub her clitoris with the pad f his thumb.

Her reaction was instant, pushing against him and queezing her eyes shut with pleasure; he continued to rub her litoris until she came, her internal muscles clutching wildly t his cock, and then he began to thrust, lengthening her rgasm and deepening it.

Susanna had never come so hard, not even when Ambrose ad brought her to her first vampire orgasm; this, she thought, as incredible, the rush of pleasure rippling through her and growing wilder and wilder as he continued to thrust.

'Oh, God, Brandon,' she cried; it was almost too much to bear, and then he was coming too, his cock throbbing deep inside her.

She couldn't lose this. Not this. Alicia hadn't been able to live without the love of her life; why should Susanna give up hers?

And then it came to her. There was a third choice. She smiled. The decision, after all, was the easiest thing in the world to make. She smiled again, rubbing her face against his shoulder, and her canine teeth began to lengthen . . .